THE SAVIOR

Silent Phoenix MC Series: Book Five

SHANNON MYERS

Cover Model: Josh Mario John

Photographer: Wander Aguiar

First Printing: 2019

Paperback ISBN- 978-1-7332748-3-8

❀ Created with Vellum

ALSO BY SHANNON MYERS

From This Day Forward Duet

(David & Elizabeth's Story)

From This Day Forward

Forsaking All Others

Standalone Novels

(Travis & Katya's Story)

You Save Me

Operation Series

(Dakota & Zane's Story)

Operation Fit-ish

(Kate and Nate's Story)

Operation Annulment

Silent Phoenix MC Series

(Grey & Celia's Story)

The Deserter (Book One)

The Protector (Book Two)

The Renegade (Book Three)

The Traitor (Book Four)

The Savior (Book Five)

The Mercenary (Book Six) *Coming 2022*

Fairest Series

(Charm & Neve's Story)

Through The Woods

(Killian & Ariana's Story)

Wait For It

Fictioned Series

(Hayden & Jake's Story)

Protagonized

For the unlikely saviors. The ones who battled their own demons to save those around them.

TERMINOLOGY

1%er (One-Percenter)- *If 99% of motorcycle riders are law-abiding members of society, the rest is the 1%. Advertised through a patch or tattoo, usually on a diamond shaped back field.*

13 - *Patch worn by a biker, usually a 1%er. May stand for the letter "M" (13th letter of alphabet), and indicate the wearer smokes pot, or uses "crank" (methamphetamine). Can also mean "The Mother Club", or original chapter of a motorcycle club.*

1916- *The nineteenth letter of the alphabet (S) and the sixteenth (P). Stands for Silent Phoenix.*

3-Piece Patch- *Configuration of back patches, consisting of: a top rocker (club's name), a center patch (club's emblem), and a bottom rocker (geographical territory).*

69 - *Patch indicating someone who has performed cunnilingus with witnesses present.*

Air Condition- *Riddle with bullets*

ATF- *Bureau of Alcohol, Tobacco, Firearms and Explosives.*

Broad- *A female whose sole purpose is being used as a sexual object; similar to a one-night stand.*

Cage- *Non-biker's car/truck.*

Church- *Club meeting.*

Club Whore- *Also known as a Mama. Sexual equivalent of a public well. Anyone can dip into her, at any time, as often as he wants. These are woman who belong to the club at large. They belong to every member and are expected to consent to the sexual desires of anyone at anytime. They perform menial tasks around the clubhouse, however do not attend club meetings.*

Colors- *Patches, logo, or uniform associated with a motorcycle club.*

Fly Colors - *To ride on a motorcycle wearing club's kutte.*

Gathering: *A scheduled social event or meeting. This is not Church.*

Grocery-getter- *A biker's car/truck.*

Hang Around- *a person that hangs around a motorcycle club and may be interested in joining.*

Jacket- *Arrest record*

Kill-Light- *A flashlight used as a weapon.*

Kutte- *A jacket which has had the sleeves cut off. All club patches are sown onto kuttes, which are worn as the outer-most layer of clothing. Most, if not all, outlaw clubs have kuttes as their basic uniform.*

Mother- *Founding/original chapter of the club.*

Nomad- *1) "Nomad" on a bottom rocker patch means that motorcycle club member travels between geographical chapters. Kind of like working in a secretarial pool, a Nomad goes where he's needed. 2)"Nomad" on a top rocker patch or car plaque means "Nomad" is the name of that club.*

Ol' Lady- *Wife or long-time girlfriend of club member. She is considered property of the member and is off-limits to other club members.*

Property Of- *displayed on a shirt, patch or tattoo to show who the woman "belongs to." Example: Monica wore a "Property of Torch" vest in Renegade. That meant that she associated herself with Torch and would do anything he needed/wanted.*

———

STRUCTURE WITHIN CLUB

National President- *Many times the founder of the club. He will usually be located at or near the national headquarters. He will be surrounded by bodyguards and organizational enforcers.*

Territorial or Regional Representatives- *In some cases called the National Vice President in charge of a specific region or state.*

National Secretary / Treasurer- *He is responsible for the club's money and collecting dues from local chapters. He also records any by-law changes and records any minutes.*

National Enforcer- *This person answers directly to the National President. He acts as a body guard and gives out punishment for club violations. He has also been known to locate former members and retrieve colors or remove the club's tattoo from them.*

Chapter President- *This person has either claimed the position or has been voted in. He has final authority over all chapter business and members.*

Chapter Vice President- *This person is second in command. He presides over club affairs in the absence of the president. Normally, he is hand picked by the Chapter President.*

Chapter Secretary / Treasurer- *This is usually the member with the best writing skills and probably the most education. He will maintain the chapter roster and maintain a crude accounting system. He is also responsible for collecting dues, keeping minutes and paying for any bills the chapter accumulates.*

Chapter Sergeant (SGT) at Arms- *This person is in charge of maintaining order at club meetings. Because of the violent nature of outlaw gangs this person is normally the strongest member physically and is loyal to the Chapter President. He may administer beatings to fellow members for violations of club rules. He is the club enforcer.*

Road Captain- *This person fulfills the role of a logistician and security chief for club sponsored runs or outings. The Road Captain maps out routes to be taken during runs, arranges the refueling, food and maintenance stops. He will carry the club's money and use it for bail if necessary.*

Members- *The rank and file, fully accepted and dues paying members of the gang. They are the individuals who carry out the President's orders and have sworn to live by the club's by-laws.*

Prospect- *These are the club's hopefuls who spend from one month to one year in a probationary status. They must prove during that time if they are worthy of becoming members. Some clubs have the prospect commit a felony with fellow members observing in an effort to weed out the weak and stop infiltration by law enforcement. Must be nominated by a regular member and receive a unanimous vote for acceptance. They are known to carry weapons for other club members and stand guard at club functions. The prospect wears no colors and has no voting rights.*

Associates or Honorary Members- *An individual who has proven his* *value or usefulness to the gang. These individuals may be professional people who have in some manner helped the club. Some of the more noted are attorneys, bail bondsmen, and auto wrecking yard owners. These people are allowed to party with the gang, either in town or on their runs; however, they do not have a voting status or wear colors.*

AUTHOR'S NOTE

Please be aware that Savior is not recommended for readers under the age of eighteen, as it contains strong language, sexual situations, drug use, and graphic violence.

If you, or someone you care about has been a victim of sexual assault, RAINN is available to provide confidential support.

RAINN Hotline: 1 (800) 656-4673

SAVIOR

\ ˈsāv-yər

noun

1. one that saves from danger or destruction
2. one who brings salvation

See also: deliverer; redeemer; rescuer.

Hell is empty
and
all the devils
are here.

-William Shakespeare

CHAPTER ONE

Grey: February 2017 (Age: 53)

My head shot up as the door swung open and I surged forward. The metal that encircled my wrists bit into the skin, warning me to back off. Instead, I pushed my body to its limit, tendon and muscle straining in a futile attempt to break free from my restraints.

"Happy... whatever the fuck today is." Cobra pulled his phone from his pocket and tapped the screen with his index finger. "Let's see, tomorrow is Valentine's Day, so why don't we just celebrate early? Isn't that what you used to do with your prisoners? Spout off all the inane holidays as if they needed to be reminded of how long they'd been with you?"

None of my captives had ever lived long enough to need to know the date, except one.

Manny.

I wracked my brain, struggling to recall how many of my men would've known that detail. To my knowledge, there were only two— Crossbones and Bear.

The chains rattled as I jerked my arms forward, suddenly convinced I was the goddamn Hulk thanks to the adrenaline that had just been dumped into my bloodstream.

Had it been one of them?

I didn't want to believe it.

"Trying to escape again? What's that—the third time this week?" Cobra sank into a chair in the corner, crossing one leg over the other with a wry grin. "Thought you would've realized by now that you aren't walking out of here."

It seemed I had nothing but time.

And I'd spent every second trying to find a way out. The chains around my wrists were bolted to a stone floor. I'd used something similar in my kill rooms, knowing that unless my prisoner knew how to tunnel through rock with his hands, there was no way out. It hadn't stopped me from trying to break my own body down, piece by piece, to get back to my family, though.

Something that had fascinated Cobra to no end.

"Tell me, did Manny think he was going to be saved?"

I shook my head and sank down against the wall, completely spent. "He knew he was a dead man the second we showed up. My club's gonna come lookin' for you, and when they do, you'll know exactly how that feels."

My fingers twitched from the tremors that had wracked my body for days. I didn't know whether it was from the wound in my chest or the stress put on my joints from being shackled to a wall. Fuck, for all I knew, it was nothing more than nicotine withdrawals.

Cobra pulled a cigar from the inside of his jacket and lit up with a smirk. "Is that so? You really think your men are out combing the streets to find you?"

I nodded, wanting nothing more than to puff on the cigar in his hand until my head cleared. "They won't rest until—"

"Until what, Grey? Do you see them going on television to plead for your safe return? Passing out flyers? What exactly is it that your men are doing?"

I didn't know.

Everything had gone dark after I was shot, punctuated by only the briefest bursts of color. I saw Rick above me, pleading with me to stay alive. At one point, there'd been a blinding whiteness directly overhead, like the headlights on a Mack truck, and then everything was a blur. Maybe that was when I'd gotten separated from my men. All I knew for sure was that I'd woken up here, in nothing but my jeans with stitches too perfect to have come from any club doctor running the length of my chest.

As long as the club was still searching for the Sons, I had a fighting chance.

"That's what I thought. Nothing." He exhaled a stream of smoke toward me and glanced at his watch. "I think it's time for a little bedtime story. You've been looking more... worn down. What do you say?"

I shook my head. It was just another ploy to fuck with my mind.

"No?" he asked. "Alright then, how about this? Your family had a lovely funeral in the middle of a goddamned ice storm; so, tell me again how hard they're looking for you. You should've seen Celia—not one tear. Why do you think that is?"

My heart plummeted to the concrete. I knew exactly why. In fact, I was probably the only person alive who was aware of how she shut down when shit got too heavy. Only this time, I wouldn't be there to shoulder the weight and bring her back.

She thought I was gone.

They all did.

I'd always known I'd never survive without her. Now, it was apparent, neither would she.

"Why the fuck am I still kickin' then?" I growled. "Saint got what he wanted, didn't he? Took a fuckin' bullet to the chest—why not end it already?"

"See, now it's interesting to me you're willing to give up so easily. Manny? Sure, I expected that cocksucker to go to his grave sniveling like a toddler. But, you?"

He clicked his tongue against his teeth with a shake of his head before bringing the cigar back up to his lips. "I had a lot more riding on you fighting until the end. Manny, he thought he knew better than everyone because he spent more time on the streets. He was too impatient to see the big picture. I cut my losses when he wanted to go after your daughters—"

"Don't sit there and act like you weren't talkin' of doin' the same goddamn thing to them. Ain't that what you said when I got here?" I was baiting him into doing something stupid in the hopes he'd give up more information. The more he talked, the more I'd learn.

If my family thought I was six feet under, then I was going to have to work twice as hard to escape; even if the wound in my chest was nowhere near healed.

Cobra freed another cigar from his jacket and held it out. "You want this? Then shut the fuck up. I have no interest in going after children, but news flash, your girls aren't so little anymore. Now, before you lose your head, just know that as long as you're cooperating, they'll stay safe."

"Like you kept my wife safe?" I growled, my wrist popping against the chain. "So, you caught a fuckin' break and got me. Just gonna leave me chained up to the goddamn wall until I die of old age? Oh, that's right. You don't call the fuckin' shots. That's what Hawk told us anyway—said you answer to Saint. What I don't get is what's in it for you?"

There had to be a plan in place. Saint had worked too hard moving us around like pieces on a chessboard for it to have all been for nothing.

I just couldn't come up with anything that made sense.

He grinned. "You still want to believe that what happened to you was a random attack, something completely unplanned. Sure, you got a little suspicious when we wiped out the Serpents—which, you're welcome for that—"

"That's where shit goes off the rails for me," I drawled, fighting against a sudden wave of dizziness. I needed water but refused to beg my captor for a goddamn thing.

"Which part? That your enemy took out another rival club, or that you saw my kutte and immediately assumed you'd found me? Speaking of, I'm going to want that back."

With a heavy sigh, he snagged a small black bag off the table beside him. "Look. Let's start over, yeah? What do we have here? Camels? Nice choice."

I watched through narrowed eyes, fighting to figure him out as he walked over and tossed the pack next to my foot. For the longest time, my enemy had been a faceless entity.

Not anymore.

If I wanted to make it out alive, I needed to learn everything I could from Cobra.

When I made no move to grab it, he rolled his eyes and bent to tap one from the pack. "And... nothing. C'mon, Grey. I'm feeling generous tonight; you might take advantage of it while it lasts."

He offered the cigarette to me, and this time, I took it. My shoulders screamed their protests as I brought it up to my mouth and leaned toward the lighter in his hand. The urge to numb myself by filling my lungs with smoke outweighed any of the risks associated with him holding an open flame near my face.

Once it was lit, he calmly stood and walked back over to the chair, leaving me more confused than ever. If he was trying to convince me he was a nice guy, he was barking up the wrong tree.

I'd seen what he'd done to my girl.

Fuck, I'd seen what he'd done with a rifle and decent aim.

"Why the fuck are you doin' this? Tryin' to earn brownie points with your boss?"

"Told you," he replied, crossing one leg over the other again like he was on the cover of a fucking fashion magazine. "I was feeling generous. Plus, the story I'm about to tell required something stronger. From what I understand, you don't drink. That's something we have in common. So, we find other ways to kill ourselves."

I took a long, desperate drag before leaning back against the wall to let my shoulders rest, hating that he made sense when nothing else did. "Fair enough."

"Haven't ridden with the Serpents in years. That's something you would've known had you actually bothered to look into the club, or, I don't know, call a meeting with them. They wanted to hold on to the old-school way of thinking and weren't big on me going after your family to get to you. It didn't matter. With the money we took from Celia, I had enough to start over with more... like-minded individuals. Remind me, what is it we call brothers who turn their backs on us?"

"Enemies," I answered, blowing a stream of smoke in his direction. We weren't friends by any stretch of the imagination. The closest I could come to describing us was death row inmate and jailer, but damn, if it wasn't nice to have some company.

Even if I was considering all the ways in which I wanted to send him to the Reaper.

"Exactly. I didn't have the stomach for a long, drawn-out death, even if it was exactly what they all deserved. Their new Pres, Viper, was a different story, though. He'd been the one to rat me out, claiming that my actions had started a war. When the fuck did that happen? When did bikers get soft? Back then, we loved nothing more than a good fight..." his voice trailed off, and he puffed on his cigar in silence, reminiscing about the early days.

He wasn't wrong.

When I'd patched in, it seemed there was always another club to go up against; someone else that needed to be reminded of who we were and what we could do.

Death had been my first love, replaced only by Celia.

Maybe it was as simple as that. We'd all gotten older and realized that there was more to life than getting bloody.

"You're thinking about her again," he said with an unreadable expression. "I can tell. Your face changes. Is that why we all became pussies in the end, Grey? Because finding a nice warm cunt to sink our dicks into was suddenly more important than keeping a stranglehold over our territory? You know, you might've just solved the entire goddamn mystery. We let our dicks do the thinking."

The vein in my forehead throbbed steadily as I bit out, "And what would you know about that?"

He laughed softly. "The club whores are all the same after a while; more concerned with their next fix. They don't care what you do to them as long as you fill their veins with something nice afterward. No, it's better when the woman has a certain look in her eyes, like maybe you're the only man who's ever gotten her. She hands over her trust, knowing you'll keep her safe. You could fuck countless women, but you'll never have that kind of loyalty."

In a fucked-up way, I understood.

"I'd never experienced anything quite like it until Celia," he mused. "It didn't matter what I did to her body, she still believed I was going to hold true to my word and keep her girls safe. I told her I was going to let her live, so she trusted me completely. Fuck, I'm getting off-track. You didn't come here to hear about my love life—"

"I'm gonna force-feed you your own cock and watch you choke on it, you piece of shit motherfucker!" I roared, rattling the chains on my arms as I reached for him, losing my cigarette to the concrete floor.

Cobra raised his eyebrows. "Is that so? And how exactly do you plan on doing that from where you are? As I was saying, before I got completely sidetracked, taking out the Serpents was my own personal brand of karma for all the ways I'd been fucked over. Knowing Viper had already ratted me out once, I decided to not take the chance of him spoiling the surprise early and cut out his tongue. Did it work? Were you surprised?"

"Surprised? Not really. When the fake prospect announced that the Sons didn't negotiate, it kinda gave away the punchline. What I don't get, though, is how he thought he was gonna waltz out of that building. Don't make a damn bit of sense."

I couldn't let him get into my head.

He bit down on the cigar and clenched his hands into fists before relaxing with a deep breath. "Kid knew it was a suicide mission from the start. That's why we're on top, and every other club is in the ground. We're willing to give our lives for our cause. Can you say the same?"

"Wait a minute, so this Saint guy is actually convincin' people to die for him? What kind of fucked-up, Koresh-soundin' bullshit is that?"

My men had always been willing to die defending our colors, as were most of the other clubs, but never once had I asked them to sacrifice themselves for me personally. I thought back to the months and years after Celia had been attacked and realized that maybe I had. For all I knew, that was what had landed me in this prison.

Wolverine had pushed us into a battle over Molly, but I'd started an all-out war over Celia.

Cobra gave me a hard smile and drummed his fingers on the thigh of his slacks as if he was bored. "We're all Saint."

CHAPTER TWO

Grey: February 2017 (Age: 53)

He held the lighter under the tip of the cigar until it was glowing red before popping it back into his mouth. "Now, here's where it gets fun. I know for a fact that you spent that entire wedding searching for a dirty cop. You want so badly to believe it was a coincidence that we showed up when we did, because it's easier than knowing one of your own tipped us off. Tell me, Grey. Who was it?"

Days and nights blended into one, making it seem as though Dakota's wedding had taken place years ago. I thought back, struggling to see what I'd missed. Almost every biker in my clubhouse had been in attendance to ensure that nothing happened to my family.

It was like searching for a needle in a haystack.

As far as I knew, it was just another trick. Another way to get me to let my guard down.

"You're wrong." I shifted forward, trying to ease the worsening ache in my neck and shoulders, fighting not to imagine Bear and Crossbones betraying me. "My men are loyal—"

"Are they?" Cobra asked with a low chuckle. "Look around you! If they were loyal, you wouldn't be with me. Why would I tell you this now? We both know you're not getting out of here. Now, think. Who wanted you gone?"

"Besides you and your imaginary friend, Saint? No one."

My list of regrets had only grown longer the more time I spent in here. If I hadn't been strung out, I could've ended the Sons before they even began.

Fuck.

Maybe if the club hadn't been my number one priority, I could've saved my wife from ever crossing paths with Cobra.

Keeping the cigar in his mouth, he slipped the jacket from his shoulders and laid it across the chair before slowly coming toward me.

As sick as it was, I was looking forward to it. The monster that was hard-wired to need violence was still in there, rattling the bars of his cage.

Cobra's face tightened in irritation as he looked down at me. "Saint wants you alive, but he didn't say jack shit about roughing you up a little. I try to do something nice, but it seems there's still only one way men like you know how to communicate."

I jerked my head back in shock when he grabbed a rope from the ceiling, looping it around my neck. A sudden coldness descended over me. I knew torture, but this wasn't it.

"What's wrong, Grey? Is this not how you do things? Last chance, tell me who betrayed you? If you guess right, I'll let you rest." He tapped an index finger against my skull. "C'mon... think!"

The implication of his words hung heavy in the air. If I told him what he wanted to know, he wouldn't string me up. For all I knew, he'd take the name for their next target, and I wasn't willing to put anyone else's life at risk just to save my own ass. I'd take whatever he wanted to do to me if it meant that my family stayed safe.

"Told you," I growled. "You and your buddy, Saint, are the only two who had anything to gain by takin' my club."

"Fair enough." He calmly walked over to where the rope wrapped around a hook on the wall. A quick glance upward confirmed my suspicions. He had a multiple pulley system almost identical to mine. If he wanted to hoist me up to hang to death, he'd have no trouble. "Last chance..."

I spit a mouthful of saliva onto his fancy leather shoes in response, and he yanked the rope, jerking my body until just my bare feet rested against the concrete. I took slow, deep breaths, bracing myself for what was to come, only to remember Cobra didn't do predictable.

He took a step back, wrapping the slack around his hand with a grin. Somehow, the cigar remained clenched in between his teeth, and he shifted it to the side of his mouth before speaking. "Do you know how hard my job was that night? I had to factor in the fact that you'd decided on a vest last-minute, on top of ensuring that your wound wasn't fatal, but something that would require more than a club doctor to fix. I go to all that trouble and can't even get a goddamn thank you?"

I looked up from the floor. "How'd you know I was wearin' a vest?"

"It's funny; I toss a rope around your neck, and you suddenly want to chat. You know the answer. The one cop you never investigated— tell me, how does it feel, knowing that your own son turned on you?"

Even though I was one good pull away from being hanged, I exhaled a laugh. The evidence against Mikey looked solid on the surface, but it wouldn't hold up. He and I might've had our differences over the years, but I knew without a doubt that there was one person he'd never turn on. One person he'd move heaven and earth to keep safe.

Lauren.

Even if he'd considered taking me down, there wasn't the slightest chance in hell that he would've partnered with the same club responsible for killing his wife's mother. They'd gone out of their way to make it look like an overdose, never expecting anyone to look into it.

Unfortunately for them, they hadn't accounted for Lauren.

Cobra's admission only proved that he didn't know as much as he wanted me to believe he did. Not only that, but he'd also inadvertently given up their mole.

At Dakota's wedding, a cop had stumbled into me on his way out of the men's room. At the time, I assumed he'd just spent too much time at the open bar and let him lean on me as I led him over to a table. Looking back on it now, it was obvious he'd been planted to check me for body armor.

It had never been one of my guys.

One dirty cop had been more than enough to give the Sons everything they needed to take me out that night.

"Detective Sullivan came to blows with another club member after your funeral; claimed the club was his to run. If that isn't a motive, then I don't know what is."

No, it wasn't a motive.

It was a sign that my son had heard me when we were sitting in the waiting room at the hospital. He was willing to become a renegade to protect our family, and I was going to have to play along to keep him safe.

"Maybe you're right," I rasped. "Told his mama to take care of it when she told me she was knocked up, but the bitch didn't listen. Kid's been nothin' but trouble since he came into this world. We covered up his shit, and he pays the club back by tryin' to kill me."

Cobra tipped his head to the side, watching me intently. "You aren't going to argue?"

I shrugged. "Why should I? You're right. I never saw it before; never imagined that he was capable of doin' it. Kid was so strung out on drugs and alcohol; I'm surprised he managed to pull it off at all."

"You know Saint's all bent out of shape over Sullivan ruining the surprise early," he slipped.

At my blank stare, he elaborated. "In the cemetery. He stayed back to open the fucking casket; realized that you weren't in it—"

"And? What's that got to do with anything?" I fought to keep my voice steady. Mikey knew I was alive and was willing to run the club to find me. Instead of feeling relieved, I was more worried than ever.

The Sons were going to be watching their every move.

Was that what Saint wanted—me, chained up, watching the people I loved getting picked off one by one?

He tightened his grip on the rope. "Saint wanted them to believe you were dead until the last possible second. Now, we're being forced to speed things up. Can't make a fucking omelet without cracking a few eggs though, am I right?"

I'd been shot New Year's Eve. It was now almost Valentine's Day. More than enough time had passed for Mikey to assemble an army. Pain shot through my chest, the rope around my neck the only thing keeping me upright.

Too fucking bad his old man was out of commission.

"So, like I said before... they're gonna come lookin' for you," I forced out through clenched teeth.

Cobra grinned. "Yes... and no. Your son wanted to take over the club to hunt you down, but Bear refused. Declared himself Pres unanimously and, even knowing you were still alive, ordered the club to stand down. Don't you see? Without you, your enemies get what they've always wanted... power."

Wrong.

I fought the grin playing on my lips, knowing he was seconds away from stringing me up. Bear wasn't my enemy, and he'd never wanted power. All he'd ever wanted was for the kid he'd raised as his own to acknowledge him. Family had always been the most important thing to Bear, and like Mikey, he never would've allied himself with the same men who'd tried to kill his Ol' Lady and son.

Initially, Saint had wanted them to believe I was dead. Thanks to Mikey, he was now going to try to convince me that the people I'd loved had betrayed me. I still didn't know how the puzzle was going to come together, but was at least aware of where a few of the pieces fit.

Cobra had yet to give up my rat, and I wondered if it was because he didn't know.

If Silent Phoenix had suddenly decided to stand down, it was because they knew they were being played.

And a plan wasn't worth shit if the enemy knew about it.

"Why does Saint want me alive, then?"

He walked around me in a slow circle, eyeing my body like a slab of beef. Having spent decades dealing in torture, I knew what he was going for even before he did. With an amused grin, he plucked the cigar from his lips and stabbed it out against the festering wound on my chest. Instead of jerking away, I leaned into the pain, letting the burn work its way down under my damaged skin, keeping me focused.

"You're the key, Grey. Without you, there's no war, and you go down like a fucking hero. It brings me back to my original point—nobody wants to fight anymore. Even Saint leaves the dirty work to everyone else. It's up to men like us to convince them to change their minds. They just need a cause." He pulled on the rope until my toes skimmed the ground, and regretfully stated, "It's gonna hurt."

I clenched my jaw and nodded. "Alright, let it hurt."

The pulleys creaked and groaned as he jerked the rope, the chains around my wrists stretching until they were taut. I'd been so preoccupied with what had been around my throat that I'd momentarily forgotten the arms shackled to the floor. He wasn't going to hang me; he was going to tear me in two.

My shoulders screamed in agony, momentarily distracting me from the rope compressing my jugular.

It didn't last.

Desperate for air, I began kicking my legs wildly, struggling to find something to hold my weight—anything that would relieve the pressure around my neck. My jeans grew warm with piss, but I was too far gone to care. A healing wound on my chest tore with the jerky movements, sending fresh streams of blood down my body. Involuntarily, I jerked my legs again, knowing I was only making things worse.

Cobra's mouth widened into another grin as he gave one last vicious tug, and my right shoulder popped. The excruciating pain sent everything into darkness just as I opened my mouth to scream.

CHAPTER THREE

Mike: February 2017 (Age: 34)

"Fred, when'd the other guy show up?" I mumbled, waving my hand toward the back of the bar. I should have been sitting in my office, fighting to break Grey's case. Instead, my ass had gone numb, sitting on a barstool watching basketball highlights.

I didn't give a fuck about basketball.

I'd been trying to shoot the shit with the old bartender, Fred, but it turned out he wasn't much of a talker. He preferred to work himself to the bone slinging drinks, over visiting with the lonely guy in the suit.

"Who the fuck are you talkin' about, boy?" he snapped. "Ain't no one back here but me. Ain't no one been here but me."

I looked up with a grin, my fingers tracing around a heart that had been carved into the battered bar top. "You got me, Fred. That was a good one. I like you a lot, you know that?"

"Drunk as a fuckin' skunk and it ain't even five o'clock," he grumbled before slapping a wet rag against the scarred wood. "That's what's wrong with the fuckin' world today."

"It's five o'clock somewhere," I sang off-key. "Okay, buddy, I gotta take a piss. Watch my tequila, would you?"

I slid off the stool and stumbled toward the back, fighting to remain upright. "Fred, my man, you gotta get someone out here to take a look at your floors. They're slanted as fuck."

"Floors are fine, dickhead."

"Good talk." I lifted my foot about three inches off the ground before slowly bringing it back down. The wooden planks sloped up like mountaintops in some areas but dipped like valleys in others. It was like climbing and descending Everest just to get to the men's room.

After relieving myself, I washed up at the sink, keeping my head down. I didn't need to see the man in the mirror—didn't need to be reminded of what an epic fuck-up he was.

I pulled the small plastic bag from my pocket and studied the white powder, my mouth already watering at the thought of taking a hit. It was the evidence that never made it into the station during a drug bust last month. Something they'd never known was missing.

The addiction I'd rewarded myself with after a less than banner start to the year.

"Don't do it," I warned myself while turning it over in my shaking hands.

I'd bitten my nails down to stubs, the skin around them cracked and bleeding. I forced my eyes up toward my reflection, seeing the wreck I'd become. I shouldn't have been surprised by the day's events. My greasy hair hung down past my ears, and I couldn't remember the last time I'd been to see my barber. I slowly ran a hand over the coarse hairs of my beard, staring at my blue eyes until I no longer saw myself, but my old man.

Grey.

The urge to pick up the phone and call him was overwhelming; almost as strong as my need to medicate. There was so much left unsaid between us, and while he'd fucked off to god knew where, I was left to wonder what he'd meant by addiction running in our family.

I was stuck with the responsibility of fixing the mess he made, yet had no way of knowing how to resist the urge to use again. It must've been nice to just leave your problems behind for your family to sort out while you disappeared.

Proving that Red had a sixth sense when it came to me, my phone chimed with an incoming text.

Lauren: Can you pick up barbecue on your way home? I suddenly have a craving for red meat again.

It didn't matter that I'd turned my location finder off. There wasn't a doubt in my mind that Lauren knew exactly where I was and what I was doing.

Like a child caught with his hand in the cookie jar, I shoved the baggie back into the front pocket of my slacks before facing the mirror again. I'd gone to all the trouble of sobering up and getting clean, only to end up right back where I started.

Michael Sullivan, Jr.

A fucking failure.

She deserved so much better.

I slapped the side of my face and growled, "What do you love more —her or the drugs? Huh? You gonna fuck away the last good thing you've got left?"

It was my voice, but Grey's words. Rage bubbled up again at the thought of him, leaving me clinging to the counter to stop myself from destroying the glass above the sink with my fists. Once I felt like I could breathe again, I tapped out a quick reply on my way out of the bathroom, assuring her I'd grab dinner on my way home.

Lauren had a way of anchoring me when I felt like I was drifting. I only hoped that when the ugly truth came out, she'd remember the man I'd wanted to be and not the man I'd become.

Any good feelings I'd conjured up died when I realized that someone was now sitting in my seat. In a deserted bar, they'd chosen my goddamn bar stool.

"Hey Fred, why don't you tell my new pal here that there are plenty of other seats for him?" I cracked my knuckles. "Would sure hate to dirty up your bar, if you know what I mean."

"Sit the fuck down, Sullivan!" Zane snapped, finally turning around to face me.

"Masterson?" I dropped onto the stool next to him and reached for the bottle of tequila, but he slid it out of reach. "Guess you heard the good news and came to celebrate my early retirement?"

His jaw tightened. "I can't believe they just let you go."

Aiding and abetting a known outlaw motorcycle gang.

Deep down, I'd always known that one way or another, Grey was going to cost me my job. Instead of tossing me into a pair of handcuffs and hauling me to a cell to await what was sure to be a lengthy prison sentence, they'd let me go under the stipulation that I not leave the city any time soon. Even without Grey, the club still had some power. Whether it'd be enough to keep me out of prison remained to be seen.

"Oh, yeah." I nodded. "It was always just a matter of time before I turned in my badge and gun to become public enemy numero uno. How the fuck did you know where to find me?"

"Ran a trace on your cell. Did you let the club know?"

I scratched at my jaw, suddenly more sober than I cared to be. "Why the fuck would I tell them shit? Bear made it clear that we weren't patching in—I'm too clean to be a biker and too dirty to be a cop. Where the fuck does that leave me?" I gestured for the bottle, but Zane shook his head. "C'mon, Big Guy. Don't leave me high and dry."

"Don't call me that," he stated flatly. "Frank, can you make this disappear? I think Mike's done enough drinking for the night."

"His name's Fred," I clipped out. "And I'll decide when I'm done drinking, okay—"

"You call me sweetie or pumpkin, or any of the other bullshit you spout off when you think you're being cute, and I'll introduce your face to the bar top and make you ride home in the bed of my truck. We clear?"

Fred raised his eyebrows before sliding the bottle off the bar and into a cabinet below. "Better listen to him, or you'll be moppin' up your own blood. I ain't in the habit of cleanin' up anyone else's messes."

"Fred," I tried.

"It's Frank, goddammit!" the old man growled. "How many goddamn times do I have to tell you? Your friend here got it in one try. Jesus Christ!" He threw up his hands before disappearing into the back.

Zane's lip twitched, but he continued staring straight ahead, refusing to give me even the smallest of glances as he muttered, "Guess that settles that."

"You know, if it's all the same to you, I'd prefer to keep this from Red for the time being… just until I pick something else up."

Despite the situation, I'd made it my personal goal to keep her pregnancy as stress-free as possible. We'd worked too hard to get those babies. The last thing I needed was her worrying about conjugal visits in prison.

"How long do you think that'll take? I haven't seen your file, but from the sounds of it, you'll be lucky to get a job as a fry cook at a fast-food joint. That is, if they don't file charges against you."

"That's just it." I stared down to where someone had gouged, Fuck Rhonda, into the wood. For all of Frank's blathering about running a tight ship, he seemed to look the other way when patrons wanted to get creative with his bar top. "Why now?"

I'd worked with Silent Phoenix for years, and while Bear hadn't wanted me anywhere near a kutte, it was heavily implied that I'd continue to use my badge to help them out. I refused. Cut ties with the club and went straight, only to lose it all only days later.

Zane mulled over my words with a slow nod. The man was so even-keeled and quiet that it was a wonder he'd ended up with the woman who never seemed to shut up.

"It's gotta be an unlucky coincidence."

I worked my jaw back and forth before voicing the concerns that had plagued me for the better part of the afternoon. "What if it's not?"

"The Sons targeted your family the night Grey was shot because you were helping the club," Zane patiently explained. "Why would they continue to pursue you after you broke away? It doesn't make sense."

He was right.

Nothing about any of it made sense.

"What if Grey's still pulling the strings?"

Zane shrugged while the tight expression on his face told me he thought I was full of shit. "Maybe?" he hedged.

I released an exasperated laugh. "Thanks for the vote of confidence there, Big Guy. Hear me out for a second, though. Grey goes dark, and the Sons immediately back down. Doesn't that seem strange to you?"

"They think he's dead, Mike. Why would they continue a war when they're convinced they've already won?"

I shook my head. "No, they have to know. Every member of the club was at Celia's house when I broke the news—"

"And one of those club members was working with the Sons!" he exclaimed, finally on the same page as I was. "That still doesn't explain how Grey's involved, though."

"The day he was shot, he told me he wanted me to run the club beside him. Said I couldn't straddle the line anymore. Well, he has to know I walked away. Maybe this is his way of punishing me for not making the right choice. Now, I've got nothing."

He ran a hand over his face and studied the bar top. "You're his kid, right? What kind of father would fake his own death just to sabotage his son's career and send him to prison?"

"Buddy, you've got no idea of the shit that man is capable of. He blackmailed me over—" I froze, seeing the look of surprise on Patrick's face as I swung... hearing the sound his head made as it connected with the curb.

"Over what?" Zane prodded.

"Over some shit I got into at eighteen... kid stuff, really." I kept my voice light, hoping he didn't start digging into my past. The tequila had loosened my lips to the point of being dangerous.

His mouth settled into a hard line. "So, your old man's an asshole. If he wanted to dismantle his family, why disappear? Why wouldn't he just do it out in the open, like every time before? Shit just doesn't add up for me."

I patted my pocket, comforted by the feel of the cocaine against my thigh. The alcohol had left my head a mess, blending my thoughts into nothing more than incoherent blobs. There'd always been a clarity with blow that helped me think.

Maybe that was what I'd been missing.

A clear mind.

Zane tracked my movements before clearing his throat. "Are you doing okay? Things at home... are they good?"

"Never better." I grinned. "Lauren's finally out of the first trimester. The headaches and morning sickness aren't as bad—"

"Then why are you here?" he interrupted. "Why are you getting fucked up in the middle of the day if things are good? Because from where I'm sitting, it looks like you just took a year and a half of sobriety and pissed it all away because you have daddy issues."

How the hell did he know how long I'd gone without hard liquor?

Was there a calendar they all kept?

It's been five hundred days since Mike's last fuck up.

"Yeah? Fuck you, Masterson!"

With a low growl, I shoved off the bar and moved toward the door. The vein in my forehead throbbed steadily as I turned to face him again. "Excuse the fuck out of my goddamn French, but you don't know jack shit about my life! I've got everything under control over here, so thanks for showing up to rub it in my face that I'm not a cop anymore, but you can shove your concern right up your motherfucking ass! I've got barbecue to get!"

My fist hit the wooden door, sending it flying open. Zane's mouth turned up in a grin. "Just one more thing before you stomp out of here..."

"What?" I snapped.

He lifted his palm in the air. "I've got your keys, but since you used your manners, I'll let you stop for barbecue on the way home. Maybe if you're good, we'll even grab some ice cream. How's that sound, pumpkin?"

I was going to murder him.

Just as soon as I sobered up.

CHAPTER FOUR

Mike: February 2017 (Age: 34)

"Help him! Oh my god—please!" Lauren screamed from somewhere near my head. I was going to be deaf.

I kept my eyes closed and tried reaching across the bed toward her, but found I couldn't move. It didn't matter. I was in a state of complete bliss.

The woman I loved had literally just fucked the life out of me.

It wasn't a bad way to go.

My dick hardened again, almost to the point of pain, and I grinned. Guess he'd decided if we were going down, he was getting his one last time. With the way Lauren's hormones had been, it wouldn't be difficult to talk her into another round.

Saliva filled my mouth, and I shook my head, wishing like hell that I had full use of my arms so that I could stroke my cock to the thought of her. Lauren had always been gorgeous, but the pregnancy seemed to enhance her beauty to where I would have happily agreed to remain in this state if it meant I got to have her as much as I wanted.

"Please," she sobbed. "Please let him be okay."

Darlin', he's just fine. In fact, I'd say he's better than fine. See for yourself.

I liked that the pregnancy hormones made her horny, but they also made her emotional as fuck. She'd cry at the drop of a hat... or dick. Just last week, I'd witnessed her falling apart over a yogurt commercial.

Nobody warned me about that before I knocked her up.

"Hold his arms," a male voice directed, and suddenly, I was no longer in a peaceful state.

If she'd gone and set up a three-way, I was going to lose it. I'd always been very specific that the only way I was getting involved in one was if she went and found another woman as hot as she was. I'd also been clear that she needed to be a redhead.

We'd have ourselves a *Ginger Snap*.

There was no way in hell I was sword fighting with another guy. Not when I'd worked this hard coming up with a clever name for a ménage.

"I'm going to stick him again."

Holy shit—again?

Had I not just been fucking Lauren? Had I been receiving a hot beef injection this entire time? What the fuck did Fred put in that tequila?

My eyelids were weighted, but I forced them open and sat up with a gasp, no longer willing to be a bottom for any man.

I was a top, goddammit.

The blurry figure above me gripped my shoulder as he breathed a sigh of relief. "There he is. Mike, do you know where you are?"

I blinked through my streaming eyes, slowly taking in my surroundings while trying to place the voice. "The bathroom floor?"

"That's right. Do you remember how you got here?" another voice asked—one I knew all too well.

Fucking Jimmy.

My lungs heaved and I began coughing violently, every muscle in my body aching. Either I was coming down with the flu, or I'd been beaten. Given what I remembered of my conversation with Zane, I was going to guess it was the latter.

"Did Big Guy kick my ass?" I rasped with a shudder. "Or was it you? You better hope it wasn't you, Jimmy boy, because so help me—"

"You overdosed, Mike," the guy above me stated flatly. "You were in respiratory distress, so I injected you with several doses of Naloxone.

The real credit goes to your wife, though. She performed CPR until we got here and could take over... probably saved your damn life."

I ran a trembling hand over my face. "Lauren? Is she—"

"Okay, I am back. How is he doing?"

I groaned upon hearing Gloria's voice, knowing it would have been better if Lauren just left me to die.

My vision cleared enough for me to see that the other guy in the room was Nate. It looked as if Dr. Husband had put aside our differences to keep me breathing. "Admit it," I taunted with a cocky smirk, shivering uncontrollably from the high fever I seemed to be running. "You wanted to let me die, right?"

Gloria's eyes narrowed, and she began speaking in rapid Spanish, jabbing a finger into my chest to drive home whatever point she was trying to make.

Nate released his hold on my shoulder and crossed his arms over his chest before leaning against the counter near the sink. "Lauren found you seizing on the bathroom floor next to a bag of what appeared to be cocaine. Given what we've seen in the ED lately, I assumed it was laced with fentanyl and dosed you accordingly. Your drugs were dirty, Detective."

I'd gone to all the trouble of busting up a drug ring, and the bastards hadn't even gotten the good shit.

Ignoring Jimmy's extended hand, I got to my feet. "I need to talk to my wife—"

"No." Gloria stopped me with her hand. "I tell Dave to take Lauren to his house. We will pack a bag for her, and then Dr. Nate will come to check the babies."

"Is this what you want out of life, Mike?" Jimmy stepped in to ask. "Your pregnant wife performing rescue breaths and chest compressions on you every time you lose control?"

"No," I snapped. "If you'd just give me a goddamn minute to talk to her, I could sort this shit out, Lurch."

He cracked the knuckles on his right hand with his thumb. "You aren't getting within ten feet of her... not strung out like you are. Jesus Christ, look at yourself! You could have hurt her. God knows you brought back memories of her mother."

The thought of Lauren on her hands and knees trying to revive my sorry ass left me with a sinking feeling in the pit of my stomach. I'd sworn that the only drug I'd needed was her; had promised to never let her see that side of me.

"I'd never hurt her," I mumbled. "She's too important to me."

Nate looked up at the ceiling. "You've OD'ed before, I take it?" When I nodded, he asked, "And who cleaned up that mess?"

"Grey."

He nodded. "I'm sure that felt good... seeing his son like that. Make no mistake, you're hurting the people who love you every time you choose that shit over them. Is this how you wanna die?"

"Is that the same crap you spout off to all your patients, Doctor?"

"Personally, I don't give a flying fuck what you choose to do with your life, but you're family now, and there are quite a few people who need you to stick around. Grey's gone, Mike. It's time to sober the fuck up and move on. Your family's relying on you."

I sank down on the edge of the tub, my thigh muscles quivering from the stress of holding up my body. "Weren't you on call the night he was shot?"

He rolled his eyes with a shake of his head. "Maybe worry about yourself first, yeah? Give that a try, and then we'll talk about me. You need to be monitored. Is there someone I can call for you?"

"I can stay," Jimmy offered.

"Fuck. That," I bit out.

Nate rubbed the back of his neck with a heavy sigh. "You're not staying by yourself."

"I know," I agreed. "I'm staying with my wife. Now, if someone could go get her for me—"

"Absolutely not," Jimmy interjected. "The last thing she needs right now is to be taking care of you. Not after what you've put her through."

Gloria nodded her approval before squeezing his arm. "Jimmy is right. *Como deseó ver a Lauren darte unas cachetadas en la cara.*" She smacked her palms together with a glare.

"She said she wants to see Lauren slap your face," Jimmy helpfully translated with a chuckle.

Gloria nodded. "*Sí*. I will move in and bring you back to health. When I am through with you, you will not want *las drogas* ever again."

I massaged the side of my aching head. "Actually, I think I'll just take my chances with Jimmy. He seems like he has a little more experience here."

Gloria's medical expertise seemed limited to Windex and holy water. There was no way that I'd survive detoxing in the same house as her.

She waved a hand in my direction. "*Estas dos tetas pueden llevar más que mil caballos.*"

"The fuck does that mean?" I snapped.

Jimmy leaned down and clutched his thighs, eyes streaming with tears. "She just said that her tits have carried more than a thousand horses. Basically, she can handle anything... including you."

Look everyone, Jimmy's still a multilingual motherfucker.

CHAPTER FIVE

Kate: February 2017 (Age: 27)

I looked down at the address scrawled on a torn piece of notebook paper and then back up at the boarded-up windows on the farmhouse.

There was no way this was the right place.

Sunlight caught the shards of glass littering the front yard, making it seem as if the dead grass was sparkling. It was the only positive I could find for a house that had either been abandoned or condemned.

The sound of my car door slamming echoing off the siding. I cautiously made my way up the porch steps. It was like the start of every cheesy horror film ever—the young and naïve therapist who took a wrong turn, ending up alone at a farmhouse in the middle of nowhere.

Any second now, a man wielding a chainsaw was going to come tearing around the side of the house, ready to dismember my body to hang in his shed.

Canceling an entire afternoon of patients to come here had been madness.

If Nate found out...

I shuddered and opened the screen door, quickly rapping my

knuckles against the scarred wooden door beneath it before I lost my nerve.

A short Hispanic woman with wavy hair approached, her eyes narrowing as she took me in. "What do you want?" she demanded, pulling the door open several inches. "You think because my grand-daughter is not here, you will come and disrespect her in her own home?"

The heel on my shoe chose that moment to snap off, and I fell over on the porch with a decidedly unladylike grunt.

"And drunk?" The older woman clicked her tongue against her teeth before yanking me back to my feet. "He will not be seeing the... *cómo es qué se llama esa mierda?*"

She waved a hand as if struggling to find the right word. Unfortunately, I knew next to nothing when it came to Spanish and had no way of knowing what she was asking.

"Uh, the word? He will not be seeing... *las prostitutas* as long as there is breath in my body. He needs to dry up."

I winced at the one word that I'd been able to understand and looked down at my modest black blouse and cream-colored dress pants, wondering which part of the outfit screamed prostitute. "Well, I'm his sister... and a therapist."

I wasn't here to counsel him, but it seemed essential to throw my profession out there, lest she think I was a lady of the night.

"His sister?" the woman all but shrieked. "Come in, come in. I fix your shoe for you. Are you hungry?" She squeezed my arm as she led me through the dark house. "You are too thin. I make you something. I am Gloria, Lauren's *abuela*, but everyone just calls me *Abuelita*. You can too, okay?"

I nodded, no longer unbalanced from the broken heel, but the complete change in the woman's personality. If I hadn't been here to visit my brother, I would have wanted to spend my time picking her brain.

"Um, okay. Is Mike—"

"In here. He will be so happy to see you. All day long, nothing but sitting and staring at the wall. I tell him he needs sunshine to get better, and do you know what he says to me?"

"Shut up, Gloria," Mike grumbled from beneath a pile of quilts on the couch. "Just shut the fuck up."

"*Sí*, that is what he says. Maybe he will do better with you. You sit." She gestured toward a chair that appeared to have bullet holes in it. "I will whip you up something. You are nothing but skin and bones."

I slowly sank down onto the chair, watching the couch for any signs of life. "Mike? It's Kate. I was just—"

"Come to shrink my head, Doc?" he muttered, still completely hidden from view.

I picked at a stray thread on my dress pants. "Oh, um, I'm not a doctor... just a licensed counselor."

"Oh, that's right. That'd be your husband. Did he send you to check on me? Is that his good deed for the day?" His hand shot out, and he tugged the quilts down toward his waist. I straightened in the chair at the sight of him, fighting to remain seated, instead of running screaming for the door.

This was worse than a chainsaw-wielding maniac.

Nate had told me he was bad, but nothing prepared me for seeing it in person. Mike looked nothing like the man who'd rallied everyone together in the middle of a cemetery just a couple of months ago. His wavy hair hung down past his chin, the matted areas looking more brown than dark blond, and the blue eyes that had always reminded me of my father and sister were no longer clear and bright but blood-shot and rimmed in dark circles.

I cleared my throat and placed my palms on the armrests, just as I'd done for countless other patients. "Nate doesn't know I'm here. I'd prefer to keep it that way if you catch my meaning."

He smirked before shuddering violently, causing him to reach for the quilts again. "Keeping secrets from old Nathaniel already? Can't see how that could backfire."

Emotion flooded my veins, and my fingers tightened against the fabric, and it took everything in me to keep my voice calm and my words professional. "What about your secrets, Mike? What would you say that's cost you?"

His eyes sharpened, and the grin faded from his lips just as Gloria entered the room. The plate she carried in her hands was overflowing with food, her mouth stretched wide in a grin.

"I fix you a little something to get some meat on your bones. You do not want to lose *tus montañas.*"

I frowned, and she held out a bony index finger, circling it near my breasts. My cheeks heated, and I nodded, indicating that I understood, hoping she didn't elaborate further. He might have been my brother, but it wasn't so long ago that I'd entertained the idea of ending up with someone just like him.

She pinched my cheek. "Enjoy it. Mike, do you want for me to make you something?"

His jaw tightened as he shook his head, and she disappeared back into the kitchen, happily humming to herself.

I stared down in wonder at the breaded steak topped with a fried egg resting on a bed of white rice. "Is this a typical brunch around here?"

"For Gloria it is." He lowered his voice. "What do you want, Kate? Why'd you come here?"

I speared the hunk of meat with my fork and cut off a tiny sliver. In my effort to avoid looking at the monstrosity that was now Mike, my eyes landed on a row of bullet holes in the wall behind the couch. "What happened to your house?"

He looked to where I was pointing and rolled his eyes. "The Sons of Death happened, Kate. Did you forget?"

The Sons.

A name that had meant nothing until the night my father was shot. Even months later, no one seemed to know anything about the elusive club. They'd disappeared just as quickly as they'd arrived.

"Well, I just thought..." I shoved a forkful of egg and meat into my mouth and deliberately chewed slowly to avoid finishing the sentence. The meat was so tender it felt as if it would dissolve on my tongue, and it took everything in me to stifle the moan on my lips.

I'd had chicken fried steak before, but this was on an entirely separate plane of existence.

"You just thought, what?" Mike pushed, before snagging the fork from my fingers and cutting a piece for himself. Bits of egg yolk clung to his scraggly beard as the steak disappeared into his mouth, taking with it any desire I had for another bite.

I swallowed. "That happened on New Year's Eve, right? I sort of thought that you would have repaired it by now."

His eyes narrowed. "Been a little busy, pumpkin. So, why the fuck did you come here? The real reason this time."

"I came because I have some questions... about our father."

He let out a rough bark of laughter, and I looked up just in time to see him wince.

"Body aches?" I asked, and he nodded. "That's pretty common during withdrawals. What about tremors? Headaches?"

He closed his eyes briefly before nodding again, his throat bobbing up and down in a swallow. "Yeah... all of that."

"What about the cravings? Are they?" I paused, trying to choose my words carefully. "Do you want to use again?"

Mike took a deep breath. "I think I'll always want to use, Kate. I'm an addict. If it'll fuck me up—make me forget for a while—I'm interested."

"What is it you want to forget?" I whispered, already feeling the sting of unshed tears behind my eyelids.

He didn't have to say anything.

I knew.

It was the entire reason for my visit.

CHAPTER SIX

Kate: February 2017 (Age: 27)

The two of us shared the same pain, the same feeling of betrayal. We'd just dealt with it in entirely different ways. I'd avoided all contact with my mother and sister, choosing to drown myself in work while he'd turned to drugs and alcohol.

Instead of telling me to fuck off, Mike pinched the bridge of his nose. "I want to forget that the man I idolized abandoned us."

I nodded. "Is that what triggered your relapse, do you think?"

I knew next to nothing about my half-brother, other than that he was a cop. I'd only found out that he was using drugs when Lauren called Nate for help the night he overdosed. It wasn't as if I was unfamiliar with addicts. I'd even counseled a few when I was just starting out.

This was family, though.

As much as I wanted to be understanding, resentment welled up within my veins. Mike had spent more time with my father than either Dakota or I had. I would have given up every measly possession I owned if it meant even five minutes alone with Grey, and Mike had taken it for granted. Then, he'd gone and fallen off the wagon, leaving everyone, including his wife, to fend for themselves.

It left me feeling anything but compassionate about his plight.

He folded the corner of one of the quilts down into a small triangle before looking over at me. "That isn't what triggered it. I—I lost my job."

I kept my face impassive, even though his revelation surprised me. I'd been under the impression that he'd been very successful as a detective. "What about the club?"

His eyes dropped to the quilt again, sounding irritated as he admitted, "Bear's running the club... said a badge would never wear a Silent Phoenix kutte." He ran a hand over his beard, trying and failing to smooth it down. "To top it off, Lauren's pregnant. So, Counselor, just how the fuck am I supposed to tell her I lost it all?"

I leaned back and shook my head, feeling every bit as trapped as he had been. "Can you fight it—being let go, I mean?"

He shrugged. "Doubtful. Whoever was helping the Sons is still pulling strings in the department. I just can't figure out why."

Already knowing the answer, I asked, "Has anyone heard from them?"

He watched me closely. "Not a fucking peep. Why would they stop now? I looked into it, and not once has a rival club backed down after taking out another MC's Pres. If their intention was to take over the area, then they would have done it by now. It was like Grey was their sole target, not the club."

I might have been ignorant about the ways of bikers but was well-versed in dealing with crazy ex-wives, enough to know that there was always an endgame when it came to the enemy.

"Maybe they think he's dead. I mean, those of us that were at the cemetery know he's alive, but they don't."

Mike clawed at an invisible itch on his arm before shaking his head. "I went out to see your mother... admitted to every biker there that the casket was empty. Before he was shot, Grey told me that someone within the club was giving up intel—"

I jumped out of my chair and crouched beside Mike near the couch as someone pounded a fist against the front door. The heel of my hand pressed to my heart to silence its thrashing.

Gloria materialized in the hall, holding a feather duster and still humming the same unfamiliar tune. The hairs on my arms stood on end, the need to warn her resting on the tip of my tongue, but I suddenly couldn't speak.

Until now, I'd listened to my husband and avoided all contact with my family. It had made sense then. My mother had chosen to live her life always looking over her shoulder, and with Dakota's lifelong obsession with superheroes and villains, it made sense that she'd be eager to tag along.

Not me, though.

I wasn't willing to risk mine and Nate's careers for a man I barely knew.

Only my husband wouldn't see it that way. When he found out that I'd been murdered along with my half-brother, he'd mistakenly assume that I'd betrayed his trust.

"I don't want to die," I whispered.

"Kate," Mike sighed heavily. "If someone came here to kill us, they wouldn't bother knocking first."

He stood and wrapped the quilt around his shoulders like a cape before slowly walking over to where Gloria stood. He didn't reach for a gun or call out a warning for the older woman to get down and stay quiet.

It was as if he'd never seen a single episode of The Devil Next Door or Evil Nightmares. Maybe the department had been right to let him go. He was walking right into danger with nothing more than a blanket to protect him.

He looked through the large glass window with a grin while I cowered near the end of the couch, ready to dive behind it once the bullets started flying.

"You're up early," he said calmly.

"Yeah, you're still lookin' like shit," a male voice stated flatly. "You want somethin' to take the edge off?"

"No way!" Gloria snapped, jabbing a bright red fingernail into the man's chest. "His body is almost dried up."

The man chuckled and held his palms up. "Okay, okay. Listen, I brought a crew with me. Thought we'd get this place put back together for ya if it's alright with the boss lady."

I strained to see the man's face, only catching glimpses of a long salt and pepper beard as he talked. Gloria's shoulders relaxed, and she patted the man's arm before stepping back with a sly grin. "Of course it's okay. I fix you something to eat and drink. This one..." She pointed toward Mike. "He is letting himself waste away to a ghost."

"Thank you, Gloria. We'll start outside and then make our way in here."

She turned and spotted me hiding. "Oh, you have not met Mike's sister, Kate! Come here, come here!"

I reluctantly left my leather sanctuary and made my way over to the entryway. As the man came into view, my steps faltered slightly, but I quickly regained my composure. His mouth turned up in a grin when he saw me, the corners of his eyes crinkling ever so slightly. It wasn't that he was unattractive, because he absolutely was, in a rugged sort of way. His long dark hair was streaked with silver straight out of a Just For Men commercial, and as he showcased a mouthful of blindingly white teeth, my knees weakened, leaving me wondering if I had daddy issues after all.

It was the leather vest that stopped me in my tracks.

He was a biker.

I extended a trembling hand, choking on the pooled saliva in my mouth as I said, "Hello, it's nice to meet you."

He gripped my hand in his with a lopsided grin. "Kate, I've heard a lot about you. I'm Michael, but everyone calls me Comedian."

Comedian rolled over on the club.

The blood drained from my face, and I jerked my hand back as though I'd been burned. "Comedian?" I spluttered, watching as the grin faded from his lips.

"Yeah... is there a problem?"

I took a deep breath, pulling air into my tight lungs before pummeling his chest with my fists. "Y-you shot my father!"

Comedian blinked several times before looking over to Mike. "Junior, how many times do we gotta do this? It's gettin' a little old."

"Kate!" Gloria cried out. "We do not hit guests!"

"He trusted you!" I screamed, my fists turning to claws, that I angrily raked down his arms.

I felt Mike at my back a half-second before he wrapped me up in a reverse bear hug, quilt and all. When I began to struggle, his arms tightened. "Kate, it's not him. It's not him, okay?"

I shook my head, still fighting to free myself. "You said—in the cemetery!"

"I know what I said. I was wrong. Jesus, haven't you talked to your mother and sister?"

"No, but I thought..." I left the rest of my sentence dangling in the air. I'd thought that Comedian had been the one to betray my father—had assumed that my mother and Dakota only wanted to involve me in more needless drama.

Comedian held me with a stare. "Why you avoidin' your mama, Kate?"

Even Gloria crossed her arms over her ample chest, giving me the same look of disappointment that I thought only my Nan could make.

"I..." I swallowed. "I don't know. I mean, we're not exactly close..."

A line of sweat ran down my spine from the interrogation, pooling near the waistband of my slacks. Mike's grip tightened, his body like a furnace, leaving me disoriented.

Maybe he was a better cop than I gave him credit for.

I'd come seeking answers, only to end up on trial.

Comedian nodded at my statement, his eyes still narrowed in suspicion. "Why is that?"

Shoving my elbow into Mike's side, I broke away with a rough pant before spinning around to face the three of them. "You wanna know why I'm not close to my mother? Maybe because she abandoned us when we were still kids, leaving my grandparents to raise us. Maybe it's because she chose gambling and a biker gang over being a mom. Or maybe..." My voice rose to a shout. "It's because I've had to scrape by for years while she lived it up on the road!"

Gloria made a sign of the cross over her chest and muttered something in Spanish before retreating to the kitchen. Comedian and Mike watched me warily, and I huffed out a breath before going to snag my purse from the floor.

I'd come for information. Information I would never get.

"You know what? I don't need this. I've got patients to see—"

Comedian stepped in front of the door and crossed his muscular arms over his chest, blocking me in. "Have you ever asked your mother for the truth?"

"What the hell are you talking about?" I growled. "That is the truth. Now, let me pass."

He stepped aside, holding his hands up as if he was afraid I was going to do something crazy.

Maybe I was.

"Ain't tryin' to stop ya, but it's obvious you came here lookin' for answers. If it were me, I'd start with your husband. He knows more about that night than any of us."

The screen door slammed shut behind me with an ominous thud, and I jogged toward my Tahoe as if a deranged lunatic were on my heels. In the cemetery, Mike had been convinced that Comedian was the one behind it all, said he'd try to run.

It didn't fit with the man I'd just been introduced to inside. He wasn't running from anything or anyone. If Mike had been wrong, then it meant that the traitor was still out there.

It meant that there was no one we could trust.

Comedian might have thought Nate was involved, but I knew my husband. He'd been fighting to distance us from my family since the funeral. There was no way he had anything to do with what happened to my father.

He wouldn't do that to me.

CHAPTER SEVEN

Dakota: February 2017 (Age: 22)

I tugged the leather pants up toward my hips while panting, "Dress for the job you want. That's what they say, right?"

Little Ricky looked up from his cell phone. "Who says that, Caparina?"

I studied my reflection in the mirror with a frown. I looked like a can of biscuits that had been left out in the sun for too long. The baby's nightly demands for ice cream hadn't done me any favors when it came to fitting into my biker-wear.

"People, Little Ricky. People say that you should dress for the job you want. Can I borrow your vest thingy? I think it'll help cover up the fact that my pants won't zip."

He shook his head. "Nah, I earned this kutte. Why don't you just wear normal clothes? You know, yoga pants and shit. Why you tryin' to look like a patch whore?"

I didn't know what a patch whore was. Judging by Little Ricky's expression, it was not something I wanted to be. "I just want them to take me seriously."

My Harley-Davidson tank top chose that moment to roll up, exposing my swollen stomach and the spiderweb of blue veins stretching across it. Everyone kept telling me how beautiful pregnancy was, but I felt like a science experiment gone wrong.

His teeth connected with a lower lip that was twitching suspiciously. "Yeah, I think you should walk up to the clubhouse like that. I can't tell if you're going for ninja or biker. Your outfits look the same."

"That's because they're interchangeable. I just wish..." I gave the pants another good tug, my cheeks reddening from the efforts, before giving up with a dramatic sigh and yanking them off. I retrieved the discarded leggings I'd carelessly tossed on the bedroom floor and pulled them on. "I just wish the designers would have considered the fact that I might be expecting."

"You know, I don't think there are a lot of knocked-up ninjas or bikers, Cap. If you wanna talk to the guys, though, we gotta go now."

The drive to the clubhouse was fairly quiet. Little Ricky messed with the radio, unable to settle on a single station. I picked at my fingernails, my nerves increasing the farther we got from the city.

Instead of traipsing out into the middle of nowhere, I could have put all my focus on being a store manager and Zane's wife. What little excitement I'd been exposed to had only left me longing for the familiar, so why couldn't I let it go?

A chill worked its way down my spine at the thought of my father being lost forever. Maybe I'd never really known Grey, but there was a small part of me that felt like I owed it to him to fight.

Grief had left me battered, but anytime I felt like quitting, I asked myself if he would have given up on me.

"Have you heard from Hail Mary?" he asked, peering at me from over his sunglasses.

I shook my head. "She still won't return my calls. Mama said she's just trying to process everything, but it's been two months. I don't understand why she shuts down like this."

He nodded before turning off onto a dirt road. His truck bounced up and down violently, causing the baby to startle. My belly contorted beneath the fitted tank top as little arms and legs fought to make their presence known.

"Holy shit, Cap, it looks like it's going to burst out of you!"

I patted my shirt reassuringly as we hit another rough patch of road. "You woke the baby up with your bad driving. Why are we even on this road?"

"You wanted to go to the clubhouse, woman! What, you think we just have it sitting on a busy street corner next to a Starbucks? *'Yeah, I'd like a mocha latte, and a side of blow, please.'* The fuck, Cap? You wanna be a biker. You gotta think like a biker."

I giggled at the image. "Geez Louise, calm down. So, I've been working on my interview questions. I wrote them down on index cards and stuck them in my purse. Do you think they would be opposed to me referencing them?"

The truck came to an abrupt halt, getting the baby all fired up again. Little Ricky cocked his head to the side and looked over at me with a smirk. "The fuck? Look, I think you've got it twisted. This ain't —wait, hold up. Actually, I think you should go over some of them with me. Practice makes perfect, yeah?"

I fished the cards out of my purse with a wide grin. "So, they're just a few hypothetical questions... things that I thought might come up. First one is..."

I shuffled through the index cards to find the one I wanted. "'Dakota, how will you increase the ROI on our drugs and guns?'" I folded my hands in my lap and recited, "I'm glad you asked me that, Sir Bear. As store manager of Bella Beauty, I have consistently been a top performer in our district. I possess excellent customer service skills and am willing to go above and beyond to ensure my clients are satisfied—that sounds sexual, doesn't it?"

Little Ricky ran a hand over his mouth, hiding another smirk. "Uh, yeah. Yeah, it absolutely sounds sexual... and what's with the Sir Bear shit?"

"Oh, well, he's the boss, so it's a sign of respect. Does he prefer Your Majesty? I can't screw this up. We have to find my dad."

Instead of laughing at me, Little Ricky's mouth settled into a flat line and reached across the console to squeeze my hand. "We will, Caparina. I swear to you."

I swallowed the emotion threatening to spill over as tears and looked out the window at the sea of motorcycles. "How are there this many bikers and we still don't know where the Sons are?"

Little Ricky shrugged easily as he navigated his pickup truck into a narrow space between two bikes. "Bear called in some of the other chapters... thought it'd be best to make sure everyone was on board with him takin' over, ya know?"

"So, they're not here to fight for my dad? They're just here to say that they think Bear should run things?" There was no hiding the judgment in my tone.

I suddenly wasn't feeling much like a biker chick. My father had given everything to the club, but it seemed as if they'd already forgotten about him.

With Mike busy sobering up, it had made sense to pledge my loyalty to the club, to let them know I would break whatever laws necessary to find my father.

Now, I wasn't so sure.

CHAPTER EIGHT

Dakota: February 2017 (Age: 22)

Alex walked up to the window with a wave. I hadn't seen the prospect since the night of my wedding when he'd stood in front of the doors, refusing to let either me or Kate pass. I'd hated him at the time, but realized his actions hadn't been some elaborate scheme to keep me away from my mother. They were meant to keep me safe.

I climbed down with as much grace as I could muster before meeting his curious expression.

"Hello Alex," I said, carefully infusing conviction into my words. Nan had always claimed that people responded well to authority. She'd only ever said it to Pops, but it was good advice, nonetheless.

He eyes me warily. "Why are you here?"

Little Ricky came around the back of the truck, his boots connecting loudly with bits of gravel. "She's with me. Why don't you get back to your post before Pres sees you?"

Alex nodded and scurried back toward the gate, still watching us with wide eyes.

"Does Alex know something I don't?" I finally asked. "He keeps staring at me like I'm about to get my head caved in, and he wants to remember how I looked before I got dead."

With a chuckle, Little Ricky looped an arm around my shoulders and led me toward a large building. "Nah, Cap. Everyone's just on edge with what happened to your old man. Bear cracked down on security—"

"Yet, here you are, bringing strays back to the clubhouse," the man in question stated flatly as he appeared in the doorway. "Why is that?"

I stepped forward. "Bear, I've come to pledge my support to the club. I want to patch in—to find my father. I have skills. Good ones. I think I could be a tremendous asset to Silent Phoenix." My words came out rushed and incoherent, nothing like what I'd rehearsed in front of the bathroom mirror.

Bear's eyebrows lowered into a look of disinterest, the muscles in his neck straining against the bandana around his throat. "Goblin," he said, using Little Ricky's biker name. "Thought I made myself clear."

"You did, but *Caparina*, she was like, 'Nah, Little Ricky, I gotta do this for my family's honor,' and who am I to stand in the way of vengeance?"

Bear covered his eyes and shook his head. "Jesus fuckin' Christ, was there a flashin' neon sign at the top of the canyon welcoming you? Or maybe you saw the help wanted ad in the newspaper?"

We both stayed quiet, standing shoulder to shoulder, awaiting our lecture.

"No?" Bear asked. "Oh, that's right. We don't fuckin' advertise what we are. And the day we open this club up to women is the day I stop bein' a biker. We clear?"

Two deep set lines ran vertically between his brows, and I got lost in thought, debating whether Botox would correct it. His skin needed a good microdermabrasion treatment... or maybe a chemical peel. I glanced up at Little Ricky's face, pleased with how well his skin was responding to the regimen I had him on.

"Dakota!" Bear snapped. "I asked you a fuckin' question."

"Have you ever considered having laser treatments done for the sun damage on your face?" I blurted.

Little Ricky went stock-still beside me, his face a blank mask as he whispered, "Fuck."

"Is this a joke?" Bear growled. "You came down here to talk about skincare?"

His voice rose, and I flinched. "I didn't mean—"

"Look around you, sweetheart. This look like the fuckin' *Clinique* counter to you? Now, I don't know if Goblin put you up to this, or if you're always this stupid, but there's only one type of facial being offered around here, and your daddy would have my balls if I let you step one foot inside to see it." He leaned back against the side of the clubhouse and crossed his arms over his massive chest, clearly waiting for a response.

The facials he mentioned had nothing to do with beauty. Instead of letting my mind venture down that rabbit hole, I pushed the unwanted images away and tried again. "You need me. I know my dad's alive, and I want to help find him."

What kind of man would deny a daughter such a simple request?

"Go home, Dakota," Bear ground out, the muscle in his jaw popping. "Goblin, she shows up again, and your ass'll be on the line. We clear?"

Little Ricky nodded and wrapped his hand around my bicep, leading me back toward his truck.

"Wait!" My throat clogged with tears as I freed myself from his grip. I had one shot. "How can you do this? How can you just pretend like everything's fine? Why aren't you looking for him?"

Bear's eyes narrowed, but he just shook his head before disappearing back inside.

I'd failed.

With Silent Phoenix went my last chance to find my father. Bear hadn't seen me as an ally, but a nuisance, a pesky bug to be squished under the heel of his boot.

I lowered my head, glancing around the gravel lot to see if anyone else had witnessed my downfall.

It reminded me of my first day of sixth grade, standing in a crowded cafeteria with my tray gripped tightly in my sweaty fists. A few kids had looked up, quickly scanning me from head to toe before going back to their conversations, smirks playing on their lips.

As if I was a joke.

I'd spent my entire life fighting to break away from the chubby girl who just wanted to be included, only to end up right back where I'd started.

I might not have been holding a tray, but I was very much still on the outside looking in. My skin vibrated with humiliation as I imagined the bikers laughing at the idea that I could be useful in finding Grey.

"Don't waste your breath," a soft voice said, and we both turned. Lauren sat on the tailgate of a truck, swinging her legs idly.

"Have you been here this whole time?"

She nodded and flipped off the empty doorway with a glare. "Yep. Outshot every single one of the bastards, and he still refused to let me patch in. Told me to go home and get ready for the babies, as if that's all I can do."

I glanced down at my own bump with a solemn nod. "It hurts, doesn't it? Maybe he's afraid of the risk. He probably doesn't understand that we're women who know how to fight."

Little Ricky made a noise in the back of his throat that sounded suspiciously like a laugh before looking away.

She clicked her tongue against her teeth. "I even checked with my obstetrician, and he said it was perfectly safe to go to war with a rival biker club until the third trimester."

My lips parted with a soft gasp as I looked up at Lauren in awe.

She'd covered all her bases.

Zane had warned me against doing anything risky when an actual doctor had given her the green light. I smiled, knowing my superhero would have no choice but to let me go after the Sons when presented with solid scientific evidence.

"Dakota," Lauren said, waving a hand in front of my face.

I blinked, pulled away from my fantasy of winning my first argument against my husband. "Yeah?"

"I'm just fucking with you, but I have a plan." She frowned at Little Ricky. "You gonna rat us out?"

He shook his head firmly. "Nah, *mi sirenita*. You know I could never turn on you. Have you come to your senses and decided you want a real man yet?"

I looked between the two of them, wondering what I'd missed. "Were you—I mean, is there something? I think you'd make a great couple... you know, were you not married to my brother and all."

Lauren cocked her head to the side. "Do you always talk this much?"

"Absolutely," Little Ricky interjected, with a rough bark of laughter. "Sometimes, I'm like, 'C'mon, Cap. Give it a rest,' you know?"

I slugged him in the shoulder and straightened. "I think we've gotten off-topic here. It's clear that Bear won't let us join their club, so what do we do now?"

Her eyes sparkled mischievously. "Silent Phoenix wants to stick its head in the sand instead of looking into Grey's disappearance. We can either do what Bear suggested, or—"

"Or what?" I asked, resisting the urge to bounce up and down on the balls of my feet as the popular girl swiped the trays off the table and gestured for me to sit down.

"Or we can assemble our own team," she finished with a wide grin. "What do you say?"

What did I say?

It was the culmination of every childhood fantasy.

My chance to wear the cape, to be the heroine my father needed.

"I'm in," I rushed out. "It's like you read my mind. I've got a notebook back at the house with some ideas for what we could call ourselves. The Avengers has already been taken, but what about The Revengers... or the—"

"You know she can't shoot a gun to save her life, don't you?" Little Ricky asked, flicking his switchblade open and closed.

"Biscuits and gravy, Little Ricky. You sound just like your dad now, doing everything in your power to keep me out of it. Your face even looks like his." I used my fingers to manipulate my lips into a sneer similar to the one on his face.

He opened his mouth to argue, but Lauren cut him off. "If you two wouldn't mind taking a moment to shut the hell up, I'd explain to you it doesn't matter. I've got a guy that might be able to help."

"Does Mikey know you're doing this?" Little Ricky asked, no longer teasing.

Her eyes flashed briefly with pain, and she shook her head. "I'm doing this for him just as much as me. He can't fight right now. So, it's up to us. We can either stay in the kitchen, barefoot and pregnant, or we can go down swinging. What'll it be, Dakota?"

I'd woken up this morning, convinced no one could understand my need to find Grey. Kate had gone back to her everyday life, and Mama had shut down emotionally.

Lauren got it, though.

She knew that if the Sons weren't stopped, then we would never truly be safe. We were bringing children into this world. How could we shield them from the ugliness if we refused to take a stand?

When the mob and the press and the whole world tell you to move, your job is to plant yourself like a tree beside the river of truth and tell the whole world-- 'No, you move.'

I'd always imagined myself as Punisher, but maybe Big Guy had seen something in me I hadn't been able to see in myself. Captain America refused to back down, even when the deck was stacked against him.

He wouldn't have taken Bear, or Hydra, or anyone else's words as gospel. I had to do this, not just for my father, but for the baby kicking in my belly and the brother who'd lost his way. I would plant myself like a tree and refuse to bend for anyone.

"Lauren," I said, sounding stronger than I had in months. "I'm with you... until the end of the line."

CHAPTER NINE

Celia: February 2017 (Age: 44)

3 *MTA3.*

The vanity license plate on the shiny red BMW greeted me as I pulled into my driveway. I stifled a groan before unbuckling, knowing exactly who it belonged to.

The only woman in the world who would think that having the mirror image of *eat me* on her license plate was the epitome of class.

I slammed the car door and stepped over the multitude of vases littering the porch. At some point, I'd given up on taking them all inside, leaving the delicate blooms to battle the freezing temperatures alone.

The inside of the house wasn't much better.

Almost every available surface was littered with flowers in various states of decay. It had always struck me as odd that we gave living things to commemorate death.

What good were flowers when I'd been given a throne of ebony by the god of death himself?

Initially, Lucy had kept up with the watering and trimming, but even she'd gone back to her normal life, leaving me with an entire greenhouse to manage on my own.

That was what happened, wasn't it?

After any tragedy, the initial outpouring of love and support was so thick you could cut it with a knife. It was in the weeks and months after that people dropped off or fade away. The same ones who'd insisted I call them if I needed anything suddenly went out of their way to avoid a conversation with me at the grocery store.

Maybe they would've stuck around were my husband actually dead instead of just missing. As it was, every day since the funeral had been spent sifting through the rumors to find a grain of truth.

He's just hiding out until the dust settles...

You know Jamie, he's a master of faking his own death...

He's working with the feds...

I'd heard it all, but didn't believe a word of it. They would never come close to scratching the surface of who Jamie Quinn was. I knew his heart and soul as well as my own, and he'd promised me he wouldn't leave like before.

The setting sun cast an eerie orange glow over the porch, and I took a deep breath before glancing toward the swing. "Did Bear send you?"

Molly raised a perfectly sculpted eyebrow before rocking back. "You know better than that, Celia. When have I ever let that man tell me what to do?"

I shifted my purse to the other shoulder before leaning against the railing. "Really? I haven't heard from you in weeks, Molly. Weeks! Look me in the eye and tell me that's not Bear."

"Things are..." She sighed. "Things are hard right now——"

"Bullshit," I snapped. "Hard is being told your husband didn't make it, only to find out later that there was a massive cover-up. Hard is having to watch your kids fall apart all over again at losing him. Hard is knowing that Mikey nearly died from an overdose. I don't know what you're talking about, but it's not hard."

Molly nodded and dropped her hands down to rest in her lap. "You're right. I've been a shitty friend to you. I just..."

She paused, looking off toward the orchard. "I don't know what to say. None of it makes any sense, and I didn't want to push you for answers that you obviously don't have."

I gnawed on the inside of my cheek. "If there's a chance he's still alive, then I won't stop searching. I'll march into the Son's clubhouse if I have to, but I won't turn my back and just forget to make your old man happy."

"You think Bear would be happy with that? He'd been riding with Grey since they were kids, Celia—"

"Then why is he doing this? Why is he making it seem as if he wanted my husband gone the entire time? Bear was quick to point the finger at Mikey, but the only one who benefitted here was him. We know for a fact that Cobra and the Sons are still out there, but the club suddenly wants to stay out of it? Why?"

Molly patted the empty seat beside her, but I remained standing. "Come here, Celia," she sighed. "Just hear me out, okay? Do you really think that Bear would have rolled over on the club—that he would've turned his back on Grey?"

"I... I don't know," I finally admitted. "Look at it from my angle, Molly. He inherited the club and immediately turned his back on my family as if we'd done something wrong. People we've known for years no longer give us the time of day. The girl I've been friends with since high school won't return my calls or texts... how does that look to you?"

Her jaw clenched, but she nodded again. "It looks really fucking guilty. You know how the club operates, though. Women are always the last to know anything—"

I laughed at the lie. "Last to know? Since when Molly? What, did you lose your 'magical powers' after Dakota's wedding?"

"You know that's not fair," she said with a small smile. "I've only ever been able to get minor details out of Bear... not a step-by-step plan for world domination."

"Well, don't leave me hanging. What minor details has he given you that left you feeling confident in the club again? I know you didn't come here for social reasons."

Molly ran a hand through her hair and slid her toes along the wooden planks of the porch, pulling the swing from side to side. "Bear is handling things," she began.

I leveled my index finger at her, just as I had with the girls when they were younger, spinning their webs of lies to avoid getting into trouble. "Don't. That club isn't doing one thing to find my husband, so don't try to convince me otherwise."

"Bear thinks Grey worked a deal with the FBI, maybe even the CIA, to disappear," she rushed out with a sigh. "It's the most plausible explanation for where he is, Celia. Maybe he's going to take down the Sons from another angle. It's... it's genius, really."

I shook my head, my jaw tightening in anger over the same worn-out excuses people kept reciting as truth. "No. He left me once before and afterward promised me he'd never do it again. We almost lost everything because of it, so enlighten me as to why he'd think that leaving us vulnerable for a second time was a lucrative option?"

"I'm not saying we know for sure... it's just one theory the club has—"

"When he faked his death before, every member of that club knew about it. It doesn't make sense that he'd accidentally forget to clue them in this time, does it?"

Her lips moved into a flat line. "Celia, someone in that clubhouse was giving up intel. Why would Grey announce his plans without knowing who the traitor was? By faking his death, he can observe the club and draw out the rat without anyone growing suspicious."

It made sense, and I hated her for it.

"But Mikey announced the casket was empty in front of the club. The traitor has to know—"

"I agree," she interjected. "But if anything, that should just make them more nervous... more likely to slip up. That's what we're counting on. If the rat feels cornered, he's going to do something stupid, and maybe it'll lead us right to the Sons."

"Why wouldn't he tell me, though?" It was the question that I'd been turning over in my mind, pulling at it like a loose thread, hoping it would unravel the mystery.

"Maybe he thought it'd make you a target again. He told you before, and you were tortured for it. He must've figured out that the Sons had eyes everywhere and decided to make it as realistic as possible. You had a funeral—"

"What if you're wrong?" I asked.

"What other explanation is there, Celia?"

I looked down at my shoes, knowing it would have been easier to believe that he was dead.

He'd promised me.

"If you're wrong, then the club is wasting valuable time going in circles when we could be out there searching for him. Did Bear put you up to this? Was this the message he wanted to send?"

Molly shook her head. "There was only one message that Bear had for you. He said to trust him. And that..." She paused as if trying to remember. "The day he takes off his kutte is the day you'll know he's surrendering."

Her words triggered a memory of being in the kitchen with Jamie, eating fried Spam sandwiches, happy for the first time in years.

I know now. Still, I chose to stay. The day I take it off is the day you'll know I've given up on us.

My hand was hidden in the evening shadows, but I could still feel the weight of my wedding band against my finger. I hadn't taken it off.

I just had to trust that Jamie hadn't either and that Bear had a plan to keep us all safe.

CHAPTER TEN

Celia: February 2017 (Age: 44)

Daddy: We have the girls' money.

I studied the text from my father, searching for the catch. It was just over two months ago that he was informed it had been stolen in the first place.

There was no way they'd been able to come up with that kind of cash in such a short amount of time, even if they'd taken every last penny from my father's retirement fund.

"What's wrong?" Dakota asked, running her fingers over the railing of a crib. Today was supposed to be about her and the baby, not my parents.

I tucked the phone back into my purse. "Nothing. It was just a wrong number. Now, tell me your theme again."

She mashed her lips together while narrowing her eyes. "I've only told you three times already. Are you sure you're okay? You've been out of it all morning."

I turned my head slightly until Crossbones came into view. He was rifling through a rounder of newborn onesies, clearly trying to blend in. Unfortunately for him, the leather vest and motorcycle boots stood out like a flashing neon sign, drawing the attention of almost everyone in the store.

Maybe Dakota had grown accustomed to Little Ricky following her everywhere she went that an added biker didn't even register.

Bear wanted me to trust him implicitly, but the added security only increased the feelings of uneasiness. I hadn't known everything that had gone on within the club walls, but if we were in danger, Jamie would have at least given me a warning.

The bell over the door jingled, and I whipped my head around, already reaching for the gun in my purse.

Lauren.

She nodded to Crossbones before making her way over to us. "Did you tell her?" she asked Dakota.

"Not yet," my daughter said with a shake of her head. "She's been acting weird since we got here."

"I'm acting 'weird' because we seem to have a security detail that I wasn't made aware of," I hissed while gesturing toward Crossbones.

"He's with me," Lauren answered smoothly while examining the price tag on the side of one of the cribs. "Now, let's get right to it. Silent Phoenix won't help us, and we won't stop until we know what happened the night of Dakota's wedding. It leaves us in a very precarious position. We can either stay in their good graces and look the other way, or we can make another enemy, but get the answers we want."

"What—you want to go after the Sons on our own?" I choked. It wasn't as if the thought hadn't crossed my mind, but we didn't have the numbers.

Even Jamie hadn't had enough men to take them out.

I'd gone after Manny on my own, only making it out by the skin of my teeth and with more than a little help from Jamie. The three of us against the Sons was a joke.

"I'm not suggesting we declare war or anything," Lauren stated, lifting a small lamp off the nightstand near the display crib. "We start small. Someone within the club is giving them information. So, we follow them... see where they lead us."

Dakota nodded in agreement, as if it was the most obvious solution.

"Absolutely not."

Lauren's eyes widened in shock, and she brought her arms up over her chest.

"You're saying no?" Dakota spluttered. "No? Just like that? Even knowing it might help us find my dad?"

"Dakota," I pleaded. "Just let it go... please. Now, we came here to shop for your nursery. Let's pick out a few things, and then we'll grab lunch."

"Celia," Lauren began. "You, of all people, should be on board with this. Don't you want to know where he is?"

I did.

More than anything.

But I wasn't willing to risk anyone else's life. Jamie wouldn't have allowed it. Plus, Bear had asked me to stand down while the club looked into things. I'd given Molly my word.

"For all we know, someone stole his body from the casket, and this is nothing more than a wild goose chase." The lie slipped easily off my tongue. It was still better than the alternative that Jamie had sold his soul to the feds.

"You really believe that?" Dakota asked, her head cocked to the side.

I busied myself with a basket of Minky baby blankets, rearranging each rolled bundle until they all looked uniform. "It doesn't matter what I believe."

"Why?" Lauren demanded.

The next basket was filled with sterling silver rattles. I bypassed them and moved on to the swaddling blankets, fighting to hold my emotions in check.

"Answer me, Celia," she tried again. "Why are you against this?"

"Because."

Lauren blew out a frustrated breath. "Because, why?"

"Because neither one of you has any idea what you're up against," I snapped before holding up a blanket. "Did you see this one, Dakota? It has baby superheroes on it."

She flicked a small glance toward the blanket in my hand before rolling her eyes. "That's DC. There's nothing super about it. Stop changing the subject and tell us why you're so against this, Mama."

My forehead dampened with perspiration. I dropped the blanket back into the basket and moved across the store with Lauren and Dakota on my heels.

"Mama... answer me."

"Because I said so," I ground out through clenched teeth.

"Why?" Lauren demanded. "Just tell us why. You at least owe us that."

The fluorescent lights overhead seemed to burn hotter, and a line of sweat ran from my temple down toward my cheek. "Because you don't know these men."

"And you do?" Lauren asked. "They killed my mother, Celia. Then, they showed up at my house and tried to kill me. I will not sit back and wait for them to come after someone else I love. And you know they will. As much as everyone wants to pretend it's over, we both know that it's not. I'm not willing to sit back and wait to be picked off. What is it that's holding you back?"

A sales associate made her way toward us with a big smile before taking in the situation. Once she saw our faces, she quickly disappeared back toward the register.

"You're pregnant," I admitted softly. "Both of you."

Lauren shook her head with a bitter laugh. "You know, I didn't peg you as being a traditional sort of woman, but I guess I was wrong. According to you, I should just be sitting at home, waiting for my blessed arrival, right?"

I spun until I was facing both of them, my chest heaving with each ragged breath. "You're pregnant, and you think that for whatever reason, it protects you. Not with these men. It makes you a more lucrative target. Don't you see that?"

My hand came up over my mouth, but I pushed the words out. "They won't hesitate to break your body with theirs, and they won't stop until they have ripped away the very thing you love from you. They won't care that you're pregnant when they leave you bruised and bloody, begging for help that will never come. I can't let you go after them."

"Mama, is that what happened to you?" Dakota whispered.

Lauren sucked in a sharp breath. "Jesus."

My eyes stung with tears that wouldn't come, and I hitched my purse up on my shoulder before moving toward the front door. I didn't stop until I reached Jamie's truck.

After climbing in and locking the doors behind me, I let my head fall against the steering wheel with a soft thud. I'd admitted my worst fears and released my demons all in one breath. I had to hope it was enough to keep them from doing something stupid.

My phone vibrated from inside my purse, and I fumbled for it without lifting my head. My fingers closed around the rectangular shape, and I pulled it into my lap.

> *Daddy: Can you come by now? I don't feel comfortable leaving the cash somewhere for you to pick up.*

For two people who hadn't lost a minute of sleep stealing from my kids over the years, it seemed as if my parents had suddenly grown a conscience.

Their insistence would've made sense were Jamie still around, but as far as they knew, he was dead.

Why were they in such a rush now?

> *Me: I'll be there in fifteen.*

I quickly tapped the reply and leaned back in the seat. What I wanted to do was go home and clear my head, or maybe rewind, back to a time when Dakota knew nothing of biker clubs.

My phone began buzzing again before switching over to the truck's system. When Angel's name flashed across the display, I cleared my throat and picked up. "Hey."

"Hey yourself. Where are you?" His voice boomed through the speakers, and I turned the volume down before pulling out of the parking lot.

"I'm—my parents texted."

He went quiet before drawling, "Didn't know Satan had a cell phone."

I grinned and made a right back toward Broadway. "Yeah, makes it easier to keep tabs on the demons."

"What'd they want, Celia?"

"They, uh, they said they have the girls' money. I'm headed there now."

He clicked his tongue against his teeth. "Just like that, huh? Why now?"

"That's what I've been asking myself. The timing is odd, isn't it?"

"Completely," Angel said, and I could picture the look of confusion on his face as clearly as if he was sitting next to me. "Considerin' that Jamie all but forgave the debt at Dakota's wedding."

"Wait—he did?" Most of the details of Dakota's wedding had begun to blur, making it impossible to remember what, if anything, we'd talked about.

Had he told me?

"He damn sure did, so why are they in such a hurry to give you the money back now? Don't sit right with me, kid." I turned on my blinker and merged into the turning lane, lost in the monotonous clicks.

"Tell me you ain't headed there alone, Celia," Angel chided. "You're too smart for that, girl. I'll meet you, but your ass ain't steppin' foot inside without me. You hear what I'm sayin'?"

"I hear you, old man," I said with another soft smile. "How far out are you?"

He chuckled. "You tell me."

I pulled into my parent's long driveway, unsurprised to see the ocean blue Chevy truck parked behind their cars. "You stalking me now?" I asked as he swung the door open and climbed out.

"Nah, just makin' sure you're safe. C'mon, let's go find out what these two assholes really want." He patted the holster on his hip. "She ain't got a yard full of cops this time either, does she?"

I pushed the doorbell. "We're not shooting anyone... we'll just get the money and go, okay?" I'd never admitted it, but Angel had given me a much-needed distraction from the conversation at the baby boutique.

Several minutes passed, and no one came to the door. Angel rapped his knuckles against the wood with a frown, keeping one hand on his gun.

After telling myself that they were in the backyard, I grabbed the doorknob and twisted. It opened to an empty den.

Angel held his arm out before moving around me and into the house. "Stay there, Celia."

"I'm not standing on the porch," I snapped. "I'm sure they're just out—"

The small breakfast table where my father sat and read the paper every morning while my mother made breakfast was now covered in money.

Large stacks of cash that completely covered the wood underneath.

It looked as if someone had robbed a bank.

"Angel," I whispered, no longer convinced that him drawing a gun was overreacting. "What's happening?"

He shook his head. "Your parents always have this kind of cash lying around?"

I shook my head. "Never."

"Let's get outside and call the club, okay?"

I'd just opened my mouth to agree when I saw it. I sucked in a sharp breath and pointed with shaking fingers towards the cabinets.

The corner of the counter near the stove was smeared with blood. It ran down the lower cabinets and had pooled on the carpet.

Home invasion.

A burglary gone wrong.

The cash on the table mocked every one of my plausible explanations. The text I'd received hadn't come from my father, but from whoever was responsible for this.

I shuddered at the realization that Lauren was right. The Sons hadn't disappeared. They'd been lying out of sight in the tall grass, just waiting for the next opportunity to strike.

And it was only a matter of time before they came for me, which meant I was going to have to break my promise to Bear.

If the Sons wanted a war, I'd give them a war.

CHAPTER ELEVEN

Grey: February 2017 (Age: 53)

Awareness settled over me, ringing loudly in my ears and pricking the backs of my eyelids even as my body fought against it; urging me to stay in a state of unconsciousness until I was healed. Saint might have wanted me alive, but Cobra was doing everything in his power to send me to the Reaper.

It was payback for the things I'd done to Manny—the ways I'd forced him to stay alive until Celia was ready to put him down.

My fingers brushed against cotton sheets, and I breathed a shallow breath of relief that I was no longer lying on the cold concrete floor. Reluctantly, I opened one eye, and then the other, before taking in my surroundings.

I was back where I started. A Hell of complete white. My nose wrinkled at the medicinal stench in the air—more evidence that I was going to be kept on the brink of death for as long as it suited them. I slowly turned my head to the side to see that my bruised and cut left wrist was back in fabric restraints while my right was in a sling, securely fasted to my chest.

A wave of nausea washed over me as I tried lifting it, leaving me to guess whether it was broken or simply dislocated. I tried swallowing past the lump in my throat, immediately wincing at the soreness. The ringing in my ears intensified, along with the urge to cry.

Even if I made it out alive, I had no way of defending myself when my shooting arm was being held together with bandages and a nylon hammock.

The room suddenly fell silent just as a familiar voice dryly noted, "Well, this all looks fuckin' terrible."

Ignoring the jolt of pain in my neck, I lifted my head and stared disbelievingly toward the center of the room. "What the fuck? It ain't possible—I gotta be dreamin'."

"Well, that sure as fuck ain't the greeting I expected," Slim said with a laugh, pulling a metal folding chair up alongside my bed. "The fuck have you gotten yourself into this time?"

"But, you're... you're dead," I spluttered. "I saw you lyin' in the goddamn casket!"

He jerked his head up and down. "Yeah, I'm still fuckin' dead. From the looks of it, you are too. Jesus fuckin' Christ, I leave you alone for three years and look at you!"

I fell back against the mattress with a heavy sigh, somehow comforted by the confirmation that I'd lost my goddamned mind and was now chatting with the ghost of my best friend.

"Yeah, well, I'm still sober," I said as I watched him crack his knuckles. "Don't that count for somethin'?"

His eyes wandered down my neck and chest before coming to rest on my arm. "Maybe if you weren't tied down to a fuckin' bed, we could celebrate. Tell me, how the hell did you end up in this mess, Jamie?"

"I don't know... just lucky, I guess." My eyelids grew heavy, and I blinked, fighting the urge to give in to oblivion. I'd spent years wishing that I could hear his voice again. I wasn't letting myself fall asleep now. "They—the men who did this—they call themselves the Sons of Death."

He let out a rough bark of laughter before leaning back in the chair. "Well, they ain't mincin' words, are they? I guess *Sons Who Like Stabbin' and Shit* would've been too long to fit on a kutte."

"You know," I groaned. "Don't remember you bein' this funny while you were alive."

"Oh, you just weren't payin' attention. I was a fuckin' hoot. Ask anybody—well, fuck. Guess you can't exactly do that, can ya? Tell me about these bikers. What do you know about them?"

I ran my tongue over my teeth, still tasting the blood from where I'd bitten down on it while being hung. "You remember us lookin' for the pricks that hurt Celia?"

He nodded. "Yeah, you ever catch 'em?"

"All but one. From what I can gather, Cobra started the Sons—met up with someone named Saint, and they fuckin' dismantled my club from the inside."

"Jesus, who rolled over?"

"That's the bitch of it," I admitted. "I don't know. Cobra wants me to believe it was Mikey or Bear, but that don't make a goddamn bit of sense."

Slim smiled. "Bear? Easiest way to find out if it's him would be to check his blood alcohol level. Fucker drinks himself into a stupor when he's stressed out. You know what I'm talkin' about."

I smiled at the truth of his words. "You should have seen him at your funeral, Slim. He'd pour a shot out for you, then knock one back. He passed out on the porch, so we dragged his ass into the bed of David's truck, left him to sleep it off. Only, we didn't know that David and Elizabeth were stayin' down in Port Arthur."

"Oh, Christ."

"Yeah," I nodded. "He woke up covered in seagull shit with no idea where the hell he was."

Slim wiped the tears from the corners of his eyes as he erupted in another fit of laughter. "Sounds like Bear. You really think he'd turn on you?"

"I don't know anything anymore. Someone put me here... just wish I knew who that was."

He ran his hands over his face before folding them under his chin with a resolute nod. "What has this Cobra guy given up?"

I shrugged, fighting to remember anything important that had been said before I'd been beaten into unconsciousness.

"C'mon, Jamie. Think. Why does he want you to think it's Mikey or Bear?"

"They want me to think the club's turned against me?"

He nodded. "Don't forget that. They'll use it to get into your head. Today, it's Mikey. Tomorrow, it might be Celia. Fight to hold on to what you know. Would Bear roll over?"

"No," I answered firmly.

"Good. Now tell me who would." Slim leaned back in the chair, somehow looking more alive as a zombie than I did with a heartbeat.

"I got no fuckin' clue. I've been lookin' into it for the better part of a year, and I'm no closer now than when I started."

Slim disagreed. "You're in the goddamn lion's den. What better place to be when you're tryin' to catch a rat?"

I held up my left palm as far as the restraint would allow. "Better place? Look at me, Slim! I'm a fuckin' mess of broken bones and torn ligaments. Even if I solved the entire goddamn thing, it don't help anybody right now."

He lifted his leg and rested his boot down near my feet. "If they wanted you dead, you'd be dead. As that ain't the case, you gotta think like they are. What's their goal?"

I closed my eyes to sort my jumbled thoughts.

Death is comin' for you...

"Celia," I croaked. "Saint wants Celia."

"Why?"

"I... I don't know."

"Okay," he said calmly. "Who do you know who would want to hurt her?"

"Betsy, but no way in hell is she behind this. No club would back a woman. There's a chance it could be Celia's parents. Norma took our girls... maybe she wasn't plannin' on stoppin' until she'd taken everything..."

"And? Who else?" Slim pushed.

I shook my head, staring blankly up at the ceiling. "Nobody besides Cobra, but he ain't the one in charge. That make any sense to you?"

He scratched at his long beard, lost in thought. "I feel like there's somethin' we're missin' here. Almost like we're lookin' at it the wrong way, ya know?"

I did because the idea that someone had orchestrated a war and taken me out just to get to her seemed like overkill. "I figured out the badge who was workin' against us."

"And?" Slim pushed. "Care to share that with the class?"

"I don't exactly know the prick's name, but I can tell you what he looked like. Maybe you can get it back to Mikey and the club."

"And how exactly do you expect me to do that?"

I shrugged my good shoulder. "I don't know... can't you go haunt them or some shit? Turn off a few lights? Maybe write it in blood on the walls?"

"Think you and I both know I ain't a ghost. I'm up here." He tapped the side of his head. "When you wake up, I'm gone."

I clenched my jaw. "Thought I was awake."

"You really think after the beating your body just took that you're awake?"

A scream echoed off the walls in another part of the building, and I lifted my head. "Was that a woman?"

Slim nodded. "Sure as fuck sounded like one."

Celia.

I thrashed against the mattress, fighting to free my wrist from the restraints. "Help me get out of this, Slim. We gotta get out of this room."

My vision blurred, and the ringing in my ears returned. "Shit... I can't see. Give me a second to let this pass, and we'll go, okay?"

When the room remained silent, I lifted my head, blinking until the fog cleared. The chair beside the bed sat empty, just as it had the entire time I'd been lying here.

A tear slipped free from the corner of my eye and ran into my ear.

I'd lost him again.

As if it wasn't bad enough, I was tied up like an animal. Life had provided a cruel reminder that no matter the outcome here, my best friend was never coming back.

CHAPTER TWELVE

Grey: February 2017 (Age: 53)

The woman screamed again; the sound piercing my skull in a thousand places. I no longer cared about breaking free to help her. I just wanted it to stop.

The ache in my neck intensified until all I could do was lie perfectly still, keeping my breathing shallow as I watched the blindingly white ceiling.

"Grey," a voice shouted from nearby. "You've got company. Wake up."

Cobra had done it. He'd gotten in my head, his voice ringing loud and clear through the empty room. I was going to die hearing him taunt me from somewhere above.

"J-Jamie?" the woman cried. "J-Jamie, h-help us!"

I closed my eyes and breathed a soft sigh of relief when I realized it wasn't Celia or my girls.

Something brushed against the sole of my foot before an arc of electricity jumped through me, torquing my body like a pretzel. My legs curled up under my ass as my hips arched up toward the ceiling. The arm that I'd been careful not to move now jerked involuntarily out of the sling, forcing a low growl from my lips.

When I opened my eyes, the room was no longer empty. Cobra

stood grinning near the foot of the bed, waving a cattle prod as if it were a flag. The screams I'd heard in my head sounded again, this time much closer than they'd been before.

I panted through an agonizing breath before turning toward it. Norma sat against the wall, arms bound in chains against her chest.

"J-Jamie," she moaned. "H-h-help him." She pushed her chained hands away from her body. I lifted my head and followed the line to where Richard lay on the concrete. Blood poured from a wound on his head. If he wasn't dead already, he would be soon enough. There was no way Saint planned on keeping all of us alive.

Cobra held up his arms, still gripping the cattle prod in one hand. "I thought you might be getting lonely and brought you a couple of friends."

Norma continued her sniffling from the corner, her eyes pleading for me to rescue them. It took every bit of strength I still possessed to laugh. "Friends? You and your buddy Saint ain't been doin' your research."

Her eyes narrowed as they met mine, not realizing I was doing the only thing I could to save her ass. I'd lost all respect for her and Dick when they stole my children from me. It didn't mean I wanted to see them die, though.

Richard chose that moment to rejoin the land of the living, jerking up off the floor with a loud groan. "Norma," he slurred, struggling to make his way toward her. "It's gonna be okay."

"What does Saint want with a couple of old fucks?" I bit out, my body still buzzing from the shock.

"Saint?" Cobra ran the handle of the prod under his chin. "Who said Saint had anything to do with this? You're the one with the vendetta against them, are you not? Don't they owe you some money?"

I used my fingers to try to loosen the bindings around my wrist. If I broke free, I could distract Cobra long enough for them to escape. Maybe they could get a message to Celia.

"Forgave the debt. Look at 'em. What threat do they pose to me? I can always make more money—"

Cobra caught Richard by the hair and jerked his head back. The old man's eyes widened in fear. "You could make the money back, but it'd take a while. I mean, they'd been stealing from your kids for years, right?"

"You got a point to your ramblin'?"

He nodded. "Since when has the leader of Silent Phoenix ever let anyone off without paying?"

"In case you hadn't noticed," I panted, trying to adjust the positioning of my arm. "I ain't the leader of shit right now."

"Maybe not, but that didn't stop you from going after your enemies. One." He dropped the prod and pulled his gun from the holster.

"By." With a grin, he pulled back the hammer and pressed the barrel against Richard's skull as Norma screamed again, begging me to stop him.

"Cobra, we both know you ain't ever been Saint's bitch. Don't do his dirty work for him." My voice was steady and even, as if his actions were of no consequence to me.

"One." He pulled the trigger, sending a spray of blood onto the opposite wall. Richard's body slumped forward, no longer recognizable from the neck up as anything other than a mass of tissue and brain matter.

Norma's screams turned to hyperventilating until her eyes rolled back in her head, her brain protecting her the only way it knew how.

Cobra straightened and placed his gun back into the holster on his dress pants with a sigh. "Tsk, tsk. Why'd you do it, Grey—going after your wife's elderly parents like that? It's unimaginable."

"You wanted to prove somethin', you've done it. Now, let her go." I ground my teeth and flexed the fingers on my left hand, testing the strength of the restraint.

He continued talking as if I hadn't said a word. "Even after they worked so hard to pay back every cent, you showed them no mercy."

"What are you talking about? They never paid me back. I forgave the debt. What part of that ain't stuck yet?"

"They texted Celia to tell her they had the money. I wonder what she thought when she got to the house and saw the cash, but no sign of her parents. Well—" He paused. "I take that back. She would have seen the blood. How long do you think it'll be before she realizes it was you?"

I shook my head. "If that was Saint's big plan, tell him he failed. Celia ain't gonna fall for it—"

"Won't she? You promised to never leave her again, yet all the evidence points to you having done just that. How many lives will it take before she sees you for what you've always been? A monster. You turned your back on her and your kids. Do you know what that did to your son?"

My blood ran cold, and I stopped fighting against the restraint. "Mikey? What the fuck did you do to him?"

"He OD'ed, Grey. All we did was give him a nudge in the right direction. Took away his job and any chance of him patching into the club. The rest was all him. Trust me," he added with a somber look. "That was never our plan. We were convinced he'd turn on you, but all he did was destroy himself."

I saw him face down on his bedroom floor, surrounded by empty bottles of tequila and his own puke. The same fear I'd felt that night as I pounded my fist against his chest coursed through my veins again.

The sheer panic as I'd breathed for him and done sternum rubs came back full force.

Only this time, I hadn't been there to save him.

"Is he?" Bile rose in my throat at the image of him being all alone, thinking that I'd abandoned him. What had been running through his mind?

Cobra quickly shook his head. "The doctor your daughter married was able to save him. His wife left, though. I guess she didn't want to raise a baby with a junkie. Makes sense, you know?"

"Lauren's knocked up?" The words seemed to lodge in my throat. It was the same feeling I'd had when Celia told me that Dakota was pregnant.

Every joyous moment in my life had always been overshadowed by the knowledge that it could all be ripped away from me in an instant.

Now, more than ever, I saw the danger.

If Mikey was using again, it meant there was no one to protect

Lauren. I wondered if Bear was keeping an eye on my family, or if the rumors were true and he'd only ever been concerned with ruling.

"She's pregnant," Cobra carefully answered. "For now. How long it'll last remains to be seen. She tends to search for danger, poking her nose where it doesn't belong. It seems she's even convinced your youngest to help."

They were going to go after the Sons without the club backing them.

My heart beat unsteadily against my chest. There was only one person who knew the exact danger they were in and could warn them. Unfortunately, the Sons' actions against her parents had all but guaranteed that Celia wouldn't stop the girls.

If anything, she was going to join them.

CHAPTER THIRTEEN

Mike: March 2017 (Age: 34)

"God grant me the serenity to accept the things I cannot change, the courage to change the things I can, and the wisdom to know the difference."

I looked around at the large group, loudly reciting the serenity prayer at entirely different paces like grade-schoolers who'd memorized the Preamble to the United States Constitution. A few even nodded after each word.

The coffee in my hand tasted like sludge, and I still wasn't sure how I'd let the old man talk me into coming. These people had actual problems. Not like me.

I'd made a mistake, one that had cost me everything I loved. But I wasn't as bad as they were.

"Am I gonna have to get up and recite some bullshit about being an alcoholic and drug addict?" I leaned over to whisper to Angel.

He shook his head. "That ain't a requirement, kid."

A woman stood up and began reading from a pamphlet in a monotone, and I lost interest again, letting my eyes wander over the filled seats. One man, who couldn't have been much older than twenty, picked obsessively at his fingernails while staring longingly at the door.

Another woman bounced her legs up and down against the carpet, her exposed skin riddled with meth scars.

A man in a suit, not much older than me, sat in the middle of the semi-circle of chairs. He waited until the woman finished speaking before standing up and introducing himself. Almost every person belonged here, except him.

I wondered if he was a member of the clergy who'd been unlucky enough to have gotten roped into leading a 12-step meeting in the fellowship hall.

"I've got fifty dollars that says he was forced to be here," I whispered, earning myself a sharp look from Angel.

"Everybody here's addicted to somethin'. If you'd sit back and keep your damn mouth shut, you might learn somethin'."

"Are there any first-timers here tonight who'd like to introduce themselves by their first name?" The man asked.

I slid down in my chair and chugged the shitty coffee, reverting to the scared eleven-year-old kid who hoped no one noticed him.

I tried to do what Angel had asked, but with every sob story, I found myself bored to tears and fighting the urge to nod off. It was a twisted show and tell of who had it worse.

They were either pressured into using by a boyfriend or had fallen into it as a way of rebelling against their parents. Not a single one had gotten their girlfriend's mom killed or found out that their dad had faked his death for the second time.

If Angel had dragged my ass here hoping I'd relate to their stories, he was failing miserably.

I snuck a quick glance down at my watch, praying they were getting close to wrapping up. I didn't know how much more of it I'd be able to take before I jumped up and told them all to go fuck themselves.

When Angel stood, I breathed a sigh of relief.

Thank fuck.

He was going to get us the hell out of here.

I leaned over and placed the mostly full cup of coffee under my chair. As I straightened, it became apparent that Angel wasn't moving toward the door but preparing to speak.

"Hello, I'm Charlie, and I'm an alcoholic."

There was a low murmur of, "Hello, Charlie," from around the room.

It struck me at that moment how little I actually knew about the man next to me. Angel hadn't been around when I was growing up, I would have remembered, and Grey had always been tight-lipped when it came to the older biker.

"I grew up around drugs and booze... never had much use for them, though. I was busy tryin' to impress the girl next door." He paused to smile before continuing. "She was real religious, so I dragged my ass down to mass with her, hopin' she'd be impressed."

His expression turned wistful, and I wasn't sure if it was the fluorescent lights overhead or if Angel was getting misty-eyed on me.

"We both moved on but reconnected down the road. Whatever it was we'd had between us had only gotten stronger over the years, and the second time around, I knew I was willin' to do whatever it took to keep her."

Thoughts of Lauren filtered in, and how she'd stuck with me after one night on the beach in Galveston. No one else had ever gotten under my skin quite like she had. I might not have recognized it at the time, but when I saw her again in David and Elizabeth's living room, that was it for me.

Instead of falling into the bottle or numbing my brain with blow, I should have spent every day showing her how much she meant to me. Maybe if I had, even with all the mistakes I'd made, she'd still be mine.

"We, uh, we got pregnant... but she lost the baby. Six years later, I lost her too," he forced out, running the back of his hand under his eyes. There were no sounds of creaking chairs or whispering. The room was utterly silent, with everyone watching Angel with rapt attention.

"Suddenly, the booze was the only way to make it stop hurting, you know? It numbed the pain enough for me to function—made it so I could get out of bed in the morning." His voice cracked again, but he held it together.

Without thinking twice, I reached up and gripped the old man's hand in mine. I'd come here convinced no one could understand why I'd relapsed—certain I wouldn't get shit out of any meeting that didn't involve an open bar. The man next to me had lost everyone he loved, but was still standing.

Not only that, but it was clear he'd beaten his addictions.

It left me with a strange feeling in my chest.

Hope.

"I decided I was gonna stay in that fucked up state until it killed me. Death didn't scare me because if I died, I knew I'd get to be with her again. Maybe I would have gone through with drinking myself to death had it not been for her son, Jamie."

My head jerked up at the mention of my father's name, and Angel gave me a curt nod before turning back to the room. "I'd known him since he was just a little boy. He might not have been my flesh and blood, but I loved him like he was my own. He would have done anything for his mama, and she seemed to come to life when he was with her."

He pinched his lower lip between his thumb and forefinger while staring into the past. "When she... passed away, he was sixteen. I could have told myself that he was damn near an adult and left it, but the kid was all alone in the world, and I knew she'd have wanted me to watch out for him."

I might have known next to nothing about Angel, but I knew even less about Grey. Minus an arrest in 1994 for assault on a police officer and a forged death certificate from 1996, there was nothing. No record of death for his parents... it was as if they never even existed.

I tried to imagine being orphaned at sixteen, forced out into the world to survive before graduation. Grey had not only survived but build an empire. With as mouthy as I'd been, I would have ended up as shark bait.

"I kept to myself," Angel continued.

"Only giving him advice when he asked for it, but still drinkin' to cope. I thought I was doin' better because I was only takin' the edge off. Wasn't until he showed up at my house late one afternoon that things got put into perspective. He'd fallen in love... wanted me to talk him out of it. Here I thought it was obvious how much pain I was in, but he didn't see it that way. Thought I'd forgotten about her..."

The man in the suit tapped the face of his watch with a regretful smile, and I wanted to tell him to shove the timepiece right up his ass.

Angel simply nodded. "I'll wrap it up by sayin' that his visit changed everything for me, made me see I wasn't living a life Mary would've been proud of. I never told him, but the kid saved my life that day. I'm Charlie, and I've been sober since February 1990."

Twenty-seven years.

The room erupted into clapping and congratulations. I just stayed where I was, still gripping Angel's hand in mine while staring up at him in wonder.

He'd done what I'd never in a million years be able to. Sure, I'd give it up for a while, but when shit got heavy, it was always going to be hovering in the background of my mind. And, just like every time before, I'd let it lure me in with its siren song until it dragged me down into the depths of full-blown addiction again.

"C'mon, Mike," Angel said briskly. "We got places to be."

CHAPTER FOURTEEN

Mike: March 2017 (Age: 34)

"Where are we going?" I asked as he maneuvered through the crowded room and out into the parking lot. The evening air was mild, a sure sign that winter was giving way to spring.

He stopped suddenly in front of his pickup before turning back to face me. "You like breakfast?"

I scratched at my beard. "Yeah, who doesn't? But you realize it's nine o'clock at night, right?"

"Breakfast can be eaten anytime, shithead. Everybody knows that. Hop in. I know a place."

"Well, since you asked so nicely, old man," I muttered before climbing into the passenger seat.

"How'd you like your first meeting?" he asked before pulling out of the parking lot. The old truck seemed to vibrate against the rough patches of road but was still a hell of a lot smoother than I'd imagined it'd be.

"How old is this truck?"

Angel grinned widely, like I'd just asked to see pictures of his kids. "1967 Chevrolet C-10. You like it?"

I nodded. "Suspension seems to be in good shape. Usually, these older vehicles shake enough to rattle your fillings out."

He looked back toward the windshield and made a left, merging onto the interstate. "Never imagined I'd be happy to ride in a cage, but Wolverine ran across this gem in a salvage yard about thirty years ago. I've always liked workin' with my hands, so I put in the work and fixed her up. It was a bitch trackin' down parts to restore her, but worth every second."

I nodded again and went back to staring out the passenger window, wondering if there was anything in life I'd ever been good at doing besides fucking things up.

"What about you?" the old man asked. "What do you like doin'?"

"That's what I was just thinking about. Not a damn thing. I was a mediocre detective, and only ever got that job because of Grey. I don't know, Angel. Maybe some of us are just good for nothing."

He jerked his chin. "That's a load of horseshit, and you know it, son. What'd you want to be as a kid? What were your dreams?"

When I grow up, I'm gonna be one of the good guys...

My laugh was hollow. "I wanted to be a hero like Brisco County, Jr. or Scandal Jackson, Jr. from Cobra. Seeing how I was a junior too, thought it was a sign from the universe or something. I wanted to be the one to save the world. Wasn't until I got a little older that I realized the world didn't want to be saved."

"So, why ain't you done it yet?"

I turned toward him with a frown. "Turn up your hearing aid, old man. I said the world doesn't want to be saved, and the good guys are all gone."

"Sound like your daddy now." He put the truck in park in front of a late-night barbershop before looking over at me. "C'mon, let's make this quick."

I studied the red, white, and blue striped awning. "This doesn't look like much of a breakfast joint to me, Angel."

"We'll get to breakfast in a minute, but first, we gotta do somethin' about your hair. And that shit on your face you're callin' a beard? You look like a goddamn hobo."

I ran my fingers over my beard, wondering if I'd missed getting the food out of it again. Maybe it had become more of a catchall lately, but

I'd made it out of the house with clean clothes on, so I was calling it a win.

The bell over the door jingled as Angel led me inside, and two men who had to be as old as God stood up and greeted him by name.

"This one here's lookin' a little ragged. Thought he could do with a straight shave and a little somethin' to clean up the mop on his head he's callin' hair."

I opened my mouth to argue, only to catch sight of my reflection in the mirror above the counter as I was led back to a chair by the shorter of the two barbers. Angel was right. I might have sobered up, but I still looked like a junkie in need of a fix.

"Name's George," the old man said gruffly by way of introduction. "Been doing Charlie's hair for years. You're by far the worst he's brought in, though."

"Thanks?" I cocked my head to the side until Angel came into view. "The worst you've brought in? Is this a thing for you?"

He shrugged. "Helped a few people out over the years when I could. Got 'em back on their feet."

"Mostly vagrants," George added while running the straight razor up and down the strop hanging on the wall. "Acts of atonement. Isn't that right, Joseph?"

The other barber nodded solemnly from the front counter.

"Atonement for what?" I asked.

Angel sank down into one of the empty chairs across from mine. "Ain't done a lot right in this life, kid. I like to think I'm makin' up for it now so that one day—"

"You end up with Mary again," I finished, and he nodded. It made sense. As much as I wanted Lauren to take me back, we both knew she deserved better.

Living without her was my punishment for Patrick and all the ways I'd fucked up my life since birth. Maybe if I spent the rest of my life atoning for my sins, I'd get a second chance with her in the next life.

"Earlier, you told me I sounded like my dad," I started as George leaned my chair back. "Were you referring to Grey or... Comedian?"

Saying Comedian's name no longer made my skin crawl. I'd been convinced he was behind Grey's disappearance, and now... now, I wasn't sure what to think. I still didn't have any answers, but Comedian was the one who'd shown up and helped me put my house back together when the club had turned their backs on me.

He'd known how important it was for me to have a safe place for Lauren if she ever came back.

In the beginning, I'd called her almost every day.

Calls that she'd wisely ignored.

It wasn't until I detoxed that I realized I was little more than a ticking time bomb. I could have convinced her to come back home, both of us knowing that my sobriety would last only until the next crisis.

I knew then that if I truly loved her, I'd either stay clean for her and our unborn children, or I'd let her go for good.

George had just laid a hot towel over my face when Angel replied. "I meant Jamie. His old man was a piece of shit, and he was always convinced that he was going to turn out the exact same way. Said it was in his blood... course, he only seemed to get like that when he was usin' or lost in the bottle."

Alcoholism and addiction run in your family.

Had I known then that he was talking about himself?

"He was... he was like me?" I mumbled from beneath the towel.

"Yeah, kid. You two are cut from the same cloth—hell, even your drugs of choice are identical."

George applied oil to my face and began lathering soap against my jawline. I couldn't remember the last time I'd shaved or done anything with as much care as the barber above me was.

Angel's boots squeaked against the linoleum floor as he moved closer. "I know you wanna believe it won't get better, but you're wrong. If your stubborn ass daddy got clean, so can you."

"How'd he do it?" I asked, doing my best not to move my mouth, ruining George's hard work.

"He hit rock bottom," Angel admitted. "You'd gotten into some trouble down in Galveston, and Celia had gotten hurt. It just seemed like everything was stacked against him."

Angel made it sound as if I'd had a failing grade on my report card, but I knew the 'trouble' was Grey finding out his son was a murderer.

The thing with Celia wasn't as easy to figure out. The day we tracked down Hawk, she'd known how to identify him based on a tattoo. That, along with Comedian's cryptic message to Kate about asking Celia for the truth, only added to the mystery.

"And?" I pushed when he stayed silent.

"Don't feel right, you hearin' it from me instead of him, but as he ain't here, it's gotta fall to me. He was gonna end it all... even called me up on the phone, sayin' he was sorry he'd let me down. I called Slim, and by the grace of the good Lord above, he was able to get to him in time—"

The straight razor passed over my skin, taking not only the over-grown coarse hairs of my beard, but the little boy I'd been only moments before. I'd always seen Grey as this invincible force, some superhero who never let anything get him down.

Angel's revelation was the equivalent of pulling back the curtain, destroying what remained of my childhood ideals. Worse than discovering that Santa wasn't real was the discovery that my hero was human.

"He was going to kill himself? Who's Slim? Was he another biker?" I asked through clenched teeth, praying George's hand stayed steady despite my yapping.

"He was," Angel replied. "And Slim had been by Jamie's side since they were kids. Well, hell, you knew him."

I did?

I ran through the list of bikers in Silent Phoenix twice as George worked diligently on my face, but couldn't recall ever having met someone by the name of Slim.

"You might be confusing me with someone else, Angel," I finally said as the straight razor began moving against the grain under my chin.

"Hold still," the old man directed. "These hands ain't what they used to be. You wanna get cut?"

I held my breath and tried communicating with my eyes so he didn't slice my throat open.

"Let's see. I guess you wouldn't have known him as Slim, but John."

"David's dad was a biker?" I asked, completely forgetting my plan to remain still.

George muttered a curse and stepped back with his arms crossed over his chest. "You two can gab all you want in a goddamn minute. Just let me finish."

John had stepped in after Grey moved us down south. No matter how hard he worked, he was never too busy to spend time with his son and the fatherless kid who always seemed to be at his house.

Maybe Grey had always known he couldn't be the father he wanted to be and had recruited John to fill in.

Maybe I was still full of shit after all these years, imagining Grey had given a damn.

Angel sighed. "Yeah, Slim was a biker until the day he died. Seemed like some days he was the only one who could get through to Jamie, ya know?"

I thought of David and how, even with his own problems, he'd been the voice of reason on more than one occasion.

Did he know who his dad was?

Did any of us truly know who our parents were?

"Why are you telling me all this now, old man?" I asked as George wiped at my face with a cool damp cloth, signaling the end of my shave.

He shifted the chair forward before spinning it around to face the mirror. I brought my hand up to touch my bare skin. It was like I was seeing myself for the first time.

Angel's eyes met mine in the reflection. "I told you all that because it's time to man up, Mike. I mean it. Jamie's gone. Someone has to take his place. That someone is you—"

"Just one problem—the club already turned me away—"

"And?" He shrugged. "What's that got to do with shit? Your daddy made it clear you'd never patch in, swore you'd never be forced to be somethin' you ain't."

I laughed. "Well, news flash, Angel. I ain't a cop anymore, either. Unless you're about to bestow some magical powers on me, I don't see that there's anything for me to run."

Instead of agreeing with me, Angel ran a hand over his mouth with a sigh. "Celia's gonna go after the Sons, kid. With or without the club's help. Several others have decided to stand with her..."

"Like a team?" I asked, my eyebrows bunching together. "Jesus, Angel, you couldn't get all of us on the same page if we were being paid."

"Yeah." He nodded. "You may be right. Be sure and tell your wife your reasons for being a pussy next time you see her, okay?"

"My wife?"

"Face looks great as usual, George. Let's get his hair cleaned up next. Need him lookin' presentable." Angel turned back to face me with a wide grin. "I can't believe I forgot to tell you... goin' after the Sons was Lauren's idea. Girl's recruited herself a nice little group. Last I checked, even Goblin had joined."

Little Ricky?

"Oh," he added. "And that tall guy... what's his name? Jed? No. Jack? Jimmy!"

Jesus fuckin' Christ.

OD'ed once and suddenly my pregnant wife was running her own biker gang with the same fuckers who'd tried to steal her from me before.

"Is that right?" I snarled through clenched teeth. "Well, you let my wife know that she just got one more."

He clapped me on the shoulder with a chuckle. "Gotta take care of your hair first, then we'll see if she'll let ya in."

CHAPTER FIFTEEN

Kate: March 2017 (Age: 27)

"Add white wine. Bring to a boil, stirring to loosen browned bits from pan," I muttered to myself while reading over the recipe on my phone screen. "Got it."

I measured out the wine and added it to the skillet before tipping the bottle back into my waiting mouth. My head had been a mess since my visit to see Mike weeks ago.

I'd been trying to work up the courage to ask Nate about the night my father was shot, but had been unsuccessful. There was no way to broach the subject without admitting I'd been talking to my brother.

Tonight was going to be different, though.

I was going to take the same advice I gave my patients and just confront my fears head-on. I was twenty-seven years-old—a grown woman, capable of making her own decisions. While my husband had a tendency to shy away from drama, this was my family, and I had a right to know.

Knowing Nate, he'd prove to me he had nothing to do with anything that happened to my father that night, and we'd both move on with our lives.

Everything was fine.

The recipe disappeared from the screen, only to be replaced with my mother's name. I tossed the empty wine bottle into the trashcan and retrieved another from the small wine fridge under the counter.

Celia Quinn: Missed Call

My phone taunted me from three feet away, reminding me that there was still one other person I was avoiding. Proving I would have made an excellent candidate for therapy. The anger and resentment I'd held toward my mother as a teen had only gotten stronger since my father's disappearance.

Have you ever asked your mother for the truth?

Comedian's words had woken me up from a dead sleep on more than one occasion, leaving my body coated in a sheen of cold sweat.

What truth?

The woman had lied to me for most of my life, starting with the day the police told me my father had been killed. She'd known the truth while I battled intense anxiety attacks from grief, but hadn't once spoken up.

She could have ended my suffering but chose not to. For him.

She'd always chosen him, hadn't she?

Leaving us with Angel when being a mother interfered with her gambling...

Shipping us off to live with my grandparents so she could live like an outlaw with my father...

I didn't know what she'd told Comedian, but Celia Quinn was a horrible mother.

At the sound of the garage door opening, I quickly shoved the almost empty second bottle of wine behind some cookbooks and turned the heat on the stove down to low before tossing the cooked chicken breasts back in with the sauce.

Nate came around the corner, bleary-eyed from a long shift. His mouth curving up into a sexy grin when he saw me. I returned it before glancing down to where his scrub pants disappeared into the top of his western boots.

My redneck surgeon.

"Hey, cowboy," I teased, tucking myself into his body as he moved closer. He let out a low growl as my lips brushed against his throat, and I belatedly realized that I was more than a little intoxicated from the wine I'd sampled while cooking.

"Katy girl," he whispered into my hair. "You feeling alright?"

I nodded and nuzzled against him like a puppy dog. Typically, I limited myself to one glass of wine and never let myself drink more than two in a week.

Right now, though?

I needed every drop.

"May have had a teensy bit to drink," I slurred before bunching his scrub top in my fists. I was supposed to be working up the courage to ask him about New Year's Eve, not thinking of how good his hard body felt against mine.

I wasn't supposed to be imagining him yanking up my skirt and tugging my panties to the side before taking me against the kitchen cabinets.

That low voice of his made it hard to think of anything else, though. We'd both been under tremendous stress with our jobs and the issues with my family. I couldn't even remember the last time we'd had sex. It had to have been up against the lockers at the gym the night everything went wrong.

We deserved an evening to pretend that nothing existed outside of these four walls. It wasn't as if there was a pressing need to have the conversation tonight.

"Shower. Now," Nate ground out, reaching over to turn off the burner.

My body was one large erogenous zone, leaving me highly sensitive and painfully aroused just by the sound of his voice. I nodded and let him lead me down the hall and into our bedroom. We bypassed the bed, leaving a trail of clothing in our wake as we moved toward the large glass shower.

Nate cranked the knobs, sending a cascade of hot water from the three showerheads along the wall and the oversized rainfall one mounted to the ceiling. It was my favorite feature on the house, hands down.

I stood swaying from one leg to the other in nothing more than my bra and panties while he stripped off his boxer briefs. He cocked his head to the side as he stepped into the shower. "You coming?"

I swallowed hard and nodded. I wanted to come... over and over and over again. It had been too long.

The hot water beat against the muscles in my back like a massage before Nate pushed me up against the wall. "Spread for me, babe. Let me see you."

I licked the droplets of water from my lips and hopped up onto the narrow stone ledge under the large frosted glass window, letting my knees fall open. "Like this?"

It didn't matter if the stones were digging into my backside or not. If he wanted me laid out like an offering, I'd do it.

Nate nodded and knelt in front of me. The corners of his lips turned up into a soft smile while he stared at me as if suddenly seeing me for the first time.

He coated his fingers with the wetness between my thighs—a mixture of the water from the showerhead and me. His eyes stayed on mine as he lifted the fingers to his mouth and sucked them clean.

The breath faltered in my chest, and I held the ledge in a death drip, fighting to keep from melting down to the floor. Nate hooked his hands under my thighs and pulled me forward until I was dangerously close to falling off.

Until his nose was buried against the junction between my legs.

"Oh," I gasped, completely unsteady.

"Oh?" He looked up with a grin. "Should I stop?"

I jerked my head back and forth. "N-no... it's good."

"Good? Let's shoot for great, shall we?" His tongue pushed into my opening before making its way up to my clit. I gave up on the ledge and brought my hands down to grip his hair, holding him firmly in place.

I was close. So close.

Nate tilted his head back to look up at me before slowly pushing a finger inside of me. Before I fully adjusted to the one, he added another and brought his mouth back down.

He knows more about that night than any of us.

I pushed the words from my mind, focusing only on the pleasure my husband was giving me. Comedian was wrong.

Nate would never hurt me.

His fingers and mouth worked in tandem, and I sucked in a breath as my orgasm hit, leaving me mumbling words of nonsense.

"Stand up, Katy girl," he demanded, pulling me from the ledge.

My legs were as limp as the spaghetti I'd boiled for dinner, and it took Nate supporting me to remain upright. He kept one arm around my waist before reaching for the handheld showerhead.

"Hold yourself up with the bar, then spread your legs for me."

I did as he asked, dropping the back of my head down to rest against the tiles. He held the showerhead to his chest, letting the water run down. His dick jutted up against his abs, and I licked my lips again, wanting the taste of him on my tongue.

As if reading my mind, he pointed to my mouth. "Open up, babe."

I did as he asked, already moving down to my knees. Nate shook his head and guided me back to my feet. "Not yet. See, I haven't fucked you in months, and I'm a little out of practice. I'm having enough trouble not coming just seeing you like this."

The fingers that had been inside my body now moved up to rest against my lips. Knowing what it was he wanted, I closed my eyes and opened up, sucking them in.

"So, I've had this fantasy," he whispered.

I blinked the water from my lashes and released his fingers before biting down on my lower lip with a smile. "Oh, yeah?"

Nate nodded and turned the handheld showerhead until it was spraying against my breasts. "Yeah." He moved it down toward my belly. "Every time I've gotten into this shower, I've wondered what it'd be like to use this on you."

I swallowed the pooled saliva in my mouth and widened my stance, giving him the green light.

One side of his mouth lifted as he positioned the shower head between my legs, forcing a loud moan from between my lips. The water pressure was intense, quickly pushing me to the brink of another orgasm.

As if sensing I needed help, Nate thrust two of his fingers inside me again while aiming the shower head at my clit. I screamed his name when it hit me, coming so hard that my vision swam in black.

I was still twitching from the aftershocks when he pulled his fingers from my body and returned the showerhead to the wall.

"You ready for me, babe?" He growled, stroking his dick. "It's gonna be hard and fast."

I was still nodding dumbly when he lifted my body up and pushed into me in a single thrust. His eyes slammed shut, and he froze as if holding himself back.

"Fuck, I missed this."

I tightened my legs around his waist and rocked forward in response, no longer capable of saying anything coherent thanks to the friction against my extremely sensitive clit.

"Nate, I—"

"Do it, Katy girl. Come on my cock." He lowered his head to my breast, sucking the nipple in between his teeth.

I made a noise of frustration and dug my fingernails into his shoulders before coming again with a scream. Nate surged forward, each shift of his hips hard enough to hurt, but leaving me panting in ecstasy.

Nate's thrusts turned erratic. "I'm close. Where do you want me, babe?"

I knew he was really asking if it was safe for him to come inside me. Like the last time... and the time before that. Things were different now.

You came here lookin' for answers...

Ask him.

"My mouth," I blurted, and he looked at me in shock.

"Yeah?"

I nodded, trying not to think of that night as I breathlessly answered, "Yeah."

He pulled out and lowered me to my knees while jerking himself off. "Open."

I obeyed, and he thrust past my lips all the way to the root, gagging me. I should have been disgusted with myself, but I liked it when he was rough with me. I liked the feel of him using my body to get pleasure.

I kept one hand on his thigh, squeezing to ensure that he was watching me look up at him from under my lashes, before slipping the other in between my legs.

He kept my hair in a death grip while I angled my lower body, rubbing myself where I needed it the most. Two simple words from him pushed me into a free fall one last time. "With me."

Come with me.

Without warning, my orgasm swept over me, sending goosebumps racing across my skin. My throat relaxed, and he buried himself deep, bringing tears to my eyes as I fought to take as much of him as I could.

Nate murmured my name over and over, praising me as he filled my throat. I continued sucking, still shuddering from the effects of my own orgasm, until his hands loosened from my hair, and he pulled away.

He shut off the water before sinking down to the tile next to me with a contented sigh. From somewhere in the kitchen, my phone chimed, alerting me to an email.

The world was fighting to break in, but it could wait. Tonight was about us.

CHAPTER SIXTEEN

Kate: March 2017 (Age: 27)

"Jesus, Katy girl," Nate panted. "I fucking love you."

"I love you too," I whispered breathlessly, letting my eyes drift shut just as my phone chimed again.

"You're popular tonight."

I wiped the stray droplets of water from my face before looking at him. His expression was unreadable, leaving me to guess as to whether or not he was joking. "Hardly. It's probably the office updating my caseload for tomorrow."

His eyes drifted closed as he asked, "Is your mom still trying to reach you?"

Here it was.

My chance to ask my husband what really happened the night my father was shot. He'd just given me the perfect segue. All I had to do was open my mouth and ask.

"No," I lied. The words I needed lodged somewhere deep within my chest.

He hesitated and rubbed at his temple before stating, "Good."

"The night," I began. "The night of Dakota's wedding—"

"C'mon, Katy girl. Let's get some clothes on. I'm fucking freezing to death in here." He jumped up and grabbed a couple of towels from the warming rack, wrapping one around his waist and the other around my shoulders.

"Nate," I tried again.

"Look." He stopped in the doorway. "I'm exhausted. Can we discuss this in the morning? I just don't see the point of rehashing the same shit we've already talked about when I could be resting, you know?"

I swallowed, the taste of him suddenly bitter against my tongue. "Yeah. Get some rest. There's chicken on the stove—"

"I'm just gonna crash, babe." He leaned down and kissed my forehead before going into the bedroom. I followed him, watching in confusion as he stripped the towel off and climbed under the sheets with a sigh. "God, what a fucking long day. You coming to bed?"

"I—" I gnawed on the corner of my lip. "I'll just clean up the kitchen. Want me to bring you a plate?"

There was no response. His soft snores filled the room, and I realized, with more than a little frustration, that he was already asleep. My concerns had been dismissed as nothing more than the 'same shit' while the dinner I'd spent an hour making went to waste on the stove.

I grabbed my bathrobe off the back of the bathroom door and tied the belt around my waist before slipping back out into the kitchen.

It wasn't the first time it had happened. There were some nights he barely made it through the door before collapsing in exhaustion.

I scraped the chicken into a large plastic container before dropping the skillet into the sink, hoping the noise had been enough to wake him.

My actions were petty, I knew that. Nate had never been one to stay up late when he'd just come off a long shift at the hospital, but tonight of all nights, I'd needed him to do just that.

"He wasn't too tired for sex," I noted wryly. I started the dishwasher before glaring down at the sink full of bubbles, deciding to leave the skillet for Nate to take care of in the morning.

"Just too tired for any conversation related to the Quinn family," I muttered as I retrieved the counter cleaner from under the sink.

I needed to put the rumors to rest, to quiet the chaos of my mind.

Didn't he understand that?

I jumped when my phone chimed again, alerting me to yet another email. The illuminated screen showed that I'd missed a call and had a voicemail from Dakota.

She usually preferred text messaging to picking up the phone and having an actual conversation. My skin prickled with worry that something might have happened with the baby. I dropped the dishtowel on the counter before playing it.

"Hey, Kate. I guess you're still ignoring all of us because... sweet potato fries! I don't know why you're avoiding us. Maybe you think if you stick your head in the sand, then you can pretend that nothing ever happened, but you're wrong. Dad's still out there and—what? I am getting to the point... just give me a second. Lauren says hi."

I shook my head with a smile, suddenly missing her so much that it made my chest ache. I longed for her long-winded rants, where even she had no idea what she was talking about by the end of it.

"Anyway, so something happened this afternoon. I was shopping for baby furniture with Mama—before you get all butt hurt, I invited you, but you never got back to me. So, we were at the boutique and Lauren met us. I don't think this line is secure. Lauren, do you think it's okay?"

Secure?

Had my mother somehow convinced her she was living in a spy novel?

"Lauren thinks it's fine, but I'm more comfortable using code, okay? So, Lauren showed up and said that she wanted to get the, um, cookies that Dad always wanted to have. Mama tried to tell her it was dangerous

because of... cholesterol. God of thunder, this is hard. Mama wouldn't let her because—"

Her voice cut off in a sob and I heard someone, I assumed, Lauren, murmuring words of comfort to her.

If I was understanding Dakota's 'code' correctly, Lauren was going to go after the biker gang that shot my father, and my mother had tried to talk her out of it.

"I'm sorry, Kate. I just can't stop thinking about it. She said—she said that these men wouldn't care if we were pregnant or not. That being pregnant made us a better target and that they would use their bodies to hurt us until—until we lost our babies. Kate, I think that happened to her. Just— just please call me, okay?"

Have you ever asked your mother for the truth?

I stood frozen with the cell phone still firmly gripped in my hand, even as the voicemail ended. Nan had spent years drilling it into our heads that my mother hadn't wanted us, that she'd been an unfit parent. I'd become so familiar with hearing it that the words had became truth in my mind.

But what if it was all wrong?

I'd counseled rape victims and women who'd suffered miscarriages. Even as separate events, the trauma could leave lasting scars. If my mother had endured both, it would have affected her ability to parent. Hell, it would have affected every aspect of her life.

Had my father known?

The anger that had been directed at my mother shifted over to my father at the thought of him leaving her to carry the burden all alone.

My phone screeched against my ear, alerting me once more to another email. I stabbed at the notification with my index finger, wondering what was so important that it warranted multiple late-night messages. The email had come through six times just in the last hour; all from the same dummy account.

Subject: The truth
Secrets don't always stay buried...

I clicked on the attachment at the bottom of the message and immediately went down to my knees on the vinyl flooring with a cry of surprise. For weeks I'd convinced myself that Comedian was wrong, sure that Nate knew nothing about that night other than what he'd already told me.

The truth was there, in grainy black and white footage from a hospital security tape. Nate, talking with a very tall someone in a hoodie, before sneaking him out of the hospital.

I tried to rationalize it, to tell myself that it was a coincidence, until I saw the date and time stamp on the bottom of the screen.

January 1, 2017.

Tears blurred my vision as I pulled up my contact list and dialed. My hands shook as it rang. If my father had been shot like the doctors had told us, then surely, he wouldn't have been able to leave the hospital on his own. I didn't even know where to begin to unravel the lies.

"Hello? Kate, are you okay?"

I tried muffling my sob with the back of my hand before giving up. "Jeremy, I need help."

CHAPTER SEVENTEEN

Dakota: March 2017 (Age: 22)

"Dakota, try to keep both eyes open this time and see how that feels."

I gave Jimmy a thumbs up before raising the Glock again, feeling less like Black Widow and more like a Stormtrooper.

Who knew aiming a gun could be so complicated?

The empty beer bottles mocked me from where they were lined up along the fence. Lauren nodded encouragingly to me before bouncing back up onto Angel's front porch. The older man had given us free rein over his house and yard while he helped Mike sober up.

"C'mon, Cap," Little Ricky called out from across the yard. "Make me proud."

"I'm trying," I said, moving my hands over the gun until they were in position. My tongue poked out from between my lips as I set sights on my target.

Failure wasn't an option.

I slowly depressed the trigger, instinctively squeezing my eyes shut. Instead of staying where I wanted it, the gun dropped. The air was filled, not with the sound of breaking glass, but that of a bullet whizzing through desert grass.

I released a heavy sigh before lowering my weapon. "I did it again."

Jimmy stepped forward with a nod. "You're flinching. That makes you a threat to everyone around you. Think about it, Dakota. If you raise your gun, you have to be prepared to end someone's life. You're overthinking it." He tapped the side of his head.

"Your targets won't sit along the fence, waiting for you to get it right either," Lauren added. "They'll likely have their own guns pointed at you. Be faster than they are. When you shoot, you're shooting to kill. Not wound... or maim."

I nodded and handed the gun back to Jimmy. "I just need some water, and we can go again."

"You're doing great, Dakota. This isn't easy, but you're trying."

Zane grinned at me from the porch swing as I climbed the steps, rubbing his shoulder as if it were in pain.

I stabbed a finger in his direction. "Not a word, Big Guy. Not one word."

"I wouldn't dream of it, Cap. I happen to like my balls where they are. Your aim's improving, though."

Pride filled my chest, and I stood a little straighter. "Yeah?"

"Yeah, babe," he said with another wide grin. "How's my son doing?"

I patted my bump. "Well, we don't know that it's a boy for sure. They said ninety percent chance... there's still that ten percent that could come into play."

He stood up and stretched, exposing a small sliver of his stomach. It was like a magnet, drawing my eyes to the trail of light blond hair running down the middle of his six-pack. "Ten percent, really? Babe, we've had three ultrasounds. Eventually, you're gonna have to admit that you've got a dick growing inside you."

My nose wrinkled. "Ew, please never say that again. I'll never be able to get that visual out of my head."

Zane caught the screen door as I opened it and followed me into the kitchen. I grabbed a glass from the cabinet and placed it under the faucet.

"Doesn't seem to gross you out when it's my dick inside you," he noted dryly. "In fact, I've gotten the impression that you liked it with all of your moaning. 'More, Zane... more.' Isn't that how it goes?"

Water spilled over the edge of the glass and onto my hand. I glanced around the kitchen before hissing, "Lower your voice."

He moved behind me, wrapping the front of his body around mine and lowering his massive hands until they cupped my belly protectively. "Hate to break it to you, Cap, but I think everybody here knows we've had sex at least once."

My cheeks heated as I squeaked out, "I get that, but they don't need to know the... the sounds I make, or the things I say."

Zane tilted my chin up to meet his gaze before turning an invisible key against his lips, as if locking them up before tossing it over his shoulder. "Your secrets are safe with me, babe."

I dropped my cheek to rest just under his chest. "Good to know, Big Guy. I gotta get back out there, or Jimmy will move on to Little Ricky, and I don't want him to get better than me."

His chest rumbled against my face as he laughed. "Yeah, wouldn't want that, would we? Is your mom still planning on coming out here later?"

"She said she was..." I hedged.

"Are you gonna ask her?" he prodded.

I lifted my eyes up to his. "I don't know. I want to, I do, but you should've seen her face yesterday. It was like she was reliving it all over again. I've tried piecing together what she told us about her gambling and the men who'd threatened to hurt her and us—"

"Threatened or did? There's a big difference."

I thought back to the day she'd appeared in my living room, remembering the way she'd had to stop to catch her breath just telling us about something that had happened decades before.

In the boutique, she'd specifically mentioned our pregnancies and how it made us more of a target, giving the impression that my father's enemies had hurt her. I understood what it was like to feel powerless, the fear of not knowing what was going to happen.

So, with Little Ricky's help, I'd learned how to defend myself. And while jiu-jitsu had saved me from being hurt before, Jimmy was insistent I learn how to handle a gun. Once I had that down, I was going to be unstoppable.

"I—" I paused to collect my thoughts. "I don't know, but I don't want to upset her by asking, you know?"

Zane turned me around until we were facing each other. "Who could you ask?"

"What do you mean?"

He scratched at his beard. "I mean, who would your mother know that you could ask? You could kill two birds with one stone, so to speak. Get answers and avoid upsetting her."

"Molly!" I exclaimed excitedly. "Little Ricky's mom has known her since they were in high school. If anyone knows what happened, it'd be her, right?"

I stumbled back into his arms at the sound of a gunshot from outside before laughing nervously. "Still getting used to that."

His face tightened. "I wish like hell you never had to. Dakota, I'm still not convinced this is the best idea—"

"C'mon, Big Guy," I said, hurrying back out to the porch. "Jimmy's waiting on us."

We'd had this conversation already, and he'd made it abundantly clear he wasn't on board with Lauren's plan. He also knew it was futile to try to stop me.

"Babe," he pleaded from behind me. "Please."

I squeezed my eyes shut and took a deep breath before turning to face him. The light was gone from his eyes, making it appear as if he was on the verge of tears.

His jaw tightened, and his nostrils flared as he admitted, "I—I thought I lost you once. I've worked undercover and seen so much shit go down, but when you got into the car with Jackson, I realized I'd never been so fucking scared in my life. It's not just you anymore, Cap. We've got a son to think about, too. If something were to happen to either of you, I wouldn't survive it."

My lip quivered, and I bit down on it before nodding. "I won't let anything happen, Big Guy. I swear."

It was a promise I hoped I'd be able to keep.

He gripped my fingers in his and brought them up to his lips before leading me back onto the porch. Little Ricky held the Glock sideways in one hand, firing round after round into the fence post.

"Like that?"

Jimmy approached him with a furrowed brow. "What the fuck was that?"

"That's how we do it in the hood, son," Little Ricky said proudly. "Bust a cap—"

Lauren reclined on the tailgate of Jimmy's truck, one hand resting lightly against her baby bump, red lips twisted up in a smirk.

Even though she was nine weeks behind me, our stomachs were the same size. And since she was carrying twins, her due date was going to fall within a month of mine.

Maybe our babies would be cousins and best friends.

"Good way to end up dead, LR," she called over to him. "Funny, I've never seen you shoot like that at the range. How in the hell did you earn a patch with an aim like that?"

"*Mi sirenita*, my aim is perfect—"

"You missed every bottle up there," she noted with a raised eyebrow. "How is that perfect?"

He shrugged with a laugh. "I was aiming for the fence."

Jimmy pinched the bridge of his nose. "We've got a lot of work ahead of us. What time is it, Laur?"

She glanced at her watch. "Quarter to two. I'd love to stay and help, but I've got a check-up. Ooh, since I'm eighteen weeks now, we might even find out the sex. Weren't you that far along when you found out, Dakota?"

"What?" I asked distractedly, still trying to figure out why Little Ricky was messing around, as if the entire thing was a game to him. "Oh, the gender thing? Yeah, they're still not entirely certain. You know, it's such a crapshoot with ultrasounds. The only way to be one hundred percent sure is to meet the baby and check between its legs."

"We're having a boy," Zane deadpanned. "Found out at eighteen weeks."

"Okay, that was... informative," Lauren said, as her eyebrows moved toward her hairline. "Congratulations."

"I'm coming with you," Jimmy stated, putting the guns back into their cases.

"I don't—" Lauren protested.

Jimmy shook his head and began boxing up the unused ammunition. "You know the rules. Buddy system. It's safer that way."

"Wait, there's a buddy system? Who's my buddy?" I asked, earning an eye roll from Little Ricky.

"Obviously me, Cap—"

Zane cleared his throat with an amused expression.

"Well, Big Guy and me. You got you two buddies, girl."

"Good, because I'm going to need a little favor while Lauren's at her doctor's appointment."

CHAPTER EIGHTEEN

Dakota: March 2017 (Age: 22)

"Are you sure I can't get you something to drink? Maybe a glass of water?" Molly hovered near the couch. "Or coffee, I have coffee. Betsy stopped by earlier and I made a whole pot, but she turned me down. Just wanted to moan about how bad Mike's gotten. Anyway, I made it extra special, just like everyone likes."

I shook my head, remembering what she did to coffee. "That's really sweet of you..."

"Ma, she's good," Little Ricky insisted. "We stopped at *Baskin-Robbins* on the way over, gave that baby thirty-one flavors of deliciousness. Right, Dakota?"

"Um, right? So, thank you for agreeing to meet with us. Is Sir—uh, Bear, is he going to be joining us?"

I had a feeling my chances of obtaining information would decrease drastically if the biker were anywhere in the vicinity.

Molly reached down to retrieve a magazine that had fallen off the coffee table and laid it with the others as she sat down in the chair across from me.

"Don't you worry about a thing about Bear," she said with a wave of her hand. "He and a few of the other guys stopped by earlier, but I doubt he'll be back anytime soon. They've got more than enough to keep them busy at the club for a while. Have you checked in with him today, Little Ricky? He said he might need your help later tonight." She moved her eyebrows up and down meaningfully while staring him down. Some silent code I wasn't fluent in.

"Ma, I got shit to do. I'll call him later," Little Ricky grumbled before reaching over into the front pocket of my purse where my phone had begun vibrating. "It's Nate."

"Excuse me for just a moment," I said to Molly before walking out onto the large, covered patio. "Hello?"

"Dakota, it's Nate." He sounded as if he'd been running.

"Yeah, I have caller ID."

Why are you calling? I wanted to ask, but held back, choosing to be the bigger person even though I suspected he was behind my sister's decision to ghost us.

"Is Kate with you? Have you talked to her?"

"Nate," I said with a mock sigh of exasperation. "This is why we have a buddy system in place. She's your buddy, so it's your responsibility to keep up with—"

"I woke up this morning, and she was gone. Her phone's going straight to voicemail. Jesus Christ, I don't know what to do. What if— what if they got her?"

"Who?" I asked, even as an icy feeling of dread settled over me. Kate hadn't been in contact with any of us since that morning in the graveyard. Why would the Sons go after her?

"Bikers, Dakota. This is exactly why I didn't want her talking to you—FUCK!" he roared the curse.

The temper I'd kept in check was dangerously close to boiling over, and it took everything in me to keep my voice calm as I bit out, "She hasn't been talking to me or anyone else. At least now I know why."

"You know it's not like that. I'm trying to keep her safe—"

"From her own family?"

There was a rustle, followed by another muffled curse, before Nate came back on the line. "I did something, Dakota. Something stupid. The night of your wedding, I was on-call when Grey came in." His voice got softer. "I'm the one who did the surgery."

The blood drained from my face, and I stumbled into a small folding chair with a gasp.

"You? You knew he was alive the entire time! Why didn't you tell us? Do you know where he is?" I asked, doing my best to quash the note of hope in my tone.

"It's not like that. I performed the surgery, and he was stable. It was fucking New Year's though, and the ED was a shit show. I was in the middle of another surgery when I got word that he didn't make it. I hadn't even rounded on him yet. I didn't know that there was a cover-up until Mike revealed it at the cemetery."

"Nate," I said slowly. "Did you see or talk to anyone suspicious that night? Maybe someone who didn't stand out right away?"

He paused before saying, "There was a man—he showed up within hours of them declaring on your father. At first, I thought he was lost and tried directing him to the right floor, but he... he told me to keep the details of the surgery to myself. He said the other club was going after anyone associated with Grey. Warned me to keep my mouth shut and stay out of it. I thought he was with Silent Phoenix, but now? Now, I don't know who the fuck I was talking to or where the fuck my wife is!"

I pulled the phone away from my ear with a wince. "Geez Louise, eardrums. Okay, so someone warned you not to tell anyone you'd done the surgery, but why? How is that important? Do you think Kate found out somehow?"

"I don't—I mean, maybe? I don't see how. Maybe they knew I was his son-in-law and how that would look to his enemies? I just did what he told me to. I kept Kate away from it all, and something still happened."

I pulled my glasses off to rest against my thigh before brushing the stray flecks of mascara from under my eyes. "Your last conversation with her. Did she say anything? Anything that might help us know where to look?"

"She wanted to talk about that night. I'd been on for forty-eight hours, though, and was delirious. I think I told her we'd talk about it in the morning, maybe. But if she's not with you, where would she go?"

"Nate, let me call you right back. I think I know someone who can help." I quickly ended the call and dialed the only person who I thought might know where my sister was.

"Hey, Dakota."

"Jeremy," I snapped. "Is Kate with you?"

"Uh—"

"Don't try to think of a lie or a way to make it sound better. It's a simple yes or no."

"Yes, but I—"

"Maybe remind her we're in the middle of a war. She can't run off without telling people." I pressed the end button before scrolling down to highlight Nate's name.

"Did you find her?" he asked, by way of greeting.

"Yes. Kate's safe, and I'm sure as soon as she's ready to talk to you, she'll call, okay?"

Nate exhaled loudly. "Thank god. Did she—did she sound okay? Was she upset? Did she say why she left?"

"Just calm down. Everything's going to be fine. You're her Bucky, remember?"

"Can you keep what I said between us? I want to be the one to tell her the truth about that night. She should hear it from me first. Fuck, I should have made a pot of coffee and just told her everything last night. Just—if you talk to her again, just tell her I love her."

I agreed and disconnected, wondering how Kate did it every day. My only patient for the day was Nate, and that had left me in desperate need of a nap.

Some superhero I made.

"Everything okay?" Little Ricky asked, holding the back door open with his foot.

I slipped my glasses back up onto my nose with a slight shake of my head. "Not really. Kate's with Jeremy. We need to know why. Also, while we're there, we need him to pull security tapes from the hospital. Nate was the one who operated on my dad after he was shot, Little Ricky."

He made a sign of the cross over his head and chest, sputtering, "Did he—he just felt like that wasn't worth mentioning?"

"That's just it. Someone warned him to keep quiet and stay out of it. If we get those tapes, we might identify who that someone was. Worst-case, we get Jimmy or Zane to use their connections and run it through some facial identification software. See if we get a match."

"One dumpster fire at a time, Cap. First, we gotta find out what happened to your ma, then we'll track down Hail Mary and Jarvis, which I totally called, by the way. Pay up."

I ground my teeth together and growled, "Does now look like the best time to collect on a bet, Rick?"

"What's that? Oh, my ma's calling us. Coming, Ma!" He jogged back into the house.

I shook my head and followed.

When Molly saw us, she shoved the paperback in her hand down in between the cushions on the couch with a yelp and quickly stood up. "I didn't hear you come back in. Change your mind on water? Maybe a lemonade? Whatever you want, I'll get."

I glared at Little Ricky before taking a deep breath. "I need to know what happened to my mother... when she was attacked."

"Sweetie—" Molly's face fell. "I don't know the details. No one does, really. You'd have to ask your mother, but even then, I know she doesn't like to talk about it."

"She was pregnant," I pushed, searching for a reaction, something to indicate that she knew what I was talking about.

"That can't be right. Let's see, the attack happened in 2000, so you and Kate would have been, how old?"

"We were six and ten." I frowned, struggling to remember my mother back then. I'd pictured the lost pregnancy as something that had happened before we were even in the picture.

Had anything happened that year?

"Oh my god of thunder," I mumbled. "It was around the holidays... we had to stay with my grandparents for a couple of weeks just out of the blue. One morning, Pops came to take us to school and then we had to pack our suitcases."

She nodded. "Lucy stayed with her for a while, said she was in bad shape. I know she was insistent that you girls never see her like that, but Dakota, she wasn't pregnant. As far as I know, it's always just been you and Kate. Your dad... he wasn't really around during that time."

"But she told us, Lauren and me, that being pregnant made us a target for the Sons... that they would use their bodies to break ours until the thing we loved was ripped away from us. What does that sound like to you?"

Molly's face took on a greenish hue, and she sank down onto the coffee table with her hands pressed against her chest. "It sounds like..." Her lips quivered. "It sounds like she went through a living hell that night."

Little Ricky made another sign of the cross before kneeling beside his mother. "Ma, is there anyone else who would know what happened? It might help us catch estos bastardos."

She looked down at her lap. "Besides Grey? It'd have to be Angel. Lucy said he was the first one there, and I know he stayed close while she healed."

I nodded to Little Ricky. After figuring out what was going on with Kate, we'd track down Angel and get the answers we needed. Maybe it wasn't relevant to finding the Sons, but I needed to know the truth.

I needed to believe that the woman who'd stayed up late baking our birthday cakes or sewing costumes for the school play hadn't abandoned us for a casino.

I'd heard it time and time again, but that wasn't who she was. Kate and I were adults now. We deserved to know the truth. About all of it.

"Dakota?" Little Ricky asked, and I came back to the present.

I'd gotten lost in thoughts of my mother while staring at the pictures lining the hallway off the living room. There was one of Little Ricky as a teen that caught my eye, and I moved closer.

"Your hair was so long." I grinned. "And this sweater? Were you supposed to dress up like someone from the past?"

"That's not Rick, Dakota. That's Bear when he was a kid."

"You and your dad could have been twins—"

"He's not my real dad, Caparina. We've been over this," Little Ricky snapped. "Now, are we gonna get shit done or sit around doin' nothin'?"

I waved a hand in his direction, still focused on the picture. "Fine, fine. We can go."

When the idea struck, I cradled my belly and turned to Molly with an apologetic smile.

Kate once told me that normal people had a tendency to look directly to the right when they were about to lie. I made sure to keep my eyes on hers as I hitched my purse up onto my shoulder and asked, "Is there a bathroom I could use before we go? I know for a fact that the minute we get in the car, this baby is gonna start tap-dancing on my bladder."

I fell silent, knowing if I said anything more, it'd seem like I was rambling. Like I was guilty of something.

"Sure. Just down the hall. It's the last door on the right."

I closed the door and turned the lock before releasing the breath I'd been holding. Adrenaline pumped through my veins, leaving me feeling like a spy who'd had too much caffeine.

A cursory glance along the bathroom counter revealed nothing useful. I turned the faucet on high before easing open the door of the medicine cabinet. There was a comb with a few short strands of salt and pepper hair caught in between the teeth. Next to it were two toothbrushes, nestled side by side in a yellow ceramic holder.

I placed my thumb and forefinger around the handle of one and lifted to find that it was hot pink.

That had to be Molly's.

The next one was royal blue. I laid it on the counter before searching for a bag. After placing the lid on the toilet seat down, I sat and began rummaging through my purse. There was a plastic bag filled with the cookies I'd packed, and another filled with orange slices.

Not willing to part with the baby's snacks, I rifled through the cabinet under the sink until I found what I needed. I tore the end off the wrapper, letting the tampon drop onto my lap before carefully placing the toothbrush inside the plastic sleeve.

"Caparina!" Little Ricky yelled from the living room. "Sometime today would be nice."

I hurriedly tucked the wrapped toothbrush into the side pocket of my purse before reaching for a washcloth to wrap the comb in.

We were going to find out why Kate had run away, convince Jeremy to pull surveillance from the hospital, swing by Angel's house and get the full story on what had happened to my mother, and then I'd have Zane run a simple paternity test on Bear.

Maybe if there was enough time, I'd even be able to sneak in a nap.

I exited the bathroom, lingering for a few extra seconds in the hallway to regain my composure and stop the trembling in my hands. A black leather vest lying on the white comforter of Molly and Bear's king-sized bed caught my attention.

My dad had been wearing one just like it the night he saved my life. I let my hands run over the worn leather before taking a closer look.

It couldn't be.

President, the patch proudly declared. Underneath were four letters that would change the entire course of my search for the truth.

Grey.

Bear had my father's vest.

He was the traitor.

CHAPTER NINETEEN

Celia: March 2017 (Age: 44)

The porch swing creaked as I settled against it, leaving me with a strong sense of nostalgia. I'd long considered the old farmhouse my safe haven. For twelve years, it had been the place I could go to escape the world.

It wasn't until Jamie went missing that I realized it was never the house. My safe place had been him.

Always.

A motorcycle slowly rumbled up the driveway, the headlight hitting my face like a spotlight. I squinted against the brightness before wrapping my fingers around the handle of the gun beside me, keeping it out of sight.

I refused to run and hide from anyone.

The lone rider climbed off the bike and removed his helmet, making no attempt to reach for the weapon on his hip.

"A man walks into a bar and sees his friend sittin' next to a twelve-inch pianist," he called up to me before stepping into the light from the porch.

Comedian.

I exhaled a shaky laugh and moved my finger off the trigger before flipping the safety on again. "You came all this way to tell me a joke?"

He shrugged. "It's my night to keep an eye on you, make sure you don't do anything crazy."

"Like what?" I asked. "Go after the men who shot my husband and took my parents?"

"Somethin' like that. Bear's just tryin' to keep you safe."

No, since he'd discovered that I'd reneged on my promise to stay out of their way, Bear was hellbent on keeping me a prisoner in my own home.

Initially, I'd stood in my parent's empty kitchen, staring at the bloodstain on the cabinets until the shock gave way to simmering rage.

I'd driven home on auto-pilot, turning Lauren's warning over and over in my mind. We were all fish in a barrel, just waiting to be picked off on a whim of a group of psychopaths.

Angel had found me in the closet, emptying the contents of Jamie's gun safe into a duffel bag. Unfortunately, he hadn't seen the logic in ending them before they ended me, and had alerted the club.

SPMC raided my house, confiscating my weapons as if I were a criminal before leaving a biker behind to 'watch over' me. Yesterday it had been Crossbones, today it was Comedian.

I adjusted my long skirt until the pistol disappeared from view. The club hadn't gotten everything. And, if the only way to recoup my firearms was by smuggling them back in under my dresses, I'd do it.

I just had to figure out how to lose my guards first.

Comedian paced along the porch, walking the same path that Jamie had when he was working through a problem in his head. It wasn't right, men who weren't him coming in and taking over.

"Are you going to tell me your damn joke or not?" I snapped, stopping him in his tracks.

He grinned before hopping up onto the railing across from me. "Right, so this guy walks into a bar and sees his friend sittin' next to a twelve-inch pianist. And he says to his friend, 'Hey, that's amazing. How'd you get one of those?' The friend pulls out a bottle and tells him to rub it. The guy does, and a genie appears in a puff of smoke, tellin' him he can have one wish.

"The man thinks it over and says, 'I wish I had a million bucks.' The genie says, 'Go outside, and your wish will be granted.' Guy runs outside, but all he sees is a sky full of ducks. He runs back into the bar and tells his friend what happened, and the friend sadly looks down at his beer before sayin', 'I know. You really think I wanted a twelve-inch pianist?'"

I mashed my lips together, fighting a smile. "That's terrible! Now, you want to tell me the one where the club finds my husband and parents?"

The grin on his face faltered. "You know I can't, doll. We don't discuss anything that goes on in church. In fact, it's best just to let the club—"

"It's best to let the club do what? Sit on their asses while my husband is lost out there? Continue to operate as if everything's normal? What is it Bear wants me to believe the club is doing to fix things?" My teeth ground together painfully, my breath coming out in short, panicked bursts.

His boot came up to rest against the railing. He pulled a pack of cigarettes from the inside of his vest, offering me one. I shook my head. "Bear thinks Grey might have had somethin' to do with your parents disappearing. Money was there—"

I ran a shaking hand over my face, feeling the vein throbbing in my temple. My blood pressure had to be dangerously close to stroke levels by now.

"Is he really that stupid?" I growled. "The money was a ruse, Michael, a way of getting me over to their house! Even the texts from my father's number were bogus. Why do I feel like I'm the one under investigation here? And for the love of all the saints, why am I the only one who seems to give a damn where my husband is?"

"Hey." He jumped down and came over to me. "Hey. I don't, for one second, believe that Grey left you willingly."

"You don't? And here I assumed Bear had everybody in the club drinking the same Kool-Aid."

"I saw how he was after you got... hurt. He could have stayed at home with you and the girls, but he refused, said he'd go home when he'd found the men responsible."

"What are you saying?" I asked.

Comedian ran his thumbnail along the edge of his jaw. "I'm sayin' that if he ain't dead, then there's a damn good reason he's layin' low. Now, between you and me, I got more than a few issues with the way Bear's runnin' shit. His focus is on widening our territory instead of on findin' your old man."

I knew it.

I'd known that Molly's reassurances were nothing more than ridiculous platitudes. The club wasn't going to find Jamie. They'd already moved on.

"Someone within that club was giving up information, Comedian. Someone wanted him dead. I need to know who that was... they can't get away with it."

"Trust me, Celia," he said. "I ain't gonna rest until I figure out what happened that night, even if I have to face every single one of those motherfuckers myself."

I wanted to say more, to inform him of our plans to stop the Sons, but I heard Jamie's voice as clear as day in my head, reciting a passage from Sun Tzu's *The Art of War* as if it were gospel.

Let your plans be dark and impenetrable as night, and when you move, fall like a thunderbolt.

Comedian served his patch above all else. He might have had his doubts and suspicions about what had happened to Jamie, but ultimately, his loyalty was with the club. If he knew what we were planning, he'd be obligated to inform the club. And, with as much trouble as I'd already given Bear, the biker would probably chain me up and leave me in their storage facility.

Imagine you're me. Where would you put him?

The storage facility.

"Celia?" Comedian waved a hand in front of my face. "You okay? You look like you just saw a ghost."

I nodded. "I'm just tired. I think I'm just going to get some sleep. I'm assuming you're staying all night?"

He nodded and reached for my hand. "You sure you're alright? You seem, I dunno, jumpy or some shit. Did I say the wrong thing? I just don't want you thinkin' that no one gives a fuck, okay? Grey was like a brother to me. Even if Bear don't give a fuck what happened, I do."

I was wound up.

The entire time I'd been going about it the wrong way. I'd been looking for my husband the way any law-abiding citizen would. I'd relied heavily on the authorities, convinced that they were making my case a top priority.

Instead, I needed to be thinking like Jamie.

I squeezed Comedian's hand in mine while wrapping the gun up in my skirt with the other, keeping it safely hidden as I stood up. "Do you need anything before I go in?"

"Nah." He held up the pack of cigarettes. "I got everything I need. You get some rest, Celia. Things'll be better tomorrow."

They most certainly would.

"Thank you for watching over me... for believing in Jamie." I sighed. "All of it."

He lowered his head with a nod. "Sweet dreams, Celia."

I closed the heavy wooden door behind me and locked it before softly calling out, "You can come out. It's just me."

CHAPTER TWENTY

Celia: March 2017 (Age: 44)

The bedroom door opened, and Kate crept down the hall slowly, hands wrapped around the base of a curling iron. "You're sure it's safe?" she whispered.

I nodded and pointed to her weapon. "Katydid, what are you planning on doing with that?"

"You know, if they got close, I'd just... I'd just hit them on the head." She swallowed nervously. "Does anyone know I'm here?"

"No, and they won't."

Kate lowered the curling iron and padded lightly across the hardwood toward the kitchen. "Who was it?"

"Comedian." At the mention of his name, she shuddered. "What? What's wrong?"

She shook her head. "It's just... it's stupid, really. In the cemetery, Mike believed Comedian was behind it all, and his argument made sense. Now, I feel like everyone's changed their minds, but I don't understand how."

"Simple. There was no evidence to back up his claims. Comedian was with other members of the club when your father was shot, and right now, he's our only ally in the club. Bear seems to think your father was behind your grandparent's disappearance."

I was giving her the watered-down version of the club's actions and didn't know why. Bear didn't deserve my loyalty after the things he'd accused Jamie of doing. Maybe I was just exhausted at the idea of having to rehash every twisted theory the club had come up with.

Kate didn't need to know everything her father stood accused of. She was going through her own battles. I'd known it since the night she'd shown up on my doorstep, completely out of sorts. Until she opened up to me, though, I could only speculate what had happened.

Instead of immediately disagreeing with the idea that her father could have kidnapped anyone, she nodded to herself before climbing up onto a barstool. "Mom, it makes sense. You have to see that. When Nan and Pops showed up at Dakota's wedding, I could have sworn he was going to kill them. Think about it. We've all remained perfectly safe, but two of my father's enemies suddenly disappear? It's telling."

I tucked my lower lip between my teeth, holding back my words for a moment. How was I supposed to convince the girl who'd grown up without her father that he wouldn't have left us voluntarily?

Not again.

"What do you think?" she asked, crossing one leg over the other.

"I think I want you to tell me why you're really here. What are you running from, baby girl?"

She slipped off the stool and moved around the island, avoiding my gaze. "I'm going to make some tea. Do you want some?"

"Kate," I tried again. "What happened? One minute, your marriage is fine, and the next, you're crying at my front door. I thought you and Nate were happy."

She filled the kettle and placed it on the stove before answering. "You have enough going on without me piling—"

I shook my head. "Stop. You could've gone anywhere, but you came here. Why?"

"Because..." The first tear fell, and she brushed at it angrily, keeping her eyes on the counter. "Because I found out it was all a façade. For months, I've felt this disconnect between us—like, we were living together, but we weren't together, you know? It's as if we've been operating on two separate planes since Dakota's wedding."

"Every marriage goes through—"

"Don't say it, Mom," she warned. "Don't tell me that every marriage goes through rough times. I know that. I see it on a daily basis. This was different. We'd just reconnected and then it was like Nate was keeping something from me. He'd been adamant that I stay away from the club and... and my family."

For months, I'd been laboring under the delusion that she was grieving and confused, the same as all of us. Suddenly, any goodwill I held toward Nate evaporated at the realization that he'd been the one responsible for all of it.

He didn't know her, not like Dakota and I did. He didn't know about the panic attacks or the night terrors. By forcing her to bottle up her emotions, he'd only made a terrible situation worse.

"I'm sorry," Kate said through another sob. "I thought he was doing it to keep me safe, but I got this email." She pulled her phone from her pocket and stabbed at the screen several times before sliding it over to me.

I watched in confusion as Nate conversed with a man in a hooded jacket before leading him toward the doors. "I'm not sure what this is supposed to prove," I admitted. "It looks like he's giving someone directions."

"Don't you see?" she asked, just as the kettle began to whistle. "That's Dad. Nate was helping him escape the hospital. It's why the club's theory makes sense. They must've known what happened, and that's why they're convinced that Dad was the one behind Nan and Pop's disappearance."

I dragged my finger to the left, restarting the video from the beginning. The man was tall, that much was obvious, but it wasn't Jamie.

I didn't know how I knew, but I did.

"Wait," I exclaimed. "When did you get this email? Was Nate home when it came through?"

Kate stayed silent, turning in a slow circle around the kitchen. Realizing what it was she was looking for, I directed her to the cabinet that contained the mugs before pointing to the ceramic canister of tea bags near the stovetop.

She added one to her mug with a nod. "Yeah, the first one was sent maybe thirty minutes after he got home."

"The first one?" I asked, scrolling up to check the timestamps. "They kept sending the same email... why?"

"Maybe to ensure I got it? I don't know. Do you want a cup?" She held up the kettle, and I nodded. "Why is it important?"

Think like Jamie.

What had he said about the Sons? Something about them being masters at moving people where they wanted them. What if they hadn't gone dark, like everyone wanted to believe, but were still subtly moving us all into position?

But to what end?

"It's misdirection," I said, moving off the barstool. "They're still calling the shots, but in a way that no one will notice. Think about it, Kate. Why would the email keep coming through? The sender knew for a fact that your husband was home... maybe they even thought you'd confront him. It doesn't matter. As long as we all end up on opposing sides, then we can't fight them."

Kate rolled her eyes, looking so much like her fifteen-year-old self that I did a double-take. "Nate and I have never had anything to do with the club. Why would they come after us? And why would a bunch of bikers care about my marriage?"

She set the mug down with a thud against the butcher block. "You really don't want to believe that my father faked his own death. C'mon, Mom. He did it before. Why wouldn't he do it again?"

"Because the last time he did, I got hurt, and he swore to me he'd never do it again," I quietly admitted, running my fingertips over the wood, tracing the grain intently as a way of avoiding her penetrating stare. "Right here in this very spot, we made promises to each other."

I glanced up when Kate turned to face the two empty barstools. "I think..." She paused. "I think that maybe it's time for the whole story. The truth. From start to finish."

"It happened so long ago," I protested. "And besides, we have bigger issues to worry about."

Kate tapped her chin with her index finger. "That's just it." She placed her palms on the island, spreading them as if laying out a stack of papers. "There's a connection between what happened to you and where we are now—"

"There is," I said with a nod. "One of the men who... hurt me connected with Saint. That's not a mystery. Anyway, it doesn't matter. He died with his former club right before Dakota's wedding."

Kate's eyes widened as she whispered, "My father was shot, and now my grandparents are missing. They're sending you a message. Mama, I think you're the key to all of it."

Death is comin' for you...

I'd assumed once Cobra died, the Sons would move on. Nothing connected me to them. Maybe there was something I'd missed.

"We're going to need Mikey," I said firmly. I thought of his arms, covered in quotes about warfare and combat. A man who had been born on a battlefield.

He wasn't all that different from his father, and if we stood any chance at defeating the Sons, we needed every member of our family on the same side. He was the closest thing to Jamie that we had.

Mikey's overdose.

Kate's marriage falling apart.

I'd gotten the Son's message, loud and clear. Now, it was time to send one of my own.

No one messed with my children.

CHAPTER TWENTY-ONE

Mike: March 2017 (Age: 34)

When I was six, my pet hamster died. We hadn't had him for more than a year, but as it was my first real experience with death, I bawled like a baby over it.

When Comedian found me in the backyard, blubbering about Mr. Pickles, he knocked me onto my ass for it. He told me that real men didn't cry like little bitches because they had problems, and they damn sure never showed their emotions.

It seemed I was always the smaller kid growing up. For better or worse, the old man's words of wisdom had saved me from getting my ass kicked by schoolyard bullies on more than one occasion.

Until tonight, I hadn't realized that the advice had also left me emotionally stunted, no better than a child in a man's body. I'd spent the better part of my thirty-four years with an almost nonexistent self-awareness and a complete lack of empathy for anyone around me.

I was the perpetual victim of my own circumstances.

At tonight's twelve-step meeting, I'd finally made the connection and promptly lost my shit, crying my eyes out in a room full of addicts.

Surprisingly, I hadn't felt like a pussy, even after sobbing on Angel's shoulder. I felt like the man I'd always been meant to be, a man who deserved Lauren Santiago-McGuire-Sullivan-Quinn—fuck, we'd figure out the last names later.

When I grow up, I'm gonna be one of the good guys...

As crazy as it sounded, for the first time in my life, I felt like maybe I could be.

"I've been completely clean and sober for thirty days," I said to the brake lights on the car in front of me, rehearsing the speech I'd been writing in my head since leaving the meeting.

In a room full of strangers, I'd only seen her face as I recounted my addictions and what they'd cost me, imagining exactly what I'd say to her if I ever got the chance.

I hadn't wanted to see it, but I'd shown her just what she meant to me when I chose to use again. And, as much as it hurt knowing that she was going through her pregnancy alone, I had no one to blame but myself.

The bridge of my nose burned with unshed tears. From the moment she came into the world, Lauren had never had any other choice but to be a fighter. Her actions had saved both of our asses the night the Sons showed up, but it wasn't fair.

She'd been my compass when I lost my way, time and time again, always there to guide me back home. I smirked at the imagery, knowing there was no way in hell I'd be able to admit that to her and keep a straight face.

I should have been her protector.

As her husband, it fell to me to keep her safe. Instead, she had always been the one to save me, pulling me back from the brink when it felt like all was lost.

According to Angel, she was preparing to do it again by taking out the men who'd shot my father. The same men who'd sent eight bikers to kill her on New Year's Eve.

The old me would have already gone in, guns blazing, just like I'd done after her mother was killed. I would have begged her to stay out of it under some delusion that I was saving her. In reality, all I'd be doing was trampling over everything she'd built.

The light turned green, and the car ahead of me began moving again. I fought to sort my jumbled ideas into something resembling a coherent thought as I pressed down on the accelerator.

What could I say that I hadn't already?

How was I going to prove to her I'd changed?

I ran a hand over my face, shocked again by the strange feeling of bare skin underneath my fingertips, wondering if I'd ever get used to it.

"Lauren, I know that my word doesn't mean shit—Fuck, I need you to know that I've changed and I'm one hundred percent committed to us. Goddammit!" I roared, slapping the steering wheel in frustration.

Why was this so hard?

I'd prided myself on my ability to sweet-talk any woman on earth, but this was Lauren. She'd see my pretty words as nothing more than bullshit before slamming the door in my face.

I glanced over to the empty passenger seat, wondering again if I should have stopped for flowers. She hated flowers, but maybe this was an occasion where flowers were mandatory.

Jesus Christ, Red had kept me on my toes since day one. She'd taken everything I thought I knew about women and turned it on its head. If I wanted her back, I was going to have to think like she did.

"If I'm Lauren, what is it I want? I've got a husband who's a crushing disappointment and two babies on the way. It's obvious that my life hasn't turned out like I'd hoped." I sighed. It wasn't exactly a ringing endorsement for her to take me back.

Torch's house came into view, and my palms grew slick with sweat as I pulled in behind the generic black sedan her dad had loaned her.

Grey had mentioned opening an account in my name as a sort of emergency fund. Maybe there'd be enough to get her something of her own. Something big enough for a family.

"Now you're thinking like a chick, Mike," I praised myself before realizing I still had no idea what to say to convince Lauren that I'd changed.

My boots crunched across the gravel, and I shoved my hands into the front pockets of my jeans before deciding it only made me look suspicious.

According to Angel, I needed to keep my body language open... whatever the fuck that meant.

I took a deep breath and knocked, watching a moth buzzing around the porch light as if it had found the holy grail. A few seconds went by, and no one answered, so I peered in through the living room window.

"*Since you left, everybody says I'm not the guy they've known. The lights are on, but nobody's home,*" I crooned softly, sounding nothing like Clint Black, before moving around to the side of the house.

"Oh, yes. Right there... right there," a muffled female voice moaned loudly as I reached a bedroom window.

I froze in shock, knowing exactly what it was I was hearing, but not wanting to believe it. The curtains were drawn, but it didn't matter.

I was going in.

God help the man who had his hands on my wife.

The front door was locked, but the back one was wide open. I slipped inside, easing the screen door closed behind me. They'd know I was here soon enough, but I wanted the element of surprise on my side.

Especially if it was Jimmy.

The goddamned tree was liable to take my head off.

"Yeah, do that again. Touch yourself, I wanna see it."

It wasn't Jimmy, I realized with a growing sense of nausea.

It was Torch.

"Torch, you motherfucker!" I roared as I marched down the narrow hallway and threw open the bedroom door. "She's young enough to be your daughter!"

My hand came up over my mouth, and I fell into the wall. "Jesus, fuck!"

"The fuck is wrong with you?" Torch growled, yanking the comforter over the woman's body before wrapping a sheet around his waist, but not before I saw more than I ever needed to. "You got a death wish, boy?"

"L-L-Louisa?" I sputtered, struggling to cover my eyes. "Does David know? God, I thought you were—I'm trying to find Lauren!"

"She ain't fuckin' here! Now, get the fuck out unless you want me knockin' some goddamn sense into that thick skull of yours."

Keeping my hand over my eyes, I stumbled back out into the hall-way. "I'm sorry. So, so fucking sorry."

Torch slammed the door shut behind me as Louisa called out, "You tell David about this, and we're going to have some real problems, Michael Sullivan!"

"I just wanna know where my wife is," I pleaded helplessly. "I never wanted to see two old people going at it like rabbits—"

"Old? I'm forty-six, you piece of shit! Still more than capable of kickin' your sorry ass!" Torch threatened.

"Forty-six?" I called back with a sudden smirk. "Why, Louisa Greene, you've gone and got yourself a younger man. Remind me again, did we just celebrate your fifty-fourth or fifty-fifth birthday?"

"Fifty-fourth," she grumbled. "Are you going to stay outside that door all night?"

"Until someone can tell me where to find Lauren, think I'll just camp out right here. Do your thing, Cougar," I encouraged.

"For fuck's sake, boy," Torch ground out. "Lauren ain't here. She's probably out at Angel's or Celia's... somewhere you can't find her. If she wants you, she knows where to look. Now, get the fuck out of my house!"

I sighed and scratched at my jaw, trying to determine where she would have gone. As Angel had been with me just a half-hour before, I knew she wasn't at his place. There wasn't a snowball's chance in hell she would have gone to my mom's, which left Celia.

I'd never get through what needed to be said if Celia was watching me with those cat-like green eyes of hers, searching for signs of Grey.

Instead of pretending I didn't exist like most women would've done, Celia had always gone out of her way to make me feel as if I belonged.

As a teen, I'd laid awake at night, imagining what it would have been like to have her as a mom. By that point, I was living down by the beach with my mother, but I'd never forgotten how Grey's knockout of a wife had never once excluded me from their family events.

Not all of my adolescent fantasies were as pure. More than a few had ended with me fucking Celia up against a wall, satisfying her needs as a widow. In 2009, when Grey turned up at my house to reveal that he was alive, I was relieved I'd never acted on the fantasies.

My old man would have snapped me in two.

I fought to clear my head just as Torch asked, "Now, where were we?" Louisa's giggling quickly turned to moans of pleasure.

"Really? Not even gonna wait until you're sure I'm out of the house?"

"That's it. Hand me my gun. I'm gonna teach this little shit-for-brains a lesson," Torch announced as I jogged toward the back door.

When I made it around to my truck, I fell against the door, wheezing with laughter.

Torch and Louisa... who would have guessed it?

I was strangely happy.

If two people who'd both suffered through such severe loss could find love again, then maybe it wasn't crazy to think that a quick-tempered redhead might still want a washed-up addict.

I might have lost my opportunity with Lauren tonight, but I wouldn't give up until she was mine again. As if a lightbulb had been turned on, I suddenly knew exactly what I was going to do to show her I'd changed.

CHAPTER TWENTY-TWO

Mike: March 2017 (Age: 34)

The miter saw whined as I pulled it down, cutting my two-by-four to length. I blew the sawdust off as I held it up for inspection.

"Michael!" *Abuelita* called from the porch. "Your dinner is ready!"

"In the garage," I shouted across the yard before going back to studying the printed diagram on my workbench, trying to decipher the next step.

The side pieces to the cribs were lying on the spare workbench across from me, the slats held together with clamps. The ends were leaned up against the wall, just waiting to be stained. I'd added a decorative triangle with some of the leftover wood pieces, hoping to give them more of a farmhouse feel.

"Oh, Michael," Gloria gasped as she entered the detached garage, carrying a large plate in one hand and a glass of iced tea in the other. "They are going to be so beautiful. You have done so much work."

It turned out that Angel was right. I just needed something to keep my mind focused. Woodworking had always been something Grey had done, but I found I enjoyed getting my hands dirty, too.

I liked the process of turning nothing into something.

Kinda like me.

"It's coming together. Might even be ready to assemble by tomorrow. I need to find out what stain Lauren used on our nightstands—"

"Oh!" Gloria held up a finger. "She used the Precipitation Gray—no, it's the word that means it's not new. It's old and worn. Michael, do you know what I am talking about?"

I nodded slowly, fighting a smile. "Weathered?"

"Yes," she exclaimed with a grin. "The Weathered Gray is her color. I will help you get it done. Now, you take a break and get some food."

"What'd you whip us up tonight?" Over the last five weeks, I'd stopped seeing her as my enemy. Sure, we still got in each other's faces from time to time, but she'd taught me a lot about family.

It meant never giving up on someone.

The woman who'd brought me into this world hadn't shown her face since finding out I'd overdosed again. Seemed only Comedian got second chances with Betsy.

She grinned. "Your favorite, *mijo*... the fried chicken steak with my sofrito on top. I am so proud of you. You stop using the drugs, and I say to myself, 'Gloria, he is trying so hard. You should make him a little treat.'"

I settled against the workbench with the plate in my hand, my mouth already watering just from the smell of it.

Gloria offered me the iced tea before saying, "I mean to tell you that Celia has called again. I tell her you are very busy and she says to tell you it is *importante* that you call her back."

"Yeah," I nodded. "I need to talk to Lauren before I do anything, you know? Can't seem to catch her, though."

"I will call her," she volunteered, but I shook my head.

"You're not calling her. Torch will tell her I've stopped by..."
Several times now.

Unlike the first time, he and Louisa were fully dressed.

"When she's ready, we'll talk. I've got nothing but time."

"Not me," Gloria grumbled. "I am nothing but an old woman who just wants to see her only granddaughter happy before I leave this earth."

I laughed through a mouthful of chicken fried steak. "You're so full of shit, Abuelita. You and I both know that you're going to outlive us all. You just say that to get what you want."

"Is it working?" she asked with a sly grin.

"Fine," I conceded. "If I haven't found Lauren by the end of the week, you have my blessing to meddle."

"You say meddle. I say, 'Gloria, you are just helping young love,'" she called over her shoulder as she made her way back to the house. "Do not stay up too late, *mijo*."

I worked until the sky was blanketed with stars before finding a stopping point. After ensuring that everything was cleaned up, I popped the tailgate on my truck and climbed up, rubbing the sawdust from my eyes while scanning the sky for familiar constellations.

It had been the one constant in my life.

No matter how bad things got for me as a kid, the stars remained. Sure, the constellations shifted, depending on the season, but it didn't matter.

They had always been a way for me to feel connected to Grey and then Lauren. I leaned back and tucked my hand under my head, wondering if they were looking up at the same sky. Maybe we were even searching the skies for the same ones.

Was Grey even somewhere he could see the stars?

There was a crunch of dead grass, and then a soft voice asked, "Did you find Leo?"

I shot up, narrowing my eyes, because I was convinced I was dreaming.

"Red?"

She tucked a strand of hair behind her ear with a nod—most of her body still hidden in the shadows. "Heard you were looking for me, Tex." She tilted her chin up, pointing toward the sky. "Do you see it?"

I thought back to my speech, all the things that needed to be said to make up for what I'd done before swallowing against the lump in my throat. "It's right there." I traced the outline of the lion with my finger.

"What's the story behind that one again?"

Her voice quieted my fears and calmed my mind enough for me to recall the mythology surrounding the constellation. "Well, let's see. Leo was a lion who had a thing for damsels. So, he got really into kidnapping and would take them back to his evil lair, all to catch the attention of a few warriors. His skin was impenetrable, so none of their 'weaponry' worked against him, if you know what I mean. I think it's relatively obvious that Leo was into some freaky shit."

"Clearly," she agreed.

"One day, he roped Hercules into coming back to his bachelor pad for some 'swordplay.' When he pounced, Hercules grabbed one of his front legs and one of his hind legs and bent him backward, breaking the beast's back. Hercules freed the women and placed Leo in the sky as a reminder to not show up at every party you're invited to."

Lauren's mouth curved up into a smile. "That's very good advice."

"Look, Lauren, I—"

"Shhh... not yet," she chided.

I brought my hand up over my mouth when she stepped into the light. My wife's body had changed entirely in just five weeks.

The last time I saw her, our babies were just making their appearance known. Now, the swell of her belly extended out over her leggings, and the tits that had captivated me since our first meeting strained against the thin material of her tank top, waking my dick from his long winter's nap.

"Not the time," I hissed.

"What's that?" Lauren asked, her brows wrinkling in confusion as she approached the bed of the truck.

"I said you look divine, darlin'. Like a motherfucking goddess. Do you need help?" I slid off the tailgate and paused in front of her. "Can I —is it alright if I help you up?"

She let out a soft exhale. "You shaved."

I brought my hand up to my cheek as if just realizing it. "Yeah, Angel got me all squared away. Apparently, I was starting to look a little rough."

"A little?" Her own hand came up to rest on my other cheek, gently stroking back and forth. "I've never seen you without a beard. It's... different. And your hair is so short."

Her fingernails grazed over my temple, leaving my dick no better than a dog fighting to get out of his cage.

I tentatively cupped her belly in one of my hands, watching her eyes for the slightest sign that I was making her uncomfortable. It might have been my babies inside, but I hadn't held up my end of our vows.

It wasn't about me or what I wanted anymore.

"You look so fucking good," I murmured. "I always thought it was a bunch of bullshit when they'd say that pregnant women were glowing, but you really are, darlin'. Pregnancy looks amazing on you."

Lauren's lower lip quivered, and I instinctively took a step back, only for her to latch onto my wrist, tugging me closer. Her nostrils flared, and she blinked several times before whispering, "Don't. Can we just pretend for half a second that we're Jack and Charlotte?"

The aliases we'd given each other the night we met in Galveston. The wayward surfer and the art dealer. Two people who probably hadn't lost a minute of sleep, worried about a war between two MCs, or whether their partner was going to overdose again.

"Come here." I gently lifted her up onto the tailgate, letting my thumbs skim along the tight skin of her belly as I did. Once she was settled, I joined her. "Found any new artists I should know about?"

Her full lips parted on a sigh before curving up into a smirk. "You know the art world, completely fluid... forever changing."

"Yeah, it's the same way with the waves. You just never know what you're gonna get out there." We were talking about nothing, yet it felt like everything to me. I'd missed wasting time with her. "Lauren, I just want you to know—"

"You've been sober for thirty-five days," she finished. "I know."

I worked my jaw back and forth, fighting to recall the beginning of my speech. "I have a lot to make up for with us. I made you a promise—"

"Don't," Lauren warned again, shifting her upper body to face me. "Don't do this right now. That's not why I'm here."

"Then, why?" I studied her face. I'd expected some push-back, but not being shut down entirely. "I owe you an explanation. You and these babies are my focus—"

Her hand came up between us. "Stop, Mike. You don't owe me an explanation. I know how hard you've been working—"

This time, it was me interrupting to confess. "No. I lost my job,

Lauren. At first, I wanted to blame it on the Sons, but lately, the more I think about it, the more I wonder if maybe they were right to drop me. I was a wreck over the Grey thing and wasn't fit to wear a badge—"

"I've looked at your file, and their reasons for letting you go are entirely bogus, Tex. Someone wanted you gone, and when I think about how close they came to succeeding—" Her voice cut off in a squeak before she composed herself. "They'll pay for that."

"Just a minute. You got ahold of my record? How in the fuck did you manage that? Do you know how dangerous—what if someone found out? You can't put yourself at risk—" My pulse throbbed steadily in my throat.

I couldn't take over.

Whatever decisions she'd made were because I hadn't been there.

"Are you done?" she asked, pursing her lips.

I nodded.

"Good. Jeremy hacked the system. I needed to know what you were being hit with and ensure that any charges against you never made it to the inside of a courtroom. Jimmy's reaching out to his contact, and we're working—"

"Jimmy?" I bit out through clenched teeth.

"Yeah, Tex. Jimmy. He might just be the one to save your ass here. Think about that before you say anything else. Look, I didn't come here to fight—"

"I don't want to fight either, but there are things you need to know. I was a shitty human and an even worse husband—"

Lauren caught my jaw as I tried to look away, bringing me back to face her. "I couldn't stand the thought of disappointing her. That's what I was, wasn't it? A disappointment? How many times had I heard that in my life?"

My mouth fell open as she recited the things I'd said at my twelve-step meeting. "But—how?"

She exhaled a soft laugh. "I was there. By the way, you are completely oblivious to stalkers. It's a good way to get yourself killed, Tex."

I couldn't fight the grin that stretched across my face. "You've been stalking me? And you didn't think about giving me a warning or a heads up before I barged in on Torch and Louisa?"

Her eyes crinkled as she threw her head back and laughed. "I thought that if I had to learn that lesson the hard way, so could you."

"Jesus, you saw?"

Her nose scrunched up. "Yep... twice. Eventually, they decided to keep their 'activities' confined to the bedroom. I hope they didn't offer you food. I'm fairly certain that the kitchen counter has been, uh, contaminated in more than one area."

I shook my head. "Torch didn't offer me anything but an ass-whooping, which I declined. Now, back to the matter at hand. Why did you keep tabs on me after everything I've done?"

"You're my partner... for better or worse. And I think you've gone your whole life just waiting for people to give up on you, and many have done just that. Those people never took the time to see all the good in there." She patted my chest. "And you have a lot of good... even if you can't see it yourself."

I mashed my lips together, holding back tears. "But those meetings, they're just for addicts. How'd you get in the door?"

Her eyes grew glassy. "I learned early on that the only person I could depend on was me. Until you. Everyone keeps telling me how strong I am... how brave."

Lauren brushed away the tears spilling onto her cheeks before admitting, "I'm not, Mike. I—"

She hiccuped through a ragged breath, and then it was as if a dam had been released. "I'm scared to death. I should be enjoying every second of this pregnancy, because we fought like hell for it, and I can't! I can't, because I know that they're still out there. It could all disappear in an instant."

I pulled her into my arms, brushing the hair back off her forehead before pressing my lips to her flushed skin. "I'm here, and I'm not going to let anything happen to you, darlin'. I swear. I know my track record is shit, but you've been my lifeline when I was ready to end it all. Let me be that for you now."

Her chest shook with another sob, forcing her body closer to mine. "You want to know why I was at your meeting? Because I'm an addict when it comes to you. I can't walk away from us without losing a piece of myself. I want to believe that you'll stay clean, if not for me, then for the babies. Because we need you, Mike. I need you. You're the only person on the planet who makes me feel safe."

I reached for her jaw, guiding her mouth onto mine with a low growl. Instead of pulling away, her hands moved over my t-shirt before gripping my shoulders with a moan.

"A man protects his home," I breathed against her lips. "Told you that once, and I know that I've failed you. I may have gotten lost, but I found my way back to you. You're my home. You're mine to protect. And if you need me to say it every day, I will."

"Mike," she protested. "Shut up and kiss me. After, you can tell me all those things again."

My lips brushed up against hers as I grinned. It was a feeling I hadn't even known I'd missed. I lifted her legs and rotated her body toward mine before pulling the flip-flops from her feet. Her eyes narrowed until I kneaded along the arch of one foot.

"Oh," she breathed, letting her head fall back with a relaxed sigh.

I used my other hand to adjust myself through my jeans with a slight grimace. Why hadn't I considered wearing athletic shorts? Right. Because I hadn't known my wife was going to be showing up to give me a raging case of blue balls. I'd take care of it later while picturing her just like this.

"I, uh, I came here for a reason."

"Oh, yeah?" I teased before switching to the other foot. "You mean you weren't expecting a foot massage under the stars?"

Lauren fumbled against the bed of the truck before managing to grab hold of the strap on her purse. "Not at all, but it feels so good. I—I came for this."

I looked at the small manila envelope in her hand with a sinking feeling. The smile that had been on her face only moments before was now gone. She used her thumb to catch the tears gathered in the corners of her eyes before placing it in my hands.

I'd seen one of these before.

When Elizabeth had David served in the middle of a bar.

CHAPTER TWENTY-THREE

Mike: March 2017 (Age: 34)

It didn't make a goddamn bit of sense.

"I thought—thought we could start over. I know I fucked up, but I'm trying here," I pleaded, the blood draining from my face. I'd botched the speech, but I'd done my best to convey everything I was feeling.

"Tex," Lauren said with a sigh. "It's not divorce papers. It's from my ultrasound appointment. I wanted us to find out our babies' genders together, and I've been waiting impatiently for over a week now, so if you could open the damn thing already, that'd be super helpful."

"It's in here?" I tore the envelope open with trembling fingers and dumped the small scrap of paper into my hand. She could have had them tell her at the appointment, could have left me out of it entirely. Instead, she'd handed me my future on a piece of paper barely larger than a Post-It note.

"Open it," she whispered, reaching for my free hand.

I unfolded it in my hands, my voice shaking as I read, "Baby A is a girl. Baby B is a... girl?" My eyes widened as I looked up at her. "We're having two girls? That's what this says, right?"

She plucked the paper from my hands, scanning it in silence for a couple of seconds before grinning. "We're having daughters, Tex."

Jesus Christ.

I mashed my knuckles against my mouth, laughing nervously. "I just—fuck! We did this—I can't! You and me, we made them. I just—"

"I, uh, I came for something else, too," she said with an almost dazed smile.

"I know. Celia's been calling. It didn't seem right to give her an answer when we hadn't even talked. I needed to make things right with you—"

"Oh, you're gonna fight with us, Tex," Lauren said. "I didn't come here for that. I came for this." Her hand cupped me through my jeans, and I gripped the tailgate, my knuckles going white as my cock perked up for the second time tonight.

I could have talked it down and insisted that we wait, or told her I just wanted to talk. Instead, I lowered her down onto the bed of the truck, while fighting to pop the button on my jeans.

"This is purely for health reasons," I said, tugging the zipper down in an attempt to give my cock room to breathe.

Lauren didn't tell me to slow down. She gripped the waistband of her leggings and arched her hips before tugging them down with a soft giggle.

"Jesus Christ, darlin'." I pulled them from her ankles and tossed them aside before dragging two of my fingers through the folds of her glistening pussy. "You're soaked."

The back of her head fell against the truck bed with a dull thud. With a slow grin, I leaned down and inhaled her scent before dipping my tongue in for a taste.

"Is this okay?" I murmured, using the same words she'd used to torment me our first time together.

Lauren nodded shakily, lifting her hips up to my mouth in offering. I slipped my hand under her thighs, kneading the flesh of her gorgeous ass with my fingers before guiding her back toward my face.

This time, her hands moved over my hair as she fought to keep me from moving.

"And this?" I whispered, letting my tongue brush lightly over her clit. "Is this okay?"

She let out a low growl, and her foot came down against the back of my neck in response. Completely pinned to her body—*hell, there were worse ways to go.*

I let my fingers and tongue take over, not stopping to ask for her thoughts. Her quickening breaths and the feel of her thighs tightening around my cheeks were more than enough of a response.

When she finally came down from her high, she relaxed her death grip on my head and pushed herself up onto her elbows, thrusting her belly toward my face. "Do you want to know how many nights I've imagined you just like this?"

My throat bobbed up and down in a slow swallow. "How many?"

Lauren grinned before pulling the hem of her tank top up and over her head in response. I fought to keep my eyes focused on her face, and not on the pale pink nipples practically begging to be in my mouth.

She crooked a finger at me, and I leaned in until her warm breath was against my ear. Her teeth nipped along the lobe before she whispered, "Every. Single. One."

I straightened and pulled her closer to the edge of the tailgate.

She watched me through hooded eyes as I pressed my lips to her belly before moving up to capture a nipple between my teeth. My hands, rough with calluses from woodworking, brushed against her tits, pulling a series of low moans from her lips.

I pulled back, letting myself take it in. It was a sight I wanted to remember forever.

That mane of red hair tossed back in ecstasy...

The pale skin of her tits, nipples harder than diamonds, thrust up toward the star-covered sky...

And her belly, filled with my babies, begging to be cradled in my hands.

I no longer cared about anything but keeping that dreamy smile on her face and my name on her lips. God knew I'd given her more than enough grief.

"Mike." Her hand slipped between our bodies, wrapping around my shaft with a squeeze. The roles reversed and my hands fisted in her hair, pulling her mouth down hard over mine. Our tongues came together in frantic desperation while her hand moved in feverish strokes against my cock.

It was madness.

Any moment now, Gloria was going to walk out to find her grand-daughter giving me a handjob in the back of my truck.

A shudder ran the length of my spine, and I dropped my hands to Lauren's knees, spreading her legs. Her back instinctively arched, bringing her body closer to mine.

"I don't fucking care if the Sons show up tomorrow. Do you hear me?" I hissed. "I have spent too fucking long without you, and I'm not rushing a goddamn second of this just because we're in the middle of a war."

Lauren's eyes widened, but she regained control of her body long enough to give me a nod. "Please?" she panted, letting her thighs fall to the side. I trailed my fingers through her wetness again before jacking myself a couple of times.

I held on to what little control I still possessed before lowering my mouth to her belly again. "So fucking beautiful."

Her lips parted on an exhale, and I traced them with my fingers. At that moment, I knew that there would never be a high that could compare to what I felt for Lauren.

Even with all of my mistakes, she was still here.

She was still mine.

I yanked her body forward and pushed myself inside of her with a growl. As I rolled my hips forward and sank into her, inch by inch, I realized that I could have her a million times, and it would never be enough.

"I've missed you," Lauren whispered. "God, I missed you so much."

I brushed the tears from her cheeks, slowly stretching her body around mine. "Look at me." She blinked drowsily, and I used my thumb to catch another tear caught on her lashes.

"You have my word." I ground my teeth together as I pushed in fully. "Right here, right now. I will never put you through that kind of hell ever again. I'm not gonna have you making excuses for my shitty behavior, so our children won't be afraid of me. Never."

"Those are big promises, Tex—"

She didn't understand, and I could no longer put it into words, but sinking into her body felt like coming home. It didn't matter how fucking far off-course I'd gotten, or how long we'd been apart. The feel of her walls shifting to fit me was a comfort I couldn't describe. Like it was her way of reminding me that in a world that had cast me out, I'd been made to fit here.

If Grey had gotten himself clean, so would I. The same blood ran through our veins. We might have shared the same vices, but I knew we also shared the same strength and willpower needed to slay the beasts in our heads.

I would either stay clean and sober or die trying.

I wanted to tell her, but all I got out was, "Please trust me."

Her eyes widened in understanding, and she nodded as if that was enough. "Okay. I trust you."

"Thank fuck," I groaned. I was a man who'd lost everything and found it all in the same woman. Lauren's hands connected around my waist, drawing our bodies closer together and cradling our babies between us.

Her feet wrapped around the backs of my thighs, guiding my pace. My vision blurred as I fought to keep from breaking, needing to give her even just a fraction of what she'd given me by showing up tonight.

It was painfully apparent that all of my free time spent sobering up and building a nursery for my babies had left me severely out of practice.

Her mouth fell open, and I gripped her tighter, knowing she was getting close. My face had gone numb. Any control I still held was quickly sucked away when she clamped down around me with a silent scream.

She sucked in a ragged breath as her entire body convulsed in a shudder. And I was a goner. I held myself inside her as I broke, feeling as if after years of fighting the current, I'd finally reached the shore.

CHAPTER TWENTY-FOUR

Kate: March 2017 (Age: 27)

"No!" I sat up in bed with a gasp, still seeing the familiar face looming over my body, the feel of hands crawling over my skin. "It was just a dream," I whispered to the empty bedroom.

My mother had decorated it to look just like the one Dakota and I had grown up in, something that left me feeling disoriented every time I woke up. I likened it to waking from a coma to find that your body had changed and grown while everything else remained as it had been before.

"Just a bad dream," I repeated.

The oversized t-shirt I'd fallen asleep in clung to my damp skin as my heart thrummed against my ribs, proof that my body wasn't buying my explanation.

I forced my head back onto the pillow, working to steady my breathing and calm my mind. The red lights on the alarm clock continued ticking up, but the foreboding feeling didn't go away.

"This is ridiculous," I muttered as I kicked off the covers and padded into the living room. I grabbed an afghan off the back of one of the recliners and curled up on the couch, prepared to wait for dawn.

The creaks and pops of the old farmhouse settling had become familiar, even welcome, over the last week. Somehow, it made me feel less alone.

Eventually, the trembling in my limbs subsided, along with the icy cold sense of dread that I was in danger. I found my phone where I'd left it on the small table beside the couch.

Nate had called again.

My thumb hovered over his name, waiting for my brain to give the go-ahead. All I had to do was tap the screen, and I'd be able to hear his voice.

If anyone could pull me out of this, it was him. He'd tell me that things weren't as bad as they seemed before convincing me to come home. I placed the phone back on the side table when I realized that he'd also want to know where I'd been and why I'd left in the first place.

Those were questions I couldn't answer.

Not yet.

"Kate?" Mama whispered from down the hall. "Is that you?"

"In here. I couldn't sleep."

"Good," she said with a weary smile as she rounded the corner. "Neither can I. Come on, I'll fix us a little midnight snack."

Keeping the afghan around my shoulders, I followed her into the kitchen. She moved gracefully around the room, pulling cheese and fruit from the refrigerator and artfully arranging them on a platter next to some crackers.

"You were such a light sleeper when you were younger," she said while coring an apple. "Your father would come in from work to find you in your PJs, rummaging through the fridge for a snack. I used to think sleep just didn't come easily for you, but now I'm convinced that you just wanted that time alone with him. Maybe you knew then that he wasn't going to be around."

I climbed up onto one of the bar stools, struggling to remember late-night snacks with the biker. "How long have you lived here?"

She added the apple slices to the platter, avoiding my gaze. "The city house felt empty without you and Dakota in it—too quiet, you know? This place belonged to Angel once upon a time, and he sold it to your dad to fix up."

Her response was elusive... vague. It was just one more thing she was keeping from me.

"That doesn't answer my question, though," I pushed. "How long have you been here?"

Without another word, she calmly knelt beside a cabinet and retrieved a large bottle of tequila from the back. "Angel," she said by way of explanation, holding the bottle up for inspection. "He found this at Mikey and Lauren's after the relapse. With your father gone, he thought he'd leave it here."

At my puzzled expression, she elaborated, "Angel knew that a bottle like this would only tempt Mikey into drinking again, but he also knew he couldn't keep it at his place—he and your father are recovering alcoholics and addicts. I asked him why he hadn't just thrown it away, and his eyes bugged out of his head. I guess this is pretty expensive stuff."

It surprised me to know that Grey had been an addict. Then again, I'd built him up to something close to a god in my mind. Up there, he could do no wrong.

"So," I said, trying to get us back on topic. "Instead of telling me how long you've lived in the country, you'd rather do shots?"

Her laugh brought back memories of the three of us belting out our favorite songs in the car on the way home from school. "This isn't the kind of tequila you shoot. According to Angel, it's meant to be sipped, like a glass of whiskey. And, if we're going to dredge up the past, I'd like a drink in my hand. What about you?"

"Tequila and I have a complicated relationship," I hedged.

"Ah, sounds like you and the rest of the world have something in common." She clicked her tongue against her teeth while looking through a cabinet. "The closest thing I've got to stemware are these jelly jars. A glass is a glass, though. Right?"

I shrugged as she poured a little into each one. My one and only experience with tequila had ended with Nate's face between my thighs and then, suddenly, my head in his toilet.

"To..." My mother paused with her glass raised. "Oh, hell. To the shit that made us who we are!"

"To the shit," I repeated, clinking my glass to hers. We each took a small sip of the amber liquid, recoiling at the burn. "You're sure we're supposed to sip it?"

Her lips puckered as she admitted, "I don't know. I got drunk on amaretto and Dr. Pepper once in high school, but that's about the extent of my knowledge of drinking."

I nodded and knocked the contents of the glass back before pouring another. "I think the only way this is going down is like a shot. We just won't tell anyone."

My mother agreed, and after four glasses, the lead in my gut had dissipated, leaving me relaxed. The afghan now hung off of one shoulder while the other side trailed along the hardwood floor, but I made no move to right it.

"So, to answer your initial question," Mama began, her cheeks flushed from the liquor. "I've lived out here since you were taken from me."

I stopped tracing the rim of the jelly jar. "Taken? You abandoned us!"

The alcohol had softened the blow of my words, making it sound as though I were merely confused, not upset.

She shook her head slowly before knocking back another shot. "Nope. Taken. Your grandmother came to the house one day and gave me an ultimatum—deliver you and Dakota to their house by four o'clock sharp, or go to jail and never see either of you again."

"J-jail?" I slurred. "What would you have gone to jail over?"

"Well, for Angel, she was pushing for child pornography charges. Me?" She tapped a finger against her lips. "I think it was drugs... maybe trafficking for the club. I blocked a lot from that day, to be honest."

Most of my childhood memories had become little more than blurs as I grew into adulthood, punctuated by only the briefest flashes of clarity.

The day we were left with my grandparents was a moment that had been seared into my brain permanently, though. I remembered watching my mother's face, searching for signs of remorse, but only seeing grief.

"I was so angry at you that day," I admitted. "Your face was pale, and I remember you were making these sounds as you sobbed. At the time, it made little sense. Why leave if it upset you that much? Why not just stay and fight for us? But you never had a chance, did you?"

She stared down into her empty glass. "I tried. Angel and your dad went to everyone they knew, hoping to call her bluff."

I knew it had all been for nothing.

Nan had gotten just what she wanted, and we'd eaten up the narrative she'd served, starving for an explanation for why our mother no longer wanted us.

"Why not just kill her?" I clapped a hand to my mouth when it dawned on me what I'd just suggested.

My mother just smiled. "I thought Angel was going to after she accused him of prostituting children—"

"How?" I asked. "How could she ever look at that man and see a predator? He needed a family, and we needed him. There was never anything more to it than that."

"You should tell him that the next time you see him. In the early days, he was so worried that you girls were going to forget about him."

She poured another glass. "When your father found out, he swore he'd kill them both before handing you and Dakota over, but she'd planned for that. They had police protection in place for years—"

I thought back to the fact that they were both missing now. "And how do you know maybe he didn't follow through all these years later?"

My mother paused with the glass almost to her lips. "You have to understand, Kate, that my parents had never been supportive of my decision to marry your dad. There were so many instances over the years where he could have retaliated, but he never did. In the end, he knew they weren't worth it."

I didn't have a lot of memories of my father, but could clearly recall tracing the tattoos on his arms with my fingers. I could still hear the deep rumble of his voice, yet couldn't remember ever hearing him say that he loved me.

Maybe bikers didn't admit to things like that.

I'd had one interaction with him before Dakota's wedding, and even that had felt like a fever dream thanks to a bout of pneumonia.

"How'd you meet him?" I asked, trying and failing to wrap my fingers around my glass.

"I'm surprised you didn't already hear about my 'mistakes,'" my mother said with a bitter laugh. "Your grandmother swore she'd do everything in her power to keep both of you from ever becoming me. Seeing how you two turned out, maybe it was for the best."

"We became the women we are because of you—not anything she did. And I don't give a damn what she told us. I want to hear the story of how my parents fell in love... from you."

Her green eyes became distant. "If you're expecting something out of a romance novel, I'm afraid you're going to be let down."

I shook my head before letting it rest against my fist. "I want the real story... all of it."

"Okay." She poured more tequila into our glasses. "Your grandfather actually introduced us—"

"Wait. Pops? How did he know my father?"

My mother sighed. "I made it sound better than it actually was. My father was a customer of the club's. Only, he stopped paying for his drugs, so the club came to collect on the debt."

"Did they beat him up?" I gasped, unable to picture Pops as an addict.

"I was home alone, Kate. They took me as payment."

I'd known what my father was, but never imagined him laying a hand on my mother.

Seeing my horrified expression, she hastily added, "It wasn't as bad as it sounds. I was scared to death because I'd heard the stories about people crossing their club only to disappear the next day. When he came into the room, I decided that if he was going to kill me, I wouldn't make it easy for him."

"You fought him?" I asked, thinking back to the night I left Nate. I might have counseled victims of trauma every day, but deep down, I was weak.

Scared.

I thought this was what you wanted...

The glass slipped from my fingers and fell to the island, sending droplets of tequila in every direction. I wasn't going to let myself think about that right now.

She helped me mop up my mess before continuing. "I did. It

turned out he wasn't there to kill me. The club had other ideas when it came to collecting debts, but I was just naïve enough to think I could talk him out of it."

"How old were you?" The tequila seemed to curdle in my gut at the thought of her being forced.

"Seventeen."

"Mama," I breathed, doing the math in my head. "Is that how... is that how you got pregnant with me?"

One tear slid down my cheek, then another. Within seconds, I was sobbing hysterically at the thought that I'd been the product of rape. The man I'd long seen as Christ-like was nothing more than a monster.

"No." She reached for my hand and rushed out, "Listen to me. He didn't force me, and you weren't conceived that night—"

"But, but you were a debt," I drunkenly sobbed. "You said it yourself."

She blew out a long breath. "I was a rule follower who'd never stepped out of line. When I found out my father had gotten in over his head with bikers, it sparked some sense of rebellion within me. Even without all that, when your father walked into the room, it took my breath away. It was in the way he carried himself, like nothing could ever stand in his way. We were from completely different worlds, but I didn't care. I gave into the recklessness and gave myself to him, willingly."

"When did you get pregnant with me?" I sniffed, wiping the tears from my face. The alcohol had loosened my tongue to the point of obscenity if I was asking about my parent's sex life.

Her mouth turned up in a distant smile. "It wasn't long after that. I was supposed to leave for college and Jamie was going to be nothing more than some summer fling that I looked back on when I was old and gray. When I found out I was pregnant with you, I realized I didn't want a life of perfects. I didn't want to do something just to check a box off my list."

She tipped the glass back with a wince. "I was supposed to go off to college and earn a degree before marrying a man who would ensure I never had to work while I raised our two children. I would have thrown myself into church fundraisers and country club lunches. Only,

I didn't want to go back to being the girl who followed all the rules. I didn't want to be my mother."

I snorted back a sudden laugh. "And here I've done everything by the book to avoid becoming you and letting Nan down. Well, until Nate, that is."

"But are you happy, Kate? My only goal as a mother was to raise my kids to think for themselves and to chase their dreams, no matter how crazy they seemed. I thought by giving your grandparents the money, it would give you the courage to do just that."

I studied the patterns in the wood. "For a long time, I think I was just checking boxes, fighting to make sure that no matter how bad things got, it always looked perfect from the outside. Do you ever think about what your life would've been like had you not gotten pregnant?"

To my surprise, she nodded. "Yeah, there were days where I found myself thinking about where I would have ended up had I just gone to college and married a man my parents approved of. Then, I realized by doing so, I'd erased the only things in my life that I was sure about. If I'd made different choices, then I would have spent the rest of my life wondering where Jamie was—imagining what our children would have looked like."

"That's how I feel about Nate," I blurted in response. "I wasted all my time checking off boxes and creating the ideal partner in my head. Do you know Nate didn't meet any of my criteria? Not one thing. And nothing about our relationship has been perfect—"

"Who wants perfection, though? I want passion." My mother placed a hand over her chest. "I want to feel it here. I want to know that if I fall apart, he's willing to go to the ends of the earth to pull me back together."

I couldn't imagine Nate going to the ends of anything for me.

He would have left it to the police, distancing himself from the entire thing. I shoved the thought back to the dark recesses of my mind before approaching a topic my mother had shied away from for too long. "Did he go after the men who hurt you?"

Now that I knew the truth about how we'd ended up with my grandparents, I fought through my drunken haze to recall the things

Dakota had said over voicemail the night I left Nate. "They didn't just hurt you, did they? They raped you."

My mother's mouth twisted up, and she let out a sharp breath before quietly admitting, "It's been sixteen years and sometimes, I still wake up convinced they're in the room with me."

I saw the face again in my head, grinning down at me from above, felt his hot breath against my neck. The shakiness returned, and I tugged the afghan up around my shoulders again, as if doing so would ward off the image.

"Your father..." She bit her lip. "He was my talisman. I could reach over and just lay my hand on his arm, and the world righted itself."

I pushed past the weight that had settled over my body, and reached for her hand, doing my best to communicate that I was with her as she recounted the night she lived through hell.

With each revelation, the walls I'd built to keep her out came tumbling down. Another long-held belief proven false.

My mother hadn't gambled out of compulsion, but because someone had been stealing from us.

Her nostrils flared out with a forced exhale. "Hawk was the one taking the money, Kate. He knew I was desperate to keep it from your father and got me into some underground blackjack games. I was too naïve to see that I was rubbing elbows with every one of your father's enemies. When they figured out he wasn't dead, but in hiding—"

"They came after you," I said

She gave me a shaky nod. "Hawk... he helped them break in one night. They demanded to know where your father was, but that was the thing. I never knew where he was going next. When they realized they wouldn't get any information out of me, they decided to send a message. All I could think about was the fact that you and Dakota were less than twenty feet away. My only thought was to keep you both safe."

The biker hadn't merely disappeared because he went to watch over another family...

Her mouth continued moving, but all I heard was a high-pitched ringing in my ears as she confessed what she'd lost at the hands of my father's enemies. Men who hadn't used words to send messages but their bodies.

"Weak men hurt women like that, Kate," she hissed, turning the jelly jar until it caught the light from overhead. "It's a hard truth that I desperately wanted to shield you girls from."

My vision blurred as a fresh round of tears fell from my eyes, and I chastised myself for being so weak.

When I was seven, two police officers showed up to tell us that my father had been killed. I remembered feeling as if nothing would ever be right again.

Hearing the truth of my childhood and knowing what we were up against now, it appeared as though that feeling had been correct.

Good existed only in fairy tales.

CHAPTER TWENTY-FIVE

Kate: March 2017 (Age: 27)

"Morning, Counselor."

I jerked my head up from the file folder in front of me, wincing at the volume of his voice. "What are you doing here?" I said, fighting through another wave of nausea.

I was never drinking tequila again.

Mike grabbed a mug from the cabinet and filled it with coffee, giving me a relaxed smile. "Celia invited me to go to war. My schedule's pretty empty these days, so I thought, why the hell not? You feeling okay? Because I gotta be honest with you, you look like hell."

I self-consciously covered my face before asking, "Does Lauren know you're going to be here?" I kept my voice low, not out of fear of someone overhearing, but because it felt like my brain was being stabbed with an ice pick. "I'm just not sure that springing something like this on her is the—" My words tapered off as the woman in question entered the kitchen.

I held my breath, wishing that I was anywhere but ground zero. The hangover wasn't helping things, either. My mother had been insistent that we needed Mike, but given what I'd seen of him the last time, I hadn't expected him to show.

The man now standing in front of me looked nothing like the man

I'd seen wrapped up in a quilt. The scraggly beard was gone, leaving his jawline with the slightest hint of a five o'clock shadow. It was clear he'd also had a haircut recently.

Those weren't what struck me the most, though. It was the brightness in his eyes again. Mike was sober.

That made one of us.

Even if he gave us a fighting chance against the Sons, it didn't mean that he was off the hook with Lauren for the things he'd done while using.

"Good morning, Lauren," I whispered, trying to infuse as much cheerfulness in my voice as I could muster in an attempt to defuse the situation.

"Morning, Kate," she answered distractedly, making her way around the island toward her husband.

"Um, did you..." I struggled to think of something, anything, to prevent bloodshed before I'd finished my coffee and sobered up. "Did you get a new shirt? It, um, it really brings out the color of your eyes."

Her mouth lifted in a grin as she glanced down at the purple maternity top. "Thank you. I got this last week... it's like nothing fits anymore."

Mike handed the full mug to her and waited until she lifted it to her lips before saying, "I seem to recall at least one thing still fitting."

A spray of coffee went flying from her mouth, onto the island and the papers I had spread before me. I dabbed at them with my napkin while she coughed and spluttered before cocking my head to the side, observing the two.

She moved as if to brush past him, letting her hand linger against his backside. He smirked and poured himself a cup of coffee while whistling a tune.

"You two aren't killing each other," I noted.

"I knew I was forgetting something," Lauren said with another strange grin.

He wagged a finger at her. "That's right. It was on the agenda after morning coffee, I believe. Drink up, Red. I wouldn't want you to be late for my untimely demise."

With a smirk, he set a bottle of aspirin in front of me. "A couple of these... maybe a little hair of the dog, and you'll be right as rain."

I winced. "How'd you know?"

"You reek of booze and bad decisions, Counselor."

The screen door slammed shut with a bang before Zane and Dakota entered the kitchen. I climbed down off my stool, feeling as if I'd entered a different dimension. "Do you see this?" I pointed to Mike. "Am I the only one confused by what's happening here?"

Zane's eyebrows moved up, and he immediately backed out of the room, leaving Dakota on her own.

"What's wrong?"

"This." I gestured with my hand. "They're acting... I don't know... weird."

It shouldn't have upset me. After all, it wasn't my marriage. Lauren wasn't the first person to go running back to an addict, but she was the first I'd seen to be so blasé about it.

Dakota looked between the two of them before moving toward the pantry with a shrug. "What's the big deal, Kate? Ooh, did Mama get more blueberry bagels? Baby Thor is craving one."

"Baby... Thor?" I asked slowly. "Please tell me that's not the name you've picked out."

She disappeared into the pantry before reappearing with the bag of bagels held over her head in victory. "Score! And I'm trying out several names just to see what feels right."

"What are some of the others?" Lauren jumped in to ask.

Dakota dropped the bagel into the toaster before leaning against the counter. "Well, there's Tyr, Heimdall, Loki—only if we're talking like Marvel movie universe, though. Obviously not comic book universe Loki. Um, what was the other one? Oh! Jake."

"Jake," Mike said. "I don't know... sounds pretty common."

"Well, Jake Olson was a paramedic who bonded to Thor for a little while. Let's see..." She paused, no doubt rifling through the Rolodex of comic books in her head. "He got killed in a battle between the Avengers and Destroyer but was brought back to life. I actually can't remember how he and Thor bonded together, but I know they stayed that way until Odin could separate them."

She retrieved the bagels as they popped up, utterly oblivious to the blank stares the three of us shared. "Hey, what do y'all think about Odin? Odin Masterson. Sounds kinda important, right?"

"Um," Lauren began. "It's unique."

"I think I'll add it to the list, but if I don't decide to use it, you definitely should, Lauren. Odin Quinn—oh, that sounds really powerful."

"Well, it could work... if we were having a boy, but—"

"You're having two girls?" Dakota screeched, sending a dagger of pain through my skull. "Oh my god of thunder, I have so many girls' names. Sif and Frigga. Brunnhilde and Freya. If you went with Brunnhilde, you could call her Valkryie for short."

"You know, that's not bad," Mike chimed in, somehow keeping a straight face. "We'll take all of those into consideration."

"Good," she said through a mouthful of toasted bread. "Now, I was thinking—"

"Caparina," Little Ricky called out as he came down the hall. "You got two seconds to tell me what the fuck you did!"

Why was everyone yelling?

She stiffened, and whispered, "Family meeting," before disappearing through the back door.

Mike cocked an eyebrow. "You see that, Counselor? Now that was weird."

"Cap—"

"She's not in here, LR," Lauren replied as he rounded the corner. "Maybe check out at the barn?" She kept the smile on her face until he left before turning to face me. "Has she told you anything?"

I shrugged. "Nothing that in any way explains what just happened."

"Something went down between the two of them after they went to see Molly." At my frown, she elaborated. "She wanted information on your mother... some event that happened a long time ago? I'm not exactly sure."

Mike's gaze darkened, and we shared a look, making it clear I wasn't the only one who knew what that something was.

After opening up about her miscarriage, my mother had clambered off her barstool and over to the sink before vomiting up the hard liquor.

As if on autopilot, I'd walked over and held her hair back, murmuring words of encouragement. I did it all while knowing that I would never be half the woman that she was. I never would have survived what she'd lived through.

"Okay," Lauren said with a slow nod, looking between the two of us. "It's obvious I've missed something, so let's round up the family for a meeting."

There was no sign of Little Ricky or my mother as we entered the backyard, only Dakota and Zane, sitting side by side on a little bench near a tree covered in pale pink blooms.

She looked up with a tear-streaked face when we approached. "I have to tell you something. I didn't want to say anything until I knew for sure, but I think it's important."

My phone vibrated against my hip, earning me a glare, and I quickly silenced it before placing it back in my pocket.

It was Nate.

Again.

"I found Dad's vest at Bear and Molly's house," Dakota said solemnly. "It was on their bed—"

"Wait," Mike interjected. "You found Grey's kutte and didn't know if that was important or not? How long ago was this?"

She swiped under her eyes. "A week ago. Look, I know I should have said something, but that's a huge accusation to make against someone. I started second-guessing myself—maybe my dad had left it somewhere, and Bear found it. I don't know. Then I thought of something Nate had said to me."

"Nate?" I choked. "Y-you talked to Nate?"

"He called when he was trying to find you. Said that someone confronted him in the hospital after the doctors told us Dad didn't make it. They warned him to keep his mouth shut and stay out of it. He thought it was someone from Silent Phoenix."

"Oh," I mumbled, before sinking down onto the grass. There had never been an elaborate plot to alienate me from my family. Nate had been trying to keep me safe. "But why go after him?"

Lauren gasped. "Because he did the surgery! He would have known that Grey was alive. I'm right, aren't I?"

Dakota grimaced. "Yeah, but I wasn't supposed to tell that part until he talked to Kate."

I'd all but begged for details from that night only to be pushed away, yet he'd given up all his secrets to my sister.

At my crestfallen expression, she quickly added, "All he knew was that Dad was stable, Kate. He was in another surgery when they told him he'd passed away."

"We need to pull those tapes," Lauren commanded. "See if we recognize the person who confronted him—"

"We already did," Zane said, scratching at his eyebrow. "The only person seen on tape interacting with Nate is Bear."

I thought of the footage I'd been sent, the man in the hoodie. "Wait, I was sent something—footage from the hospital, I mean. There was another man he talked with. At first, I was convinced that it was our dad—"

"Why are you just now telling us this?" Dakota shouted, and I squeezed my eyes shut, longing for a dark room and eight hours of uninterrupted sleep.

"You just admitted that Bear has Dad's vest," I said calmly. "When I showed Mama the video, she said it wasn't Dad, so I didn't see the point of bringing it up again. We need to tell her about this, though. Maybe the guy in my video is the one who threatened Nate."

Dakota's face paled. "Well, that's part of the problem..."

"Where's Celia?" Mike asked, looking around the empty yard.

Her lip trembled, and another stream of tears fell from her eyes. "I'm sorry. I didn't have all the facts when I showed her the footage and told her about the vest. I didn't know she'd react—"

"Dakota," Lauren said firmly. "Where is she?"

"She went to the clubhouse," she admitted through a sob. "She said she's going to kill him."

CHAPTER TWENTY-SIX

Celia: March 2017 (Age: 44)

Angel frowned at me. "You wanna explain why you wanted me to meet you here, of all places?"

Wolverine exhaled a stream of smoke from his mouth with a raspy laugh. "We're gonna torture the shit out of ya, Angel."

Muscles and veins strained against the skin of my forearms as I looked up at the storage facility with clenched fists. "Because there's a chance they brought Jamie here—"

"Celia," Wolverine began. "You and I both know that the Sons wouldn't get within ten feet of this place before the club knew about it."

I checked the magazine on my gun and forced a smile onto my face as I said, "Oh, I think they knew more than they're telling you. Now, are we staying out here all day, or can we get on with it?"

They pulled their weapons with simultaneous sighs of frustration before following me up to the door.

"Thought I told you on the phone that just because you had a video of Bear chattin' with the doctor, it don't mean he's behind it all," Angel grumbled.

"Dakota found Jamie's vest on Bear and Molly's bed," I hissed back, wishing that she hadn't chosen today to give up the traitor. I would have liked to have spent my first hangover lying in bed.

"You're sure it was Jamie's?" Angel asked, keeping an eye on Wolverine. What he was really asking was whether I was ready to start a war over it. Angel might have lived like a mercenary, but Wolverine would bleed Phoenix red until the day he died.

The former Pres had made it explicitly clear that he'd only shown up to prove me wrong. If he got wind of the intel I had on the club, I'd lose my ally from the inside.

I nodded discreetly as Wolverine unlocked the heavy door and shoved it open. "See? Not a goddamn thing in here—"

"This place gets raided by the cops, do you think they want my husband strung up like a goddamn Christmas tree where anybody could see him when they walk in?"

Wolverine's silver eyebrows shot up. Instead of getting in my face, the old man just crossed his arms over his chest and cocked his head to the side. "Alright, good point. So, where the hell is he?"

I strode past him toward the back office, suddenly jittery. "Basement. It's soundproof and has hidden doors. You need to think like a criminal. Didn't Jamie teach you that?"

"Where the fuck do you think Jamie learned it from, kid?" Wolverine growled from behind me. "You think he just came into this world knowin' how to run a club? That ain't the way this shit works!"

I turned around to him as I reached the door, teasing, "See, now I'm confused. He said he taught you everything you know."

Angel let out a low whistle and shook his head. "Fuck, you got some balls on ya, Celia."

"Did he now?" Wolverine asked, fighting a grin. "Well, hell, I almost hope he is down here now. I got a little somethin' to remind him where he came from."

In actuality, my mouthiness had nothing to do with the size of my lady balls and everything to do with the nervous anticipation coursing through my veins.

I was going to find Jamie, and then I was going to go after every single person who had a hand in hurting him. There was a strong chance that this would go down as more than just the day I survived my first hangover.

The three of us didn't attempt to hide our presence as we reached the base of the stairs. At the powerful stench of death, our guns moved just a little higher and my hopes of finding Jamie alive dwindled.

I went straight to the last door on the left, half-expecting to see Hawk or Manny strung up from the ceiling. Instead, the room was empty—the chains dangling over patches of dried blood on the concrete.

The blood could've come from anyone at any time, but the cigar butts littering the floor were a different story. I lowered my gun to grab one, confident that Angel and Wolverine would have my back if something happened.

"Cobra." I rolled it between my fingers, letting the stale scent fill my nostrils. "He was here."

It didn't make sense. He was supposed to be dead.

Wolverine's eyes moved over the pulley system along the ceiling, to the stains on the concrete floor. "These look fresh to me, but I know for a fact the club ain't had anyone here in months."

"Fuck! Celia!" Angel roared from the next room.

My heart, which had been thumping heavily in my chest, moved up into my throat. My numb fingers curled around the handle of the gun. I stumbled toward the sound of his voice with Wolverine fighting to move in front of my body.

He'd found him.

We were too late.

I lifted the back of my wrist to my nose as the stench of rotting flesh grew stronger, fighting the urge to vomit. A moldy cot had been shoved up against one of the white walls, stained with blood.

"What the hell is this?" I asked, fighting to see around Wolverine's torso.

"Jesus Christ," Wolverine exhaled softly. "Celia, go upstairs and wait for us."

I gave up any pretense of being brave, or strong, or any of the other crap Kate seemed to think I was as I gripped the material of his shirt in my fist. "Tell me it's not him!" I begged. "Please!"

"Doll, listen to him," Angel added. "It's better that way."

Goosebumps spread over my arms, but I stayed where I was. Jamie had fought to restore me. Even the parts that I'd become convinced were lost forever. He'd never given up, and no matter how badly it hurt. I wouldn't leave his side now.

The breath fled my body as I surged around the wall of bikers, my feet stuttering to a stop when I encountered the island of fluids surrounding the body on the floor. Insects fed on liquefied flesh of what had once been a head, making it almost impossible to determine identity other than that the victim was male.

Angel looked up from where he knelt with a handkerchief covering his nose and mouth and somberly shook his head. "It ain't Jamie, Celia. Now, go upstairs."

I nodded, flooded with guilt over my relief that the person on the floor wasn't my husband. I looked down at the ring on the man's left hand, wondering if his wife was out searching for him like I was for Jamie.

When she found out what happened, would she fall apart blaming herself, or decide to go after the men responsible?

Wolverine placed a hand on my shoulder, silently urging me to leave. I looked away from the anchor on the man's forearm and turned toward the door, fighting not to think of the man's loved ones.

When it registered, the blood drained from my face, and I careened into Wolverine's body with a hard groan. "No! No, it can't be!"

The proof continued to stare up at me from the concrete, a tattoo with one word woven through it—Norma. A symbol that represented his time in the Navy and his love for the woman who would become his wife.

"Daddy," I gasped. However bad things had gotten between us, he'd deserved better than this. He'd deserved better than being discarded like trash.

My vision blurred as Wolverine helped me up the stairs, but the tears wouldn't fall. The grief left me feeling as if I were going mad, wild with rage that they were going to pin this on Jamie too, and people would believe it.

They would believe that my father had died at my husband's hands, because to them, it made sense.

And while everyone was busy shaking their heads in shame, Jamie slipped farther out of reach. The Sons and the man who betrayed him got away scot-free.

Not today.

I broke away from Wolverine's side with a low growl and ran for Jamie's truck, hitting the lock button as the door slammed shut behind me. The gun I hadn't realized I was still holding dug into my palm, and I reluctantly placed it in the passenger seat before starting the ignition.

Wolverine rapped at the window in a panic. "Celia, open the door!"

My resolve slipped until I remembered my father's body, left to rot in that hell all alone.

"It's Bear. He's the traitor, Wolverine!"

The leathery skin around his eyes stretched thin in surprise as he yelled back through the thin pane of glass, "No. Celia, it ain't him."

But it was.

"He has Jamie's vest," I choked out, sounding as if I was on the verge of crying even as my eyes remained dry. "I'm going to kill him."

"Don't do it, doll. Just open the goddamn door!" His fist connected with the glass, making it rattle.

"Move," I pleaded. "I don't want to hurt you."

He pulled back. "You go down to that canyon, and you're askin' for death! Ain't one person gonna be able to save your ass! Think about Jamie! You want to turn his brothers into his enemies?"

"They already are," I said before shifting the truck into drive, leaving him behind in a cloud of dust.

CHAPTER TWENTY-SEVEN

Celia: March 2017 (Age: 44)

Within seconds, my cell phone screen was lighting up with Angel's name, the cheerful musical tone filling the cab of the truck. I let it go to voicemail, only for it to start up again almost immediately.

I switched it off while keeping my foot pressed against the accelerator, daring any cop to pull me over. I navigated the narrow road leading down into the canyon with ease, no longer a scared, pregnant teenager, but a cynical woman with a vendetta.

I bypassed the open spots and threw the truck into park behind a row of bikes, watching in amusement as the prospects shared looks of wide-eyed panic.

Jamie's newest prospect, Alex, ran up to the side of the truck, demanding I get out. Only, he didn't answer to Jamie anymore. He answered to a traitor.

"Hey there, Alex!" I kept one hand on the door handle and the other on my gun, praying he'd back down once he knew who I was.

"C-C-Celia?" he stuttered as I climbed out, keeping the weapon tucked close to my body. "Jesus Christ, you damn near took out Pres's bike!"

I brought my hand up to my mouth in mock horror. "Did I? I'm telling you, I just got these new contacts, and my depth perception is all sorts of messed up. I need to talk to Bear."

His eyes moved to the hand I had concealed in the folds of my dress before he replied, "Uh, he ain't around—"

A gun is the fastest. Get the guy on his knees, press the barrel against his skull, and pull the trigger.

"That's funny. Wasn't it his bike I almost hit? Now, which one was it again? Oh, it's right there." I pulled the gun free and brought it to the side of his head before he could reach for his own, gripping the patch-free vest right between his shoulder blades to keep him from bolting on me. "Get on your knees."

My head jerked from left to right as the remaining prospects raised their weapons without hesitation. They didn't know me. Even if they did, my husband wasn't the one running things anymore.

"Get Bear!" I called out through a clenched jaw.

"There's six of us and one of you, bitch!" a prospect taunted from over my left shoulder. "Those ain't the best odds."

I spun with Alex still locked in my grip, fighting to keep them in my sights. "Bear!" I screamed, knowing I had about thirty seconds before they started putting bullets in me.

Better to ask for forgiveness than permission.

Sweat was clinging to almost every part of my body when Bear finally appeared in the yard, flanked by his usual guards. "Celia," he said patiently, seemingly ignoring the gun being held on his prospect. "To what do we owe this pleasure?"

"You know damn well why I'm here!"

He made eye contact with someone behind me and shook his head, causing me to crane my neck to see all of my enemies.

"Don't have the slightest fuckin' clue, but I'm gonna go out on a limb here and say it ain't because you missed me," he replied with a smirk.

I wanted him unsettled, but Bear looked as relaxed as ever. The hands clenched into tight fists at his sides were the only indication I'd caught him off-guard.

Somehow, that was scarier.

The sinking feeling in the pit of my stomach intensified when I realized he wasn't calling off his dogs. "I want to talk. Alone."

"See, if you wanted to talk without an audience, you should have left the gun in the truck," Bear said, raising his palms in a helpless shrug. "It don't come across as real fuckin' friendly, if you know what I mean."

"I just came from your storage facility." I relaxed my hold on Alex before calmly firing a round into the dirt between Bear's feet. "I saw what you did to my father! Now, tell me where Jamie is, or I won't hesitate to put the next one in your head."

Bear's eyes flashed briefly with surprise before he nodded to his men. Two prospects took me down to the dirt, knocking the gun from my hands and the breath from my lungs.

"Everyone inside!" Bear demanded as I lay gasping on the ground.

The men moved off of me, and I forced myself up onto my knees, slowly breathing in through my mouth while pushing my stomach out in an attempt to get my diaphragm working properly again.

The biker who'd always felt more like an older brother than Jamie's second-in-command watched me warily as he emptied the bullets from the magazine on my gun before tossing it into the dirt. "Which storage facility were you at?"

"The one off the interstate," I rasped.

"You found your father there?" he asked softly, no longer smiling.

"Don't pretend like you don't know!" I pushed myself up and staggered toward him.

"There are a lot of things I don't know, Celia!" Bear growled. "Like, how did Grey's kutte end up at my house after your daughter visited—"

"She found it on your bed!"

His nostrils flared, and he took a step forward, placing us toe to toe. "And why the fuck would I have it?"

"Because you're the traitor!" I looked down at the leather vest caught in my fists, knowing by laying hands on him I'd just sentenced myself to death. Sadly, I no longer cared. "You turned him over to the Sons, killed my father—"

Bear laughed. "You still believe that I'm behind it all! The fuckin' mastermind who sold out his own club for an enemy! Jesus fuckin' Christ!"

The sound of tires moving over gravel drifted through the trees, but I kept my focus on the biker in front of me.

"Just tell me what you did to him, you son of a bitch!" I screamed, driving my fist into his chest. "Tell me... put me out of my misery!"

For months, I'd clung to this naïve hope that we'd find Jamie alive. Today, it had been my father's body. Tomorrow, it might be my husband's.

If the Sons hadn't killed him yet, there was a reason. I just didn't know what that reason was.

Bear stood motionless, letting me batter him with my fists. "Celia." His voice was low—a warning, vibrating beneath my arms.

"Where is he, Bear?" Mikey called out from behind me. "Don't make this hard on yourself."

"Fuck you, Sullivan!" Bear spat.

I sucked in a ragged breath before launching myself into his large body again, knowing that if he wanted to, he could easily take me down.

"If your club isn't responsible, then why did I find my father at your storage facility?" I growled, striking him across the face with an open palm. I had crossed every line to get answers, or at the very least, a reaction that proved his guilt. "Where. Is. My. Husband?"

At the mention of the storage facility, Bear snapped out of his trance, quickly capturing my wrist in his hand and bringing it down. "You're seein' exactly what they want you to see," he said, so softly that I almost swore I'd imagined it.

"Stop fucking around and tell us what we need to know," Mikey demanded. "We aren't leaving until every inch of your clubhouse has been searched."

"Sullivan, unless you brought a motherfuckin' warrant, you ain't gettin' within ten feet of the door. That goes for every last one of you." He glared down at me, still squeezing my wrist to the point of pain. "Now, I'm gonna tell you one last time. I didn't lay a fuckin' hand on Grey."

"But—" I protested, thinking of all the evidence that seemed to point directly at him. Dakota had shown me footage of Bear confronting Nate. In my severely dehydrated and sleep-deprived state, it had all made sense. "I saw you."

"He's right," Kate spoke up. It wasn't her presence that surprised me, but the strength in her voice as she stepped forward. Her hands trembled, but she straightened her spine and faced us. "Mama, the other video. I think that's the key."

I lifted my chin up to Bear. "You confronted Nate... told him to keep quiet—"

"Kate, pull up that damn video." His brows drew together in confusion, anger rolling off of him in waves. "Is that what you think?"

He gripped me tighter. "Yeah, I fuckin' confronted the doctor that night. I wanted to know who had access to Grey before he died. I thought I tied up every loose end, and guess what? I still completely fuckin' missed the fact that someone took him!"

We all had.

Because the sheer number of people who would have had to have been paid off to keep quiet was staggering.

Impossible.

Kate handed Bear the phone with a mumbled, "It's, um, it's all here."

He released his hold on me, running his hand over his beard as he watched the video. "This ain't one of my guys. Sullivan, is he one of yours? Oh, that's right, you're not a fuckin' cop anymore."

Bear's mocking laugh triggered some protective instinct within me. Mikey may not have been my blood, but he was still my son, and no one attacked my kids and got away with it.

Even a biker who could very well break me in half.

For someone smaller, a sneak attack is better.

I bent down as if I was going to tie my shoe before retrieving the trench knife from its holster. The laughter died on Bear's lips the moment I shot up and pressed the tip of the blade to his throat.

"Do not speak to him like that," I drawled. "You can take your anger out on me for showing up here, but you will not involve my kids. Are we clear?"

"You're on dangerous ground, Celia," Bear ground out. His face was mottled with red. Whether it was from the pressure of the blade against his skin or a temper on the verge of exploding remained a mystery.

"Are we clear?" I repeated.

Bear jerked his head in assent, and I released him before returning the knife to the holster on my thigh. He rubbed at his throat before pointing to all of us.

"You've got sixty seconds to jump back in your cages and get the fuck out of here. You show your face around here again, and I won't hesitate to put a bullet in every one of your fuckin' heads. Am I makin' myself clear?"

I nodded on behalf of the group and sent them ahead of me before turning back to the biker. "I won't stop looking for him, Bear."

The muscle in his jaw ticked in anger, but he nodded. "You're fuckin' with dangerous men, Celia. You keep lettin' them lead you into these traps, and it won't be long before you end up dead. The next biker you attack might not hold back." He patted the gun on his hip, a reminder that he could have killed me at any point.

"And Celia?" he added, handing me Kate's phone. "The day I take off this kutte is the day you'll know I've given up on findin' him."

I nodded and retrieved my unloaded gun from where it lay in the dirt, emotionally beaten down and with no more answers than I'd had when I arrived.

Mikey stood by the open door of Jamie's truck with his arms crossed over his chest, looking just like his father did when he was angry. "What the actual fuck was that?"

"I found my father at their storage facility."

"And what? Just thought you'd go after an entire goddamn MC on your own?" He ran a hand roughly over his face before turning to a stricken Kate. "Call Nate. Tell him to meet us back at your mother's."

"But he might—" she protested, leaving me to guess why she was still avoiding her husband.

"Does now seem like a good time to make excuses, Counselor? We're fucking lucky that Bear didn't kill every last one of us."

My head chose that moment to remind me just how hungover I was. I massaged my temple, and abjectly replied, "But he didn't. We're all still here to fight another day."

"Celia, sweetie," Mike snarled. "What good is finding Grey if we're just going to have to tell him you went off and got yourself killed? No more secrets, from here on out. We communicate, and we sure as fuck—"

"Don't go running into things with our dicks out," Dakota finished somberly. "Got it."

Mike squeezed his eyes shut and pinched the bridge of his nose. "Okay, anyone else have anything they need to confess to or share with the class before we get the fuck on the road?"

Lauren squeezed his hand. "Need me to drive?"

"Mikey, I'm sorry. I—" I tried, only to be met with more resistance.

"We either work as a team or not at all, Celia. If we're all off doing our own thing, then we're as good as dead."

"So, tell us what to do."

He glanced around. "Not here. Your place. Kate," he singsonged, without turning to face her. "I'm not hearing a phone call."

———

The drive back to the farmhouse was a quiet one, filled with nothing but the sound of static from the radio. Instead of turning it off, Kate and I had each gotten lost in our own heads.

When she'd offered to ride back with me, I assumed it was because she wanted to talk about what had happened to her grandfather, or at the very least, to give me some clue why she was still avoiding Nate. Her fingers darted over the screen of her phone, but otherwise, she remained silent.

My mind was all over the place. I quickly moved from thoughts of Jamie and where he was being held, to Kate and the secrets she was keeping.

Wife.

Mother.

I shifted between the two like a ping-pong ball, coming away from both with nothing but more confusion.

"You're staring at me," Kate said, still staring at the phone in her hand.

"Do you want to talk about it?"

With a sigh, she asked, "What's there to talk about? My grandfather is dead. No one seems to know anything about where my dad is. Oh, and my husband, who hates drama, is about to be thrown into the middle of a shit show. Did I miss anything?"

I pulled into the driveway, watching as Kate's already pale face seemed to lose more color at the sight of Nate's black BMW idling beside the house.

"Why won't you tell me what really happened the night you left him?"

As if I needed proof that I was on the right track, her breathing became little more than shallow pants, a clear sign she was spiraling. She rubbed her palms against her black slacks and lifted her eyes to meet mine. "Let it go. Please."

I put the truck in park and touched her shoulder. "Kate—"

Her body immediately twisted away from mine. She backed toward the door, one hand already on the handle while the other came up in defense. "Don't touch me!"

"No." The word was an exhale, a plea. I saw Angel holding a washcloth to my battered face. I felt Jamie's lips on mine, his arms caging me in, making it impossible to draw a breath.

Wetness hit my cheeks when I shook my head, the feel of the tears almost foreign.

I'd failed her.

"Mama, you're crying," she whispered as if she knew that until now, only her father had held the power to break through the veil of numbness that surrounded my heart.

As a mother, how was I supposed to tell my daughter I knew the truth without her saying a word? Even with all that I'd done to keep them safe, someone had hurt my baby.

Nate rapped at the window, and Kate jumped in fright. When she saw who it was, her shoulders visibly relaxed, and relief flooded her face.

Someone had taken my little girl and left her a skittish, frightened mess. But, without a shadow of a doubt, I knew that someone wasn't her husband.

CHAPTER TWENTY-EIGHT

Kate: March 2017 (Age: 27)

Nate knocked on the window again, the smile on his face wavering slightly when I held up a finger. "Just give me a minute."

I inhaled deeply, and the panic began to subside, taking with it the weight on my chest and the feeling that everything was lost.

He nodded and stepped back, tucking his hands into the front pockets of his jeans. The movement left my heart racing, and I realized that instead of spending the entire ride trying to work out what to say, I should have worked on curbing my body's reaction to the sight of him.

When I shamelessly continued to stare, his dark eyebrows drew together, and he licked along his lower lip as if trying to figure me out.

My cheeks heated and his eyes, the same color as the tequila my mother and I had spent half the night drinking, suddenly widened with cautious hope.

My mother.

I reluctantly tore my gaze away from the man I loved and focused on the broken woman across from me. For the life of me, I couldn't remember the last time I'd seen her cry.

It had to have been after she helped me bail Dakota out of jail, or when she found out I got married in Vegas. Either way, it was a rare enough occurrence to have caught my attention.

Maybe she'd learned to keep a tight rein over her emotions after years of living with a biker.

Notoriously stoic, even with the world burning around her.

She pasted a smile onto her face when I reached for her hand. "I'm f-f-fine." With that, she hiccuped loudly and promptly dissolved into tears again.

"Mama, you've been so brave," I said, adopting my counselor's tone. "And today has been exceptionally heavy. You lost your father—"

My voice wavered when I realized I'd never hear Pops call me Katydid again, or watch as he made goofy faces from over the top of his newspaper when Nan's back was turned because he thought she was being unreasonable.

My grief was overshadowed by knowing he'd never have to answer for taking us away from our mother or the stolen money meant for mine and Dakota's futures.

I cleared my throat. "You also confronted Bear—"

"Mary Katherine, I am well aware of what today has been," she stated while dabbing at her eyes. "Now, if you're finished with your counseling session, I'd like to give you some advice."

I nodded and slumped back in my seat, waiting for the inevitable lecture. "If this is about Nate..." I turned to see if he was still watching, but he was deep in conversation with Zane. "I'm going to—"

"It is... and it isn't." She blew out a breath. "Do you remember last night when I told you that if I'd only told your father the truth, how everything could've been so different?"

"Yeah... and I just said I'm going—"

"You don't want to talk about it with me, and I get that," my mother interjected. "But please, for the love of all the saints, tell him what happened to you. Just... just don't shut him out is all I'm trying to say."

"What happened to me?" I parroted, even though I knew exactly what she was talking about. My face grew warm, and I reached for my seatbelt. "I just—excuse me."

"Kate—"

I took a deep breath and opened the door, deciding how to best approach my husband. Despite my mother's advice, there was no way I was ever talking about what happened that night. I was going to bury it and pretend like it never happened.

We had more important things to worry about.

"Hey." I stroked Nate's arm. "You're really here."

"Is it true?" He turned to face me. "You didn't text me because you wanted to reconcile. You brought me out here for questioning?"

"I—" I swallowed. "Well, maybe partly—"

The hope I'd seen in his eyes extinguished, along with any chance of us working things out. "Just when I think that there's nothing else left for you to do to rip my heart out, you go and surprise me."

He turned and held his palms up to Mike, his jaw settling into a hard line as he asked, "Do you need to pat me down or am I okay to be interrogated like this?"

"I already told you this wasn't anything official. We're just trying to establish a timeline for the night Grey was shot." Mike shot me a look of apology. "I thought you told him."

Nate laughed bitterly. "That this was nothing more than a fucking ambush? No, she kept that to herself. Let's get this over with. I have things to do."

I stood rooted to a patch of yellowed grass as he stormed up the steps and into the house. Where I expected tears, there was nothing but numbness.

My mother and Dakota approached me cautiously, but I waved them off. "I'm fine."

Dakota reached over to squeeze my arm. "This is all a disaster. I'm sorry, Kate. If I would have just told you—"

"Don't do that," I said with a shake of my head. "Seriously, it's fine. We'll see what he knows, and then he can go back to his regular life."

"Tell him, Kate," my mother demanded, her eyes filling with tears again. "Mikey can wait. If he knows—"

"If he knows... what, Mama?" I snapped. "What will that change? Absolutely nothing."

Mike watched the entire exchange from the porch with a pinched expression and crossed arms. "If we could just—Kate, I'm really sorry, but we need to save this shit for later—"

"Don't worry, Detective," I bit out. "I won't hold up your investigation. Just one thing, though." I stopped in the doorway and looked up at him with a cruel smirk. "You're going to be dealing with so much more of 'this shit' with two girls on the way. Good luck."

Dakota immediately began asking my mother for answers from the porch, but I continued on into the house, moving toward the sound of voices coming from the kitchen.

Nate had his back to the doorway, but turned when he heard me come in. His jaw tightened, and he shook his head before looking away again.

I reached out a shaking hand to steady myself against the cabinets when I realized the real reason I was afraid to tell him about what happened. Deep down, I knew. When the truth came out, Nate wouldn't hesitate to leave me.

Just like my father had.

"Hey," Dakota tried to capture everyone's attention when she entered the kitchen. When no one acknowledged her, she let out an unholy screech that made my skin crawl. "I said, hey!"

Mike dug a finger into his ear from behind her. "Jesus Christ, Dakota! What the fuck was that?"

She shrugged. "A whistle. Well, I can't actually whistle, so I just make the sound."

Zane shook his head and gestured for her to get to the point. "But that's not important right now. Today has been a little hard for our team."

Today had proven that none of us knew what the hell we were doing. We weren't a team. We were nothing more than a group of people, all convinced that our way was better than the next guy's.

"I'll take it from here." Mike patted her awkwardly on the back before moving into the center of the kitchen. "Everyone in this room is family, but we're not acting like a family. Why have the Sons been successful?"

"Because they have better weapons?" Dakota guessed.

I felt Nate's eyes on me and slightly tilted my head to look up at him. The expression on his face was hard to read as he lowered his head to mine. My heart beat wildly, sending the blood from my extremities down to the more lucrative organs between my thighs.

"Is this why you wanted me to come out here?"

I exhaled shakily as his warm breath hit my ear, fighting the urge to throw myself into his arms and admit to everything.

"To witness your kumbaya shit?"

The breath left my lungs in a heavy sigh, and I took a step back.

"Nate," Mike called out. "If you could pay a little bit of attention, this does concern you. Okay, sweetie?"

"How does any of this concern me? I told you I'd give you the details of the night I was on call, but I don't need to be involved in whatever team-building—"

"The Sons are successful because they work as a unit!" I snapped over him. "No one goes off on their own. It's why it never seemed to matter how many you arrested. There were plenty more to take their place. They are completely committed to the cause."

"Like Hydra," Dakota whispered to no one.

I took a deep breath for courage and turned back to Nate. "As much as you don't want to believe it, this does concern you. They're going after the people I love. First, it was my father and then my grandparents. Tomorrow, it might be you."

"Katy—"

My eyes burned with the need to cry. "Mike, you were right. We either work as a team or not at all. So, tell us what we need to do."

He picked up a pen from the island and clicked it several times with a slow nod. "Bear—he mentioned something about the guy in the video being a cop. Do you still have it?"

"Right here." I pulled my phone from my pocket, carefully avoiding looking at Nate. I kept my eyes down, knowing that if I looked up, the tears clogging my throat would spill over onto my cheeks. "It was sent to me that... um, night. They wanted me to believe you helped my father get out of the hospital without being seen."

Nate nodded. "So, you left."

Mike plucked it from my fingers before snorting. "Fucking hell! Masterson, this prick look familiar to you?"

"Son of a bitch," Zane cursed. "Well, now we know how they were able to take your fucking job from you. Corruption goes all the way to the top. "

"Let me see," Nate said before walking over to Mike. "That's the guy who warned me to stay out of it. I thought he was with the club—"

"Nope," Mike said, clicking his tongue against his teeth. "That'd be Sergeant Rogers, the bastard who cost me my job. Change of plans, kids. I think it might be time for a little surveillance work."

Hadn't we had enough excitement for one day?

Was I the only one who wanted to sleep off the remnants of last night?

"Lauren, you're with me. We'll stake out Sergeant Rogers' house tonight, see if he leads us anywhere. We know the department had multiple moles, so maybe he'll give up a few or at least get us on the right track."

Zane pushed off the counter with a nod. "Dakota and I can take Bear. He says his hands are clean, but there's only one way to know for sure if he's talking to anyone outside the club."

Mike nodded. "Good. We know that there are weak links within both. Who else do we have? Wait, where the fuck is Goblin?"

I moved until my back was against the wall, praying I somehow blended in enough to not be called on. It was the same thing I'd done to get out of most team sports in high school.

"Um," Dakota began, gnawing at the corner of her lip. "Okay, so no more secrets, right? You said that. Okay, I guess now is a good time to mention that I may have done something to upset Little Ricky, but I was only doing it in the interest of information. Information is the key to a long—"

"Dakota ran a paternity test on Little Ricky and Bear," Zane interrupted with a shake of his head. "Then, she delivered the results to Molly like she was Maury fucking Povitch."

"You what?" Mama exclaimed. "Why would you do that? Little Ricky's father—"

"Is Bear," Dakota finished for her. "The test proved it. In my defense, I thought Bear was the traitor, and I wanted to ensure that my best friend didn't share the same blood, but I messed up, and now Little Ricky won't talk to me."

Mike massaged his temple with a heavy sigh. "Okay, that is more than I needed to know. Celia, we're going to need to pair you with someone else—"

"Jimmy," Lauren offered. "We don't have a buddy for him."

"That was intentional," Mike said through his teeth. When Lauren continued staring him down, he growled, "Fine. Jimmy and Celia can work together."

"Doing what exactly?" My mother asked, her hand already moving up onto her hip.

"Celia, pumpkin, you went to the storage facility on your own. Did you ever stop to think what would have happened if the Sons were there?"

"I had Wolverine and Angel!"

"Oh, good!" Mike roared. "The Decrepit Duo totally could've handled it. Jesus, it's obvious you've had quite enough adventure for one day, so you and Jimmy will do research. Deep web searches... anything and everything that might relate back to the Sons. I want to know where they are, and I want to know what they're planning next. We'll do a sweep of the storage facility tomorrow and search for anything that might've been left behind."

My mother didn't respond well to being told what to do, but instead of arguing, she let the slamming screen door answer for her as she stormed outside.

"Who am I forgetting?" Mike scanned the room. "Nate!"

"Oh, no," my husband held up a hand. "I'm not getting roped into this—"

Mike nodded. "I get it. You're off the hook. Kate, looks like you'll be reviewing hospital surveillance tapes with Jeremy. He's got everything from the night Grey was shot."

Jeremy.

At the mention of his name, stillness filled the kitchen. The blood roared in my ears and pulsed in my neck. Last night's tequila reared its head within my abdomen, and the bile rose in my throat.

The airways in my lungs narrowed, forcing short agonized wheezes from my chest, and I risked a glance toward the screen door, wondering if I'd be able to make it to my car without being caught.

"Jeremy?" Nate growled, the muscles rippling along his jaw. "I don't want him anywhere near Kate."

I felt myself falling and stumbled into his side without a second thought, clinging to him like a small child would a parent on the first day of school. His body stiffened in response before he allowed one of his arms to rest around my shoulders.

"Then, I guess you'll be going after all," Mike said with a grin.

Nate's arm tightened around my body before he ominously stated, "Alright. Let's get to work... buddy."

CHAPTER TWENTY-NINE

Dakota: March 2017 (Age: 22)

"I think I might need to pee." I bounced my knees up and down with a slight wince.

Zane handed me an empty soda bottle, keeping his eyes on the dark building in front of us. "Just climb in the backseat if you need to."

"Um, Big Guy? I can't pee in this. It's barbaric. Listen, I saw a 7-Eleven a few blocks back. You stay here, and I'll just go take care of business."

"You don't really have to pee, do you? You just want snacks."

I pushed my lips out into a pout and nodded. "I'm hungry."

"Babe," he stated calmly. "Told you to pack a cooler before we left. Surveillance takes time."

We'd been tasked with tracking Bear. Initially, it seemed more exciting than reviewing hospital security cameras or trying to identify the man seen on the video sent to Kate, but now I wasn't so sure.

We'd been sitting in here for an hour, and not one thing had happened. The only thing that had left the body shop was a bat, and as he wasn't a criminal, Zane didn't care to hear about it.

I bet the others were having more fun.

They probably had snacks, too.

I traced my finger around the window control button on the

armrest. "What if he's not even here? What if we're just sitting here for no reason and he's at home watching sports and laughing at how stupid we are?"

"He's here. My source saw him arrive about a half-hour before we got here. We'll wait him out and see where he leads." Zane drummed his fingers lightly against the thigh of his jeans, perfectly content doing nothing.

I pulled my phone out to text Little Ricky again, only for Zane to pry it from my fingers with his giant bear paw of a hand. "No phones. The light could draw unwanted attention. We want this to look like any other vehicle parked along the street."

With a grumble, I leaned back in my seat and closed my eyes. I wondered what Little Ricky was doing right now. I'd thought that he would've been happy to know that Bear was his real dad, but both he and Molly had seemed upset by the news.

Maybe it was because they knew that Bear really was the traitor.

"Why do you think that Little Ricky is mad at me?"

Zane shifted to face me. "Besides the fact that you took his DNA without his consent? Probably because you meddled. Put yourself in his shoes. Kid spent his whole life thinking that his dad died before he was born, and now you drop the bomb on him that he's alive."

"And how is that any different from what I went through? Until six months ago, I thought my dad was dead. Finding out he was alive was the greatest thing to ever happen to me—"

He cleared his throat with raised eyebrows. "The greatest thing?"

"Well, besides meeting you and finding out I was pregnant with baby Thor. I just..." I sighed. "I just really thought he would have been happier. Now, we may never speak again."

"He'll come around. I'm convinced it's impossible to stay mad at you."

"Really?" I said, a smile creeping onto my face.

"Really, Cap. Now, get comfortable and watch for anything suspicious."

"Is this something you used to do a lot?"

He nodded. "Yeah, as long as you stay inconspicuous, it's a good way to get information. I did surveillance on you." The corner of his mouth lifted in a smirk. "I even peed in a bottle to avoid blowing my cover."

It wasn't a romantic thing to say, but I found myself turned on, regardless. "You watched me like this? Just hours and hours, doing nothing but watching me?"

"Yep. Camped out in the parking lot of the mall one night and waited for you to come out. Then I followed you back to your apartment—"

"Did you watch me get undressed?" I interrupted with a giggle.

His eyebrows pulled together as he frowned. "No. It was the night that Jackson Blake showed up at your door. I left when he did."

I frowned. The big lug was ruining my fantasy by bringing up my ex-fiance. If we were going to pass the time, it was up to me to get him back on track. "What if he hadn't been there?"

"What do you mean?" He lifted the binoculars and studied something near the door before lowering them again.

"I mean..." I ran a finger lightly down his arm. "What if it had just been me? Would you have stayed?"

"I don't know," he admitted. "It was pretty late. I guess I might have observed you for a bit longer, just to see if there was anything I could have used on our case."

I bit down on my lip, fighting a grin. "I remember there being this one area of the parking lot where you could clearly see into my apartment if the balcony blinds were open. What if you'd parked there?"

Zane rubbed at his beard, clearly thinking through the scenario like a cop would. "I guess it's possible. If I had reason to believe that you were working with the Blake family and I didn't know you'd be coming into the gym, it's entirely possible that I might have camped out in the parking lot and watched you."

Another fantasy entered my mind of me showering alone in the locker room while he watched from one of the nearby couches.

One fantasy at a time, Dakota.

My mouth went dry, and I swallowed before continuing. "So, you're camped out in front of my apartment, and I come home from, say, comic book club. I look really hot, by the way. I go into my apartment and kick off my heels before stripping down. I don't even look to see if the blinds are open before doing it. So, there I am in just my under-wear, walking around my apartment without a care in the world."

Zane's face remained blank, but I watched as he shifted uncomfort-ably in his seat before reaching down to adjust himself through his jeans. "What's the underwear look like, Cap?"

Welcome to the party, Detective Masterson.

CHAPTER THIRTY

Kate: March 2017 (Age: 27)

The vinyl on the chair squeaked as I leaned forward to study the computer screen again. My head ached from straining to make sense of the sometimes blurry footage, and my leg bounced restlessly between two men who were seconds away from coming to blows.

My stomach, which had been unsettled all day, tightened into another knot when Jeremy broke the silence.

"So, right here..." He paused the video and reached for my hand, letting his fingers brush against my thigh before lifting it back to the computer. "Do you see anything that seems out of place?"

"You touching my wife," Nate warned.

I pulled my hand free and moved it back to my lap before shaking my head. I just needed to focus on the task in front of me, and then I could go back to my mother's to scrub his touch from my skin. "I've already told you I don't remember seeing anything unusual that night."

"And I've already told you I saw a lot of fucking things that were unusual, Lucky," Nate said with a growl, poking fun at Jeremy's red hair.

Jeremy's gaze moved between me and Nate, a smile pulling at the corner of his mouth. "Hey, Doc? You might wanna watch your step. Be a shame if something were to happen to you because you couldn't keep your fucking mouth shut." He clicked the mouse, and the video started again.

A man appeared on the footage from one of the emergency room cameras, and I tapped the screen. "Stop. Right there. I know who that is. From the gym. What did Dakota call him? Um, uh, Doucheface!"

Jeremy's mouth curved up in a wide smirk. "Is that his given name or just a nickname?"

"I don't remember his real name. He hit on me at the gym when I went once with Dakota—"

"Kyle Barton," Nate finished. "I'd recognize that sleazy mother-fucker anywhere. Do you remember him being at your sister's wedding? Drunk off his ass, trying to convince a bridesmaid to blow him in the bathroom because he was a detective."

I grimaced at the thought of any woman being desperate enough to willingly let him put his hands on her body. "Ugh, no."

"Did it work?" Jeremy asked.

My skin crawled at his sudden interest in the topic, and a flush crept its way onto my face. I tried to swallow, feeling as though something was lodged in my throat. I shoved my chair back and got to my feet. "Just need a drink—"

"Hell no!" Nate shifted his chair to the side to let me pass before continuing his conversation. "Instead, he just moved from one seat at the bar to the next. There was even one point where he came stumbling out of the bathroom and ran right into Grey. Like, so sloppy drunk that he was falling all over him."

I stumbled into the kitchen and grabbed a bottled water from the fridge before pressing it to my forehead. The two men continued laughing over Kyle's behavior while I stewed in the next room. Suddenly, they were best friends.

I didn't know what I expected—that Nate would've jumped up and offered to come with me? Maybe given me a secret look that meant we were going to sneak out?

So far, all he'd given me was the cold shoulder. Perhaps I'd gotten him to my mother's under false pretenses, but he'd kept things from me too.

I glanced down at my watch, trying to calculate how many hours of footage we had left to review before it would be appropriate to leave.

"You okay?"

I jumped at the sound of Jeremy's voice, backing myself against the cabinet near the sink. "You can't touch me," I hissed. "It's not right."

Jeremy rolled his eyes and grabbed a beer from inside the refrigerator. "I think you're overreacting—"

"No," I whispered, blinking back tears. "You can't just cross lines like that."

"Jesus." He let the fridge close with a soft thud and sauntered over. "Is this about the night you stayed over? Let it go, Kate. We had a few drinks. I thought you wanted me and decided to shoot my shot. You weren't down for it. End of fucking story. Nothing happened."

"But—" I paused, scrambling for a rebuttal. His explanation seemed simple when my feelings on the matter were complicated and confusing.

"But what?" Jeremy asked, reaching around me to open a drawer. He grabbed the bottle opener and popped the top on his beer. "It's not like we fucked. Trust me, I would have remembered that."

I took a deep breath and held it in as he left the kitchen, hating that his words made sense.

Nothing had happened.

I was so used to looking for loose threads I'd magnified a simple misunderstanding, blowing the entire night out of proportion.

"Stop being ridiculous," I chided under my breath. "Just be an adult and do your job so you can go home."

Nate and Jeremy were studying a still image of the detective when I came back in, neither raising their heads to acknowledge me.

I pushed my wounded pride aside and studied the timestamp on the bottom of the screen as I sat down. "Wait." I looked over at Nate. "What time were you called in?"

"Uh..." He thought it over. "Twenty-two hundred hours, give or take. Why?"

I looked at the footage again and pressed play. "Look at the time. It's just after midnight. You said he was stumbling around at the reception. Does this look like a man who was falling down drunk just a couple of hours before?"

Kyle looked directly at the camera before speaking into his cell phone and moving off screen. I went to the next camera, but he never appeared.

"Christ," Jeremy noted before rewinding the footage. "She's right. He's as sober as a fucking judge here. Either he metabolizes alcohol better than any human I've ever met or—"

"Or he was never really drunk," I finished for him.

Just two adults having a simple conversation.

"Why fake it?" Nate asked the room. "Surely, that wasn't his way of picking up women."

"I can think of more effective ways to get a woman." Jeremy leaned back in his chair with a stretch. The tattoos on his forearms peeked out from under the sleeves of his dress shirt, and I forced my eyes back to the screen.

I wasn't the first woman to lose her virginity to a biker, even if he had been wearing a suit and masquerading as a realtor. I remembered being shocked by the multitude of tattoos covering his body. Shocked, and more than a little turned on.

I would not let my mind even go there.

Especially not with my husband's thigh up against mine. I looked to my left, noting the sleeve of tattoos coating both of Nate's muscular arms.

Obviously, I had a type.

"I mean, the best way to do it is to not even be trying. Maybe you're thinking about work." My ears perked up, alerting my brain to the possibility of danger. "Maybe she wants you to stop thinking about the job and just take her home."

Hadn't that been how it had happened?

I'd just found out my boyfriend was cheating on me with another man and had forced myself off the couch to attend the chamber of commerce's after-hours event. The co-worker who had begged me to attend never showed and Jeremy had approached just as I'd convinced myself to leave.

Unbeknownst to me, he'd been tasked with keeping me safe by my father. I'd been reckless when I pushed the biker to take me home, blissfully ignorant of the fact that he was breaking every rule the moment his hands touched my body.

"Does that happen a lot in your line of work, Carrot Top?" Nate asked, still looking at the cameras. If he'd been looking up, he would have seen the smirk as it crossed Jeremy's face and known immediately where the conversation was headed.

"You know, it's only happened to me once..."

I clutched my stomach and tried to make myself smaller as nausea reared its ugly head once more.

"When Kate here was down on her knees, begging me to fuck her—"

Nate's chair fell with a resounding clang against the hardwood floor before he launched his fist into Jeremy's jaw.

I instinctively turned my torso to protect myself, and Nate shoved my chair to the side before landing a second strike near Jeremy's mouth, splitting his lip wide open.

I'd thought that was going to be the end, but Jeremy caught Nate's legs with his, sending both of them crashing to the floor in a tangle of limbs.

"What's the matter, Doc?" Jeremy taunted with a bloody grin, blocking the third blow. "Don't like knowing I got there first?"

I stumbled out of the chair with a strangled cry, my hair falling across my face to shield me from the venom in his words. The tingling in my chest only intensified amid the sounds of fists connecting with flesh, leaving me to wonder what it was about sex that turned men into Neanderthals.

"Guys!" I begged as Jeremy landed a solid hit to Nate's jaw, sending a spray of blood from between his lips. "Stop! Please stop!"

"Kate," Jeremy panted as he grabbed a fistful of my husband's shirt, forcing the back of his head down against the floor with an ominous thud. "Just let it happen."

Just let it happen...

The heartbeat that had been sluggish only moments ago now raced to the point of exploding.

Just let it happen...

I stared straight ahead, no longer seeing anything but Jeremy's face looming over mine. The breath burst in and out of my lungs, and I realized why I couldn't forget.

He'd defiled me with his touch under the assumption that because we'd been together once, it would automatically happen again. He'd twisted his actions until he was the hero and I was nothing more than the frigid bitch who'd led him on.

I'd taken the blame for him.

Muscles and veins I wasn't even aware I had strained against my skin as I whirled away from the two of them and headed toward the front door, fully prepared to leave them to their schoolyard fight.

Nate could beat Jeremy to death for all I cared before going back to ignoring me, but I refused to stick around and witness it.

"I warned you to keep your fucking hands off my wife!" I looked back over my shoulder as Nate spat a mouthful of blood onto the floor. "That includes talking about her like she's some fucking trophy you won. Don't fucking disrespect her like that!"

My hand hovered over the doorknob as Jeremy glanced another blow off Nate's jaw, stunning him into silence. This was no pissing contest between two jealous males fighting to become the alpha.

This was my husband defending me.

The pounding in my ears drowned out Jeremy's next words, and I limbered up my shoulders and neck before stalking into the kitchen.

I was tired of cowering. Sick of waking up with the image of his smile burned into my mind.

CHAPTER THIRTY-ONE

Dakota: March 2017 (Age: 22)

"So I'm wearing that black lacy set you like so much. You know, the one where the material is so sheer you can almost see my nipples if you look hard enough?"

Zane's hand dropped back down to the crotch of his jeans.

"Maybe that's what I'm wearing when you're watching me. I get thirsty and grab a bottled water from the fridge. I'm drinking it so fast that some spills from my mouth and down my chest. It's so cold, and now my nipples are hard, just rubbing against the lace."

He groaned softly and clenched his hand into a fist. "Yeah? Then what?"

"Oh, I don't want to wear a wet bra around the house, so I reach back and unclasp it, letting it fall to the floor. And I look at the clock and realize it's almost time for the news to come on. I'm a single girl living in the big city all alone. I need to stay informed about current events."

"The news?" he asked through his teeth, forcibly restraining himself.

"Oh, yes," I said, trying for sultry.

"I go toward the couch before noticing how big the moon is. Without another thought, I pull the vertical blinds to the side and open the sliding glass door to see it better. Only, now you can see me better too. You wanted to stay hidden, but I know you're there and now you're worried. Maybe I'm about to bust your entire case wide open. But then I do something surprising."

Zane had given up any pretense of hiding his erection and was now openly stroking himself through his jeans. "What do you do, Cap?"

I grinned. "I go back inside and close the door, but I leave the blinds pulled so you can see me. I've seen you around the complex before, and from what I remember, you're incredibly sexy. I keep my eyes on your truck as I move my hand down to my panties. As I slip my fingers under the waistband, I realize it's not my hand I want... it's yours."

"M-mine?" he forced out. "What are you going to do about it?"

"I walk up to the glass door, letting my nipples brush against the cool glass before gesturing for you to come up. What would you have done then, Big Guy?"

He hissed out a ragged breath. "I would have been out of my truck and up those stairs within seconds."

"And then what?" I whispered, slipping a hand under the waistband of my leggings. Zane's eyes followed the movement, and he clenched his jaw. "What would you have done if I opened the door and invited you in?"

"This." He unbuckled his seatbelt and leaned across the console, his lips parting on a warm exhale against my skin. Suddenly, being forced to spend hours in his truck together didn't feel quite like the punishment it was an hour ago.

I lifted a finger and traced it around his mouth, similar to the very first time I kissed him. "Hey, Big Guy," I whispered. "Now that you've got me, what are you going to do with me?"

Zane grinned down at me, his eyes drunk with lust, before lowering his mouth over mine. He tugged my lower lip into his mouth with a sigh. One hand went behind my head, holding my hair back, while the other stroked small circles over the baby.

"Unbuckle," he murmured against my lips.

When I complied, he resumed sucking and nipping at my lower lip, letting his hand wander down to the top of my leggings. As his fingers slipped beneath the waistband, much like my own had only moments before, my body grew slick with need.

"If I'd just watched you do a strip-tease in your apartment, and you answered the door for me in nothing but your panties," Zane panted against my cheek. "I wouldn't have wasted time pulling them off."

His fingers brushed over the lace before he yanked it to the side with a growl. "See, I would have known what you needed and just... repositioned them for easier access."

When his hand stilled against me, I opened my eyes with a huff of frustration. "Big Guy, I'm... I'm a little uncomfortable."

He froze. "Is it Thor?"

I shook my head with a hiss. "Um, no. I'm just really turned on and wearing too many clothes and—"

"Kick your shoes off," he directed, before freeing my lower half from the confines of its cotton and spandex prison. True to his word, the lacy panties stayed exactly where they were. I didn't have the heart to tell him they weren't maternity, and had left indentions and patterns on my skin. It would have ruined the fantasy.

"Where were we?" Zane asked with another sly grin. "Oh, right. You've just answered the door." His teeth grazed along my jawline. "And now I've got you up against the wall with my hand between your legs."

"I—I would've begged you to touch me..."

"Oh, yeah? How?" His eyes sparkled with amusement. "How would you have begged me?"

There was only one thing that I could have said. The one word that never failed to turn him on. Pushing my lips into a pout, I whispered, "Fuck me with your fingers, Big Guy."

"Jesus," he growled before plunging one inside me, my body completely ready for him. "You know what it does to me to hear you talk like that."

My head fell back against the seat, and I arched my back, forcing his finger deeper. "D-don't stop."

He added another before crushing his mouth to mine again. His kisses became rougher, his beard scraping against the delicate skin around my mouth with every one. I twisted his long hair up in my hands, fighting to keep his mouth on mine.

I didn't care if I had the world's worst case of beard burn afterward as long as his fingers continued moving just... like... that.

My belly tightened, and I dropped my forehead to his as I clenched around him with a strangled cry. Zane didn't slow his movements, just thrust his tongue past my parted lips, silencing the sound.

I slowly came back down, my body still pulsing around him with mini-orgasms. "Oh," I managed.

"Oh," he agreed before pulling his fingers from my body, bringing them up to his mouth to suck clean. "I need a bigger truck because you taste fucking amazing, and a man like me needs room to eat."

I pulled the damp hair off my forehead. The breath faltered in my chest at the image of Zane down on his knees in front of me. The man was going to give me a heart attack.

His own breathing had gone ragged, and I cracked one eye open at the sound of his zipper coming down. His dick tented the front of his boxer briefs, clearly in need of attention.

"Sit back," I directed, before moving up onto my knees. Baby Thor shifted, contorting my belly as he stretched before settling back to sleep.

Zane let his eyes drift down to rest on my stomach, the look of love so intense on his face that it made me want to cry. "God, I fucking love watching him move like that."

I dropped my mouth down to his with a happy sigh. We were definitely going to be doing more surveillance. It had really brought us closer together.

He caught my hand and brought it down to circle his dick. "Touch me, Cap."

I gently squeezed his shaft in my hand before lowering my head. "If you came into my apartment and made me orgasm like you just did, I would have felt the need to return the favor."

"Yeah?" His voice was strained.

I swirled my tongue over the tip of him with a low hum of pleasure. "It wouldn't have been fair to leave you like this, would it?"

"Definitely... not."

I let my hand glide up and down for a few strokes before taking more of him into my mouth. At our wedding reception, one of Zane's buddies had stumbled over to drunkenly tell him that now he was married, he'd never get a blow job ever again. At the comment, I'd choked on my ginger ale and promptly had to excuse myself.

Before Zane, I would have agreed, but there was something about watching my superhero lose control because of my mouth that turned me on.

Maybe I was the exception to the rule.

It wasn't as if Kate would have been open to questioning. My sister kept the details of her sex life locked down tighter than Fort Knox.

I swallowed around him, and he thrust deeper with a low groan, keeping my hair twisted up in his fist. We quickly found a rhythm—the cab of the truck filled with the sounds of me pleasuring my husband.

"Come here." He tugged my hair, just until my mouth slipped off of him. "Straddle me."

I looked down at my belly and then back at him. "Babe, I'm not sure—"

He reached in between the seat and the door, and the seat hummed to life, reclining his chair until he was almost laying flat. "Ride me."

My tank top slipped over my head before joining the leggings on the floorboard. I clambered across the console and placed my legs on either side of his, painfully aware of the dampness clinging to the inside of my thighs.

Zane hadn't missed it either and reached between my legs to coat his fingertips. "If we were at home right now... I'd want you to sit on my face and let me fuck you with my tongue."

"Z-Zane," I stuttered, suddenly wetter at the thought.

"It's what I would have done if you'd invited me into your apartment," he said with a grin as he lined the head of his dick up with my opening.

"Wouldn't have let a single drop go to waste," he growled before pulling me down onto his thighs. "That's my girl. Fuck, I wish you could see yourself like I do. You are so goddamn sexy that it's almost fucking impossible not to come right away."

"Mmmm..." I moaned at his words of praise. "Not yet. I need more."

"I know you do, babe. Let go, I've got you."

I rolled my hips forward until he was where I needed him, digging my fingernails into the hard muscles of his chest as I came apart with another loud cry.

Zane's hand moved over my mouth, muffling the sound before he thrust up, forcing me to take all of him. His other hand stayed against my belly as if he was reassuring our son that I was okay.

I wasn't okay.

Another wave of pleasure washed over me, and I shuddered through my next breath, wondering how it was possible that sex still felt this good.

I rocked back with a whimper, my hand sliding over the fogged-up window as his thrusts became shallower. Even my glasses were coated in condensation. Knowing I was good for one more, I moved my hips faster, chasing my next high.

Zane came up off the seat, wrapping his arms around my shoulders and back as he filled me with a roar. Our heavy breathing filled the small space, and I began to giggle.

"What?" he panted.

I wiped the sweat from my head with a smile. "I just imagined what it would have been like if you would've come into my apartment and made love to me like that. I would have never let you leave."

"Who's to say I would have left? Maybe I would have broken out the handcuffs and stuck around for extra questioning." He exhaled a laugh and buried his face between my breasts with a playful growl.

The radio that Mike had insisted we needed crackled to life from the cupholder. "What are we seeing, Big Guy?"

Zane lifted his head and whispered against my ear, "Let's see... a pair of fantastic tits and the woman I love wrapped around my cock."

"I don't think you can tell him that," I whispered back, as if Mike might somehow hear us.

He reached around me for the radio and brought it up to his mouth. "Yeah, we got nothing so far. Pretty quiet—"

We both jumped as something heavy rapped against the driver's side window. The radio fell from Zane's hand as he tugged himself back into his jeans before lifting me over the console and into the passenger seat.

Just as Zane reached for his weapon from the side pocket of the door, it was thrown open. I saw the barrel of the gun as it dug into Zane's temple before the man holding it came into view. "Thought I made myself pretty clear—" Bear said in a low voice.

"Masterson, come in," Mike's voice crackled from somewhere under the seat. "Is there a problem? Do you have eyes on the target?"

I kept one arm over my chest and the other between my legs, fighting to remain semi-decent. "Bear, we didn't mean to—"

"Jesus Christ, Dakota! Put your goddamn clothes on!" he snapped, looking away with a wince. "Some spies you two make. What happened, Detective? Took a wrong turn and got lost in your wife's cunt?"

"Don't talk about her like that," Zane growled through a clenched jaw. "We weren't here for you."

Bear laughed. "Right, you were just here to fuck."

I hurriedly replaced my clothing before trying again. "Please, we didn't see anything. Just let us go, and—"

"Out. Let's go. I gave you both a warnin', one you obviously didn't pay a goddamn bit of attention to. Maybe you'll listen a little better this time around."

Zane brought his hands up to rest against the steering wheel before calmly stating, "Let her go. She can take my truck. You and I both know the last thing you need is Grey's daughter's blood on your hands—"

"No," I argued, tears already leaking from the corners of my eyes. "I'm not leaving you alone, Zane."

"Dakota, listen to me. You are going to—"

"Shut the fuck up, both of you. Jesus Christ! No one's goin' anywhere—no one's gettin' special treatment, okay? She ain't a kid anymore, Masterson. See..." He kept the gun on Zane before dragging him from the truck. "In my club, we have rules. Apologies and second chances don't exist. We live by code, and we die by code."

Panic held my body in a vise as I threw my door open and scrambled down after them, feeling as if I was on the verge of hyperventilat-ing. My bare feet landed on broken glass, but the feeling of pain barely registered in my rush to get to Zane.

"Uh, uh, uh," Bear warned, keeping the gun trained up at Zane. "Stay where you are unless you wanna be scrapin' your superhero's head up off the pavement. Now, I've let a lot of shit slide, but this has crossed a goddamn line. I ain't your villain!"

"You didn't even look for him!" I choked back a sob, knowing the only reason Zane hadn't tried fighting back was because of me. "You just gave up—"

"Gave up? You don't know a fuckin' thing about what I've done," he snarled.

"The reason you don't know? Because I've got a goddamn traitor in my clubhouse. And, if I have to sit back and let everybody think it's business as fuckin' usual, I'll do it to catch the rat who gave up your old man. But I'm not lettin' a fuckin' civilian come in and tell me how to run my club!"

"Is this because of Little Ricky?" I cried. "I shouldn't have done it. I didn't mean to hurt him, I swear!"

Bear froze. "What'd you do to Rick, Dakota? Where is he?"

I swiped away my tears. "I didn't mean to... I only wanted to help—"

The gun clicked, and Zane winced as the barrel dug into the base of his skull. "Last chance, what the fuck did you do to Rick?"

"I took some of his hair... and yours. Well, I also took your tooth-brush, but I swear that my heart was in the right place. You know when you're trying—"

"Dakota," Zane growled out. "Get to the goddamn point!"

"It was a simple test. I saw the picture of you from high school, and I thought it was Little Ricky. I thought he'd be happy to know that you were really his dad, but he and Molly seemed upset, and now he won't talk to me. And I know you're mad too—"

The hand holding the gun fell uselessly to his side. "Wait, what the fuck are you sayin'?"

I sighed. "I'm saying that I did a paternity test without anyone's consent. Little Ricky is your son. I am very ashamed of my actions and the pain I may have caused your family, but please don't kill my husband because I was only trying to help."

Bear shoved the gun back into its holster before running his hands over his face with a loud inhale. Zane took the opportunity and moved in front of me.

"That's impossible," Bear muttered to himself. "I—we used a condom—Jesus, you're sure?"

I nodded. "It was a solid match. I mean, sometimes accidents happen. Look at me and Zane. Well, that's not really the best example because we didn't use protection—"

"Dakota, shut the fuck up and go. As far as anyone is concerned, we never saw each other, and you were never here."

We quickly agreed and headed toward the truck when Bear called my name. I turned back. "Yeah?"

"Tell Celia that the Sons have eyes on her. I haven't figured out how they're pullin' the strings, but they are. Motherfuckers have eyes everywhere. Until then, none of you are safe. Next time, it might not be me knockin' on the window. So, stay the fuck out of it and let me do this my way, okay?"

"Okay. Thank you again, sir—Bear. Good luck with your, um, family things."

"Dakota." Zane tugged at my arm. "We need to get the fuck out of here."

The radio was still crackling with static and Mike demanding our location. Zane buckled me in before jogging around to his side.

My foot stung from the glass I'd stepped on, and when the dome light overhead kicked on as Zane's door opened, I made the mistake of lifting it up to inspect the damage.

"Oh," I said in surprise, watching the bright red blood as it flowed from the cut.

Zane had just retrieved the radio when he realized what was happening. "No, no, no. Don't look at it!"

I watched him move across the console in slow motion, reaching for me before everything went black.

CHAPTER THIRTY-TWO

Kate: March 2017 (Age: 27)

By the time I made it back into the living room, Jeremy had his hands around Nate's throat, squeezing. A strange sensation flooded my veins, leaving me feeling as if I was invincible.

"Get the fuck away from my husband!" I roared, holding my weapon to the side of Jeremy's neck just like I'd watched my mother do to Bear.

He released Nate's throat and rocked back onto his heels with his palms in the air. "Christ, Kate! Calm the fuck down!"

Nate's left eye was rapidly swelling shut, but his right one focused entirely on me. Something like confusion came over his face before he drew in a ragged breath.

I continued staring down at Jeremy in an attempt to frighten him, ordering, "Get away from him," through a clenched jaw.

"You can't be serious." He stood up and stumbled back into his chair with a pant before glancing down at Nate with a cruel smirk. "You rely on her to finish all of your fights for you?"

Nate made a sound that might have been a growl before moving into a crouch.

"Babe," I said, no longer feeling like a superhero as tremors wracked my hands, leaving me struggling to hold on to the butcher's knife. "We got what we came for. Take me home."

Please.

Nate placed a thumb on his jaw, working it back and forth, before giving me a slow nod. I stepped across the overturned chair and reached for him, keeping the knife pointed in Jeremy's direction.

I noted, with more than a little horror, that the knuckles on my husband's right hand were split open. "Come on, Rocky. I'll drive," I stammered before linking my arm through his.

Nate's nostrils flared as he forced his injured hand into a fist, but he let me lead him out of Jeremy's house and into the passenger seat of his car.

My knees buckled as I slid behind the wheel, and I let out a huge breath before asking, "Oh my god, what the hell were you thinking? You could have broken your hand, and then how would you perform surgery? We need to get some ice on it before it swells."

He let his head fall back against the headrest with a forced laugh. "What the hell was I thinking? He disrespected you, Katy girl—made it sound as if you were no better than the girls that hang around their clubhouse. Like you're just a fucking object!"

"Well, he's a biker," I said weakly, realizing it sounded as if I was making excuses for the things he'd said. Jeremy might not have grown up around bikers, but he'd had no trouble acting like one.

I could have told your father, Kate. If I'd just told him, things could've been so different for us. Instead, I held onto my pride and kept the truth locked up tight.

"You know what? No, my dad's a biker. Jeremy's an asshole. Uh..." I winced, trying to decide how to best approach it. "So, you know how I left you because of the video?"

He nodded slowly, but remained silent.

Tears welled up behind my eyelids, but I blinked until my vision cleared. "It was just that you'd been taking on more shifts and acting so distant. At first, I thought it was because you were giving me time to work through the stuff with my dad, but then it felt like maybe you might have changed your mind about us." I ran the back of my thumb under my eyes, angry at the stray tears that had escaped.

"Katy," Nate said softly, finally turning to look at me.

"Don't. Just let me finish. When I got that video, it was like things finally clicked. I felt like that was the reason things had felt off between us. I drove to Jeremy's..." Nate's jaw tightened, but I forced myself to keep going.

"I showed him the video, thought he might help me make sense of it. We watched it and re-watched it until I could barely keep my eyes open. He told me I could sleep on the bed in his guest room and I didn't even bother undressing... just collapsed on top of the comforter."

For the love of all the saints, tell him what happened to you.

Nate's undamaged hand moved over the console to rest on top of mine. "Babe, what happened?" The worry in his voice only made my tears fall faster.

"I, um—I woke up—" I saw Jeremy's face in my mind, back-lit by the light from the hallway, his teeth somehow still blindingly white in the dark room. "One hand was under my shirt and the other—" I fought against rising nausea. "The other was between my legs, but still over my clothes."

I left out the part about Jeremy being naked, with his erection pressed against my thigh, and waited for the laughter... for Nate to tell me I was overreacting about nothing. Instead, he let out a rough exhale before tightening his hand around mine.

"After a well-placed kick on my part and multiple groaned apologies on his, I drove to my mother's. I knew Dakota would just grill me for answers before deciding to become Punisher and you..." I paused. "I wasn't sure what you would do."

That wasn't true.

He would have left.

"I couldn't tell my own mother," I admitted with a bitter laugh as more tears gathered in the corners of my eyes. "I'm a damn therapist, and by the time I pulled up in front of her house, I'd convinced myself none of it would have happened if I hadn't put myself in that situation. His actions were so out of character and I—I blamed myself."

"Turn the car around," he said softly, stroking his thumb over my knuckles.

"Nate, I can't—"

He nodded briskly. "Yeah, you can, babe. Just go back. You don't even have to get out of the car—"

"Enough. Your hand is in bad enough shape as it is. I don't even know how you're going to go to work. Let's just get you home. Please."

He let it go, and we drove in silence for a few minutes before he stated, "It wasn't your fault—"

"Nate, I could have called anyone that night... made a better choice—"

"Don't do it," he warned. "Don't justify his actions. It's not that fucking hard to keep your goddamn hands to yourself. Jesus, I imagine him touching you and—turn the fucking car around!"

I let out a shaky laugh. "He's not worth it."

His voice was almost inaudible as he asked, "Were you scared?"

I pressed the garage door opener before answering honestly. "No. I was mad as hell."

"So am I, Katy girl. So am I," Nate said with a chuckle before climbing out. "Are you—I mean, if you're not comfortable—"

"I thought I'd stay, if it's okay," I finished for him as I opened the door.

The house looked exactly as it had over a week ago. The small pile of mail that we swore we were going to sort through was still stacked up on the corner of the island. My cardigan lay across one of the dining room chairs, exactly where I'd tossed it before making dinner the night I left. Even the faint scent of balsam from the plug-in I'd gotten on clearance after the holidays still lingered in the air.

My entire life, I'd wanted a place to call my own. I'd longed for the stability of staying in one place.

This place was my home.

Nate stretched his fingers with a wince, pulling me from my reverie and forcing me into action. I grabbed several ice packs from the freezer before leading him over to the couch. "Sit." I placed one on top of the swollen joints on his hand and settled in at his side to hold the other to his puffy eye. "Let's see if this helps. I can grab you some ibuprofen—"

"I should have told you the truth." He reached up and tucked a few stray hairs behind my right ear, letting his fingers linger against my throat.

"Nate—" I swallowed. "We don't have to talk about that."

"We do. I think we've kept enough secrets from each other." The muscle in his jaw twitched in anger. "Fuck, I wanna drive back over there."

I let my forehead rest against his collarbone with a groan. "Stop. I meant what I said. He isn't worth another thought."

And this time, I believed it.

The fingers on his left hand curled under my chin, lifting my face to meet his. "In the car, you said that I'd been distant. You were right." A shadow passed over his face. "I fucking threw myself into work to try to lessen the guilt over what happened that night. He was my patient, Katy. Mine. And I fucked it all up—listened to the wrong people. If I stayed with him, none of us would be in this mess. Jeremy would have gotten nowhere near you—"

"They would have found another way, Nate. If it wasn't you, they would've tried to make someone else the fall guy. Just look at the people they have working for them." I shuddered with the realization that though we'd unmasked one tonight, there were countless others still lurking in the shadows.

"How do we keep getting it all wrong, Katy girl?" Nate hesitated. "With us, I mean. It's like we're both still afraid of getting our hands dirty."

I moved in a little closer, breathing in the familiar scent of him. "I know what you're saying. I just got so focused on things being perfect out of some fear that I'd end up like my mother. I didn't want anything to threaten what we had."

Like Cinderella waking up the morning after the ball to discover her carriage had returned to a pumpkin.

"And now?" His voice was quiet.

"Knowing what I know now?" I propped my elbow up against the back of the couch. "I think I'd consider it the highest compliment to be compared to Celia Quinn. She's a warrior."

"She's a warrior? Babe, I watched you hold a knife on a biker like it was nothing. You looked like, I don't know, some badass goddess sent to save the entire fucking world. Speaking of bikers, let's—"

I sighed. "We're not going back, Nate. Look, I know you wanted to stay out of this, but my father is still out there—"

"Oh, we're not backing down now," he said, staring toward the black screen of the television.

"We're... we're not? Why the change?"

He cocked his head to look down at me, knocking the ice pack from his eye onto my lap. "Isn't it obvious? I told them I'd stay out of it, and they still involved my wife. When it comes to protecting you, Katy girl, there isn't a fucking thing I wouldn't do."

"You'd break the law?" I whispered as I placed it on his face again. "Potentially even risk your job—"

I'd been convinced he'd never do anything to blow up his perfect life...

Nate lifted the pack off his bruised hand and held it up. "This is just a fraction of what I'm willing to do for you."

My mouth gaped like a fish's and I sagged against him. A slow smile spread across his face as he lowered his head, pressing his lips against my forehead and catching my tears with the pads of his thumbs. "Someone's gotta take care of you, Katy girl."

"I thought that's what I was doing for you," I said weakly.

Nate's fat lip looked almost comical when he smirked. "It might surprise you to know, but that wasn't my first fight. Hell, it wasn't my tenth fight." He leaned closer to whisper, "And in medical school, they teach you a thing or two about first aid."

I pushed against his chest. "You're making fun of me after I saved your life."

He nodded. "You damn sure did. The Bonnie to my Clyde—"

"Considering they both died in a shootout with the law..." I shuddered at the image his words conjured up. What if we ended up like that?

Running from the enemy, only to die in a hail of bullets.

As if he was thinking the same thing, Nate flinched and curled his arm around my body possessively, rubbing a trail up and down my spine to ward off the sudden chill.

He cleared his throat. "How about we distract ourselves for a bit?"

Warmth flooded my body, and this time when I shivered, it was from pleasure, not fear. My eyes popped open in surprise. Instead of the feel of Nate's mouth on mine, I was met with the sound of the television being turned on and the incessant clicks of a man channel surfing.

"Um, babe?" I shifted my focus up to his face and leaned in, letting my lips brush against the stubble on his jawline.

"Yeah?" He flicked a glance in my direction, seemingly unaffected by my advances. His act would have been more believable if his dick wasn't digging into my thigh.

"Kiss me." I was shameless in my begging, but my body was craving his touch. Maybe it was a normal human reaction to the threat of imminent death. Before, it had been my father's war or something I'd been mistakenly involved in.

We were in uncharted territory now.

No longer casual observers, but willing participants.

A slow smile lifted the corners of his mouth, but he shook his head. "C'mon, Katy girl. Watch a movie with me."

Despite my racing heart, I extricated myself from his embrace and move off the couch. "I said I'd take care of you."

The ice pack fell from his eye and landed against the cushions again, but Nate made no attempt to reach for it as I began unbuttoning my pants, working them down my hips. I fought against the urge to look away and kept my eyes locked on his as I tossed them aside.

"We don't..." His throat moved up and down in a swallow. "We don't have to do this. That's not what I expected—"

"Nate," I said as I pulled my blouse over my head and settled across his lap. "You're not him. So, shut up and kiss me."

He pulled me down hard into his kiss, tracing the line of my jaw with his thumb while his fingers kept a steady pressure against the back of my neck.

My lips parted to welcome his tongue, leaving me to wonder whether I'd always been addicted to his taste, or if it was a recent development, like our decision to go to war.

When he pulled back, I brought my fingers down to his swollen lip with a wince. "Babe."

"It doesn't hurt." He loosened his grip on my neck, dropping his hand to the clasp of my bra. "Is this okay?"

I slipped the straps from my arms and nodded. "Please."

It fell between our bodies before Nate tossed it aside to join the forgotten ice pack. I ground my hips against him when his teeth scraped along my jaw before moving down to my breasts.

His hand moved from the middle of my back down to my ass, squeezing and palming my flesh with enough force to make me moan. He gave me a victorious smirk before lapping at my nipples until they were stiff.

I tugged on the waistband of his jeans, fighting through the haze of lust to find the button. As much as I wanted to lose myself to his touch, a part of me felt like I'd just slept through my alarm.

We were running out of time.

I tugged at his jeans before rocking back onto my heels with a growl of frustration.

Nate patted my thigh with a patient smile. "Move."

When it became apparent that he wasn't faring much better without the use of his right hand, I lowered myself to my knees. "I've got it."

With a solid yank, Nate's t-shirt sailed over my head and landed against the coffee table, and he arched his lower back as I tugged the denim down to join my clothes on the carpet. I shimmied out of my thong before ultimately losing focus at the sight of his dick curving up toward his abdomen. The tip was already glistening with moisture, filling me with something like pride.

I did that to him.

"No," he said, pinning my hands between his thighs as I reached for his solid length, imprisoning me with a shake of his head.

"But..." I pushed my tongue out, tracing a line around my top lip as I moved closer.

His hand came to rest against my cheek. "You put your mouth on my cock, and I'm coming down your throat, babe. I want this to be about you."

I swallowed a moan as his hand threaded through my hair and he tugged, directing me onto his lap again. I rearranged the ice pack against his knuckles before straddling him. "What do you want?"

"To be inside you," he said, his words barely controlled. "Is that okay?"

My eyebrows drew together in confusion at the repeated request until I realized he was asking for my consent.

As soon as I nodded, his middle finger moved between my legs in slow, deliberate strokes. I lifted my hips to control the speed of his movements, eliciting a low chuckle from his lips.

"So impatient," he whispered, letting his head fall to my breast, his teeth roughly connecting with the sensitive flesh.

I was, too.

Here, we'd found a sense of calm, but just outside, a storm was raging like we'd never seen before. Our enemy was at the gate, and if we had to come together like savages before going to face them, I'd take it.

I'd take it over not having him again.

"Fuck me, Nate," I panted, rolling my hips forward in search of him. "Fuck me like you'll never get another chance to."

He didn't question my logic—he didn't tell me to stop being morbid. Instead, my husband pushed into me with a barely restrained growl. "You good?" he ground out between his teeth once he was fully seated.

I nodded dumbly, no longer capable of complicated things such as consonants and vowels.

He pulled out before thrusting back in slowly, giving my body a chance to accommodate all of him. When I began rocking against him, he pumped his hips faster, forcing me to keep up with the pace he set.

Nothing existed but us and this stolen moment.

Our bodies quickly settled into a rhythm that left me gasping for air and clawing at the back of the couch.

"Close." My body tightened around his, and I cried out something unintelligible as his hand clenched my ass, keeping me in place.

Sweat ran from his hairline, but the look of intense concentration on his face remained as if he'd made it his life's mission to keep me coming on his cock.

"Katy," he groaned when his thrusts became unsteady. "Where?"

"Inside me—come inside me!" I begged.

Nate jerked his head in a nod. "I'm almost there."

I squeezed his shoulders in desperation as I rode out my next orgasm, moving only on pure instinct. He thrust one last time, his entire body arching up off the couch as he filled me with a hoarse groan.

I rolled my hips forward, chasing the last of my high before collapsing against his chest in exhaustion. Still, our mouths sought each other out, coming together in a frenzy that surprised even me. We feasted on each other as if it were our last meal before breaking apart with a pant.

"Fucking love you, Katy girl," he murmured against my hair as my head slipped down to rest under his chin.

"I love you too, Nate." My hand moved down against his beating heart, and I realized my mother was right. In his arms, I hadn't thought of Jeremy or that night once.

Nate was my talisman.

CHAPTER THIRTY-THREE

Mike: March 2017 (Age: 34)

"Masterson, do you copy?" I repeated the question, slower this time, just in case the big lug hadn't understood my other fifty requests.

"Maybe they're hooking up," Lauren offered with a grin. "Like someone in this vehicle has suggested more than once."

"Jesus Christ, darlin'. You're gonna drain me dry. What would that make—the third time today?"

She lifted her shoulder in a shrug. "Fourth, but who's counting?"

Fuck.

As much as I tried to shut her comment out, my dick nudged against the zipper of my jeans, entirely on board with the idea. He was fully committed to spending his time surveilling the inside of her body.

"Darlin'," I pleaded. "As soon as this job is over, I am all yours. But right now, I need to set an example."

She bit her lip with a small grin before reminding me, "You set an example in Celia's laundry room earlier."

I tried thinking of historical documentaries... of baseball statistics... anything but the vision of her coming apart on top of the old washing machine.

It had surprised me that with as much money as Grey had, he'd held on to the piece of shit. Until it hit the spin cycle. Then it became crystal clear.

"Fuck, Red," I growled. "You know how uncomfortable this fucking zipper is?"

Her hand snaked across the console. "Here, let me help."

I caught her wrist and held it while working on getting my breathing and my cock under control. "Just—"

She nodded and pulled her hand back to rest on top of her belly. "You're right. Now's probably not a good time to do that thing I did for you on our porch swing."

"Fuck me, Lauren," I groaned, letting my forehead drop onto the steering wheel. "Not. Helping."

We could have made love twenty times today, and I would've been up for it. The only thing that kept me from moving our party to the back seat was the fact that my former sergeant's house had remained dark all evening, leaving me with a severe case of déjà vu.

The Sons didn't leave loose ends. If they suspected that we'd identified the cop, they wouldn't hesitate to eliminate him.

Just like they'd done with Detective Rangel.

The only difference between this time and last time was that I wasn't being backed by a squad of bikers with military backgrounds. And maybe it made me crazy, but I wasn't too keen on dragging a horny pregnant woman into an active crime scene.

"Sullivan?" I bolted upright as the radio crackled to life.

"Masterson," I said. "Give me something."

"We, uh—" His voice cut in and out. "Fuck, there's no easy way to say this, but our cover was blown."

I pinched the bridge of my nose with a muttered curse. "Did you get anything we could use?"

"Negative. How's it going on your end?"

I glanced out the window and back at the house. "Think I might need some backup."

After giving him my location, I punched the steering wheel. "They're onto us, Lauren. I feel it. It's like they're always one fucking step ahead!"

"There has to be a way to outsmart them," she said. "A way to force them to slip up. I've been thinking about it all day, you know? Like, if we just had one ace up our sleeve, it might be enough to bring the entire operation down."

I took in the crease between her eyebrows and the stubborn set of her jaw with a wry grin. "You've been thinking about it all day? Huh. Could have fooled me."

There was just enough light coming in from the street lamps for me to see the flush as it worked its way up her chest.

"Now who's making it all about sex?" she asked with a raised eyebrow. "I'm serious, though. If we could just find a chink in their armor, we could exploit it."

"Darlin', the king of bikers himself, wasn't able to figure it out. What makes you think we'll be able to?"

Lauren gnawed at the corner of her lip, no longer consumed with thoughts of getting me naked but with outsmarting the Sons.

It was a damn shame, too, because I'd just warmed up to the idea of a quickie before Zane and Dakota arrived.

Coincidentally, the change of heart occurred right around the time my stomach started growling, and I remembered why I'd missed dinner. After a late afternoon nap to recharge, I'd found myself hand-cuffed to our bed with a gorgeous redhead straddling my thighs.

The headlights from Zane's truck hit the back window, and I bit back a growl before getting out.

Dakota waved weakly before limping over, and I looked to Zane to fill in the blanks.

"Had a little run-in with a broken bottle," he said, as if that suddenly explained everything.

Lauren asked the next obvious question. "But you're wearing shoes. How did that happen?"

"Well, I was wearing shoes, but I took them off. When Bear pulled the gun on Zane, I didn't think and just jumped out of the truck to run after—"

"In the truck," I hissed. "Now."

As soon as the doors closed, I turned to the backseat. "Bear pulled a fucking gun on you, Detective?"

Zane winced. "It sounds worse than it was."

"I find that hard to believe. And Dakota, care to explain why the fuck you took your shoes off on a surveillance mission?"

"Yeah, I took them off so I could get my pants down—" She clapped her hand over her mouth.

"Told you they were hooking up," Lauren exclaimed with a giggle.

I leaned over the seat and into Zane's view when it became apparent he was avoiding eye contact with me. "Sweetie, you wanna tell me why your wife needed to take off her pants and how you ended up on the wrong end of Bear's gun?"

His jaw tightened. "Thought I told you not to call me your bullshit pet names, Sullivan."

"And I wouldn't be forced to resort to that had you not used your surveillance time to screw your wife, pumpkin—"

Zane moved forward with a growl, only to be stopped by Dakota before he could batter my face. "Hey there, Big Guy. Sun's getting real low."

She began petting his arm as though he were a kitten before turning to me. "I know how it sounds, but Bear's not the one behind this. He said the Sons have eyes on my mother—that they have eyes everywhere."

I nodded and turned back to the dark house in resignation. "In that case, we've all been wasting our time. Rogers is dead."

"How do you know that?" Lauren asked. "Maybe he's just sleeping."

"Only one way to find out. Masterson, you coming with or do you need more time in the 'calm down corner?'"

"You keep running your mouth, and you'll be in the calm down corner," he muttered before climbing out.

"I'm guessing he means dead."

Dakota's lips pinched together in response.

"Alright, great. You two stay here. Maybe listen to the radio... see if Celia's found anything—find a way to stop the Sons. You know, whatever feels right."

Zane was waiting by the back gate with his gun drawn when I approached. "You thinking it's just like Rangel?" he asked, acting as though he hadn't just been on the verge of ending my life.

I nodded and whispered, "Probably, because why should we be given even one goddamn break?"

Zane picked the lock on the back door. Neither of us bothered with gloves or made any attempt to conceal our identities. We both knew what lay on the other side of the door.

The house was eerily quiet, minus the sound of steady dripping from a faucet in the kitchen. For a fucking giant, Zane crept silently down the hall, keeping his gun up as if expecting an ambush at any second.

Instead of taking the lead, he paused outside the first closed door and looked at me. I nodded, and we entered an empty room.

Empty as in nothing but the carpet and bare walls.

We moved to the next and found the same. By the time we reached the master suite, I knew this was nothing like Rangel.

Rogers had known he was a dead man when the surveillance cameras caught him and had packed up shop to run.

Zane checked the master bathroom before re-entering the deserted bedroom with a shake of his head. "Does he really think he can outrun them?"

I paused when it hit me and began moving back down the hall. "But there was still furniture in the living room, right?"

"Christ," Zane croaked when he flipped on the light.

Rogers' wife sat in what looked like a dining room chair on the other side of their large entertainment center, her chin resting against her chest as if she was napping.

The position had kept her hidden from view of anyone coming in through the back door. Even without a drop of blood anywhere on her, it was obvious she was dead.

"Drugs?"

It was the only thing that would explain the lack of blood. The Sons hadn't bothered giving Rangel's wife a quick death, so why change things now?

I looked at the gag in her mouth and back to Zane, struck again by the sound of a dripping faucet coming from the kitchen.

"The gag," I said at the same time he concluded, "Rogers is still here."

We lifted our weapons and moved into the kitchen. The Sons might have given the missus a speedy trip to the underworld, but they hadn't extended the same courtesy to him.

"Oh fuck," Zane murmured, bringing his fist up to his mouth.

It looked like something out of a slaughterhouse.

My former sergeant had been stripped of his clothes and hung by his belt from the wrought iron pot rack bolted into the ceiling.

As if there'd been a concern that he might survive, they'd sliced from throat to groin, eviscerating him. Blood dripped steadily from the organs hanging from his body, mimicking the sound of a leaky faucet as it splashed onto the counter and floor.

My phone vibrated against my thigh.

Lauren: 911. We need to go now.

"We need to leave."

Zane nodded, lowering his hand. "Do we—fuck—do we call it in?"

I stared at him in silence, waiting for a punchline or grin—anything that would give me some sign he wasn't as stupid as he looked. "Call it in?"

"Yeah, we can't just fucking leave him like this."

"Sure," I said casually. "Let's call it in and explain how we picked the lock to find them like this. I'm sure we'll find a way to explain how our fingerprints are all over the fucking place. You know, when we're sitting behind bars!"

"A simple no would have sufficed, asshole." He shouldered past me and out the back door.

"What?" I called after him. "You're the guy who does his job like a good Boy Scout, and I'm the guy who's keeping us out of a cell. Takes all kinds, right?"

Zane stopped right before we reached the truck and hissed, "Look, I'm not a fucking criminal. I didn't grow up in this world, and I'm a little out of my goddamned element here. If you could just cut me a little slack or, I don't know, give us some fucking clue what we're all doing, it'd be great. Okay... pumpkin?"

The sharp retort died on my tongue when I saw Lauren's face

through the window.

"What happened?" I asked as I climbed in.

Her jaw settled into a hard line, and she shook her head. "Jimmy called. The Sons knew we'd be busy here, so they torched the storage facility. Any evidence that might have helped us find them is currently up in flames. Did you get anything in there?"

I ground my molars together. "They got Rogers... and his wife. As the list of things we don't know keeps growing longer, can anyone here tell me what we do know?"

Dakota looked up from her cell phone with a grin. "Kate got something. They were reviewing the hospital tapes from the night my father was shot."

"And?" I waved my hand, silently urging her to get to the point. Every second we spent sitting here was another second the Sons had to come up with new ways to fuck with us.

"Does the name Kyle Barton ring any bells?"

Zane let out a heavy sigh. "Barton's in with them?"

Barton...

The name briefly registered as the rookie who'd pulled me over a couple of years prior. Instead of hauling me off to jail for drunk driving and indecent exposure, he'd let me off with a warning. Other than the one encounter, the name meant nothing to me.

By now, it seemed as if everyone in the department was on the Son's payroll.

"You know him?" I asked.

He nodded. "Worked undercover together. He was also at our wedding, probably gave the Sons all the intel they'd ever need, too."

"I'd say we could track him down, but it's pretty fucking apparent that if he isn't already dead, he will be soon enough. So, back to square one with *absofuckinglutely* nothing to go on."

"That's not necessarily true," Lauren said slowly. "Dakota and Zane were able to figure out that Bear isn't the one behind this—"

"About that," Zane spoke up from the backseat. "At the clubhouse, he had his armed guards with him. Tonight, he was all alone, though. There's still a chance that he's working against Silent Phoenix."

Using my thumb, I cracked the knuckles on my left hand before moving over to the right. While I did it, I tried to piece together everything I'd learned from watching Grey over the years. "If he was working against the club, then he would have killed you both tonight."

"The Sons have killed off anyone who could be used as a witness against them." Lauren's eyes widened. "Bear's not the traitor."

I shook my head. "He's trying to find the rat, but the Sons have eyes everywhere. It won't be long before they figure out that it's not business as usual at the club."

"And then he'll be their next target," Zane added.

"If they have eyes everywhere, we need a blind-spot," Dakota mused. "Some way of moving without being seen."

Lauren drummed her fingers against the armrest. "She's right. What is it Bear told Celia? We keep letting them lead us into traps, but what if we led them into one?"

I pulled my lower lip between my thumb and forefinger, wondering what in the hell we could try that hadn't already been done before.

We sat in silence, each of us fighting to come up with a way to defeat the giant. The fatal flaw in every one of our plans was the fact that we were being watched. It was why Grey had never gained the upper hand.

I felt like the answer was staring me right in the face.

"I've got it," I exclaimed suddenly. For the longest time, I'd approached the Sons the same way Grey had. I'd seen them as just another club looking to encroach on Silent Phoenix territory. They weren't motivated that way, though.

If we stood a chance in hell at surviving this, I had to stop thinking like a biker and go back to the eleven-year-old kid who'd sworn he was going to be one of the good guys.

"They're watching our every move. So, we use someone they'll never see coming." I turned to Lauren. "Darlin', as much as it pains me to say it, we need Jimmy."

I flexed my left arm, struck by the truth in the Sun Tzu quote spanning the length of my forearm.

All warfare is deception.

We'd seen what they wanted. Now it was time for a little sleight of hand.

CHAPTER THIRTY-FOUR

Mike: March 2017 (Age: 34)

"I can't believe I'm fucking doing this," Zane muttered for the one-millionth time since I'd given him the plan.

"C'mon, Big Guy," I said, feigning a pout similar to one I'd seen Dakota make when she wasn't getting her way. "I'm doing this for us. With our fingerprints all over the goddamn place, you would have ended up someone's bitch in prison and, well, let's be honest, I don't like to share."

He inhaled deeply through his nose before turning to look at me. "One of these days, Sullivan, I'm gonna break you in half."

I grinned and doused the inside of a kitchen cabinet with gasoline. "Oh, you tease!"

His jaw tightened. "Jesus Christ, do you ever stop?"

"*Can't stop, addicted to the shindig. Chop Top, he says I'm gonna win big. Choose not a life of imitation...* something... something... something *reservation*," I rapped before moving into the living room.

Celia looked at her watch when I entered before lowering the mask covering her nose and mouth. "Sunset in twenty minutes."

"You hear that, Big Guy?" I called back into the kitchen. "Sun's gettin' real low."

Zane muttered something vaguely threatening in response.

"You know, he's gonna destroy you, right?" Dakota said from behind her military-grade gas mask. She continued delicately pouring fuel onto the couch as if she was watering a damn garden.

It was like something out of a post-apocalyptic thriller.

I'd insisted on the full face shield, thinking it'd keep her quiet while we worked. Obviously, it wasn't working.

"And then when we find Dad," she continued. "I'll have to tell him, and then he'll kill Zane. It'll be a disaster."

"Don't worry." I clapped her on the shoulder. "He's gotta be able to catch me first. Where's Red?"

Celia pointed toward the back door. "She said the fumes were getting to her."

I frowned. She had the same mask as Dakota and Jimmy had assured me that nothing was getting through.

"I tried talking Dakota into getting some air too, but—"

"But we're almost done, and I'm wearing the mask thingy," she argued. "Remind me again, how is burning this place to the ground part of the plan?"

"Cap, sweetie, we're destroying evidence. Evidence that would look really bad for me and Big Guy should the cops decide to show up. Your mom's right, you need to stop huffing the gasoline and get some fresh air. By the way..."

I was going to straight to hell, but couldn't resist. "How's the old foot doing?"

Her cheeks reddened, and she turned her back to Celia before flipping me off, mouthing: You're a dead man.

"What happened to your foot?" Celia asked as I made my way down the hall.

"You should ask Zane," I called over my shoulder. "I hear he has in-depth knowledge of the situation. From what I understand, he went deep undercover. Really penetrated the fortress of, uh, mystery." At Dakota's snarl, I added, "Alright, good talk, kids. Five minutes. Let's finish strong... or high—whatever."

The bedrooms reeked of accelerant, but I forced myself to enter each one, ensuring that everything was in place. Rogers and his wife lay awkwardly against the large whirlpool tub in the master bathroom, their bodies still stiff with rigor mortis.

It had taken both Zane and me over an hour to move them, neither of us keen on the idea of the girls seeing the Sons' handiwork up close. Celia had already dealt with one dead body in the last twenty-four hours. She didn't need another one.

I'd helped clean up more than a few messes for Grey over the years, but never imagined I'd be covering up a double homicide for the Sons.

If we wanted to come out on top, we had to stay one step ahead. With or without our fingerprints, there was still a trail leading back to us.

I smiled at the thought of the Sons second-guessing themselves when they realized we were here, wondering if we'd found something they'd missed. Some clue that was going to lead us right to their front door.

It was time they had a taste of their own medicine.

To know your enemy, you must become your enemy.

They burned down our storage facility. I was simply returning the favor. Tit for tat.

As planned, everyone was gathered on the back porch by the time I came out. "Alright, time for phase two."

Beads of sweat appeared on my forehead just as a wave of nausea swept over me. I barely made it over to the rose bushes before I was vomiting up what little food I'd eaten throughout the day.

Once I finished, I ran the back of my hand over my mouth and placed my palm against the brick siding to steady myself before dropping my mouth to the garden faucet. I lapped up the cool water, swishing and spitting, until the bitter taste of bile no longer coated my tongue.

"It's alright," Celia said softly, rubbing in between my shoulder blades. "It's going to work."

I waved off her concern as I straightened. "Think the fumes just got to me. Let that be a lesson to all of us. Don't do drugs, kids. Anybody got a breath mint?"

Lauren appeared out of nowhere, throwing herself into my side with a terse, "Are you sick? Should we call it off?"

The dizziness persisted, along with a feeling of weakness in my legs. I wrapped my arms around her body, anchoring myself just as much as her. "Calm your tits, darlin'. I'm fine."

Her chin rested against my chest as she looked up at me with eyes that seemed overly bright. "Are you sure? What if they figure it out? They've already taken so much from us. My mother... Grey—"

"They won't," I assured her. She'd been a nervous wreck since we'd come up with the plan, even though this was the last place the Sons expected us to be. "Is Jimmy ready?"

She nodded. "He said to text as soon as it caught. Kate's got the truck in position."

I crushed my lips to her forehead. "Good. Last thing we want is the house burning down around us and no getaway car."

Celia stood rigidly off to the side, spinning her wedding band in a slow circle around her finger. "Mikey, we have to be prepared for things to get worse once we do this—"

"Oh, it's gonna get worse. See, those motherfuckers have called the shots for years now. They're convinced they have us all figured out." I pulled the matches from my back pocket with a smirk. "What do you say, Celia? Ready to blow those misconceptions to shit?"

She clapped me on the back again before pressing a kiss to my temple. "You're just like your father. Alright, let's do it. Lauren, the minute it goes up, alert Jimmy. Dakota, you've got Kate. And remember, stick with your partner."

"Hey," I interrupted. "Who's robbing this train—me or Jesse James? Now..." I turned back to Lauren, lowering my head until our noses were touching. "You good, Red? Practiced your breathing? Remember what I told you, there's no crying in biker wars—"

"But it's completely safe to fight until the third trimester," Dakota added, tapping the side of her nose with a wink.

I pulled back to run my hands over my face with a shake of my head before bringing them to rest against my wife's belly.

Lauren jutted her chin up with a defiant smirk. "Any more words of wisdom you care to impart, Tex?"

"Yeah. Let's all play a great game out there." I swatted her ass and moved until my mouth covered hers, swallowing the witty retort resting on the tip of her tongue. My hands moved to her hips, squeezing as if to remind myself she was real. Lauren tilted her head to the side, deepening the kiss while greedily exploring my mouth with her tongue.

As a kid, I'd wanted to be the hero, never imagining that the world I wanted to save would someday rest under the palms of my hands.

Knowing it was now or never, I reluctantly pulled back, wondering if the men who'd dropped the first atomic bomb felt like I did—this fear that the world would never be the same.

By lighting the match, we were changing the entire game, and that came with a lot of fucking variables.

"Hey, Mike?" Lauren called softly. "I've got some advice for you now."

Thank Christ.

Finally, someone realized I shouldn't have been the brains behind the operation.

Her nose wrinkled, as if what she was about to say caused her pain. "You, um, you might want to find that mint now."

The crease disappeared from between her brows and, as much as she tried to fight it, her laughter echoed across the empty porch.

I shook my head in mock disappointment. "Jesus, darlin', you're gonna blow our cover. Maybe we tackle the issue at hand first. Then I'll guzzle a bottle of mouthwash if it'll make you happy. Zane, you ready?"

He propped the back door open and poured a line of gasoline out into the grass. "With the breeze, it's gonna catch fast. Dakota, maybe you go on ahead."

"I'm not that slow," she grumbled, pulling her phone from the waistband of her leggings. "I've got the text ready to send to Kate. Just tell me when."

Lauren nodded. "Good to go here, Tex."

"Ma?" I cocked my head to the side and looked at Celia.

"Don't call me that," she said, keeping her eyes on her watch. "Okay... now."

I struck the match and dropped it. Any fears that we hadn't used enough accelerant were quickly alleviated by the sight of a bright orange fireball, spreading through the inside of the house like a tornado.

Light gray smoke began pouring through the open doorway and from under the roof like a thick fog, the heat forcing us to hurry through the side gate toward the street.

We went down as the front window exploded, sending fragments of glass and wood through the air like something from a pipe bomb. Any minute now, the neighbors were going to come running out to investigate.

"Debris!" I announced. "We got debris!"

Dakota did her best to keep up, but ended up stumbling and falling into the grass. Zane scooped her up before looking back at me with a shake of his head. Right about then, another window exploded from the side of the house.

So, there was a slight chance we'd gone overboard with the gasoline.

The wind quickly caught the smoke coming from the broken windows, drawing it around us until the other houses disappeared from view.

It was exactly what I'd been hoping for... in another two to three minutes, when we were speeding away. We might as well have been caught in a blinding snowstorm with as much visibility as we had.

Kate pulled up in Grey's truck, her mouth hanging wide open in shock. She'd have to save all questions until the end. With as fast as the fire was spreading, first responders were probably already en route.

The ground vibrated beneath my feet, and I jerked my head to the right and left, straining to see the threat through the veil of smoke.

Even with Dakota in his arms, Zane reached the truck first. When he heard the deep rumble, he cocked his head to the side as if trying to place the sound. "Mike?"

"Everybody in the truck!" I roared.

I knew exactly what I was hearing, but thought we had more time.

Like something out of a movie, everything seemed to slow as the first motorcycle turned onto the street. Lauren turned back, her eyes widening in horror.

The sounds from the fire faded away as the other bikes came into view and I reverted to the nine-year-old kid hiding in the closet.

"Mikey?" Celia's voice called to me. "It's okay. Please talk to me."

My mama talked real sweet to lure me out sometimes, knowing it was better to give the monster what he wanted. "Just get it over with," she'd whisper.

I pulled my knees up to my chest and rocked back and forth, wondering how long I'd have to wait Celia out.

I hadn't meant to break it... I'd only wanted to help...

The sound of footsteps grew louder, and I held my breath, knowing that if she found me, she was going to take me to Mr. Grey for a beating.

What if he was like my old man?

What if he didn't stop until he was tired?

The closet door popped open with a loud creak before Celia knelt beside me, taking my hand in hers. "You're hurt."

I looked down at the blood on my palm and shook my head. "I'm okay. I didn't mean to—you just seemed so tired and Katy was real fussy. I wanted to help you and wash up the breakfast dishes, but I used too much soap, and it was too slippery—" I held back my tears because real men didn't cry like pussies. They took their punishment with their heads held high.

"Hey," she cradled my palm. "I'm not mad. Accidents happen. I wish you would have just told me, but it's easier to run and hide, isn't it?"

I nodded and whispered, "I'm sorry. Is Mr. Grey—"

"He's not here, Mikey. This will be our little secret, okay?"

I nodded again and lowered my head with a sniff. She'd never know I was crying.

She sighed. "Look, I know that it's hard to believe, but someday you're going to grow up to be big and strong. And, instead of running away from the things you're afraid of, you'll stand your ground and fight. Right now, though? I want you to promise me you'll run and hide. Promise me you'll stay safe."

When she saw the bikers, Dakota began fighting to get out of the truck. Zane caught her in his arms, wrapping his body around hers like a shield. Lauren's mouth opened in a scream I could no longer hear as she reached for me before Celia pulled her inside the truck.

They were safe... that was all that mattered.

The men pulled their guns just as the driver's side door opened and Kate stumbled out, her eyes wild with fear.

Promise me you'll run and hide...

Stand your ground and fight...

She stood frozen in the middle of the street, directly in their path. I tried waving her off, screaming over the roar of the bikes, "Katy! Run!"

My sister shook her head and mouthed the word no, pulling me into my own worst nightmare. It was the same every time. My legs moved as if fighting a current while the person I loved lay just out of reach.

Only this time I wouldn't wake up...

She reached my side at the same time as the first biker, and I didn't even think before knocking her down to the grass and facing them head-on like a human shield.

There was no time to draw my weapon.

My body jerked as the first pop filled the air amid Kate's screams of terror. They came in succession, and it wasn't until my ass landed beside her, and the breath left my lungs, that I realized every single one of them had been accurate.

I stared up at the smoke-filled sky until Kate's face came into view. Her mouth moved, screaming something that looked like my name over and over, but my ears were still ringing from the gunshots. As my eyes drifted shut, and the sounds from the bikes faded into the distance, I took comfort in the fact that she was safe.

When I grow up, I'm gonna be one of the good guys...

CHAPTER THIRTY-FIVE

Celia: March 2017 (Age: 44)

While Athena represented intelligence and military strategy for the Greeks, Ares represented the violent and physically untamed aspects of combat.

The god of war was not a favorite among his people because of his dangerous and uncontrollable tendencies on the battlefield. He was also known to react savagely to even the smallest of slights.

Ares.

The embodiment of violence and destruction.

A man governed by hedonism and bloodlust.

Just like the Sons.

The entire time I'd been laboring under the delusion that there was a motive, something they wanted from us. But they were no better than Ares, fighting just to fight.

Which meant we had to become Athena. The fierce and ruthless warrior trusted enough to wield the shield and thunderbolt of Zeus. She protected civilization from those who sought to destroy it.

Lauren's hand tightened around mine, and I squeezed back, both of us fully aware that our salvation lay just beyond the locked doors of the surgical unit.

"We have one shot at getting the Sons," I mumbled, retracing every step of the plan in my mind.

What was it Mikey had said?

War could either be approached with brutality or intelligence.

As we weren't able to outnumber them, we had to outsmart them.

Lauren's chin dropped to her chest, her arm resting against her belly as if reassuring her daughters that their daddy was going to be okay.

Comedian burst into the family room, his gaze darting from face to face, looking for answers. He crossed the room when his eyes landed on mine, dropping to his knees in front of me. "Is he?" His eyes pleaded for me to lie, to tell him there had been some mistake.

My shoulders curled forward as I shook my head. "We don't know anything. He was—" I mashed my lips together. "He was hit five times."

"Christ." Comedian rocked back onto the heel of his boots before running a shaky hand over his eyes. "My boy."

Lauren's fingers twitched against mine, her teeth sinking into the flesh of her bottom lip until it turned white as if to keep herself from screaming.

Comedian reached out and placed his palm against her thigh. "He's gonna be okay, sweetheart. I'm gonna handle this shit, you hear me?"

Her head bounced up and down like a bobblehead doll's, but she continued staring right through him with glassy eyes.

"Good girl." He squeezed her leg and stood up.

We jumped as the door opened suddenly, expecting the doctors, but it was Betsy. She mashed a fist to her mouth, moaning, "My baby boy!"

Comedian went to comfort her, but she brushed off his attempts before approaching me with rage in her eyes and venom in her words. "You did this to him!"

Lauren squeezed my hand until my fingers went numb while keeping her focus on the door.

"You took my baby and tried to make him a soldier! Did you think this was a game? Did you think he wouldn't get hurt?" she all but screeched.

As much as I wanted to remind her she hadn't lifted one finger when her baby relapsed, I kept my mouth shut. For better or worse, she was his mother. If blaming me eased her mind, I'd take it.

I curled my hand into a tight fist. This would be the last time I sat in a private room, waiting to hear the fate of my family.

We had to end it.

Unable to sit still for a moment longer, I released Lauren's hand and got up to move. As I set a manic pace around the room, I continually checked the clock on the wall, fighting to recall how long we'd been waiting.

I'd sent Zane and Dakota home when it became clear we wouldn't know anything for hours. Nate came off-shift and had done his best to give us updates before convincing Kate to get some sleep. She'd been almost catatonic with grief, blaming herself for what happened, as if she could've changed the outcome.

Angel sat silently in the corner, picking at his lips with trembling fingers. "Should have been me, Celia."

I paused, sure I'd misunderstood.

"Should have been me," he repeated. "Kid just got sober and had his whole life ahead of him. Babies... a wife."

"Hey," I sank down in the chair beside him. "Don't talk about him like he's already gone—"

"Ain't he?" His watery brown eyes met mine. "You heard the doctors. He'd lost so much blood..."

His jaw settled into a hard line. "Should have been me. I ask myself every day why I'm still around, you know? Tryin' to figure out what unfinished business the saints need me to handle. I think I finally know what it is."

"What?" I whispered.

"Jamie. Maybe they ain't gonna take me 'til I find my boy. Just tell me how in the hell I'm supposed to do that, knowin' his son is dead? His mama trusted me to take care of him when she was gone, and I couldn't do the same for his kids—" His voice broke off in a sob.

I lay my head on his shoulder and squeezed my eyes shut, going over every step of the plan in my mind, refusing to accept the idea of failure.

And then I did something I hadn't done in years.

I prayed.

The doctors entered, and I fought my way back over to Lauren, my feet heavy as if they were being weighed down with concrete blocks.

Once, when I was younger, I'd gone to the local amusement park and purchased a ticket for the main attraction—the Death Scream roller coaster. As the car slowly climbed the first hill, each ominous click along the wooden track seemed to ratchet up my anxiety, leaving me to question what had possessed me to put my life in danger in the first place.

My fear increased when we finally reached the top, only to stop moving altogether. It seemed as if we hung over that drop for ages.

"I'm so sorry, Mrs. Sullivan," the older doctor began with a shake of his head. Lauren choked out something unintelligible, and I felt the car shift almost imperceptibly. "We did everything we could—"

Just when I'd become convinced we'd remain suspended forever, the car rocked forward, and we entered a free-fall.

CHAPTER THIRTY-SIX

Kate: April 2017 (Age: 27)

"*Katy! Run!*"

    I jerked awake suddenly, still hearing Mike's warning echoing through my skull. His voice was the strongest in the middle of the night, pulling me from a dead sleep to alert me to the danger surrounding us on all sides.

Nate's breathing remained deep and even as I slipped out of bed and into the bathroom. I softly closed the door behind me, not bothering to turn on the light. As I stared at my reflection in the mirror, I noted there was more than enough moonlight streaming in from the window above the tub for me to see the dark circles rimming my eyes.

I flipped on the faucet, splashing some of the cold water onto my face before pulling my bath towel from the hook. My knees buckled beneath me. I sank down to the tile, mashing the fibers against my face to stifle the sounds of my sobs.

In some weird ritual born out of tragedy, I left the faucet running, as if my body needed a soundtrack of running water to grieve properly.

For the past three weeks, the bathroom had become my sanctuary, my safe place, to purge the overwhelming guilt I felt when I thought of what Mike had sacrificed in his final moments.

He was dead because of me.

One minute he was here and the next, he just wasn't.

His daughters were going to grow up without their father because he'd died protecting me. I wailed into the expensive cotton towel while my brain replayed every second of that night in slow-motion.

Mike had been standing in the yard, seemingly lost, as he looked up and down the street. I saw the motorcycle at the same time he did, and when the others turned to follow, my only thought had been to get him into the vehicle.

Why had I run after him?

If I'd just waited even half a second more, he would have come. Instead, I put myself in harm's way, forcing him to make a split-second decision.

His life... or mine.

After deciding on cremation, Lauren announced there would be no funeral or memorial service, widening the ever-growing rift between her and Mike's mother.

She was in denial, refusing to accept the fact that her husband was gone. It had also been made abundantly clear that I was the last person she wanted counseling her.

With Mike went our only chances of finding my father and ending the war. Any plans that had been in place withered and died on the vine.

Dakota returned to her job as store manager of Bella Beauty, while Zane went back to his badge—even with the knowledge that the department was corrupt.

The only reason we weren't all sitting in jail for arson and homicide was because Jimmy had moved heaven and earth to make it seem as if we were never there.

When my weeping became hiccups, I lowered the towel and pressed the heel of my hands to my heated eyelids. My head ached from the force of my tears. I knew, even without the mirror in front of me, my face resembled that of a boxer who'd lost his big fight.

I let the back of my head rest against the lip of the bathtub while contemplating my next step. It was clear with my all night crying jags and days spent in a permanent fog of lightheadedness that I was suffering from survivor's guilt.

Why had I lived, and Mike hadn't?

Another sob tore from my throat, and I hurriedly brought the towel back up to muffle the sound.

"Katy?" There was a light tap against the door. "Babe, you okay?"

At some point, he'd dropped the girl, and I'd become just Katy. Mike had been the only other person to call me Katy—something I hadn't remembered until he was screaming it to save my life. My mother later told me that when we were kids, he'd insisted everyone call me Katy, just like everyone called him Mikey.

"I'm okay," I blubbered unconvincingly, lowering the towel back into my lap.

The door opened, and Nate let his eyes adjust before coming over to kneel beside me. He brushed the hair off my sweaty forehead, and I realized his was sticking straight up on the right side of his head.

"Bad dream?" he asked, fighting a yawn.

I mashed my lips together and nodded. "I just keep going over it, picking apart every detail in my brain as if it'll change things."

Nate sighed and sank down onto the bathroom rug before taking my hand in his. "Babe, I think that's pretty common after something like this—"

"I think I need professional help," I interrupted. "I have a constant headache from crying all the time, and I'm tired, Nate. I'm so tired. It doesn't matter how much sleep I get, it's like I'm working in a fog."

As if on cue, more tears leaked from my eyes. "See?" I pointed. "I'm a wreck!"

He pulled me into his arms, dropping his chin to the top of my head. "You're not a wreck, you're grieving. And the exhaustion is just your body's way of demanding a break."

"I don't think this is grief, Nate," I mumbled against his chest. "It's guilt, and I don't feel like I deserve a break. There's this part of me that believes I should have to live with the crying, headaches, fatigue, and dizzy spells, because I'm the reason he's not here anymore."

Lauren herself had told me it wasn't my fault, but it didn't lessen the guilt any. I sniffled, waiting for a similar reiteration from Nate.

Instead, his muscles tightened beneath my cheek, and the hand rubbing my back froze mid-stroke. "How long have you been feeling like this?"

I tilted my head up toward his face to see if he was joking. "Um, since Mike died?"

He shook his head. "The fatigue and lightheadedness... how long have you been experiencing that?"

"Um..." I thought about it. "It's gotten worse over the last week—"

Nate released me and flipped on the light before squatting down by the vanity. We both squinted, letting our eyes gradually adjust to the sudden brightness.

"Just, uh..." He let out a rough exhale before throwing open the cabinet under my sink. "Just humor me here for a second. Your symptoms are very similar to those of early pregnancy—"

"What?" I practically spluttered, tears completely forgotten. "Nate, no, I'm not pregnant. Trust me, I had really bad dizzy spells and panic attacks after my dad died—well, when he went away the first time."

He continued rifling through the cabinet before holding up the box of pregnancy tests I bought not long after my father was shot. "You're probably right, but let's rule it out, yeah?"

I took the box from his hand. "Are you staying in here with me?"

"Yeah... but I'm a doctor, so it's okay."

"You're a trauma surgeon," I snapped as I sat down on the toilet. "When's the last time you had to give someone a pregnancy test? And why are you smiling like that?"

Nate leaned against the wall, running the back of his thumb over his lips with a grin. "You gonna pee on the stick or not?"

I placed the cap back on the applicator when I finished and set it on the counter before washing my hands, fighting to ignore my puffy eyes and splotchy face. "There. You happy?"

He met my stare in the mirror with another broad smile. "Completely. Come here."

"You seem pretty confident you know what the results are going to be," I said as I padded over to where he stood.

"I just thought before you convinced yourself there was something wrong with you, it wouldn't hurt to consider you might be pregnant." His arms circled around my back, drawing me up against his chest.

The possibility rocked me to my core. We'd just found solid ground as partners. Adding a baby to the mix now seemed like a recipe for disaster.

"Are you upset?" Nate's brows pulled together.

"I just…" I paused to gather my thoughts, letting my chin rest against his chest. "It just seems as if nothing has gone according to plan with us, you know? I thought we'd get to our first anniversary before discussing children. It just feels rushed."

"This is—" He sighed. "This is hard, which is something I swore I didn't want. Been there, done that, you know? But ever since we met, you've captivated me, Katy. You saw me when no one else did—not my job or the money. Just me. And I fell, babe. I fell so fucking hard for the girl with the big heart. Yeah, it's messy and complicated, but it's us, and I'll take that over easy any day."

The stress and guilt I'd been carrying for weeks melted away at his words, leaving me feeling as if I could finally take a full breath. "I don't want perfect… I just want you."

I want passion. I want to feel it here.

His hand moved to cup my jaw, his thumb lightly tracing along my cheek. "Katy?"

"Hmmm?" I asked, sleepily staring into his bright, whiskey-colored eyes.

"It's been three minutes."

I nodded and took a deep breath before going back to the vanity. I was greeted by the sight of two pink lines in the oval window, and instead of the initial rush of panic, I embraced the mess and imagined a little person who was the perfect blend of the two of us.

"Does that mean what I think it means?" Nate's lips brushed against my neck, his hands already settling against my abdomen.

I tilted my face up, and his mouth captured mine in a slow kiss that left me struggling to put my thoughts into words. I pulled away just long enough to whisper, "We're having a baby."

Nate grinned and turned me in his arms until we were face to face before lowering to his knees. In a moment I would remember forever, he lifted my t-shirt and pressed his lips to my still-flat belly.

"Hey, babe?"

I blinked back the tears in my eyes and nodded, unable to speak.

Keeping one hand on my shirt, he lowered the other and ran his fingers over the skin he'd kissed in reverence. "I hope the baby has your eyes."

I gripped his hair, feeling as though I'd just stepped off a plane after a long journey.

I was wrong before.

Home wasn't the house, with its stack of mail and shoes left on the floor.

It was him, down on his knees, worshiping the life we'd created.

CHAPTER THIRTY-SEVEN

Grey: April 2017 (Age: 53)

"We're not getting out of here, are we?"

I forced my eyes open and turned to face Norma. "Ding, ding, ding," I croaked. "What do we have for her, Johnny?"

She licked her cracked lips and shifted against the concrete. "I'll take that as a no. Look, I know we've had our differences—"

"If you're tryin' to apologize, you're about eleven years too late. You took my children. Only your God can save you now."

Tears fell onto her cheeks. "Is that why you're doing this? To get back at me?"

"Look around you, Norma," I growled. "It look like I'm in charge of a goddamned thing?"

She cleared her throat and blinked away the moisture in her eyes before jutting her chin up at me in defiance. "I did what I thought was best for those girls. Celia was gambling—"

"Is that what you think? Jesus, you've got no fuckin' clue what your daughter went through. All you ever cared about was how it made you look." My vision blurred, forcing my head back down to the mattress with a grunt.

"You're bleeding again." The chains around her wrists rattled as she slowly made her way over to my cot. The cold metal brushed against my skin as she examined the wounds on my chest and shoulder. "Jamie, they're looking worse."

"Probably because they're gettin' worse," I noted dryly, wondering again why Saint was keeping the two of us alive. It had been weeks since they dragged us from a building that looked a hell of a lot like my storage facility, driving for hours over rough terrain until we reached what had become our new home.

The walls were different, but it was still the same hellhole as before.

"You need a doctor and strong antibiotics—"

"I know this is gonna come as a shock to you, but we ain't exactly at a resort—"

The large door vibrated as it was unlocked from the outside, and we fell silent. Norma cowered between the head of the cot I was tied down to and the wall, using my body as a shield when she saw who it was.

Cobra had been gone for weeks, leaving us in the care of men who weren't comfortable laying a hand on an elderly woman, but seemed to have no qualms about beating the shit out of me.

I'd almost come to believe Saint had redistributed him.

The lines on his face seemed more pronounced, as if he'd been gone for years. Cobra snagged a chair, the metal legs scraping loudly against the concrete as he dragged it over to us, but there was no grin or reminders of what day it was as he sank down onto it.

"Grey..." He paused. "Something happened—"

"Your boy Saint get cold feet on killin' us all of a sudden?" I taunted, even as the hairs on my neck and arms lifted. "That why you've been gone for so long?"

He shook his head. "It's about your son—"

Mikey?

"Son?" Norma moved in front of me to face Cobra, fear suddenly forgotten. "He doesn't have a son. He has two daughters—"

I flinched as fragments from the cinderblock wall rained down from above my head before watching Norma drop to her knees with a forced exhale.

"Shut the fuck up," he calmly stated, before kicking something away from his shoe. It hit the wall and bounced off before I realized it was a piece of her skull.

Norma fell to the side, facing me, her eyes blinking rapidly as if she couldn't fathom how she'd ended up on the floor. Bloody bubbles of saliva burst from between her still moving lips.

Cobra slipped the gun into the holster at his shoulder and fell against the back of the chair with a muttered, "Fuck... Fuck!"

I kept my focus on the woman who'd brought my wife into the world, wondering if she'd struck a bargain with the devil himself to stay above ground. Her eyes, which hadn't been focused on any specific thing, suddenly locked on mine as she mouthed one word repeatedly.

Celia.

She began convulsing and then, whatever deal she'd made, expired.

I felt nothing.

"Grey." There was something in his voice that made me look up at him. It sounded like regret. "There's no easy way to say this, but your son was—"

"No," I growled, feeling as though the cot was spinning out beneath me. I lifted my left wrist, testing the limits of the restraints. "Don't you fuckin' say it—"

Cobra closed his eyes briefly. "He's dead—we didn't want to believe it at first, either. But after looking into it—"

The pressure in my head increased until my ears popped, and the truth in his words filtered in. "Looking into it? What the fuck does that mean?"

I never should have left you with them...

Tears stung the backs of my eyelids, and I thrashed from side to side, fighting to stay in control, refusing to accept my son had been taken from me. I closed my eyes, no longer seeing Mikey as a grown man, but a scared little boy who'd needed protecting.

"Mr. Grey, it's okay. I was climbing trees, and I fell. Didn't shed one tear, though, because I'm a man... like you." Mikey puffed his chest out in pride, doing his best to draw my attention away from the fingerprint-shaped bruises along his neck and shoulders.

Injuries that hadn't come from any tree.

"Hopefully, that tree learned its lesson, kid," I finally said when I'd regained the use of my tongue.

The grin on his face slipped, but he covered it up with a shrug. "Trees are pretty big, Mr. Grey."

I clenched and unclenched my fist. "Sounds to me like you need an ax..."

His blue eyes went wide. "An ax?"

"Somethin' to defend you should that tree get in your way again. Think of it as protection—"

Mike barreled into my legs, his tiny chest heaving with sobs. I sank down to my knees and his hands moved up around the back of my neck. "I got you—"

"I'm not a pussy, Mr. Grey. I just got something in my eyes," he sniffled, keeping his face against my chest. "You think you know where I could find me an ax?"

He was so fucking small...

"Yeah, kid," I said quietly, resisting the urge to stroke his dark blond hair, knowing it would only embarrass him further. "You got me."

Mikey pulled back to look up at me, wiping the stray tears from his cheeks. "You? How can a person be an ax?"

"Look at me. You think that tree's gonna lay a hand on you when I'm around?"

He quickly shook his head. "No, sir."

I cupped the side of his face in my hand. "I'll be your ax 'til I draw my last breath, kid. Ain't one thing gettin' past me to hurt you—"

A sharp pain pierced my chest, and I understood completely how someone could die from a broken heart. The jagged pieces of mine cut through walls of muscle and cages of bone as if they were made of butter.

I'd lost two children at the hands of bikers.

A body could only hold so much grief before it came spilling out in the form of blood. This time, no doctor could put me back together.

"Mikey!" a broken voice wailed. I looked to Cobra in shock before realizing the sound was coming from me. Muscle and bone shifted against old and new wounds as I pulled myself into a sitting position, but I no longer cared. I pushed past the crippling effects of dehydration and electrical jolts of pain, willing to tear myself to shreds for what I'd lost.

I no longer cared.

CHAPTER THIRTY-EIGHT

Kate: April 2017 (Age: 27)

"Fuck," Nate cursed from the bedroom.

I looked up from my laptop with a frown. "What? What happened?"

"Oh, the hospital just called me in for a case." He walked out to where I was sitting on the couch, already in his scrubs and cowboy boots.

I discreetly minimized the nursery furniture website I'd been browsing and pulled up a psychological study on the link between empathy and sexual harassment. "That's okay—"

"No, it's not. I wanted to spend the day with you. We just found out you're pregnant." He laughed and ran a hand through his hair as if he still couldn't believe it. That made two of us. "Tell you what, I want you to take it easy today, and tonight, we'll celebrate. Dinner, anywhere you want to go. How's that sound?"

"Okay, deal." I tried and failed to keep a straight face. "But you better be careful, Doctor. A girl could get used to this kind of attention."

His suddenly heated gaze dropped to my mouth. "I forgot to mention that after dinner, I plan on bringing you back here and giving you a thorough examination, Mrs. Davis. It could be physically exhausting, so you'll want to rest up."

Red-hot need flared up within me, but instead of saying something clever or sexy, I just nodded dumbly, my mind already tangled up in the sheets.

Nate leaned down for a quick kiss. "You make me so fucking happy, Katy."

I locked my arms behind his neck, enjoying the rough feel of his stubble against my cheek. My brain helpfully reminded me of other places I enjoyed feeling it, too, before I finally regained control of my speech center.

"I love you," I sighed against his lips. "Are you sure someone else can't do the surgery for you?"

He pulled away with a reluctant groan. "I wish. I'll let you know if I can get out of there early. In the meantime, relax... browse every baby website—yeah, I saw that. I'll be home soon."

The door closed behind him, and I caught sight of my reflection in the screen of my laptop as it switched over to screensaver mode. My lips curved, and while I wasn't glowing, it was impossible to miss the excitement in my eyes.

I continued grinning at the screen, imagining how Nate was going to be as a dad. My smile wavered when thoughts of Mike filtered in, and I realized I'd gone almost the entire morning without the memory of that night at the forefront of my mind.

It felt like cheating, finding joy in the middle of tragedy.

At the sound of the doorbell, I set my laptop and thoughts of Mike aside, suddenly grateful for a distraction. When I saw who it was, grateful suddenly wasn't the right word. "What are you doing here?"

"Before you call in the firing squad..." Jeremy held up a paper cup. "I come with a peace offering. Earl Grey with two packets of honey... just like you like it."

Reluctantly, I took it from his hand. "Why?"

He looked down, scuffing the toe of his boot against the welcome mat. "I heard about Mike... and I'm an asshole who owes you an apology. Is Nate here? I owe him one, too."

"He got called into work—"

"Can we talk? Out here, I mean. I don't want to cross any lines." Jeremy moved his hand protectively over his groin with an easy laugh. "I'd like to keep my balls intact."

I pointed toward the small bistro set tucked into the corner of the porch. "We can talk over here."

He sat down with a heavy sigh. "First, I just want to say that I'm sorry about your brother."

My nose burned with the threat of tears, but I kept them at bay by sipping the hot tea. "Thank you," I finally said, studying his face. Maybe it was the fact that we were sitting on the front porch in broad daylight, but the feelings of fear were gone.

"And the shit between us. I fucked up, Kate. I never should have pushed you for something that you weren't ready to give—"

I held up a hand. "I'm married, Jeremy. You say not ready like it's some temporary thing—"

He glanced up and down the sidewalk before leaning in with a wince. "I meant the night you lost your virginity. I shouldn't have pressured you into going home with me. It only complicated things."

"Oh." I took a long drink, more to keep myself from blurting out that I'd pushed for him to take me home that night, knowing the conversation would only lead to trouble.

A young mother waved as she walked by, pulling her toddler in a little red wagon. I lifted a hand in return, watching the leaves rustling on the trees lining the street. Someday, they'd be tall enough to provide shade.

I could picture us pulling our baby in a wagon under a canopy of green, waving to the neighbors sitting out on their porches.

"You seem different," Jeremy noted. "Happier than the last time I saw you."

I frowned, still watching as the mother and her baby became dots on the horizon. "The last time you saw me, you made extremely inappropriate comments and then got into a fight with my husband."

"Fair enough," he said with a chuckle. "So, what are you going to do?"

"About what?" I turned back to look at him.

"The case... Avengers assemble and whatever else Dakota says. I thought with what happened to Mike, you'd be out searching for answers. Speaking of, did you ever track down the cop? What was it you call him?"

"Doucheface? No, we never found him." My head suddenly felt heavy, and I stretched, sliding down until it rested against the cushion. This felt different from the average, everyday fatigue I'd been experiencing.

Like being weighed down with a warm blanket.

"You doing alright, Kate?"

I took another sip of tea before the cup fell from my fingers and onto the table between us. "My tongue feelth thick," I slurred, sounding more than a little intoxicated. I planted my bare feet against the patio pavers and stood, only to begin swaying violently—the ground tilting beneath me.

Oh my god, I felt drunk.

"Whoa there." Jeremy caught me before my face introduced itself to the stamped concrete. "Are you feeling okay? Let's get you inside."

I nodded, letting him lead me through the living room and onto the couch. "I'm gonna grab you some water. Just lay here."

"Dizzy," I mumbled as if Jeremy could somehow interpret that I'd been dealing with lightheadedness. The room spun slow circles around me, and I watched in wonder as the ceiling fan multiplied before fighting against a wave of nausea.

I needed a doctor.

My hands closed around air twice before I managed to pluck it off the coffee table. There were six missed calls from Nate.

But he was in surgery...

"*Do you want ice?*" *Jeremy called from the kitchen, and I nodded.*

Up and down means yes.

A text box appeared underneath my thumb as I tapped at the screen, struggling to remember how to unlock it. I stared blankly at the arrangement of letters, struggling to make sense of them in my addled state.

Nate: Hospital says they didn't page. Must've been a glitch in the system.
Heading home now.

Glitch.

I thought you knew Jeremy was a hacker...

The answer had been staring us in the face the entire time. My foot slipped off the edge of the couch, falling to the hardwood floor like a boulder from the side of a cliff. The trap had been set, and we'd walked into it without another thought.

Jeremy was the traitor.

I reached for the coffee table, only to end up in a heap on the floor. The pulse thrummed in my throat as I tried lifting an arm to pull my body up, but it was as if someone else had taken control. With a low moan, I dragged myself a few inches, stopping to cool my overheated skin against the hardwood.

When I tried again, my fingers just twitched in response.

"Here we go, Kate," Jeremy called as he came into the room. "Jesus Christ, I told you to stay on the couch. You're in no condition to be moving around." He lifted me into his arms and placed me back on the couch, smiling as he gently brushed the hair from my eyes.

"Y-y-you," I forced out through a clenched jaw. "Why?"

The biker wiped the sweat from my forehead. "Now, before I lose you to the drugs completely, can you tell me what happened with Mike? Do you know who shot him? We want to help."

Who wanted to help?

My lips parted, and a small puff of air escaped, but the ability to speak had fled. I just wanted to let go and drift away. My body was begging for it. The sleep I'd been craving was within arm's reach. All I had to do was take hold.

Katy, you make me so fucking happy.

The corner of my mouth pulled up in a smile.

We were happy.

"Kate," Jeremy's voice sang from somewhere high in the trees, pulling me back to shore. "We want to help you, but we need answers. Who wanted your brother dead?"

I thought of the baby growing in my womb, so small and defenseless. It was the push I needed as my eyes became heavy and my consciousness ebbed.

Keep breathing, Katy.

Deep breaths.

In and out.

"W-w-who?" I pushed the word out like a breath, before being pulled back down to the depths of relaxed oblivion, my cheeks damp with tears and my husband's voice echoing inside my head.

Jeremy lifted my hand, pressing a kiss to the inside of my wrist. "I kept you safe—the night you came to me. I would have protected you from all of it. I wanted you to remember how good it was between us like I did, but you pushed me away."

He paused to wipe the moisture from my face before clearing his throat. "Now, it's too late. Saint wants you, and I don't have a fucking clue what he's got planned, Kate. Just tell me what you know. Tell me, and I'll ask him to let you go. Was it Bear? Silent Phoenix? Just give me a name!"

How did he not know?

"Kate," Jeremy growled, his lips brushing against a tear on my cheek. "For fuck's sake, answer me! I'm trying to keep you alive!"

When they realized they wouldn't get any information out of me, they decided to send a message.

I registered the sound of the patio door opening and hope surged within me, propelling me back to the surface.

Fight! Nate's voice roared in my head, and I ground my teeth together before reaching up to weakly shove Jeremy's mouth away from my face.

I did it.

I'm saving us, baby. Hold on.

"We're out of time. We need to go," a familiar voice tersely stated before moving over my body.

Recognition slammed into me like a rogue wave, sending me tumbling back down into the depths, the darkness closing in all around me.

I forgot to keep fighting.

I forgot to focus on each breath.

But I remembered her face before everything went black. Then I remembered nothing.

CHAPTER THIRTY-NINE

Grey: April 2017 (Age: 53)

All this time, I'd kept my mouth shut and let them break my body down, thinking I was keeping him safe. If they were hurting me, they couldn't hurt them. It was the same deal I'd made with my old man to keep my ma safe, but someone had broken the fucking rules.

I should have known better.

"Your family's in danger," Cobra said solemnly. Something flashed in his eyes, but he blinked before I could guess what it might have been.

"I'm gonna rip your throat out," I said calmly before tugging at the restraint. In some last-second burst of strength bestowed upon grieving fathers, I yanked my arms forward, and the fabric tore from my left wrist, fluttering back down to a cot I was no longer lying on.

The first time I betrayed Death, I half-expected Hades to show up to drag me back to the underworld. A part of me had even craved it— this need to be done with all of it. He never showed, though, and I eventually ventured out of the shadows and back into my role as leader, convinced I'd never be caught.

The second time Death appeared, he hadn't come alone. Ares was with him. They had the element of surprise— had ambushed me when I least expected it. Still, I was alive.

I was forced to keep drawing breath when they couldn't.

I'd been questioning why Saint hadn't pulled the trigger since day one, never realizing they had decided to take my son's life in exchange for mine.

I stalked toward Cobra, waiting for him to draw his gun and end it. My luck had run out. There'd be no cheating Death for the third time. Instead of killing me, he kept his hands by his sides and let me swing. My fist connected with his jaw weakly before he took my legs out from underneath me, sending me down to the concrete.

Tears ran down my cheeks as I begged, "Do it, Cobra. End it right here and now."

He shook his head, standing his ground before me. "There's no victory in this, Grey. You're nothing more than a wounded animal—"

I sucked in ragged breaths. "You wanted to break me... you did it."

"Not us. The Sons had nothing to do with this. Who were your enemies?"

I jerked my chin up and growled, "You."

"No." He pursed his lips. "We wanted a fight, not a massacre. Your family is being picked off, one by one. Tell me, who would want to hurt you?"

I ran the back of my hand under my nose with a sniff. "Who would come after my family when it's clear the Sons have the upper hand?"

I'll be your ax...

He'd been all alone, had died because of my arrogant pride. I'd started a war, thinking I was a god. Now, I was nothing more than a broken man, down on his knees, begging for death.

"Mikey," I wept, watching my tears mix with the dried blood on the concrete beneath me.

"You have my word, Grey." Cobra's voice was quiet. "The men responsible for your son's death will be brought to death."

I rubbed at the back of my neck before slapping at the cinderblock wall with a howl of rage, screaming his name until my throat was raw and my voice was gone.

I wanted to drown myself in booze until I didn't feel as though I'd been flayed alive.

It wouldn't bring him back.

Nothing would bring him back.

The monster used his body to batter the sides of his cage, begging for a kill, craving vengeance. I ground my teeth together. "Put a bullet in my head, Cobra. It's what you wanted—"

"Don't mistake my kindness for weakness. I'm going to be the one to end your life, but not like this. I want you fighting back."

"You want a fight?" Using my good arm, I got to my feet before staggering toward him. I reached out and gripped the lapel on his fancy dress shirt in my hand, surprised at how much strength such a simple action had taken.

Cobra looked down at my hand. "Grey, I've told you the Sons aren't responsible for this. We've kept tabs on your family, but I swear to you, we didn't lay a hand on your son."

"If you didn't, then who did?"

The vein in his temple pulsed rapidly, even as his face remained passive. "That's what we're trying to figure out. Was there another club? The cartel?"

"I don't know." I slumped against his body, unable to hold myself up any longer.

Instead of letting me fall to the floor, Cobra hooked his arm under mine and led me back toward the cot. "Let's get you back to bed."

"Ain't my fuckin' mother," I snarled. It would've been more menacing were my head not resting against his shoulder.

"No," he laughed. "But I'm the closest thing you've got to a friend here."

The door vibrated as it was pulled open, and my hand fell away from his shirt. "Jarvis," I choked, recoiling at the sight of a man I'd trusted.

Cobra stepped away from the cot. "What the fuck is this?"

At the question, the woman being supported in his arms lifted her head with a sloppy smile. "Daddy?"

Kate.

Her long dark hair fell around her face like a curtain, but it didn't hide the fact that her green eyes were almost entirely black from her blown pupils.

"Saint wanted her—"

"The fuck did you do, Jarvis?" I growled, fighting to stand. "The fuck did you give her?"

He straightened, but I didn't miss the sweat beading on his upper lip. For all his swagger, he was still afraid of me. "Just gave her the drugs. They should wear off soon."

"I just finished telling him we had nothing to do with his son's death and you parade his daughter in here. You see how this looks, don't you?"

He shifted Kate, and her head flopped back like a doll's. My heart thrashed wildly in my chest when her chin began to quiver. The corners of her mouth turned down, and she mashed her lips together, just like she had as a baby.

Only this time, it was drug-induced.

"I trusted you with her life, and you were going behind my back this entire time?"

Jarvis tipped her head forward, and she watched him curiously. "Not gonna let a damn thing happen to her, Grey," he murmured, keeping his eyes on hers.

I made it to my feet, and Cobra placed a hand on my shoulder to steady me. The old me would have knocked his teeth in. The old me also wasn't suffering from a severe case of vertigo.

"She's here to keep you compliant."

Jarvis tightened his hold, thrusting Kate's head up against his. "Saint said he just had a few questions—"

"You really that fuckin' stupid?" I spat the words. "You had to have known what you were doin' by bringin' her here."

Kate tried bringing her hand up over her mouth but kept missing and hitting her cheek. "I don't feel good," she moaned, and I swore my teeth were going to crack from the pressure.

"Lay her on the cot, Jeremy," Cobra demanded. "And clean up this mess."

I prayed the drugs were still in effect enough to hide the fact that her grandmother's body was lying on the concrete.

He hesitated. "She doesn't know anything. If Saint lays—"

"Saint will do what he thinks is best and you'll run back to your club like a good soldier. You want to be paid? Do your fucking job."

I tried reaching for her, but my right arm flopped uselessly back to my side, another reminder that my shoulder was shot.

When Jarvis didn't move, Cobra exhaled a long sigh and released his hold on me. I kept myself upright by squeezing the metal headboard but swayed from side to side as if on a ship.

"Give her to me," he said through his teeth. "And clean the fuck up."

I prepared my body to fight as Cobra took Kate in his arms, knowing the things he'd done to her mother. She blinked up at him in confusion, lashes fluttering against her cheeks as the drugs tried to pull her under again.

He carried her to the cot, laying her down as if she was made of glass. I sank down beside her, ready to rip out the throat of anyone who got too close.

"She looks just like her mother," Cobra mused, ignoring the warning growl in my throat.

"You wanna know why I did it, Grey?" Jarvis asked as he dragged Norma's body across the floor. "Because it should have been me. I kept her safe. Me."

Kate jerked beside me, fighting to break away from the hold the drugs had on her. I stroked her forehead with the pad of my thumb like I'd done to soothe her when she was fussy as a baby. When she sighed and went still again, I turned back to Jarvis. "She didn't choose you, so you abandoned your brothers and broke your oath to the club. You don't deserve to wear that kutte."

"I obeyed every one of your goddamn rules," he hissed. "Kate was the one thing I wanted. But bikers weren't good enough for your little girls. You're such a fucking hypocrite, Grey."

He reached the door and turned around. "Oh, and one more thing. I broke rule number one... and rule number two—fuck, remind me which number her sucking me off was? You only have yourself to blame for her being here right now."

Cobra began clapping slowly. "Good for you, Jeremy. You traded your patch for pussy. It's clear you've served your purpose. Now get the fuck out of here."

My hands shook with rage. I wanted to watch him struggle for air as I choked the life out of him.

"Hey, Jarvis," I growled. "I'm gonna take pleasure in retrievin' your colors before sendin' you to the Reaper."

He nodded. "Yeah, we'll see about that. I'm not liking your chances, Pres."

When the door rolled shut behind him, I shifted to face Cobra, tucking my daughter behind my body. I didn't have much left in me, but I'd give it all to keep her safe.

"I'm not interested in your daughter, Grey. But if Saint is, you have cause to worry."

"You didn't know, did you?" I stroked Kate's hair when she whimpered, mumbling strings of gibberish.

He leaned against the wall. "No. Maybe it's his way of keeping her safe until we know who killed your son."

Tears stung my eyes as I thought about Mikey. I'd broken so many of my promises over the years, but knowing that I'd failed him in this was almost too much to bear. I tightened my hold on Kate and fought against the urge to close my eyes.

They'd already ripped two children away from me.

I'd be damned if I let them take another.

"I'm gonna get us out of this, Katydid. I swear to you."

CHAPTER FORTY

Dakota: April 2017 (Age: 22)

"Dakota, focus," Jimmy pushed. "Keep your eyes open and use your chin to guide your head, like we talked about. You're getting in your head and overthinking it."

I nodded, keeping the target in focus. "Got it."

After several more missed shots, it was clear I didn't have it. I released the magazine from my gun with a groan. We were running out of time, and my aim wasn't improving.

Lauren got up from the porch swing and moved inside, leaving me alone with Jimmy and the overwhelming stench of failure. She was going to lay down. It seemed if she wasn't sitting on the porch, staring down the driveway, then she was sleeping.

We needed a plan to avenge Mike's death. Instead, we'd all gotten lost in our own heads.

"Hey." Jimmy patted the top of my head as if I was a small child. "You don't give up, and that's commendable."

I pressed my lips together, briefly debating the pros and cons of fighting an ex-CIA agent. "Jimmy," I said, with as much sweetness as I could muster. "Did Zane ever tell you how he got that shoulder injury of his?"

Zane looked up with an arched eyebrow at the mention of his name before going back to his laptop with a shake of his head.

Jimmy leaned down to inspect my gun. "His shoulder?" he asked distractedly. "No, I don't think it's ever come up."

"Pat me on the head again, and you'll have one just like it."

"Did you just threaten me?" He asked, fighting a smile before looking at Zane. "You heard her, right? She just threatened me. Come here."

I staggered backward, suddenly wishing I'd kept my mouth shut. "I didn't mean it," I blurted.

Jimmy pulled me into a hug and let out a rough laugh, causing my face to bounce up and down from the vibrations. "Fuck, that's what I like to see. You've got spark, Dakota, and that's not something that can be taught. Now, reload and let's go again."

I frowned, following him into the barn. "You're not going to make me sleep with the fishes?"

"No, there's not enough water around here. You'd be found too quickly." Jimmy unlocked the gun safe and began taking stock of what few weapons we had.

I perched on the edge of an old sawhorse, suddenly curious. "How would you do it?"

"What—kill you?" He turned to look at me. "Well, first, I'd ensure that I'd gotten all the intel I needed from you."

"Intel? Oh, like force me to crack kinda thing?"

"Yeah." He inspected one of Mike's special guns, a cobbled-together fully automatic. "Waterboarding... auditory overload... sleep deprivation... stress positioning—the possibilities are almost endless for breaking someone down."

I swallowed. "So, you do all that and then you kill them?"

Jimmy nodded. "By the time you put them down, it's more of a mercy than anything else." He picked up a box of ammo and gestured for me to follow. "But that shoulder thing you mentioned sounds intense, too. I might have to add that to my repertoire."

I slugged him in the arm playfully. "Jerk."

Our heads shot up at the sound of a car coming down the driveway. Zane closed his laptop and hopped out of the bed of his truck, already reaching for his weapon. It wasn't until Jimmy's hand went to his holster that I realized he'd positioned himself in front of me.

"Wait a minute," I said when the red BMW came into view. "It's Little Ricky and Molly!"

When he stepped out of the sports car with a wide grin, I didn't even think before running and throwing myself into his arms. I made a noise that might've been a laugh, were tears not streaming down my face. "Does this mean you've forgiven me? Because I'm so so so sorry—"

"Hey, Caparina..." Little Ricky pulled back to look at me. "Why you cryin', girl?"

"Because I just missed you so much," I blubbered, no longer a confident gunslinger—but a hero who'd needed her sidekick.

He laughed easily. "Missed you too, Cap. Had to get my head right, ya know?"

"I'm sorry. I know what I did was wrong. And the thought of you and I never speaking again just—" My voice broke off in another loud and decidedly unladylike sob.

"Nah, Cap, it's all good in the hood. You and me are like this." He crossed his fingers. "Tight. How's my boy doin'?"

I patted my belly with a sniff. "Getting bigger."

He squatted down and placed his hands on either side of my tummy with a wide grin. "Yo, Thor. It's your Uncle Little Ricky. Yeah, I know, my dude. I missed you too! Okay, keep, uh, bakin' and shit."

"I can't believe you're here," I choked out. "So much has happened..."

He stood up, no longer smiling. "I heard about Mikey. That's actually why I came. Club's been lookin' into it—"

"Molly?" My mother stepped out onto the porch. "What are you doing here?"

"Haven't been the best friend to you, Celia," she said matter-of-factly. "I told you to let the club handle shit. And then this one went and meddled."

I looked around for the culprit before realizing she was talking about me. "About that," I began. "I can explain... maybe."

Molly threw her head back with a laugh. "I can't wait to hear you explain how you smuggled Bear's DNA out of our house—"

"Simple." Little Ricky flashed his teeth. "Cap's a ninja."

"Well, ninja or not, it led to some uncomfortable conversations in our house."

"It's true, then?" My mother asked. "But, you said—"

"Little Ricky, would you mind running inside to get me some water?" Molly interrupted.

"You got it, Ma."

Once he was gone, she turned back to both of us, lowering her voice. "One night, I went to *Leather & Lace* by myself—"

Mama's eyes widened. "You didn't. By yourself?"

I knew nothing about *Leather & Lace*, other than it was a biker bar. Judging by my mother's reaction, it obviously wasn't the sort of place a woman went alone.

"Kate was still a baby, and I don't know. I wanted what you had," Molly argued. "I thought if it worked out for you, then there was a chance I might find love there, too. I drank way too much, but Bear was there to drive me home."

I tried imagining the biker twenty-five years younger but kept seeing Little Ricky's face, which ultimately killed any chance of me getting a lady boner.

"He was thirty at the time and, compared to most of the men I'd known, seemed to know what he wanted out of life. I thought that included me, but when I woke up the next morning, he was gone. I chalked it up to a one-night stand and met Carlos not long after."

I thought back to what Bear had said the night I revealed that Little Ricky was his son. "When you found out you were pregnant, you didn't think it was Bear's because he used a condom, right?"

Molly scratched at her temple. "Yes, but how did you—"

"Bear might have mentioned it—when we told him. Look, woman to woman, I get it. When I found out I was pregnant, I—"

"Knew immediately who the father was," Zane said from behind his laptop. "We didn't use protection, remember?"

Molly and my mother both averted their gaze, suddenly finding the dirt beneath their feet fascinating. "Celia, maybe we should continue this conversation—"

"Elsewhere?" my mother suggested.

"No," I pleaded. "I won't interrupt again, I swear."

"Anyway." Molly glanced at Zane again before clearing her throat. "When Bear found out I was pregnant, he showed up on my doorstep, demanding to know if it was his. By that time, the doctor had given me my due date and, based on the likely conception date, there was no way it was Bear's."

"You never considered that maybe the doctors were wrong?" I asked, slightly skeptical, but still completely invested in the story of how my best friend came to be.

"Dakota, I'd just survived one man who didn't want to be a father," Molly said, exchanging another strange look with my mother. "I'm not going to lie and say that I didn't take pleasure in telling Bear that the baby wasn't his, either. I wanted to hurt him like he'd hurt me."

"Wait, so that means that Little Ricky wasn't born prematurely," Mama said suddenly. "Was he?"

Molly shook her head. "My periods were a goddamn nightmare back then, making it almost impossible to predict an accurate conception date. When he was born, I swore he looked like Bear, but I felt like I was seeing things that weren't there, stupidly hoping we could be a family."

"But you are a family," I said, patting her arm. "He loves you."

Molly's laugh caught in her throat. "Yeah, he's just over the moon for me right now."

"How is he taking the news?" I asked tentatively, secretly wondering if the biker still wanted to murder me.

"Heads up," Jimmy said suddenly. "Anyone know this vehicle?"

The truck came tearing down the long driveway, leaving a cloud of dust in its wake. As everyone drew their weapons, I realized mine was still back in the barn and grabbed the closest thing I could find.

A gardening fork.

The truck hadn't even come to a complete stop before Nate threw open the door and stumbled toward us, completely unsteady on his feet.

"Nate?" Mama asked. "What's wrong?"

"She's gone." His voice shook. "I was too late. They took her—"

CHAPTER FORTY-ONE

Dakota: April 2017 (Age: 22)

"Kate?" My bravado was gone, leaving my voice sounding small... fragile. The gardening fork fell to the dirt, completely forgotten, as I approached Nate.

A man dressed as a cowboy came around from the other side of the truck and laid a steadying hand on Nate's shoulder, his gaze darting from one person to the next before he asked, "Kate's not here?"

I shook my head, mashing my lips together to keep it together.

The cowboy led Nate over to the tailgate of Zane's truck before introducing himself with a reluctant wave. "Garrett, Nate's brother. He called me when he realized she was..." He bit down on his lip. "When he got—fuck, this is really hard."

"Nate," I said. "Tell us what happened."

"I got a page from the hospital, but when I got there, no one seemed to know who sent it. They said it must have been a glitch. I just—" He shook his head, his voice choked with emotion. "I knew something was wrong. I started calling, but she didn't answer. When I got there, the house was empty—"

"Does she have her phone?" Jimmy asked.

"She left everything—phone, purse, keys—fuck, even the damn car was still sitting in the garage! We have to find her, she's—" Nate mashed his fist to his mouth, suddenly looking a little green. "She's pregnant."

Kate was going to have a baby.

I lurched forward just as a pair of muscular arms locked around my body. "It's okay, babe," Zane said, directing me up to the house. "Let's sit for a minute."

"But Kate," I protested weakly as he led me over to the porch swing. "Who would take her?"

His boots came down against the wood, putting the swing into motion. "We're gonna figure that out, but I need you to sit here and stay calm—"

"I'm not sitting here doing nothing when we don't know where she is, Zane!"

"Dakota." He sighed. "Just let me and Jimmy handle this—"

"No!" The vise around my chest seemed to tighten, leaving me lightheaded. I forced myself to take several deep breaths before continuing. "You and I work as a team, Big Guy."

Zane rocked forward suddenly, tilting the swing as he rested his forearms against his thighs. He ran a hand through his long hair and worked his jaw back and forth. "No."

It was just above a whisper, in a tone that left no room for arguing. We sat in silence while I processed the pronouncement, and he worked to get his emotions under control.

"We haven't talked about it, but the night of the fire put things in perspective for me, Cap," he said quietly. "As your husband, my job is to keep you safe. It's a job I take seriously. When I was trying to get you in the truck that night, you fought back. You would have willingly put yourself in the line of fire without a fucking weapon."

"Zane." I placed my hand across his muscular thigh, remembering our first conversation after I stole the quadriceps machine right out from under him. "I didn't think. I just saw Mike, and I knew I had to stop them."

"You didn't think. In my line of work, if you don't think, you end up dead." He dropped his hand down to cover mine. "I had to go thirty-one years without you. Don't make me go a lifetime."

The swing rocked back abruptly as he stood up, and I gripped the chain to keep from falling off. "Hey, Big Guy," I called as he reached the edge of the porch.

Zane's shoulders stiffened, but he turned until I could see his profile. "Yeah?"

"I love you too." He exhaled a soft laugh, and I added, "But I'm not sitting this one out. She needs me."

He jerked his chin and moved down the steps, each stomp sending vibrations all along the porch.

The screen door flew open, slamming against the siding like a bullet leaving a gun, and I scrambled again to keep myself on the swing.

"What happened?" Lauren asked.

I watched Zane retreat toward the barn before giving her the rundown.

She curled her arms overhead and blew out a breath. "Why? Why take Kate? It makes no sense."

That was what I'd been trying to piece together. I felt like the answer was staring me right in the face. I slipped off the swing and paced the length of the porch, turning Nate's words over in my head. "The page—Jimmy!" I called across the yard. "Can we trace the page?"

He looked up. "Not if it's a one-way pager. It's a passive receiver only. No GPS, no location. It's okay, Dakota. We're going to find your sister."

If Mike were here, he would have at least pretended to listen to what I had to say. He probably would've even jotted it down in his little notebook, just in case.

That was it.

I had to take what I knew and make a timeline. "Lauren, do you have some paper and a pen?"

While she got me what I needed, I focused on clearing my mind. So, maybe I couldn't shoot a gun or join a biker gang.

Maybe my purpose was to lead the entire operation.

"Here you go." Lauren handed me a pen and paper. "Making a grocery list? If so, can you put coffee on there?"

I sat down and actually wrote the letter c before shaking my head.

"No. Lauren, I'm not going to the store. I'm trying to make a timeline."

She sat down beside me. "A timeline of what?"

"Nate got a page from the hospital saying he had a case. Obviously, we can't trace that, but maybe there's something else... like a text or phone call from a blocked number, maybe?"

She tucked her hair behind her ear with a nod. "The night my mom was killed, Mike got a text from a blocked number. Not long after, I received something similar. Jeremy cracked the code on those already, though. Guy was a detective. Mike went after them, but the Sons got there first."

I scratched both out. "Okay... maybe the surveillance footage that got emailed to Kate. We could run a trace on it—"

"Yeah, that's been done, Dakota," Lauren said patiently. "It led nowhere. I like where your head's at, but this isn't going to help us find Kate. Come on, let's see what Jimmy's come up with."

Ooh, Jimmy was in the CIA. Better listen to him. Never mind that Dakota spent years studying the Marvel universe for insight into villains and their tendencies.

I trudged down the porch steps with a black cloud hanging over my head. I just wanted to be taken seriously for once. Was that too much to ask?

Guy was a detective...

Jimmy was talking about setting up a perimeter with Little Ricky and Garrett when it hit me.

Someone who would know how to manipulate technology.

"Jimmy?"

"Just a sec, Dakota. Now, if we start—"

"Jimmy, it's important," I insisted.

His jaw clenched for a brief second before he gave me his attention. "Yep, go ahead."

"I'm just curious, the surveillance footage that was emailed to Kate. Did we ever find out who sent that?" Lauren's eyes narrowed, and I jabbed a finger in her direction, willing her to be quiet.

"Uh, last I heard, Jeremy didn't have any luck on that. Something with a firewall... why?"

Bingo.

"Well, I just find it interesting that Lauren and Mike received texts from blocked numbers, only to track the guy down and find that he'd just been murdered by the Sons. We get video surveillance of the sergeant threatening Nate, but arrive too late again. Then, we have the glitch with the pager—"

"What's your point?"

Nate's head lifted, and he looked up at me in shock. "Holy shit, Dakota."

"It's Jeremy," I whispered. "He's the only one who would have the means to do it. He's been feeding us information this entire time, but only when it won't do us any good."

Nate's jaw tightened, and the cords in his neck stretched taut as he ground out, "He's the motherfucking traitor."

Jimmy brought his hand up to rest under his chin. "It was staring us right in the fucking face, and we missed it. Everything he's given us has been at their discretion."

One of us didn't miss it.

One of us was looking into everything—no stone unturned.

"Oh my god," I breathed. "Jimmy, I know why they took Kate! It's what you said—back in the barn. My father's still alive—"

"Fuck, they're going to use her to break him."

"We're not ready," Lauren mumbled to herself before disappearing back inside the house.

Nate jumped off the tailgate. "We have to find her... you don't know the things he'll do! Somebody get me a goddamn gun!"

"Follow me." Molly tugged him toward her car. "Dakota," she said as they reached the trunk. "You wanted to know how Bear was taking the news."

When she hit the release button, my eyes went wide. It was filled to the brim with weapons.

"Let's just say I'm doing penance for my sins. Little Ricky, call your father. Tell him we've smoked out his traitor, and we'd like an army. We're going to war."

"How soon can we leave?" I asked, running my hands reverently over the steel of a Glock.

"Dakota, while I appreciate the help, I think it's best if you let the professionals handle this—"

"But I solved the mystery," I argued. "Me, Jimmy. I discovered the traitor. Oh, and newsflash, they've got my sister. I'm not sitting this one out."

He bit his lip. "I just think that maybe until you're a little more comfortable—"

I loaded bullets into the magazine before sliding it back into the Glock and calmly unloaded it into the paper target on the tree. I resisted the urge to blow the smoke from the barrel like they did in the movies. "I think I'm comfortable."

"Are we just ignoring the fact that you faint at the sight of blood?" Zane asked from behind me.

I smiled, knowing that was as close as he was going to get to giving me his blessing. I looked over my shoulder with a wink. "Then I guess I just won't look, will I, Big Guy?"

CHAPTER FORTY-TWO

Grey: April 2017 (Age: 53)

"Get up."

I jerked awake at the sound, reaching for Kate even as my body screamed in agony from the movement. She continued snoring softly beside me, blissfully unaware of the danger lying just feet away. Her hands curled around her stomach as if she was giving herself a hug.

I would have smiled had there not been someone else in the room. Reluctantly, I rolled toward the voice. "You can torture me here, Cobra. Ain't leavin' her alone."

When he moved, a shaft of light from the doorway hit me in the face. He'd never left it open before. "I'm getting you both out of here."

I cocked my head to the side, certain I'd misunderstood. "You're bustin' us out? What does your buddy, Saint, think about that?"

"Saint lost control of the situation the moment your son was killed. I have little time so, unless you've decided to rot in here, we need to move."

"Katydid," I whispered, gently shaking her shoulder. "Need you to wake up, darlin'."

She smacked her lips together, exhaling a soft sigh.

"Drugs are still in her system. She'll have to be carried." When I went to lift her, he chuckled. "By me, Grey. You won't make it to the door with her."

Bile surged in my gut at the thought of what I was about to do. I was handing my unconscious daughter over to the motherfucker who'd raped my wife. I was putting the very thing that had pulled me back from the brink of death and given me purpose into the arms of a monster.

Celia would have had me by the balls if she knew.

Probably would have sent me to the Reaper herself.

As we didn't have any other options, I decided it'd just be one more thing I took to my grave.

The fluorescent bulbs flickered overhead as we stepped out into the hall, and I winced at the brightness until my eyes adjusted. At first glance, it looked like we were inside an aircraft hangar, but without windows or some form of natural light coming in, we could have been anywhere.

Dizziness sucker punched me in the jaw, and I placed my left hand on the wall in front of me, fighting against a body that wanted death.

Kate.

I had to get Kate somewhere safe.

With that thought, I pushed off the wall and forced myself to keep moving. "Where are we?"

Cobra turned, and I was struck by Kate's arm, dangling limply at her side. If I hadn't seen her chest rising and falling, I would have thought she was dead.

"New Mexico. Place was used as a nuclear missile vault for the military back during the Cold War. We don't have much time—"

I looked down the deserted hallway, suddenly wary of taking another step. "How do I know Saint's boys won't be waiting around the corner?"

"You don't," he stated flatly, keeping his back to me this time. "If you'd feel more comfortable staying behind, be my guest. But I gave you my word. I have no desire to kill a man who's already broken—an opinion that Saint doesn't share."

I nodded, suddenly too tired to talk.

"The best games are the ones that get pushed into overtime.

Evenly matched adversaries, if you will. No one wants to watch a game that's won right out of the gate."

"Not really," I huffed. "Not really a sports fan."

"Of course not," Cobra answered cryptically. "Men like us prefer a different sort of playing field, don't we?"

We moved at a slow pace down hallways and up flights of stairs. I clung to consciousness with everything I had and forced my legs to keep moving. When Cobra threw his back into a metal door, I went down to my knees, blinded by something I hadn't seen in months.

The sun.

I dug my hand into the soft soil, letting the grains slip through my fingers. Everywhere I looked, I was met with vibrant bursts of color from the crayon blue sky to the green on the trees. I'd been surrounded by whites and grays for so long that it was almost overwhelming.

The scent of pine was everywhere, and I breathed it in, silently weeping at my first taste of freedom.

"You can cry later," Cobra reminded me. "Right now, we need to get away from here."

I composed myself and, ignoring the twinge in my shoulder, pushed to my feet with a low grunt. It was cleverly hidden in the side of a mountain. I would have rotted away for decades before anyone ever came across it.

I took one last look at my prison before following Cobra through a narrow clearing, paying close attention to the sticks and pinecones littering the ground. One wrong step and I'd be finished.

Kate.

I had to stay strong for Kate.

A tan Jeep Cherokee straight out of the seventies sat just off a worn dirt road. Otherwise, the place was deserted. Not a motorcycle in sight.

"Where is everyone?" I asked gruffly.

He opened the passenger seat and slid Kate's limp body across the bench seat. "I imagine they're following up on the lead into your son's death—"

"There's a lead?" The ignorant sound of hope in my voice shocked even me. It wouldn't matter if every single one of them was brought to justice, it wouldn't bring him back.

Just like killing Donald hadn't brought Ma back to me.

"False lead," he corrected. "I just needed to buy us some time."

Despite my misgivings, the Jeep fired up with a deep rumble. Cobra threw it into drive and branches scraped along the windows, pleading for us to stay. The tires dipped into a muddy rut, but he managed to get us back onto the road.

Kate cried out, not quite asleep, but not fully awake. With a sudden gasp, she sat upright—her eyes were wild and frantic as she searched the cabin. "Mike."

She relaxed again. But that one word was enough to detonate the bomb residing where my heart used to be.

"Kate was there," Cobra stated, keeping his eyes on the winding road. "When they shot him. It's why Saint wanted her—maybe he thought she'd reveal the killers with the right motivation."

How far was she willing to go to save her old man?

"Thought you were all set to build your cult leader's compound. What changed your mind?"

"Truthfully?" He glanced over at me. "He lost sight of what we were doing. Going after your in-laws instead of dismantling Silent Phoenix and killing you."

Kate's head fell against my shoulder, and I shifted to keep her from falling forward. "What do you know about Saint, anyway? Where the fuck did he come from?"

"Honestly? I never met the guy. Wouldn't surprise me if he was some politician with the power he has—"

"Wait a minute," I argued. "You're tellin' me you went to war for someone you never met and now you think you're just gonna walk away without him findin' out?"

Saint had taken over the Sons without revealing his identity.

I was wrong before. This wasn't some David Koresh-sounding bullshit. It was straight out of the Wizard of fucking Oz.

"Saint's become obsessed with finding out who killed your son. Wants to start another war before finishing this one. I'll be long gone before he realizes anything is wrong. I never gave a fuck about who capped the kid."

I clenched my jaw and leaned across the seat, ignoring the flashing in my vision. "You don't give a fuck about my kid?"

He clicked his tongue against his teeth with a shake of his head. "You seem to have me confused with Mother Teresa. I only ever cared about what happened to you—"

My nostrils flared. It was the same shit he'd been saying since day one. "Yet here you are, helpin' me escape when you should have put me down months ago."

"Do you know what it's like to set out with a clear goal? This one thing you just have to accomplish, only to wake one morning to find you can't remember why you started in the first place?"

I shrugged my good shoulder and slouched down until the back of my head rested against the seat. I needed sleep. We could talk later.

"Grey." Cobra snapped his fingers. "Stay awake."

"Why?" I groaned. "Don't know how to fuckin' drive without me givin' directions?"

He slammed on the brakes so suddenly that I barely had time to get my left arm out in front of Kate before my right shoulder slammed against the dash with enough force to leave me gasping for breath.

"As I was saying..." Cobra took his foot off the brake, and the Jeep began moving downhill again. "I started the entire fucking thing to avenge the Serpents. The club may have turned on me, but my mission never changed. I was always going to kill you."

"Oh, yeah? What's stoppin' you now?" I wheezed out through clenched teeth before bracing myself for the next impact.

He surprised me by laughing. "I've told you. I want to know I took you down at your best." The Jeep slowed to another stop, and he retrieved a cell phone from the glove box. "So, this is where I leave you—"

I looked out at towering pine trees lining either side of the mountain trail and then back to him. "And where the fuck is this?"

"Couple miles outside Mirror Lake." He held the phone out. "You may have service, you may not. Just know that they'll trace the phone, so you'll want to ditch it soon. I think this makes us even now, no?"

Mirror Lake?

I wracked my addled brain for the memory, almost weeping with relief when it came to me.

"What if we took the girls to Mirror Lake?" Wolverine asked with a sly grin. "Got a cabin up there—all the fishing gear. Might keep 'em entertained for a weekend. Always kept you busy as a kid."

"I'd be willin' to get in on that," Angel added. "Just leaves Celia, all alone in that house. Might be a good chance to reconnect..."

I shook my head, hiding a smile. "You two just got it all figured out, don't you? Alright, if you take the girls, I'll see what I can do to win their mama back."

Wolverine clapped me on the shoulder. "That's a fine idea you've come up with, kid. A fine idea."

The door swung open underneath my hand, and I checked the side pocket door for a weapon before pulling Kate to the edge of the seat with my good arm. I wasn't sure what I would've done even if I found something. I couldn't shoot, and I didn't have one-tenth of the strength I'd need to use a knife.

It didn't mean this was the end of the road for us, though.

"You of all people should know we'll never be even 'til blood's been drawn," I said, as Kate brought her hand up to pat my cheek. "Soon as I'm healed, I'm comin' after you with everything I've got. Made a promise to my girl that I'd send you screamin' to the Reaper."

Cobra's eyebrows went up in surprise even as his face lit up with a manic grin. "I wouldn't expect anything less, but I think I'll be working alone from here on out."

"Tell you what," I said, draping Kate's body over my left shoulder. "Figure I've got a couple of weeks to a month before I'm in any shape to fight. Seems like a fair head start to me."

As I moved to slam the door, he leaned across the seat. "I'm looking forward to it."

The terrain was uneven, and despite my attempts to wake her, Kate was nothing but dead weight. I raised my shoulder, trying to reposition her several times. Within minutes of hiking into the forest, my skin was soaked in a layer of sweat.

Trees seemed to bend and arch onto the overgrown path, slowing us down. If we didn't move faster, the Sons would be on us before sundown. I was so focused on the low-lying branches that I missed the exposed roots and stumbled to the forest floor with a low groan. Instead of blinding pain, something soft broke my fall.

When Kate cried out almost immediately and began struggling, I realized my soft landing hadn't been dirt. I rolled away from her to assess the damage.

"My leg," she whimpered, rocking back and forth. "Help."

Her bare foot was twisted at an abnormal angle and already swollen to twice its normal size.

"Oh, fuck, Katydid!" I pressed my fingers into the tender flesh, and she came up off the forest floor with a roar. Her fingernails dug into the battered skin on my chest, and tears filled her eyes as she fought to free herself from my grip.

I'd broken her foot when I fell.

In the middle of goddamned nowhere, with armed bikers that were going to be looking for us any fucking second, I'd just crippled my daughter.

CHAPTER FORTY-THREE

Grey: April 2017 (Age: 53)

S he shifted against the dirt floor before squeezing her eyes shut with a wince. "My foot hurts... and my head hurts—" With another low moan, she leaned to the side and began vomiting.

I squeezed Kate's shoulder and rubbed along her spine as her body purged the remnants of the drugs. When she finished, she sat up, only to collapse against my chest with a whispered, "I'm sorry."

"Don't you apologize to me, darlin'."

"Where are we?" she croaked.

My throat was so dry that it hurt to swallow. "Somewhere outside of Mirror Lake. Do you remember coming out here with Wolverine and Angel?"

She nodded, studying the dense trees. "I don't see the lake, though."

"Yeah, we got a few miles to go, darlin'. Think you could use your old man as a crutch?"

A tear streaked down her dirty cheek, and she shook her head. "No, Daddy. I need to sleep. Just let me sleep for a little longer, okay?"

"Okay, sweetheart, but just for a minute." I settled her against the trunk of a nearby tree before getting to my feet. As much as I wanted to collapse beside her, we couldn't stay here. They'd be combing every inch of these woods once they realized we'd gotten free.

I pulled the cell phone from my pocket, surprised to see that there were three bars of service. Cobra's warning to ditch it echoed in my head as I punched in the number and hit send. "C'mon, princess. Pick up."

"Darlin'—" I said before realizing I'd gotten her voicemail. My throat tightened just hearing her voice, but I held it together long enough to get out what needed to be said.

"Celia, it's me. I need help—we're outside of Mirror Lake. Me and Katy. Gonna try to make it to Wolverine's old cabin, but we're in bad shape, darlin'. If—" My nostrils flared, but I forced myself to say it. "If I don't make it... need you to know that you were the best thing that ever happened to a poor fuck like me. I—I love you, princess."

Swiping the tears away, I dialed the only other person I thought might be home. I had to ditch the phone soon before they had Jeremy track us down.

"Who's this?" Angel said by way of greeting. "Got the caller ID now, so if you little shits think you're gonna pull one over on me again, you better think the fuck again."

I swallowed. "It's me—"

"Jamie? Christ, kid, where are ya?" I could hear him moving around.

"Somewhere near Mirror Lake. There was a military bunker built into the mountain. Fuck, Angel—I'm turned around—"

"Okay... okay," he said soothingly. "What'd I teach you as a kid? You remember? Get you a stick about three feet long and find a spot where it'll cast a shadow. Make sure it's level and then mark the end of the shadow with a stone or pinecone. That's west."

I nodded before brushing away more tears. "Yeah, uh, then I wait, right?"

"That's my boy. Wait a bit and then mark where the shadow moves. Straight line between the two'll give you an east-west line. If it gets dark—"

"Look for The Big Dipper and trace up from the front of the bowl to the first bright star they point to," I answered dutifully, surprised I'd remembered jack shit about something that happened over forty years ago.

"Pole Star will give you true North. Now Wolverine's cabin was on the south side of the lake. You get turned around, just keep movin' downhill. Lake is at the base of the mountain. I'm comin' to you—"

"I got Kate," I admitted. "We're pretty fucked up—won't be long before the Sons come lookin' either. I can't keep this phone, but I'm gonna try to get her somewhere safe. If I don't make it—"

"Don't you talk like that, Jamie. I'll search the entire goddamn mountain if I have to, but I ain't leavin' without the two of you. Keep together and stay out of sight."

I nodded and looked up at the sun shining brightly overhead. Staying hidden was easier said than done.

————

"I can't, Daddy," Kate pleaded. "I can't go any farther—"

I tightened my hold on her hip and pulled her forward several more inches. "We've gotta keep movin', Katydid. Can't stop now. Angel's comin' for us."

She kept her hand on my arm for balance before leaning over to retch again. "I can't—oh my god," she panted, her words still slightly slurred. "We're going to die out here, aren't we?"

The moonlight hit her face, illuminating the terror in her eyes. We'd been limping along for hours now, narrowly avoiding steep drop-offs and forest debris hellbent on taking us down again.

"Ain't a goddamn thing gonna happen to you, darlin'. Look up at those stars." I lifted my arm toward the sky. "See those stars up there? It's like a giant map, guidin' us right to Angel. Just a little bit more and we'll be at the lake. You remember which cabin was Wolverine's?"

Kate wiped her mouth and gave me a shaky nod. "Yeah, it's green. Everyone else painted their cabins red or yellow, but Wolverine's was a deep green, like the color of the trees. And it's not with the others, it's off by itself."

"That's right," I encouraged, cautiously taking another step. I had to keep us moving. If we stopped to sit, we weren't getting up again. "You remember why he built it so far away from everyone else?"

"Because he wanted peace and quiet."

In reality, it was because we used the smaller buildings on the property for cooking, and the last thing he wanted was nosy neighbors calling the badges in over a weird smell.

The feds would have had a field day.

Kate exhaled a soft laugh that turned into uncontrollable sobbing. She brought her hand up to cover her face. "Everything is blank. Like, I can remember things that Wolverine said forever ago, but I can't remember the past twenty-four hours!"

"Don't cry, Katydid. Don't cry, baby." I wrapped my arm around her shoulders in a half-assed attempt at a hug. Someone gunned a vehicle down a nearby mountain road, and we fell silent, holding our breaths as we listened. "I don't think it's comin' this way. Just keep movin'."

"I want to stop," she whispered. "I just need to sit down and try to piece together what happened. I remember I woke up—" Her voice cut off in another sob and she stumbled.

"What is it, darlin'? Your foot?"

She shook her head and mashed her lips together, even as her nostrils flared. "It's not that. I couldn't sleep because I was thinking about Mike, and Nate came in—"

By this point, Kate's grip on my arm was loosening as she tried moving down to the ground.

"No, you don't, baby. Gotta stay on your feet. What happened to Mike..." My own throat tightened. "It wasn't your fault."

I couldn't let myself think about him right now. We had to keep going with what little strength we had left.

"It's not that," she hiccuped, twisting the diamond ring on her finger. "I'm—I'm pregnant. I just f-found out."

The drugs.

We'd had club whores who'd gotten hooked on their club drugs, not even stopping when they got knocked up. The ones that didn't pay a visit to Vic carried to term with no issues.

But they weren't Kate.

I thought of Celia miscarrying on the bathroom floor, and my molars came together. I should have killed him with my bare hands when I had the chance. For that matter, I should have lured Cobra out of the Jeep and slammed his head in the door. Fueled by nothing but sheer rage, I lifted Kate with my left arm and began powering through the trees. I'd live just so I could watch them die.

"Daddy?" she questioned.

"Gonna get you to Angel, and then I'm gonna rip that motherfucker's heart out of his goddamn chest," I panted. "Jesus fuckin' Christ!"

"Y-you're going to kill Nate?" she squeaked. "He saved your life—the night you were shot."

I'd known those stitches were too perfect to have come from any club doctor. Eli could handle a lot of things, but a bullet to the chest wasn't one of them.

"Nate? Why the fuck would I kill Nate?" I asked, pushing through a tangle of branches. "I'm gonna kill Jarvis. Nate can help."

Kate fell silent again, except for the occasional sniffle, and I wondered if she'd fallen asleep. The sounds of water lapping against the shore grew louder. We had to be getting close.

"Daddy?"

"Yeah, darlin'?"

She hiccuped again. "Do you think the baby—"

I jerked my chin. "Baby's gonna be just fine, sweetheart. Now, just hold on. We're almost there."

"But Mama," she protested. "I know about what happened. How do you know that won't happen to me?"

My jaw tightened. "Cause I ain't gonna let it. If I have to trick the sons of bitches into following me out onto the lake, I'll do it if it'll keep you safe."

"When you said you were going to kill him, did you mean Jeremy?" Her voice was starting to sound drowsy again, her body fighting to shut down and recuperate.

"Jeremy's goin' to the Reaper for what he did to you—"

She gasped. "He told you about that?"

I pressed my arm a little tighter around the backs of her thighs. "Tell me about what? Drugging you to get you here?"

"He drugged me?"

I sighed. We'd been over the events several times, but the sedative kept wiping her memory clean.

"Jamie?" a voice whispered a few feet ahead.

I moved against a tree and lowered Kate back to her feet, signaling for her to keep quiet. The only person who knew we were here was Angel, but I wasn't putting it past the Sons to call me by my given name to draw me out.

"Goddammit, kid," he cursed. "I just walked into a fuckin' spider-web, so if you're there—"

I let out a low whistle. "Right here, old man. Comin' towards you." Kate draped her arm over my shoulders, and we began hobbling toward him.

The moonlight made the ripples on the lake shimmer like bits of silver as we broke through the trees into a clearing. Angel stood, looking every bit like a guardian angel that had come down just to save us.

"Christ, kid," he finally said after looking me over. "Look like ya got one foot on a banana peel."

"Says The Crypt-Keeper himself. What are you now—two hundred?" I joked as he moved to Kate's other side, supporting her weight fully.

We'd done it.

"Three hundred, but who's countin'?" he fired back before pointing toward the little green cabin. "Wolverine has a first-aid kit inside. Let's see if we can't get the two of you put back together for the ride home."

I glanced around, but the forest was quiet. Too quiet. "Make it quick. Sons'll be all over the place before long."

"Katydid, thought you'd keep your old man company?"

Her gaze moved from the water to the trees and then back to the cabin. "Can we just go, please? I've got a bad feeling."

"Sweetheart," Angel said calmly as he led her up the steps and picked the lock on the front door. "Me and your daddy ain't lettin' those motherfuckers anywhere near—"

The sudden blast forced Kate into my side, the momentum sending both of us down in the entryway. My ears were still ringing as I called out, "Angel?"

I was met with ragged pants. "I'm here, kid."

"What the fuck was that?" I reached back toward the porch, feeling along for his boots.

"Everything's just fine. Get—get Kate in my truck. Can you do that... for me?"

"Angel?" Kate cried out. "Angel, where are you?"

Headlights kicked on from behind us, and Kate began screaming. Angel had made it back up to his knees, a growing red stain spreading across his chest. As he fumbled for his holster, a second blast sent him sprawling face down onto the porch.

I worried I'd dislocated Kate's arm as I dragged her away from the open door before moving back onto the porch for Angel. The mother-fucker with the gun could take me out right now, but I wasn't leaving him out there alone. "I'm right here."

My ma was always rescuing wounded animals when I was a boy— said the trick was to keep your voice low and calm.

They're scared already, Jamie. You don't want to make it worse.

He lifted his head and reached for my hand, letting me drag him over the threshold. I reached up and flipped the lock, knowing it wouldn't be enough to keep them out for long. The headlights streamed through the window, just enough for me to see how bad it truly was. Both bullets had hit him in the back and torn through his chest.

"It don't hurt, Jamie. Don't hurt a bit." He began coughing violently, and a line of blood ran from his mouth and down toward his chin.

"You're a shitty liar, old man," I said through my tears, leaning over to take both of his hands in mine.

"Daddy, I need your shirt. We can use it as a tourniquet," Kate begged, as she crawled over.

"Katydid." Angel shook his head. "Ain't gonna do me a bit of good right now. You know what I need for you to do?"

"What?" she wept, lowering her cheek down to his.

"Need you and Kota-Bear to take care of your old man for me." He swallowed, forcing the corner of his mouth up into a half-smile. "Ain't the easiest gig in the world—"

"Don't—" I choked on the rest of the words.

Don't leave me.

Don't make me figure this shit out on my own.

"Hey," he said softly, bringing his hand up to cup my face. "It's time, kid. Your ma's been waitin' on me for a long-ass time. Someone's gotta keep Mikey in line up there."

His hand fell away, and he reached into his pocket before pressing the keys to his truck into my hand. "Run," he whispered. "I'll hold 'em off long enough for you to get her out of here. Go out the back door."

"Angel, no." I shook my head.

"You wanted to be just like me, my boy, but you were so much better. Might not have been my blood, but I was proud to call you mine." His body began shaking as the shock from blood loss set in.

I pressed my trembling lips to his forehead, fighting to stay strong for him. "I love you, Charlie. Take—take care of Ma and Mikey for me."

"Love you too, my boy," he said through chattering teeth. "And Katydid, you tell that sister of yours that I couldn't have asked for better granddaughters. You made my life worth livin'. Now, go."

"Ain't leavin' you—"

"Now ain't the time to play superhero, Jamie. Take the g-gun—" He exhaled loudly, but didn't take another breath.

The heavy tread of boots hit the front porch, and I reluctantly let go of his hand to reach for Kate's. "We gotta go now, sweetheart."

She covered Angel's body with hers and shook her head. "We can't leave him. We can't leave him for them."

I bit down on the inside of my cheek as my resolve cracked. "I can only carry one of you, darlin'. We gotta keep you and that baby safe."

With that, she let go and reached for me. I had her climb onto my back like I did when she was a child, and we crawled under the windows, making our way to the back door.

I didn't know how we were supposed to get around Saint's men, but in here we were sitting ducks. They could burn the goddamn thing down around us if they wanted to—at least out there we stood a chance.

The back door opened just as we reached it, the corner catching me in the temple hard enough to blur my vision. I blinked to clear it while fumbling to get Angel's weapon up, but my movements were sloppy and uncoordinated. I found myself staring down the barrel of a gun and into the eyes of someone I knew all too well.

"The fuck are you doin' here?" I managed to get out before Kate was pulled away and everything went dark.

CHAPTER FORTY-FOUR

Celia: April 2017 (Age: 45)

I looked out at the caravan coming down Lauren's driveway. "Why are there only two bikers?"

Molly avoided meeting my eyes as she arranged our weapons on the large wooden table. "About that—Bear and quite a few of the others had to make a last-minute run to Colorado, so this was the best we could do on such short notice."

"The best?" I questioned as Wolverine climbed off his bike before turning to help Lucy. "You're joking. You're sure you told him about Kate and Jeremy?"

Lauren walked out onto the porch, crossing her arms over her chest. "What the hell is this?"

I jerked a thumb over my shoulder. "This is the army Molly got for us."

Torch and Lou pulled up alongside Wolverine. With her magical ability to squeeze information out of Bear, I sort of imagined him sending us something a little more menacing and definitely a lot younger.

"We're not ready," Lauren said simply. "We need more time." It was all she'd been saying since we discovered Kate had been taken. "Wait— Abuelita? What are you doing here?"

Gloria waved cheerfully and held up a covered dish. "Do not worry, LoLo. I am not here to make the war. I brought tamales."

"You brought... tamales," Lauren repeated before running a hand over her face. "This is what you got us, Molly? This is how we're going to defeat the Sons?"

"What?" Molly shrugged. "Nate and Garrett are sharpshooters, Jimmy's ex-CIA, Wolverine can probably kill people just by looking at them now—and that's not even getting into what we can do. But if you're still worried..." Molly pointed behind us with a grin. "I got him too."

We turned, and I sucked in a quick breath. "Carnage?"

Other than a red scar on his temple, he looked the same as he always had. It was miraculous considering the Sons had shot him twice.

"Celia." His mouth lifted mischievously. "Heard you were going to war with those cocksuckers and you didn't invite me."

I let out a huge breath and walk down the steps into his arms. "I can't believe you're here. Are you healed? You're all better, right?" I traced the scar with my fingertips.

"Better than ever, and ready to kick some ass. Thought I'd see if my old partner needed any help."

"You mean the 'kid' you used to babysit?"

He shook his head and flexed his fingers. "No, I meant partner. We worked well together in Celia's little house of horrors."

"House of horrors?" Lauren questioned, her gaze darting between the two of us. "What does that mean?"

"Celia's a master at torture," Carnage proudly stated, just as I opened my mouth to assure her it was nothing. "Seen her make grown men cry."

"Is that so? Celia, you've been holding out on us. Molly, did you know about this?"

Molly shifted a gun over several millimeters as if adjusting a place setting at a table before bringing a hand up to her hip. "Yes, I knew."

Lucy patted me on the shoulder in greeting before going up the stairs to her niece. "Oh, you knew about it, did you? Lauren, these two went after an entire gang on their own once."

I cringed, knowing if Dakota was within earshot, I'd never hear the end of it. "That was a long time ago, and we would have gotten ourselves killed were it not for the club showing up."

"And that's how I ended up spending my free time with Celia." Carnage grinned. "Learned a hell of a lot, too."

Lauren leaned back against the house with a thoughtful look. "You did it before. You could do it again, right? Carnage, what sort of things did you learn?"

He lifted a shoulder. "Torture, mostly. Oh, and she's a badass at jiu-jitsu."

"Interesting," Lauren said cryptically before winking at Molly. "You did well."

I'd spent the afternoon biting my nails down to the quick while Jimmy and Zane worked to trace Jeremy's cell, knowing there was a good chance he'd already turned her over and disappeared. Carnage's trip down memory lane had been a good reminder that we hadn't always had a Jimmy or a Mike telling us what to do.

Once upon a time, I'd been a warrior...

"Got him!" Jimmy yelled from the bed of his truck, pulling me from my thoughts. He held up his laptop. "Bastard's good, I'll give him that. But I'm still better. Got him down south, maybe headed toward the border—"

"No!" I roared. The noose around my neck tightened and rage flooded my veins at the thought of Kate being handed over to traffickers. "We need to go. I have to leave. Has anyone seen my purse?"

I was rambling—my brain caught between preparing for battle and doing what I was told to do. I'd only ever been good at one of those things.

"Celia, we're going to get her back. I swear it. Now, I'm going to need a team—"

"Me," Lauren stated.

Jimmy's face fell. "You know I can't let you—"

"*¿No puedes o no quieres?*" she asked in a low voice. "You know we don't have the numbers to go up against them, yet you refuse to let us fight."

"Doll..." Wolverine stepped in. "Let me share a little secret with you. You're never gonna have the numbers you want for war. Never gonna be fully ready. Know what, though? Worn these colors for longer than I can remember and they don't run. So, you gotta look in the mirror and decide that today's as good a day to die as any."

Lauren's mouth settled into a hard line. "Thanks, Wolverine, that was really... motivating."

"Lauren," Jimmy called as he leaped down from the back of the truck. "Lauren, come back!"

She stalked back into the house, slamming the screen door behind her. A woman after my own heart. While I'd initially been reluctant, we'd gone into this together, only to have it stripped from our hands as we approached the goal line.

"Where's Angel?" I asked, scanning the yard. "Wolverine, did you talk to him?"

He frowned. "Ain't spoken to him today. Was he comin'?"

"I called right after Nate arrived." I patted the front pocket on the jeans Lauren insisted I wear, the denim almost rough against my skin. "Let me find my phone, and I'll try him again."

"Alright, boys," Wolverine turned back to the group. "We ridin' or plannin' the best spots to fish?"

Jimmy looked back at the house before nodding. "Wolverine, Zane, Torch, and Little Ricky, you guys are with me—"

"Wait a second," I argued. "You're leaving now? What are we supposed to do?"

"You also seem to have forgotten someone," Nate added.

Jimmy pinched the bridge of his nose. "Just—fuck! Celia, if you can, just keep everyone here. Nate, I know you want to go—"

"You're fucking right, I do. She's my wife."

"And that's why I need you to stay here. You're too close."

"Too close?" he roared in response. "Too close? Do you have any fucking idea what I'm going through right now, not knowing where she is or even how she is? I show up, and you say we're going to war, but now we're being asked to sit this one out? Where the fuck do you get off?" He stepped back, panting heavily, fists clenched at his sides.

I'd never been more proud.

Jimmy took a deep breath. "I know exactly what you're going through, but you're still too close. You're liable to react emotionally, which will get you or your loved one killed. So, if you don't mind, I'd like to do my job and bring Kate home safe."

"Come on, Nate," I held out an arm. "You're wasting your breath."

Garrett pushed off the tailgate and wrapped an arm around his brother before turning back to Jimmy. "Anything happens to her. It's on you now. Remember that."

We stomped up the wooden steps, utterly dejected, as vehicles began firing up all around us. I retraced my steps, looking for my cell phone, checking first the living room and then the kitchen. Lauren was somberly eating a plate of tamales while Dakota chopped an onion. Using her forearm, she pushed her glasses up onto her head and wiped at her streaming eyes.

"No, no," Gloria chided. "*Con ganas*, mija. Take pride in your work."

"Did you see the target outside? I took pride in that."

Gloria must have been some type of sorceress to have roped Dakota into a cooking lesson. She was about as likely to learn how to cook as she was to be seen reading a Batman comic.

"Baby girl, have you seen my cell phone?" I finally asked when it seemed that I wasn't interrupting.

She nodded and pointed upstairs. "It was dying, so I plugged it into Lauren's charger in the bedroom. That was over an hour ago, so it should be good now. Do you need me to help you get it?" Her head bobbed up and down in a slow nod, as if she was attempting to hypnotize me.

"No, I think Gloria needs you here—"

"I need to be out there," Dakota insisted. "What good am I doing? Cooking? That's not getting my sister back—"

"*Mija*," Gloria scolded. "You are preparing food for the soldiers. They will need full bellies to have minds that are clear. So, we have the most important job of all."

Dakota picked up the knife again and went back to cutting. "Can you at least tell me what the plan is?"

Her hopeful expression tugged at my heart. "Uh, Jimmy, Zane, and several others are heading down south—"

"What?" she screeched. "They're leaving us? After all the hard work we put in—"

"Dakota." Lauren rubbed her forehead. "Just chill. I'm working on it, okay?"

I left the two of them to sort out all our problems and jogged upstairs. When I reached the top of the stairs, I stepped into the bathroom, closing my eyes in an attempt to remain calm. The Sons had taken Kate because we were getting close. I couldn't believe anything else.

We'd just leave it in Jimmy's hands and wait.

It felt like a cop-out.

"You can stay here and continue to live like a mouse, Celia Quinn," I told my reflection with a jerk of my chin, repeating words I hadn't spoken in years. "Or you can stand up and fight for what's yours."

The warrior met my gaze, and my lips tipped up into a smile as she urged me to fight.

It was time to do things our way.

CHAPTER FORTY-FIVE

Celia: April 2017 (Age: 45)

My cell was lying on the comforter, fully charged, just as Dakota had predicted it would be. I was about to call Angel when I saw a missed call and voicemail from a blocked number.

"Celia, it's me. I need help—we're outside of Mirror Lake. Me and Katy. Gonna try to make it to Wolverine's old cabin, but we're in bad shape, darlin'. If—" My nostrils flared, but I forced myself to say it. "If I don't make it... need you to know that you were the best thing that ever happened to a poor fuck like me. I—I love you, princess."

I dropped to my knees against the hardwood floor with a startled cry. Jamie was alive, and he had our baby. The Sons were leading Jimmy south when we needed to head west.

"Nate!" I screamed. "Dakota!"

Everyone in the house came charging up the stairs in a panic. I mashed the speaker button and replayed the message, my heart filled to bursting with frantic hope.

"Mirror Lake! I know where that is!" Dakota exclaimed. "What are we waiting for? Let's go!"

"Wait." I stopped at the top of the stairs as my brain played Devil's advocate. "If they're at Mirror Lake, it means the Sons are too."

Was this Saint's big plan? To send half of our team south while lining up the other half like dominos just to watch us fall?

"We've been chasing them for years, Celia," Lauren reminded me. "If this is our only chance to get them, we have to take it, ready or not."

"We need to call him, Lauren," I urged.

No more walking into traps.

"The minute we do, they'll know. Celia, Grey got away. If we alert the others, then the Sons will be all over that cabin. Let the boys create the diversion for a change."

I clasped my fingers over the bridge of my nose while wracking my brain for another solution. There had to be another way to get my family without drawing the Son's attention.

"It is true?" Gloria made a sign of the cross over her chest from the foot of the stairs. "You are going to go to war now?"

Lauren winced before nodding slowly. "Now, before you call my dads and get them all—"

"We must pray to the saints for their protection. I bring my deck. Come, come."

"*Abuelita*, we don't really have time for that. The lake is at least three hours away. We need to leave now."

Gloria jerked her chin up, staring daggers at her granddaughter. "I am nothing but an old woman now. If you are going to the war, I insist we pray. Now, come."

I released an exasperated breath as she ushered us into the kitchen. Several pots were still bubbling away on the stove and our chances of getting to Jamie and Kate in time were dwindling with every second we wasted here. "I think we will have time for the last supper, but..."

Lauren pressed her fingers against her eyelids and leaned against me with a groan. "Please, just hurry. For the love of all that is good and holy, woman! We need to go!"

"You have a deck... of saints?" I asked when she held up the cards, deciding it was the most Catholic thing I'd ever heard.

"*Sí*, let's sit." Gloria shuffled the cards as if we were about to play a rousing game of Name That Saint. "Let's see—St. Erasmus? No, he is more for the cramps. Do you have a patron saint, Celia? You and Lauren are the leaders. We must keep you safe."

I thought back to when Mike was taken to the hospital, knowing I hadn't been praying to one specific saint as much as anyone who would listen. "I'm sorry. It's been quite a few years. Can we just skip to the praying part?"

"Who was it?" The older woman demanded, rifling through her cards.

I sighed. "St. Teresa of Avila—"

Her eyes narrowed. "The patron saint of headache sufferers? Mija, are you sure?"

Teresa was a wicked sinner, Celia. It was only by the grace of the Lord that she was redeemed and made whole. When you pray, pray to her. And remember where your lust will lead you if you stray.

I cleared my throat and moved my hand down to smooth my skirt, disappointed to find that I was still wearing pants. "My mother had very strong opinions about what sort of saint would work best for me, Gloria."

She snorted. "You mean, she found you too likable. Teresa was charming, but always convinced she was full of the sin. No, she is not your saint. I come back to you. LoLo, for you and Dakota, we pray to St. Gerard."

Lauren took the card from her hand. "A man?"

"*Sí*. And a virgin. When we must approach the gate of death, we ask St. Gerard to open the door of life for our little ones. I bring the medals to put into your pockets. He will keep you both safe. Will there be lightning?"

We shrugged, and I stole another glance at the clock on the wall, watching the minutes tick by.

"Okay, I will set St. Barbara aside for now. Now, let's see." She shuffled through, flipping cards over and discarding others with an accuracy I hadn't expected. "Celia, I think we should consider St. Gianna for you. She is the patron saint of mothers and unborn children. Read this."

"It says that she was willing to give her own life to save the life of her child." I looked up in surprise, and Gloria smiled encouragingly before gesturing to continue. "'*If you must decide between me and the child, do not hesitate: choose the child. I insist on it. Save the baby.*'"

The card shook in my trembling fingers. A woman who knew nothing about me had somehow just assigned the perfect saint to intercede on my behalf.

"And here it is!" she exclaimed. "St. Michael. We need him. He is technically an angel, but the defender in battle—"

"Archangel," I corrected automatically. "He's above the angels—"

It's, uh, it's Michael. Like the archangel. Do you remember what he does? He's a protector and a warrior.

I sucked in a ragged breath, a sudden coldness descending over my body as the pieces fell into place.

You look so beautiful...

Mama, I think you're the key to all of it.

Bear was right.

I'd let the Sons push and pull me from one suspicion to the next, convinced they were nothing more than savages with no apparent motive in mind.

But there was a goal.

Death is comin' for you...

Hadn't Hawk warned me? I'd seen it as an omen, but maybe it had been a clue. For years, we'd been strategically positioned like pawns on a chessboard. With Kate's abduction, the final exchange was made, pushing us into the endgame.

Only, instead of going into the final showdown blind, I now knew exactly what Saint wanted.

Me.

"Celia." Lauren touched my shoulder. "Are you okay?"

I pointed to the card in Gloria's hand. "Saint—I think Saint is Comedian."

CHAPTER FORTY-SIX

Celia: April 2017 (Age: 45)

"You're sure this is going to work?" Dakota whispered from the trees. The only light around came from the moon, but even with that, it was a struggle to see her.

"It'll work," Lou responded from another spot in the forest.

"They started this war, but we're gonna be the ones to end it," Lucy said from somewhere off to my left, clicking her magazine into place.

Once we knew who we were dealing with, a plan formed. Dakota had gone to work, camouflaging hers, Lou's, and Lucy's faces with makeup before scrounging up some of Mike's hunting gear from the barn.

The three of them were now damn near impossible to find.

"Nate and Garrett are in position," Carnage said softly from behind me, and I nodded.

The two brothers were in charge of securing the perimeter and checking the smaller buildings on the extensive property. We'd discovered Angel's old truck hidden under a pile of branches during our initial search, but nothing else.

The thick trees that kept us hidden also prevented us from seeing anything going on inside the cabin. We might not have seen them, but there wasn't a doubt in my mind that we were being watched.

Jimmy would have blown a gasket if he knew I was about to parley with the enemy. Hell, all of them would have if they knew I planned on exchanging myself for Jamie and Kate.

Molly checked her weapons before sliding them into the holster on her waist. "Did you see what Lauren loaned me?" she hissed, pointing to it. "Holds both of my Glocks back here. I feel like Lara Croft, ready to raid some tombs."

I shook my head. "Is Lauren in position?"

"Should be close," Molly said, pointing across the lake. "She said to keep an eye on the ridge just over there."

I glanced toward the spot, waiting to see the signal from her flashlight. As much as I'd wanted her by my side when we confronted Comedian, I wasn't willing to put her on the front lines.

It had to be me.

The full moon cast an almost eerie glow on the water, and I watched, lost in thoughts of my husband. I'd always seen him as the sun and myself as Icarus, but that hadn't been true in quite some time.

If Jamie was the sun, then I was the moon, each of us continually chasing the other. For years, we'd been destined to miss one another. But on the rare occasions we met, the power of our love blinded the world.

I'd lost faith in most things, but if there was an afterlife, I'd wait for him there. Maybe then we'd truly be at peace.

The ridge lit up in a small burst of light before going dark again. As we rechecked weapons, I paused, listening for anything that didn't belong.

The forest was filled with the songs of crickets and gentle chirps from a few late-night birds looking for a snack, but nothing unusual. I turned to Carnage and Molly. "Let's go."

We stayed low as we moved through the brush surrounding the cabin. It seemed as if every light in the house was on, something Jamie never would have done if he and Kate were hiding out.

"You think Angel left the lights on?" Molly whispered in my ear.

I shook my head. The old biker might have been a lot of things, but stupid wasn't one of them.

"Comedian knows we're coming. Stick to the plan. Once I distract him, get Jamie and Kate out." I thought of the truck. "Probably Angel, too."

"I got it, Celia," Carnage assured me. "I can carry them both if I need to." I didn't doubt it. I'd long considered him half-biker, half-mutant.

We moved around the cabin until we came to the front door. My stomach churned in a jittery mess of fight or flight, my body screaming for me to run away from the danger and not toward it.

"Remember, don't come back for me," I warned, before climbing the worn wooden steps. I prayed Comedian didn't have a sudden urge to fire through the door and ask questions later.

We had one shot to end this.

Hades might've been the god of death, but the queen of the underworld still controlled the spring, and she had no qualms about using the roots to bind her enemies.

Giving myself one last jerky nod, I turned the handle and reclaimed my throne.

My throat clogged with the coppery stench of blood. As much as I wanted to turn back, I forced my feet to follow the trail to where Angel lay on his back. I knelt and placed my hands over his wounds. Tremors wracked my fingers as I tried to staunch blood that had already begun to congeal.

He was gone.

I knew it, yet I couldn't let go. He was my friend, and he'd needed me. His blood soaked through my jeans, just like mine had done to him the morning he saved me.

"I'm sorry," I choked softly. "I'm sorry I couldn't save you like you saved me."

An ugly sound forced its way out of my throat, filling the air around me and alerting my enemies to my presence. I'd burned once before, on the floor of my bathroom.

This time, I didn't fight it. I let the flames lick along my skin, burning away the last bits of softness inside—leaving behind what remained of the naïve girl who still believed there could be good in the world. I scorched myself until nothing but ashes remained.

And then I kissed Angel's head and pushed myself back to my feet.

"Celia?"

I jerked my head up at the sound of his voice, letting the rage rise to the surface. For the first time, I saw the monster behind the man. The madness that I'd long mistaken for complacency shone brightly in his eyes.

Comedian's eyes moved down, and he paled. "Fuckin' Christ —is he?"

"Wouldn't you know?" I bit out, forgetting the role I was supposed to be playing. "You did this!"

He shook his head and held his hands up. "I got a call from the detective I hired to look into Mike's case—said he had information."

I balled my hands into fists before taking a deep breath. If I wanted this to work, I had to stay calm. I needed to play along.

My head bobbed up and down in a jerky nod. "So, you just drove out to the middle of nowhere?"

"I know what it looks like, but if—" He ran a hand over his face, suddenly looking as if he was on the verge of tears. "I thought if there was even the smallest chance it'd help me find the men who killed my boy, I had to take it. Swear to you, though. Didn't have shit to do with this."

"You were set up," I stated, keeping the accusation out of my voice.

Comedian nodded, his eyes narrowing. "Looks that fuckin' way, don't it? Who told you to come?"

"I—" I swallowed.

"Was it you? Were you behind it?" His face fell. "Tell me you didn't have nothin' to do with this, Celia."

My chest rose and fell rapidly. "Where's Jamie, Michael? Where's my daughter?"

I skittered away when he took a step toward me, painfully aware of how he seemed to tower over me. He hadn't reached for his gun because he didn't see me as a threat, but I knew the imminent danger I was in.

"Someone took one of the girls?" His scowl deepened the lines on his face. "That how they got you here?"

"You," I whispered. "You're Saint. I know."

I whirled away when he took another step, confusion clouding my head. My knee caught an end table, and I collided with a wall.

"Hey." Comedian reached for me. "Hey, take it easy, Celia."

I jerked back, only to find I'd boxed myself into a corner. "Don't touch me!"

He moved, faster than I would've thought possible, hooking an arm around my waist and drawing me up against his chest. "Ain't Saint, Celia. Goddammit, don't fuckin' fight me!"

A scream wrenched from my throat and I flailed helplessly as his grip tightened. His touch resurrected thoughts of that night. Instead of his hands, I felt Cobra's digging into my hips. Flashbacks of being crushed beneath the weight of a man's body stole the breath from my lungs, leaving me gasping for air.

I knew how men like him worked. Beads of sweat ran down my face when I realized there would be no quick death. He was going to finish what three men had started.

"Close your eyes," Comedian demanded.

I shook my head and jerked my chin up at him in defiance. If he wanted to take my life, he'd have to look me in the eye while he did it.

"Celia." He lowered his voice. "Close your eyes, and take a deep breath."

"No," I forced out through clenched teeth.

"Just tell me, who's in charge?" He relaxed his hold enough for me to move.

"What?" I sputtered. "Where did you—"

"Heard Pres say it to you, doll. Said it kept you calm. Ain't tryin' to hurt ya, 'cause I ain't that motherfucker Saint. I'm gonna let you go now."

I spun away as his arms came down before doubling over against a wave of nausea. My breaths came in short, panicked bursts, my body convinced it was reliving my nightmare. "Saint Michael," I whispered. "It's you."

The muscles in his body tensed. "You really believe that? You think that I'd side with the same men who killed my son?" He pinched the bridge of his nose. "Did you think I'd just forget what those cocksuckers did to you? Held you in my arms while you lost a baby, Celia. In what fuckin' world would I want to hurt you?"

"If it's not you—oh my god, I got it all wrong! I led everyone here, thinking I knew. We're going to die."

He shook his head. "Ain't no one dyin' on my watch. Now, who told you to come here?"

"Jamie. He, uh, he left a voicemail. Said he and Kate were hurt, but that they were going to try to make it to the cabin. But they're not here," I finished weakly.

We'd walked right into a trap.

I jumped at the sound of footsteps on the porch. Michael pulled his gun free and signaled for me to stay quiet. The heavy tread seemed magnified, as if the person wanted us to know they were coming.

He positioned himself between me and the door, willing to risk his life for the woman who'd been stupid enough to enter without a gun.

"Celia!" a voice yelled from just outside the front door. "Found Annie Oakley and her friends hanging out in the woods all alone. Why don't you let us in?"

Michael raised his gun, but I moved in front of him, shaking my head. Panic left me wanting to claw my throat open, but it wouldn't change a damn thing about our situation. "They have Lauren."

We couldn't run.

Not anymore.

The door fell open, and Lauren was forced down to her knees, the barrel of a gun buried in her red hair. Blood ran from her nose, and she tried focusing on me with the eye that wasn't swelling shut before mouthing: *I'm sorry.*

Behind her was the cop who'd been at Dakota's wedding. The same man who'd later turned up on the hospital's surveillance tapes.

"Very clever, having her hide up there. It wasn't easy to take her down. I had to put everything into it." He touched his jaw.

Michael growled, and I knew he would have put the cop down were it not for the army of bikers directly behind him.

Dakota came through next, seemingly uninjured, and eyes filled with murderous rage. "You chose the wrong side, Doucheface."

A biker dragged her into the middle of the room, kicking Angel's body toward the corner before binding Dakota's wrists behind her back. Her nostrils flared, and tears spilled over onto her cheeks, before she matter-of-factly stated, "You'll die for that."

I watched in horror as my friends were led in at gunpoint, the blood turning to ice in my veins. When the cop slammed the door behind Carnage, I looked at Lauren in confusion. Nate and Garrett weren't with them.

Right now, they were our only hope of making it out of this alive.

One by one, their hands were bound behind their backs before they were forced into a straight line against the wall.

This wasn't a parley.

It was an execution.

"Let them go." I raised my shaking hands. "I'll stay to meet with Saint. Just let them go. Please."

The cop shook his head with a laugh. "I'd be more willing to believe you if your funny guy here wasn't pointing a gun at me."

"Michael," I said softly, placing my hand on his arm. "Please. We have to keep them safe."

If you must decide between me and the child, do not hesitate: choose the child.

"Sons don't negotiate, Celia," he growled. "They ain't lettin' any of us leave."

"He's right, I'm afraid."

I knew that voice.

CHAPTER FORTY-SEVEN

Kate: April 2017 (Age: 27)

The nightmare began the same way it always did, with his hands roaming freely over a body that didn't belong to him. No matter how much I fought back, I couldn't free myself from his grasp.

The throbbing pain behind my eyes intensified, bringing with it an awareness that forced me back to consciousness. Instead of seeing the ceiling fan that hung over mine and Nate's bed, I found my nightmare had become a reality once again.

Jeremy's face hovered inches above mine, his grin widening when he realized I was awake. The fingers that had been digging into the flesh of my breasts moved up to stroke my cheek. "Hey, there she is."

Panic clogged my throat when I realized my hands were bound behind my back with rope, the fibers chafing the skin around my wrists the more I struggled.

I opened my mouth to scream, only to choke on the thick material mashed against my tongue. He'd gagged me. My breaths turned shallow, the air wheezing loudly through my nostrils as I took stock of my situation.

My clothes were gone, my ass resting on the dirt floor of what appeared to be a small shed. Shafts of moonlight broke through the wooden slats, but not enough for me to gauge where I was.

How had I ended up here?

The day's events replayed at high speed in my head.

Daddy.

Angel.

I inhaled again, fighting against tears to get my body the oxygen it craved. If I started crying, I'd suffocate.

Think, Kate.

"Deep breaths," Jeremy encouraged, letting his hands move back to cover my breasts. "You're safe now. I convinced Saint to let you go. We can go anywhere we want now."

I shook my head from side to side, squirming to get away from his touch.

"No?" He rocked back onto his heels. My heart sped up at the fury reflected in his eyes. "I saved your life, Kate."

Jeremy lowered his mouth to the gag, and I twisted my neck while tugging at the rope around my wrists. With a grin, he reached up and pinched my nostrils closed.

"Did you know I killed a club whore just like this? She reminded me of you with her dark hair and green eyes. It's what caught my attention. I even pretended she was you as I fucked her."

I bucked backward against the wall, trying to break his grip.

"Had her tied down to my bed and gagged. As she came, I held her just like this and watched her eyes widen when I didn't let up. Her body was so fucking tight around mine I couldn't have let go if I wanted to at that point."

Just as black spots moved where his face had been, he released me. I fell back, sucking in as much air as I could get while my limbs shook uncontrollably.

"What I didn't expect was how much of a fucking mess she'd make. Thought I was done for, but Saint helped me get rid of her body like nothing ever happened. I told Grey she'd packed up and left town. No one even cared."

His fingers rested against the base of my throat. "All I've ever done is help. Grey wanted me to babysit you. I did it. Needed me to break through a firewall. I hacked it. I jumped through every goddamn hoop, but no one was ever grateful. My road name was Jarvis, as if that's all I was... a fucking computer."

He tightened his grip. "All I wanted was a little gratitude... to feel like maybe I meant something."

Knowing there was only one way out, I nodded until his hand fell away and pushed my face up toward his. He ripped the gag free and gripped the hair at the base of my skull. The movement forced the front of my body up against his. I sucked in a deep breath before his lips roughly brushed against mine.

He took my mouth as surrender, as a white flag going up—when, in reality, it was a declaration of war.

"Suck me," he murmured before releasing my hair. He patted his belt buckle. "Show me how grateful you are to be alive."

I crouched in front of him, lowering my head as if I was his submissive. He lowered his head as he reached for the zipper. "See? Was that so—"

My skull exploded into a thousand slivers of jolting pain as I surged up onto my knees, thrusting the back of my head into his chin.

Jeremy fell back with a roar that pierced my ears—my momentum sending me sprawling onto his chest. My shoulder landed hard against his exposed throat, cutting off the sound. When he began struggling beneath me, I used my legs, fighting to keep him pinned down.

I was no match against him. His left fist knocked me back to the dirt, leaving me stunned and panting for my next breath.

"You little bitch," he growled, yanking me up by the hair. Instead of dealing another blow, he stuffed the material back into my mouth with such force that part of it ended up in my throat.

Jeremy flipped me over and thrust my face into the dirt as I choked around the gag, my eyes streaming with tears.

I heard his zipper coming down, felt him against my back. His fingers dug into the skin around my hips, and I sucked in a pained breath, filling my lungs with dust.

With the last of my strength, I tried lifting my head, but he brought a hand down against the back of my head, plugging my nostrils with dirt. I was being buried alive.

He was going to kill me just like he'd killed that girl.

CHAPTER FORTY-EIGHT

Celia: April 2017 (Age: 45)

"I wasn't sure you'd come. Thought you and your little girl gang would have gone south with the men." She pushed the back door closed and surveyed the small room with a grin.

"Betsy?" Michael asked, lowering his gun. "The fuck?"

"You know..." She tapped a finger against her chin with a vicious smirk. "I could have sworn you'd have killed him by now, Celia. Never mind. I'll do it myself."

I watched her hand as she flicked her wrist, not realizing it was a signal until I heard the loud pop. Michael stumbled back, and the cop lowered his gun like a well-trained dog.

Blood pumped from the wound on his chest, and he swiped his fingers through it before looking up at me in shock. "Celia?"

I stripped off my flannel jacket and dropped to my knees. "It's okay. You're going to be alright." I could feel his pulse through the material. He was losing too much blood.

"Let her take care of you now, Michael. Isn't this what you always wanted? Grey's girl, down on her knees in front of you?" Betsy taunted.

"You're Saint." It was no longer a question.

"How long did that take you, Celia? You really thought this

dumbass was behind it all?" She jerked her thumb to where her husband lay, bleeding out.

Michael reached up and gripped my hand, keeping pressure on the wound. "You?"

"You can't imagine the planning that went into this, and yet you were so quick to give credit to a man whose concerns revolve around his next high and his next fuck."

I watched warily as she circled the room, eyeing the people I loved as if they were outfits she was considering trying on.

"You got me here. Let them go. I'm the one you want."

"I'm the one you want," she mimicked. "Be honest. You thought Saint was in love with you. Look around you, Celia. This is how much I hate you. I've hated you since the day you turned up at a clubhouse you didn't belong in and just snatched up the Pres as if he were yours for the taking."

"You were married," I pushed out.

"Oh, yes. Married to a man who fell all over his dick once you came into the picture. Do you know how many times he slipped and called out your name while he was fucking me?"

"How is that my fault?" I watched the windows by the front door. If I kept her talking, Nate and Garrett could go for help. I just had to keep her talking. Michael grew paler by the second, his skin bathed in sweat.

"Nothing is ever your fault, is it?" Betsy shook her head. "Grey was mine. We had a child together—do you know how many club whores I killed just for looking at him? I gave them the good stuff, and the club turned a blind eye, convinced they'd just OD'ed. Kinda like your mom, Lauren."

Lauren mashed her lips together, looking as if she was going to burst through her skin. "Why?" she finally got out. "Because she was onto you?"

Betsy smirked again. "She knew too much."

"Is that why you sent the Sons after me too? Convinced she'd told me?" The dried blood on Lauren's face cracked.

"All I wanted was one man I didn't have to share with Celia. Was that too much to ask? I thought if I kept Mike around Grey enough, he'd see how good we could be together. Instead, Mike just fell under her spell, too. It took years to undo that, and then you..." She pointed at Lauren. "You took him from me, just when we were getting close again—"

"You were a shit mother, Betsy," I snapped, hoping to draw her anger away from the others. "You and I both know it. We tried to help Mikey for years, but you kept dragging him back—"

"To keep you away from Grey!" she screamed, as if it was the most logical explanation in the world. The bikers seemed unaffected by her outburst.

Dakota's shoulder dropped at the same time as Carnage leaned into her. To a casual observer, it looked as if they were just holding each other up, but from my crouched position near Michael, I realized they were working to free themselves.

There were four Sons and the cop.

Not the best odds, but not impossible.

As if sensing my thoughts, Betsy looked toward the front door. "My men have the cabin surrounded, Celia—"

"See, what I can't figure out is how you got a biker club to back you."

"No?" She pursed her lips. "You wouldn't, would you? I didn't build this overnight. When Mike killed that kid on the beach, Grey revealed he was alive. I realized I'd been grieving for a man who abandoned his own son... and me. Once I got over my initial anger, it gave me an idea. If he could fake his own death, then why couldn't I create someone more powerful to show him that we were meant to be together?"

"But how?" I pushed, watching as Dakota freed one hand. She discreetly shifted closer to Carnage and began working on his bindings.

"Easy. I tracked down the men who raped you." Her lip twitched in amusement at my gasp. "Told them I worked for a powerful man who wanted to take down Grey's organization from the inside out. They had the cash they took from you, but had already blown through most of it. I simply gave them more. Grey always told me I thought with my cunt, but look where it got me."

Carnage cracked his neck before letting the back of his head rest against the wall as if he was tired.

Two down.

Four to go.

"Money," I stated, as though I was bored. "Seems if it were that easy, then there'd be a woman running every club."

Betsy jerked her head from side to side. "Nobody could pull off what I have. Do you know how I came up with the name Saint? Fucking Michael lived for months on how he saved you—the things he said when you went into shock. I heard so much about St. Michael that I was ready to hang myself until I realized I could just as easily slip his head through the noose. The only people who know the real Saint are in this room. The rest of the world will see exactly what I wanted them to. For once, Michael will take the fall for my crimes, and I'll move on somewhere else, finally free of him."

"You've yet to answer my question, Betsy. How did a woman who dropped out of high school end up running the Sons?"

She bristled at the school comment, but quickly let it go in favor of talking about herself some more. "In the beginning, I was Saint's messenger, delivering money and plans. Never underestimate the power of a woman to lead a man around by his own dick. Can you imagine what Silent Phoenix could've been had Grey chosen me?"

"So, you worked in the shadows for years..."

"Until Saint was something like a god. The mice won't play when they don't know what the cat looks like or where she might be lurking. I sat back in the clubhouse and listened as Bear got shit-faced and spilled club business to anyone within earshot. Knowing how Grey liked to torture people came in really handy—"

"Fuck you, Betsy!" Molly snapped. "You fucking bitch."

"Jesus Christ." Betsy spun on her heel with a roll of her eyes. "You talk a lot of shit for a woman who's tied up. One more word out of you and I'll have Kyle give you the same treatment that the old ball and chain got. You know how easy it was to leave Grey's kutte in your house? I really expected you to take the bait and start second-guessing your old man, but you disappointed me, Molly."

"You put the flowers in Grey's casket and left behind Comedian's card, didn't you? You set him up to take the fall for not only Grey's death, but my mother's as well," Lauren snarled.

"I did," Betsy replied. "Nobody gave a fuck about me, but I knew everything there was to know about them. I used that to my advantage to take down the woman who stole my throne."

"What throne?" I asked, knowing full well she'd never been equipped to handle the problems that came with the crown.

Her eyes seemed wistful. "If you hadn't fucked it all up, my family would be together. My son would still be alive! You took everything from me, so I simply returned the favor. Tit for tat, Celia. Grey... your parents... Angel... Kate. How does it feel, knowing you've lost it all?"

I risked another glance toward the wall.

Five down.

One to go.

"Where is my family, Betsy? Where are Jamie and Kate?"

She pushed her lips out into a fake pout. "I sold Kate to the highest bidder. Apparently, he got a taste and wanted more."

Jeremy.

"Who's to say what he's going to do with her... see that's the difference between me and these other guys. I reward my men. Maybe if Grey had done the same, you never would have been raped. Now, I can't say the same for Kate." Her cheeks flushed with excitement.

"And where is Jamie?" I fought to keep my voice steady, balling my free hand into a fist.

"Right here." She gestured to one of the men, and he disappeared into a bedroom, only to reappear moments later, dragging something behind him.

"Not sure you're going to want him, though. Even broken, he still refused to turn on anyone within his own club. I led him right to the water's edge, but couldn't make him drink. So now, I'll watch him drown."

The man bound before me was unrecognizable as the man who'd left me on a dance floor just over four months ago. Old and new bruises covered almost every part of his emaciated body. His right arm hung at an awkward angle, as if it had been broken.

Jamie blinked up at Betsy before weakly turning his head toward me.

For so long, the events from the night I was attacked had held me in their grip. But as I faced another monster, I realized my weakness had never been the men who'd used their bodies to wound me—it was the broken man lying near my feet.

A man who was still wearing a wedding band on his left ring finger. The man I'd vowed to love until I took my last breath.

The day I take it off is the day you'll know I've given up on us.

I touched the diamond on my own hand and met his gaze, watching as the first signs of hope ignited in his blue eyes before tilting my face up to meet Betsy's.

"Your plan would have been perfect were it not for one little thing," I said as Molly worked to free Lauren's hands.

"And what's that?" Betsy sneered. "Because from where I'm standing, it looks like I'm winning."

"Mikey." The color drained from her face. "You got distracted from taking me down because you were looking for his killer—"

"And once I kill you, I'll keep looking."

I shook my head, my mouth lifting into a half-smile. "That'll pose a problem because I'm the only one who can tell you who killed him."

Six down.

Zero to go.

CHAPTER FORTY-NINE

Kate: April 2017 (Age: 27)

An explosion reverberated through the dirt like an earthquake, and then the weight on my back was gone. I tried to expel the gag, my body jerking violently against the hard earth.

"Katy!" a deep voice shouted as someone cut through the rope around my arms, pulling me up.

"She's choking! Fuck, she's choking!" It sounded almost like Nate's brother, Garrett.

I had to be dreaming.

The gag was yanked free, and I turned my head to vomit up a small amount of liquid before taking in as much oxygen as I could get. My limbs trembled from exhaustion, and I wanted nothing more than to sleep for days, but I let my rescuer slip his jacket around my shoulders.

I snuggled into the warmth and relaxed, only to be jolted back to reality amid the sounds of a struggle. The tears I'd been holding back fell freely when I opened my eyes and took in the scene in front of me. Nate had a knee on Jeremy's chest, and his hands locked around his throat in a death grip.

"Nate?" I rasped.

"I got you, babe," he growled, panting from the exertion. His eyes met mine and his jaw tightened. "Did he?"

He couldn't finish the question.

My dry tongue stuck to the roof of my mouth, making it hard to talk, but I shook my head. My head screamed in agony from the movement. Had they been just a few seconds later, he would have raped me.

Jeremy continued struggling, not putting up as much of a fight as he had with me. The crimson stain on his shirt might have had something to do with that.

"You shot him?"

"Well, technically, I did." Garrett stood in the doorway, holding the rifle across his body. "Took first place every year in the county's 4-H field-shooting contest. Just maimed him for Nate, really. What are brothers for, right?"

He rambled when he was nervous or worried, something that only ever seemed to occur in situations involving his son, Daniel.

"I'm... okay," I whispered before letting my head fall back against a solid chest.

"Shit's about to hit the fan in a big way," solid chest man said in a low voice. "Got a vehicle across the lake. Take it and get as far away from the cabin as possible."

Jeremy gave a final jerk under Nate's arms before going still. It was over. He would never hurt anyone again. I looked away and tipped my chin up to see who was holding me.

"But you're dead," I croaked.

He grinned. "Not yet, Counselor. Figure I still got a little fight in me. Now, let's get you some goddamn clothes."

CHAPTER FIFTY

Mike: April 2017 (Age: 34)

I stood frozen outside the storage building, trying to pinpoint what felt different. There was nothing. The woods had gone deathly quiet around me.

The cabin sat over a half-mile away, hidden behind a multitude of evergreens. Shaking my head, I took one last look at Jeremy's body before turning away.

"See you in Hell, motherfucker," I bit out.

"We've got a problem—"

I spun toward the sound, reaching for my gun before lowering my hands with a sigh. "Jimmy, sweetie, the fuck are you doing here? You're supposed to be leading the Sons down south so that Daddy can wrap up things here."

He stepped into the clearing. "And we were, pumpkin. But, Masterson had a wild hair and decided to track his wife's phone."

"And?" I asked, the back of my neck prickling in fear. "They're at the house, right?"

Jimmy straightened uncomfortably. "They're here, Mike... along with all the Sons. Wolverine spotted them along the ridge just over there. We get within ten feet of that cabin, and they're gonna light us up."

Please be wrong.

I rubbed at the stubble on my cheek. "Lauren? Celia?"

He shook his head. "I'm sorry. I swear to god, I told them to stay put. I've wracked my brain, trying to figure out why the fuck they'd come here."

"She led them here, which means I've got to work quickly. I called Bear—said he and his crew can be here in..." I checked my watch. "Twenty minutes. It's not a lot of fucking time. We've got to stick with the original plan."

"They'll shoot you the minute you're in range—"

"Not if they know who I am, they won't." I grinned. "Jimmy boy, let's end this without getting dead, okay?"

He clapped me on the shoulder and glanced at the storage building with a grin. "Let's see if Torch can't create a bit of diversion for you."

Within minutes, Torch had all three buildings lit up like the goddamn Fourth of July. I wound my way through the woods to the cabin, pausing in the shadows as the Sons raced toward the inferno.

"What are you gonna do, Sullivan?" I asked myself. "Stroll up to the front door like you own the joint? Why yes, yes I am."

The two bikers on the porch scrambled to their feet as I came into view. I had a bullet in each of them before they'd even drawn their weapons.

"You step one foot onto this porch, and I'll kill everyone in here," my mother called through the door.

I'd spent weeks tracking her movements, wanting to believe it was someone else. I hadn't wanted to believe that the woman who'd baked pies and run charity auctions at church could be the mastermind behind it all. When she left the state, I forced myself to follow, knowing she was going to lead me right to my father.

Only, she hadn't.

"Is that any way to treat the prodigal son?"

The front door opened immediately, and Betsy swayed on her feet, staring at me like she was looking at a ghost. "You—you died!"

I climbed the steps, keeping my gun down by my side. "See, we in the biz call that misdirection." I waved my fingers mystically. "Good to see you, Ma. Care to chat inside? Okay, cool."

She continued staring out onto the porch as I brushed past her, scanning the faces along the wall until I found Lauren's. The others looked relatively unscathed, but my girl had put up a fight. "Darlin', thought we had an agreement. No more running off to war without my permission."

Her lips curved up into a small smile. "Thought I could handle it, Tex."

"Wanna tell me who battered your pretty little face?" I kept the grin on my own while staring down the men in the room. "Anybody? Anybody here wanna admit to laying a finger on my pregnant wife?"

"Kyle," Lauren stated. "Asshole sucker punched me."

I shoved the gun back into the holster and stormed toward the miniature cop. "Barton?"

"It was—I was just—"

I drove my fist into the side of his head, laying him out on his back. Unconscious. "That," I panted. "That's a motherfucking haymaker. One and done. Comedian taught me that—"

"Junior?" a broken voice cried out.

I'd been so focused on getting to Lauren that I hadn't even looked to the other side of the room. Celia knelt beside Comedian, holding a blood-soaked piece of clothing to his chest. His head slumped forward, and his eyes fell shut as his body fought to conserve what little strength it had left.

The man who'd been my hero my entire life lay nearby, nothing more than a walking skeleton. I'd wanted to believe Saint was a man because it seemed impossible that a woman could be that sadistic.

When my eyes landed on the body in the corner, I brought my split knuckles up to my mouth in a growl.

Angel.

"Now, Mike, I did this for us," Betsy began. "I thought you were dead—"

"Everything you saw, we wanted you to see." I forced a bitter laugh. "You had eyes everywhere. Knew our next move before we did, but I figured out a way to beat you at your own goddamn game. So, if you're the saint, then I guess that makes me the motherfucking savior."

The timing couldn't have been more perfect. The wooden floor vibrated beneath our feet as the air outside filled with the thunderous sound of motorcycles.

Something like confusion crossed Betsy's face before she snapped, "What'd you do, Mike?"

"Brought a few friends to even the odds, Betsy. You're Saint, don't you wanna see a good fight? What the fuck am I saying? Of course you do. It's what you've kept us doing for years."

Dakota began squirming on the floor. "Um, excuse me. I really need to pee! This baby is on my bladder."

The biker nearby looked at my mother in question. "What do I do?"

"What do you do? You take her to the bathroom, genius. She's a pregnant woman. What the fuck is she gonna do? Just stay in there and make sure she doesn't try to run." Betsy threw up her hands before turning back to me. "Mike, I want you to come with me. We'll leave all of this behind and start a new life together. Just you and me."

"And my family?"

"I'm your family. Me! These people are nothing!" Her voice rose, drowning out the thump of a body hitting the floor in the bathroom. She continued rambling, but I couldn't hear a word she said as I made my way toward the bathroom.

Just as I reached for the door handle, it opened beneath my hand, and Dakota stepped out, straightening her hair. The biker who'd escorted her lay on the floor, unmoving.

"Jiu-jitsu. I'll teach you someday."

"Fine," I whispered. "Need you to help me get everyone out of here. Zane and the others are nearby, but it's gonna get ugly here real quick. Stay hidden."

She nodded, and I walked back to the main living area, calling over my shoulder. "Jesus Christ, how long can one woman pee?"

Carnage jerked his head. "Now."

Molly pulled a gun from behind her back and fired, hitting one biker in the chest. Carnage fired on the other, hitting him in the head and sending him to the floor. The first one got two shots off before collapsing, striking Molly in the chest and abdomen.

"No!" Lauren shouted, covering Molly's body with hers.

I didn't even think about the ramifications before sending two rounds into the guy's forehead. For good measure, I walked over to Kyle's unconscious form and unloaded the rest of my mag into his skull. "You cocksucking pieces of shit," I growled.

Gunfire erupted outside, echoing off the mountains and turning the woods into a war zone. Sun Tzu believed it was crucial to end a battle strongly. We'd chosen to follow his principle of shock and awe by striking on the military that had backed my mother.

We were cutting the head off the snake.

Without an army, there was no Saint.

"Mike, put the gun down. Let's talk." Betsy had Celia's hair gripped in her fist and the barrel of a gun pressed to her temple. With the way she positioned her, Celia had become a human shield.

"Carnage," I said calmly, keeping my eyes on my mother. "Get them out of here and kill the one in the bathroom before he wakes up."

"You got it, boss."

"Nobody move or I'll do it. I will end her."

Grey struggled to free himself, thrashing wildly against his restraints. "Let her go, Betsy. It's me you want."

She looked down at him as if he were something stuck to the bottom of her shoe. "Not anymore."

"Take the shot, Mikey," Celia demanded, stoically resigning herself to her fate.

I shook my head. "I'll hit you."

"Then hit me," she ground out. "Just end it."

"He won't," Betsy gloated. "I'm his mother. He couldn't even put down Michael, and I gave him every opportunity to do that. What makes you think—"

I'd always thought it was bullshit when people talked about time slowing down, but as Bear kicked in the front door and bikers swarmed the cabin, it felt like we were all moving underwater.

"Comedian," Grey rasped. "Punchline."

My old man suddenly grinned, his teeth stained with blood. His hand moved down to his boot, retrieving the .38 Special he used as a backup weapon. "Betsy, why'd God give men dicks?"

When she turned around to face him, he took the shot, sending her and Celia tumbling to the floor. Celia immediately rolled away, hands up in defense, but my mother was gone.

"Bet you're wantin' the punchline," he panted, his breaths growing farther apart. "It's so we'd have at least one way of shuttin' a woman up."

I lowered my gun and went to him, peeling the shirt away from his chest. It was a miracle he was still conscious with as much blood as he'd lost. "We're gonna get you some help—"

He jerked his chin to look up at me. "It's okay, Junior. The monsters—the monsters are all gone now." He exhaled loudly, and then his body went limp.

I stared down at the bodies of the people who'd raised me, both of them monsters in their own way. My mother had hidden her darkness well, letting everyone around her take the blame.

My old man had come into the world a villain, but he had died a hero.

"Molly!" Bear roared from across the room, dropping to his knees beside her limp body. He dragged her into his arms and kissed her forehead. "It's okay, baby. We're gonna get you help—"

She reached up and stroked his beard, her eyes closed as if she was slipping away. "I didn't know Little Ricky was yours. I wanted it to be true so badly, but I swear to God I didn't know. Please forgive me. You have to—"

"There's nothin' to forgive. I just need you to stay with me. I can't do it without you, baby."

I frowned when her eyes suddenly popped open and her lips curved up into a smile. "Good. Because I need to be honest with you, bullet-proof vests don't absorb the shock like I imagined. Feels like I got hit with a sledgehammer," she groaned.

"Wait. You're wearing a fuckin' vest? So all that talk of me needin' to forgive you—"

"I thought now was as good a time as any to get back in your good graces."

"Jesus Christ, woman," he grumbled. "I oughta take you over my knee."

"Please do," she purred.

I turned away with a grimace, trying to get the mental image of them fucking out of my head. I'd seen enough old people going at it to last me a lifetime.

Those were scars that didn't fade.

"Jesus fucking Christ!" Jimmy announced as he stepped over broken glass and blood. "Looks like you pulled it off, Sullivan."

I watched as Grey was carried out by a team of bikers. He'd known I couldn't take the shot and had saved us all with one word to Comedian.

He still owed me a conversation.

We'd put it off for too long.

We'd kept silent out of fear of Comedian, never once seeing that Betsy had been setting him up for years. From now on, there would be no more secrets between us.

I gestured toward Molly. "Hey, Jimmy, someone else here backs up my claim that, even with a vest on, a fucking 9mm feels like taking a bat to the chest."

"Hmm... I'll take that into consideration the next time I want to shoot you."

"Sweetie, not sure if you remember or not, but we'd agreed on two shots. Do you remember how many times you shot me? Five. You shot me five fucking times!"

He shrugged with a relaxed smile. "Five seemed more believable."

"I'll show you more believable," I growled, just as Lauren stepped in between us.

With her palms planted firmly on my chest, she led me away from the giraffe. "Easy there, Tex."

I dropped my hands to her belly; the tension leaving my body instantly. "The fuck were you thinking, Red? You were supposed to let me know of any changes in the plans." I mashed my lips to her forehead. "How are you? Fuck! Your nose and your eye—Jesus! You just—my girls, are they okay?"

My shoulders shook uncontrollably, and I clenched my jaw, fighting against the strange sound I seemed to be making. I managed a ragged breath before the floodgates opened, and I began bawling like a scared kid. "Thought I was gonna lose you—"

"Shhhh..." She let her forehead rest against my chin. "We're okay, Mike. It's over. You saved us. We're safe now."

Safe.

When was the last time I'd felt that?

I wrapped my arms around the redhead who'd saved me on a beach in Galveston, throwing out a lifeline and towing me to shore. She'd put my feet on solid ground and challenged me to be a better man than I was the day before.

Lauren was my Charlotte, my front porch swing partner and the woman who was going to be holding my hand when I left this world.

I'd sacrificed myself once before. If anyone stood against my family, I wouldn't hesitate to become their savior again, exchanging my life for theirs.

Until then, I was going to spend every day showing her and my daughters just how much they meant to me. I would be their protector and their rock.

CHAPTER FIFTY-ONE

Grey: April 2017 (Age 53)

My eyes opened to the face of an angel with green eyes. She smoothed the dirty and damp hair off my forehead and kissed my brow before whispering, "You saved me."

"No, princess. You saved me." I licked my cracked lips and shook my head, unable to put into words the strength I'd drawn just by seeing that she was still wearing her ring. "Kept me fightin', even when I wanted to give up."

"You can rest now," she whispered. "It's okay."

Maybe by sending one monster to hell, I'd earned myself a few extra minutes with my family in purgatory before the Reaper showed up to collect.

I could have slipped into oblivion and forced Mikey to pull the trigger, or demanded that Bear take Betsy to one of our facilities to be put through the same hell I had.

In the end, I tried to give my family what we'd chased for seventeen years.

Closure.

As much as I wanted to watch her die over and over again for the things she'd put my family through, it wouldn't change the past. No kill in the world could set things right.

The memories of the things we'd lost were like scars. They might fade over time, but they'd never truly go away. The war might've been over out here, but we'd forever be sifting through the rubble in our heads.

They loaded me into the backseat of someone's truck, and I reached for Celia's hand, needing to free her like she'd freed me. "Need you to do somethin' for me."

She followed me in and settled against my side with a solemn nod. "Whatever you need."

I lifted my left arm, ignoring the stiffness in my joints as I let it rest against the back of her neck. "Doesn't have to be now, but when you're ready, I want you to know that I'm here."

Her eyebrows moved together. "What are you saying?"

I caressed the nape of her neck, touching her skin with my wedding band as if it had healing properties. "I'm sayin' that it's okay to cry."

Moving on was a foreign concept for both of us. We'd always been running, from one thing to the next—never had time to come to terms with the past.

Her eyes filled, and the tears spilled over onto her cheeks as she let go. I sat in the pain with her as she grieved the seventeen-year-old girl who'd envisioned a fairy tale and been given a horror story.

I held her when she broke apart over the loss of her parents and the people she'd needed them to be.

My thumb stroked her heated skin, mourning the family we never became, and all the years we spent apart.

And when it seemed that neither one of us had anything left, we tore ourselves open and grieved the loss of the biker who'd saved our lives on more than one occasion. He'd kept us moving forward when we were on our knees, ready to quit.

A man who had been not only our closest friend, but family.

Angel.

I kept her tucked against my body until her sobs turned to sniffles before giving her a reset the only way I knew how. "Who's in charge right now?"

"We are," she whispered, tucking her head into the crook of my neck.

As we drove around the lake, I noticed that the water was calm. The light reflected so perfectly off the water that it appeared as if there were two moons. I was flooded with a sense of peace, as if the calm waters were a sign of things to come.

Maybe after years of fighting, we could drift toward the shore and rebuild.

———

"You even think about gettin' that spoon anywhere near my mouth, and we're gonna have problems," I growled.

"We're just trying to get your strength up," the male nurse protested.

I eyed the pathetic spoonful of lime green gelatin. "That shit ain't gonna do a goddamn thing for me. Bring some meat and potatoes in here, and then we'll talk."

He scurried out of the room, and I let my head rest against the pillow again. At the sound of a throat clearing, I cracked one eye open to find Celia glaring down at me.

"Was that necessary?"

"Fuck, princess," I grumbled. "I just want some real food. Tired of being hooked up to all this shit."

"You went without real food for a long time, Jamie. You've got to build up to that stuff."

There was a tap at the door, and then Mikey poked his head in. "Is the coast clear?"

"Darlin, why don't you go see if he'll bring that green shit back. Like to give it another go."

"Jamie Quinn," she said sharply, and I grinned, suddenly struck stupid by her beauty. After almost thirty years, she still had me hooked on her like a drug. "What? Why are you smiling?"

"Goddamn, am I in love with you—"

"Is this another one of your ploys to get me out of the room?"

I shook my head, drinking in the sight of her, as if it'd be my last chance to. "No, just can't believe you're still here and that I'm the lucky bastard who gets to call you mine."

Her cheeks turned red before she leaned down to press her mouth to mine with a soft exhale. It was pure torture, a silent reminder of everything I couldn't have as long as I remained in this goddamn bed.

She broke away with a pant and winked before calling out, "Come on in, Mikey."

To the kid's credit, he tried keeping the brown paper bag concealed when he strolled in. Unfortunately, Celia had trained herself to identify outside food from a mile away. "Mikey?"

He tucked the bag into his side. "These are just clothes I brought from the house. Nothing to see here."

"Mmm-hmmm..." Celia clicked her tongue against her teeth and went off in search of the nurse.

After double-checking to ensure she was gone, he handed over the bag. "Got a cheeseburger and tater tots—I know you wanted the onion rings, but that's a dead giveaway. I think there are even some pepper-mints down in there for after you finish."

"You bring your old man a pack of smokes?" I asked.

"While you're hooked up to an oxygen tank? No, thank you. I'd prefer we didn't blow up a goddamn hospital." He pulled up a chair and dropped onto it with a sigh. "So, how are you... really?"

I looked down at the various tubes connected to my body. My right arm was back in a sling and, as I'd refused the good stuff they kept pushing on me, I was relying on ibuprofen to deal with the pain.

"I, uh, I've been better. But the docs seem hopeful that I'll regain mobility in my right arm. May never get it all back, but it's better than bein' dead."

I took a deep breath, repeating the same words I'd been saying for the past three days. "Thought you were gone, kid. Worst fuckin' feelin' of my life."

Mikey's mouth went flat. "Wasn't my first choice, believe it or not. Just seemed like the Sons were going to out think us on everything."

Between Mike, Jimmy, Celia, and Lauren, they'd executed a plan so perfect that it left me in awe. Jimmy even had some type of special effects vest that sprayed blood when he was hit. The rest was just a matter of paying off the right people, and then my son was free to move where he needed without arousing suspicion.

He winced and rubbed his chest. "Still not sure that Dakota's forgiven me for tricking her. Your girl's got a mean right hook."

"According to Bear, she's got a strong kick, too." I mashed the remote on the bed, forcing myself up. "They're still okay? Doctors have checked them over?"

It didn't matter that Celia had assured that everyone was healthy. I'd believe it when I could lay eyes on them for myself. In my mother hen state, I'd even forced Bear to bring Molly in so that she could show off the massive bruises left behind on her torso.

Mikey nodded. "Lauren and I saw the OB this morning. Girls are growing strong—"

"Twin girls," I murmured, still in shock over the news.

"Yeah, Pops. Twin girls. You're gonna have your hands full."

I laughed before grimacing at the pull in my shoulder. "I guess so."

"Dakota's still doing well. Zane said she's been taking it easy, but seems content as long as Little Ricky stops by with ice cream."

I swallowed. "Katy?"

"Hey," Mikey said, placing his hand over mine. "We've been over this. Katy's gonna be just fine. Doctor put her on bed rest, so she doesn't even need the crutches for her broken foot." At my expression, he added, "The baby's good. You just need to worry about resting. I got this. I know how to keep these girls in line."

"Got another request." I slipped the wadded up paper out from under the covers and placed it in his hand. "Need you to see if you can help me find someone. Got a little unfinished business."

He looked it over before raising an eyebrow. "Cobra? You mean he didn't die before this all started?"

I shook my head and settled against the pillow. "Soon as I'm out of here, I'm gonna go lookin' for him."

"One step at a time."

I'd failed him in so many ways as a father. It was why I'd encouraged Comedian to take the shot that night. I knew what it was like to send a parent to the Reaper. That burden was never meant to be on his shoulders.

"What do we do now?" I finally asked, pulling myself out of my head.

He shrugged. "I don't know. I thought about maybe going back to school—"

"About that," Jimmy began, before closing the door behind him. "Got some news I thought you both might like to hear. Police department's undergoing a bit of a transition. Turns out there was some corruption and falsifying of records. Effective immediately, Detective Michael Sullivan-Quinn has been reinstated, and his record with the department wiped clean."

Mikey's jaw dropped. "You got me my job back? I'm a cop again? Jesus fuck, Jimmy. If I didn't hate you for shooting me five times, I might consider giving you a hug."

"Couldn't resist throwing in the number, could you?" Jimmy grinned and threw an arm around him. "Love you too, pumpkin. As for you..." He shifted his focus to me. "As far as the world is concerned, James Quinn has been deceased since October 18, 1996. The patient residing in room 4821 is none other than James Grey, a family man without so much as a speeding ticket to his name. So where you two go from here is completely up to you."

"What do you think, Pops?"

"You keep callin' me that," I said carefully, trying not to let my heart read too much into it. I'd been Grey his entire life, but ever since the night he saved us all, he'd taken to calling me Pops.

He grinned. "Thought Daddy made it seem like we had a different sort of relationship, but if you're into that, just remember that I'm a top. Fuck, I'm kidding. You're my old man. What do you want me to call you?"

I mashed my lips together, my nostrils flaring wide as I held back my tears. "Pops is good," I choked out.

"Alright, Pops, what's it gonna be? Gonna go back to running the club?"

Jimmy cleared his throat. "You should know that they've reinstated the biker syndicate, thanks to Bear. With the Sons wiped out, it looks to hold up, too. Well, you probably already knew that, though."

"What do you mean?" Mikey and I asked at the same time.

"At the cabin, did you really think that all of those men were Silent Phoenix?"

I shrugged. Honestly, most of that night was a blur.

"From the time you were shot to the night at the cabin, Bear was building an army with every club he could find. As the Sons hadn't made any friends, it wasn't hard to convince the other clubs to fight. Over one hundred chapters rode in that night—"

"But if anyone asks, I was still the hero, right?" Mikey asked with a mock frown.

"Christ, Mike," Jimmy muttered. "Yes, you're still the one who discovered who Saint was. If it weren't for you following her to the cabin, we'd still be hunting."

"Oh, Jimmy." Mikey fanned his face with a smug grin. "Gonna make me blush."

"You got Bear on board when Celia couldn't—"

"Well, I didn't fire a gun at him or hold a knife to his throat, so there's that," Mikey reminded him.

"What?" I threw the covers off my legs, fighting to get out of bed. "Goddamn, my girl's got balls."

Jimmy shook his head. "I was convinced Bear was a lost cause, but he really came through for you, Grey. So, what'll it be?"

Celia pushed the hospital room door open and held up two cups of lime green gelatin with a grin. "I got you two." Her smile faded as she watched our faces. "What? What happened?"

Jimmy spoke up. "I just gave Grey his new identity and was asking what his plans are. If he's going back to the club or something else."

"Mikey," I said, my voice suddenly hoarse. "Did you get it?"

"Yeah, Pops. I got it." He placed the black velvet box in my hand, and Celia's eyes widened.

"What are you—" Her hands came up over her mouth when I popped it open to reveal a diamond ring.

"Been carryin' this around for fifteen years, waitin' on the perfect moment. But darlin', there ain't ever gonna be a perfect moment." I gripped the side rail and tried swinging my legs over the side, only to be met with Mikey's hand, pushing me back down.

"The fuck are you doing, Pops? Look at that damn yellow bracelet on your wrist. It says 'fall risk.' Means your ass has gotta stay in bed."

"Already proposed to her once before in a bed. Wanted to do it right and get down on one knee this time," I grumbled.

He grinned and shook his head. "Unless you're sitting on my lap, you're shit out of luck."

Reluctantly, I let go of the railing and let him guide me back onto the bed, the wind completely knocked out of my sails. I'd wanted it to be perfect—she deserved that and so much more.

I finally looked up at Celia, expecting to see an amused smirk or narrowed eyed. Instead, her expression took my breath away and left me clenching my jaw to stay in control. She was looking at me as if she truly saw me—not the invalid lying helplessly in a hospital bed, or the biker club Pres.

Just me.

My entire life, I'd wanted to be loved in a way that the world could never taint. Celia Quinn had come after me, over and over again, when I didn't deserve it.

She could have given up on me, but hadn't. She did it because she'd known that same hunger, this desire to be seen for what she was and loved, anyway.

Her monsters called to mine, and I would fucking love her until I took my last breath.

"Made you a promise, princess. Said one day I'd take you to the place you dreamed about." I tugged the old diamond ring off her finger, a ring I'd given to satisfy an addiction.

Only, she was so much more than that.

She was my salvation.

"What do you say, wanna get married again on the beach?"

A slow smile spread across her face as I slipped the new ring over her knuckle. "I say yes." A curtain of dark hair fell over my face as she brought her mouth down over mine.

"You hear that, Jimmy? My girl said yes. So, if it's all the same to you, I think I'd like to hand over the club to Bear and give this civilian life a try."

I was going to be a nobody.

EPILOGUE

Grey: Summer 2020 (Age: 56)

"Now, this minnow is our bait, see?" I threaded the hook through the tail of the small fish. It instantly began squirming, much to the delight of Hazel, who started screaming and clapping her hands.

Her twin sister, Olivia, wasn't as impressed and took a step back, catching a bucket with the heel of her shoe. She stumbled over it before going down onto the dock on her ass with a loud cry.

"Darlin', he ain't gonna hurt you. Come here and see." She stuck her chubby little hand out and let me pull her up into my lap. "Look, he wants to go for a little swim. You wanna put him in the water?"

Olivia nodded and rubbed the tears from her eyes. "Him okay?"

I looked down at the minnow, fighting to free itself. "Uh, sure, darlin'. He's just ready to swim, so let's drop your line in, and you sit right here."

"Mine." Hazel made a grab for the fishing pole, nearly going off the dock in the process.

"Whoa there!" I caught her in my arms and moved her away from her sister. "Not yet, Hazel. Pops is gonna get yours going next. Where's Thor?"

I turned just in time to see a minnow disappear into his mouth.

Hazel began clapping again as the tail slapped against her cousin's lips angrily.

"Jesus fu—let's not eat the bait, okay, buddy?" I cupped my hand under his chin, and he spit the fish out with a wide grin.

"Looks like you got your hands full here," Wolverine noted a little too smugly as he walked onto the dock. "Need some help?"

"Like wranglin' cats," I muttered as I baited Hazel's pole and got her situated a few feet from Olivia.

"Alright, Thor—Thor?" I scanned the deck and then the water for his bright orange life vest.

"I twicked you, Pops!" he roared, popping out from under the five-gallon bucket.

I sighed. "You got me, buddy. You ready to fish now?"

"I eat da fish with my mouf like dis!" He began exaggeratedly moving his jaw up and down. "I no need da pole!"

"Okay, buddy. Let's try the pole to start and then we'll toss you in if that don't work." I baited his hook and settled him next to his cousins before falling into the folding chair next to Wolverine's.

"Their hair looks like fire under the sun, don't it?" Wolverine pointed to the twins. "You think that's Karma? Mikey gettin' twin girls with red hair like their mama?"

"And they have their daddy wrapped around their little fingers."

"Always pictured Mikey ending up with three women, just maybe not in this capacity," Wolverine deadpanned.

I chuckled, watching as Hazel reached over and patted Olivia's knee.

"Seestew, yook!" She pointed to her pole. "We awe fishing!"

Olivia held her finger to her lips with a smile, loudly whispering, "We awe supposed to be quiet!"

I'd told them that the fish liked things nice and calm, something it seemed they'd promptly ignored. Thor sat holding his pole and making angry faces at the water, even going as far as clenching his teeth and shaking.

"What the hell's he doin'?"

"Catchin' fish, old man. Ain't you aware of the technique? You mind keepin' an eye on them for a minute? I'm gonna check on my other little one."

He shook his head and lit up a cigarette. "Last I checked, she was sittin' in the orchard. You might wanna grab some sunscreen while you're by the house."

I looked back at the kids. "I coated them in sunscreen a half-hour ago."

"Not them. You. Lookin' a little crispy, Grey."

"I'll just throw a shirt on. It'll be fine." I waved him off and headed for the orchard. When I found her, I shook my head. She'd gotten into the markers again and was happily drawing on her arms.

"Hey, there's my girl," I said softly, trying not to startle her.

She lifted her head and pushed the jet black hair off her face before her green eyes widened. "Pops," she said solemnly, thinking she was in trouble.

And she was—just not with me.

Her mama could handle that.

"Whatcha doin', Charlie?" Just saying her name left me with a lump in my throat. When Kate told us she and Nate had decided to name their baby after Angel, I'd nodded and smiled before falling apart like Thor when he missed his nap.

I brought his body back here, to the place he'd bought for my ma. When we finally worked up the courage to clean out his house, I found a navy blue urn with butterflies on the side. For years, I'd wondered where they'd buried her. It turned out Angel had never really been able to let go.

He'd kept her on the nightstand next to the bed, along with a rare picture of the two of them I'd completely forgotten I'd taken. It only clicked when I studied the camera angle and realized the photographer was a lot shorter than the two of them.

I kept the old photograph, but buried him with her in his arms. Just like he would have wanted. They were laid to rest next to a Texas Redbud tree where I could visit anytime I liked.

"Pops," Charlie breathed. "Twyin' decowate my awms." She traced her fingers across the ink on my skin with her little fingers. "Yike you."

"Is that right, little miss? Who else has decorated arms?"

Charlie mashed her little teeth together with a grin that crinkled her nose. "Daddy!"

I tapped the dimple on her cheek with my index finger. "Yep, and who else?"

She bounced her legs up and down in excitement. "Unca Mike!"

"And?" I could have sat out in the orchard with her all day. She reminded me so much of Kate at that age. I'd never get the time back that I lost with her, but I was going to soak up every second with my grand-babies to make up for it.

"Unca Zane!" She threw her hands in the air before happily adding, "Mommy!"

"Wait, your mama has a tattoo?"

Her eyes sparkled with amusement that she knew something I didn't. "On hew boob!"

Holy shit.

She pointed to her ribcage. "Wight heew."

"Is that right?" I asked. "What does it say?"

Charlie shrugged and held her arm out to me. "Decowate... pwease!"

"Got somethin' else in mind. Wanna get your helmet and go for a ride with Pops?"

She dropped the markers and jumped up in excitement. "I get it. Wait."

I let her get about ten feet from the house before scooping her up and jogging the rest of the way while she shrieked like a banshee in my arms. Mike looked up at the sound before going back to the smoker with a grin when he realized it wasn't one of his kids.

"Down!" she demanded. "Cece, save me!"

Celia stood on the porch with her hands on her hips. "Save you? Is mean old Pops getting you?"

"Old?" I cocked my head to the side and set Charlie down before stalking toward Celia. "Did you just call me old, princess?"

"Wun, Cece!" Charlie warned, before taking off through the paddling pool, kicking water over the side.

"I got her." Dakota jumped up from the picnic table and took off after her niece with a growl.

A hint of a smile played on Celia's lips as she watched Charlie tear across the yard like an excited puppy. "I'm not scared of him!" she called before walking inside.

As if she was concerned that I wasn't going to follow, she looked over her shoulder with an arched eyebrow and licked along her top lip. "If I run like that, would you chase me?"

Every part of me hardened at the thought of chasing her through the orchard. "Guess it depends on what you're wearin'..."

She lifted her chin. "Nothing."

We were expecting a crowd within hours, but all I could think about was getting inside my wife. Nothing else mattered at the moment. Charlie would just have to wait for her ride.

I looked up at the clock on the wall. "What time's everyone gettin' here, princess? Need to fuck you. Hard."

Her eyes flared with lust, and she popped the top button on her sundress with a wicked grin. "Do you need to take something first?"

"Goddammit. Bedroom. Now." I swatted her ass as she slipped around me and down the hall. We both froze at the sound of a groan coming from the bathroom.

"You think someone's sick?" Celia whispered with a frown.

I adjusted myself through my jeans and tapped lightly on the door, listening to the faint sound of running water. "Everything okay?"

When there was no answer, I turned the handle and immediately wished that I hadn't. My daughter sat on the counter with her legs thrown over Nate's shoulders, the back of her head resting against the mirror.

The tattoo I'd been so curious about was Charlie's name woven in script. I knew because Kate wasn't wearing a goddamn thing.

"Fuck," I cursed, slamming the door behind me.

"Daddy!" Kate shrieked, sounding just like her daughter. "What the hell are you doing?"

"Thought you were sick, sweetheart. Obviously, I was wrong. Christ, was I wrong." I fell back against the wall with a groan before looking over to where Celia was hunched over, shaking with laughter. "The fuck are you laughin' at? They're fuckin' in our bathroom!"

"Because we thought we had a few minutes to ourselves," Kate grumbled from the other side of the door. "Kinda hard to find time alone with a toddler."

"Your father and I were just going outside to check on the kids. I assume we'll be gone for twenty... maybe even thirty minutes."

I frowned and jerked my thumb toward the bedroom. "I thought we were gonna—"

"Later." She pressed a kiss to the corner of my mouth and walked toward the front door, leaving me with a raging case of blue balls.

"The world's in a sorry state when a man can't fuck his wife in his own house," I grumbled as I followed her outside.

Mikey waved me over to the smoker when I stepped out onto the porch. "Settle this for me, Pops. Hurricanes would be nothing without Killian Reed."

I looked to Zane for a translation. "The baseball team out of Houston. He thinks that the only reason they've done as well as they have is because of Reed; not the organization as a whole. It's bullshit. You're just pissed that your Oilers are in a slump."

I nodded dumbly. "Sure. Okay, well, I'm just gonna find Charlie and take her for a—"

"Wait a second. Can you watch this for me, Big Guy?" He pointed toward the smoker.

Zane rolled his eyes. "Because you've been so much help. Don't worry, sweetie, I'll make sure we have dinner."

"That's why I love you, pumpkin," Mike crowed, holding his middle finger in the air. He ran a hand through his short hair before asking, "You got a minute to talk? I got something I wanna show you."

I followed him out to the barn, surprised to see that Olivia was still sitting on the dock with Wolverine, fishing pole in the water. The other two had run back up to the house to splash in the pool.

"Look at your girl." I pointed to the dock, loving the way his face softened when he looked at his kids.

"Livvy's the patient one. She'll sit out there all damn day until she catches something. Mark my words. Gets that from me, obviously."

"Looks like she's chatting Wolverine's ear off about something. She gets that from you, too."

His eyes narrowed, but he grinned. "Yeah, that's probably right. So..." He dug in the front pocket of his jeans. "Close your eyes."

I closed them. "You ain't gonna whip your dick out, are you?"

"Jesus, Pops. What kind of maniac do you take me for? Just, uh, just let me tuck this back in." I shook my head, and he began laughing. "Kidding. Open your eyes."

He held his palm out with a triumphant grin, and I squinted at it before retrieving the glasses from the front pocket of my shirt. I slid them onto my face. "What do you have—"

I gasped when I realized what he was holding. A gold ring with the number thirteen encased within a diamond. A ring I hadn't seen since the man wearing it had dropped me in the middle of the mountains.

"How did you get it?"

"Me and Zane tracked him down outside of Oklahoma City. Knew you'd been looking for him for a while now, so I handled it."

I turned the band over in my hand. "It's done?"

He nodded. "It's over. Anyone who's laid a hand on our family is in the ground now. We can move on."

The old me would have been angry that I hadn't been the one to send him to the Reaper, but I'd wasted too many years seeking revenge. I'd seen where that path led.

Betsy had let the little slights and hurts build until they consumed her. She'd wasted her life and missed out on so much because she was hellbent on destroying my wife.

Mikey blinked a couple of times and took a shaky breath before continuing. "When I was a kid, you told me something that's stuck with me."

"Oh, yeah?" I grinned. "Your old man taught you something?"

"Not a lot, but you got a few things right. No, you told me you'd be my ax, that you'd fight for me. Even when you were at your weakest, you gave the order that saved us all. You held up your end when I couldn't take the shot."

His lip quivered, and he paused, working his jaw back and forth a couple of times before continuing. "Time for me to be your ax now, Pops."

I pinched the bridge of my nose and nodded, letting him pull me into a hug. "I, uh, I got somethin' for you too."

"Better not be your dick," Mikey joked before releasing me and swiping a hand over his face.

I held the sobriety chip out. "Found this a few weeks ago in the back of the old dresser we took from Angel's house. I was getting ready to sand it down and get some new stain on it when I ran across it. Thought it was fitting since you just hit three years."

"Love you, Pops," he gulped before swiping at the tears on his face.

"Love you too, kid."

"Fuck," he groaned. "My mascara's gone to shit. I'm just gonna go freshen up."

I stayed back in the barn, needing a few minutes to get myself under control. The final string connecting us to the past was severed with Cobra's death, allowing us to finally move on.

"Thought I might find you in here," Celia said from the doorway. "Olivia says she's sitting on that dock until the fish come out. And Thor insisted you told him it was okay for him to eat the fish right out of the pond."

I grinned. "Whatever works for him. What about the other two?"

She stepped closer. "Well, Charlie talked Hazel into visiting her arm decorating shop."

"Kid's gonna be a tattoo artist, just you wait. Where's everyone else?"

Her hands moved up to slip the second button on her dress. "Lauren's finishing up the deviled eggs, Kate and Nate are presumably still in the bathroom, Dakota was supervising the arm decorating, Mike just passed me headed back to the house, and Zane's on smoker duty. Did I miss anyone?"

With each name, she'd undone another button before slipping the straps from her shoulders. The dress puddled near her feet, and a growl left my throat. She hadn't been wearing anything underneath.

"Goddamn, darlin'. You should wear this more often."

"Yeah?" She did a little twirl before crooking a finger at me. "Come here."

There was a pile of horse blankets tucked into the corner of the barn. It was just secluded enough that if we stayed quiet, no one would know where we'd gone. Celia lowered herself onto her back and spread her knees, inviting me in.

I dropped a hand to my belt, and her gaze moved lower. "Someone's fighting to get out of his cage."

"I can't imagine why." I laughed and peeled the denim off before slowly lowering myself to my knees. My body had been through the wringer, and all the physical therapy in the world couldn't get me back to what it was before, but I was still alive. I was in the arms of my girl.

I lapped at her with my tongue, her body an altar that I never tired of worshiping at. People talked every day of losing the spark after so many years together. They went outside of their marriages to search for it, desperate to recreate the feelings they once had.

It made me think that maybe with all of my wrong turns, I'd done something right by being so fucking gone for the mother of my kids that laying my hands on another woman never crossed my mind.

Celia eventually grew impatient with my mouth and arched her hips. "Please."

"Who's in charge here?" I asked in a low voice.

She looked up at me with drowsy eyes. "Me."

"What do you want? All you have to do is say it."

"I want..." she glanced around before whispering, "I want your cock."

"I'm sorry, baby. Did you say you wanted somethin'? My hearing just ain't what it used to be."

Celia groaned as two bright spots of color appeared on her cheeks. I loved that she still couldn't say the word without blushing. "I want your cock, husband."

I nodded and sank into her with a ragged exhale. "So fuckin' tight."

"I feel it," she panted beneath me, forcing her cunt down around me before pulling back. She did it again, finding a rhythm that had her gripping my cock like a vise within seconds.

When she came down, I pulled out and rolled her legs to the side. Celia's lips parted on a gasp when I drove back into her with a rough thrust.

Her tits bounced, and I ignored the twinge in my shoulder as I moved into a pushup position and sucked one into my mouth. Fingers tangled in my long hair, tethering my mouth to her chest. She went sailing over the edge again with a cross between a moan and a scream.

I clapped a hand over her mouth and thrust deeper, the electric tingling in my spine making it impossible to hold back. I dragged my cock in and out of her tight walls, sucking against the tender skin on her tits until I was sure there'd be bruises.

Sensing I was close, she reached back and locked her right hand around my thigh, pulling me deeper. I came inside her with a groan, continuing to thrust until my body shuddered violently before collapsing on top of her.

"Jesus, princess," I murmured, still feeling the shock waves of pleasure. "Hope you weren't expectin' me to be useful after that."

"Mama?" Dakota called out from nearby. "Torch and Lou are here!"

I dropped my forehead to Celia's, fighting to keep her pinned beneath me, even as she began squirming to move away.

"No, stay here," I begged, like a petulant child.

"Greedy man. Come on, we have guests."

Reluctantly, I rolled away and got dressed, remembering the ring in the pocket of my jeans. Someday, I'd give it to her and admit that Cobra hadn't died in the early morning hours of Dakota's wedding day.

Maybe I'd tell her how he became something of a friend in my darkest hours. How, in what I was sure were my last days, I learned about the kind of man I didn't want to be. I saw what built-up anger could do to a person, the type of monster it could turn a person into.

I wouldn't mourn his loss, but I would remember the lessons he'd taught me at my lowest. Vengeance and protection were two completely separate things. A person could only choose one.

I chose her.

I chose family.

Celia pulled the straps back up on her dress and straightened it. "Maybe once everyone goes home, we could go skinny dipping in the pond again. Now, come on, they're waiting for us."

We joined hands and stepped out into the late afternoon sunshine, squinting against the brightness as if we'd never seen the light.

Olivia had moved up onto Wolverine's lap, entrusting him with her fishing pole while she dozed open-mouthed on his shoulder.

Zane said something to Mikey, their laughs carrying across the breeze. Lauren and Dakota worked on setting the large picnic table that Mikey and I had built together, while Lauren's Abuelita and Little Ricky provided direction. Torch and Lou stood with Lucy, the three of them admiring something in Celia's flowerbeds.

Nate was sitting on a lawn chair by the paddling pool with Kate on his lap and their feet in the water, neither complaining as Thor pretended to be a shark and splashed them. Charlie was still working on Hazel's arms, their little heads bent together under the shade of a pecan tree.

Bear's bike was parked near mine, but he and Molly were nowhere to be seen. Probably making use of the open bathroom.

"It's what you wanted," I said, more to myself, as I took it all in.

Celia's head popped up. "How'd you know?"

I exhaled a soft laugh. "It's what I always imagined family looked like, what I wanted more than anything."

"Me too," she mused, tightening her hold on me. "They say you don't know the value of a moment until it's a memory, but this right here?" She mashed her lips together. "This is something I'll remember for the rest of my life."

"Hey, Mama," I said, looking at the life we'd built. "We did it. Now, what do you say we take those little ones for a spin on the old bike before dinner?"

I used to think that if I had a chance to do it all over, I would have found her sooner—would have tried to be someone else. I'd lived my life in scenarios, always wondering how much better things would have been had I made different choices.

It struck me now that even with the mistakes I'd made, I still had this. I'd taken all the wrong paths, only to find that they all led me home.

They'd led me to my family.

Keep reading for a special bonus chapter...

BONUS CHAPTER

Angel

I spluttered as a stream of water hit me in the face before sitting up with a sharp gasp, suddenly wide awake. The sprinkler began moving away from me, and I patted along my chest, taking stock of my injuries.

My t-shirt was white, not a trace of blood anywhere. I poked two fingers into my chest, waiting for the inevitable sting of pain, but felt nothing.

"Hey, Charlie. Took a bit of spill, did you?"

I looked across the lawn and toward the small brownstone in confusion. Nobody had called me by my given name since Mary.

The man stood on his front stoop, hand held up in a wave. He was wearing a vintage bowling shirt and khaki shorts that were rolled up his thigh to the point of being obscene. A cigarette hung from the corner of his mouth, but there wasn't an ounce of suspicion in his eyes.

"You know me?" I ran my fingers over my kutte, surprised to find the leather firm as if I hadn't been wearing the damn thing for the past fifty years.

He exhaled a stream of smoke and pointed at me with a wide grin. "Is this another one of your practical jokes? Careful now, the sprinkler's coming back your way."

Convinced I was dreaming, I patted the lawn, letting the blades of grass tickle my palms. When that failed to wake me up, I got to my feet and stumbled over to the sidewalk.

"Oh, I get it. You're still trying to guess how I get it so green. It's nothing more than a little elbow grease, you know?"

I nodded along, not really paying attention as I studied the 1970 Plymouth Barracuda parked in his driveway. Damn thing looked practically new. "You restore this yourself?"

He chuckled and exhaled a puff of smoke. "Now, I know you're pulling my leg. What's gotten into you? Been hitting the Mary Jane a bit early today?"

"Somethin' like that," I mumbled, looking at the vintage cars lining the street. Only they all seemed to be brand new. I rubbed my eyes, but everything stayed the same.

If it was a dream, it was the most vivid one I'd ever had.

The longer I stared, the more familiar everything seemed as if I'd been on this street before. Without saying goodbye, I moved on, headed straight for the Rambler wagon parked in front of a bungalow I'd recognize anywhere.

The last time I'd seen this place, weeds had sprouted up between the cracks in the sidewalk before taking over the lawn entirely. The old screen door had been hanging on by a single hinge, and the windows had all been boarded up.

That wasn't the house I was looking at now.

I was greeted by the sight of a well-manicured lawn and a house that had obviously had a fresh coat of paint recently. Whoever was living here had put a lot of work into the place to make it shine. Even in the early days, it had never looked this good.

I didn't know how long I stood admiring the old place before realizing how it must have looked. Neighbors were probably already calling the cops about the elderly vagrant casing the joint.

Knowing it wouldn't be long before I either woke up or got picked up by a badge, I ran my hand reverently over the old Rambler, remembering how good it had felt to drive it with my girl by my side.

When I caught sight of my reflection, I froze and brought my hand up to my cheek, stroking the jet black hair on my beard in awe.

The gray hairs and deep lines that had been on my face longer than I could remember were gone. I looked just like I had in the seventies.

I glanced back at the old cars lining the street and then back to the Rambler underneath my palm.

If it was still here...

Before I lost my nerve, I strode up the stone path and knocked on the screen door.

Initially, I didn't see anyone when it opened, until I caught movement in the bottom corner of my eye. A dark-haired boy no older than three stood watching me, clad only in a pair of shorts similar to ones I'd seen Jamie wear as a boy.

I opened my mouth to apologize when I was struck by his eyes. An almost electric blue that rendered me speechless.

"Who is it?"

At the sound of her voice, I reached out and gripped the doorframe in my hand, fighting to stay in what I now knew had to be a dream.

The little boy stayed silent, but his eyes held a certain curiosity to them, as if he was waiting to see what I did next.

"It's me, Mary," I said hoarsely.

She came around the corner, wiping her hands on the frilly apron tied around her waist. "We've been waiting for you, Charlie," she said with a grin. "Supper's almost ready."

I covered my mouth to hide my sobs.

It felt real.

So fucking real.

When I stayed where I was, she approached me with a shake of her head, taking my left hand in hers. "You're soaked. Took a nap on the lawn again, did you?"

"I—I—" I pointed helplessly to the little boy. "Who's this?"

Mary stood on tiptoe and pressed her lips to my jaw, whispering, "Are you telling me you don't recognize your own son, Charlie Stewart?"

I looked into his eyes again and knew she was telling the truth. I'd gotten shot and ended up in some alternate reality where my entire world hadn't been ripped away from me.

She squeezed my hand and spun the simple gold band on my ring finger. "Did you forget me too?"

"Not one day," I breathed, touching the ring on her finger; something I'd never seen her wear before. A piece of jewelry that hadn't been tainted by Donald Quinn.

"Daddy?" the little boy asked, stretching his arms out to me. "Up?"

"Remind me what we named him, baby?" I asked as I lifted him onto my hip, keeping my other arm around her waist.

She threw her head back and laughed. "Charles, your daddy is being silly today, isn't he?"

"Silly," my son repeated.

My son.

I swallowed past the lump in my throat and held on tighter. "I'm gonna make you so happy, Mary. Both of you."

Her blonde curls settled against the crook of my neck as she pressed another soft kiss to my face. "You already do, Charlie. Now, let's eat before it gets cold."

Charles squirmed out of my grasp and tugged my hand toward the kitchen. "C'mon, Daddy."

With one last look at the sidewalk, I closed the door behind me and let my son lead me to the table.

It had taken thirty-seven years of atonement for me to find my way home.

The End.

———

Not ready to leave Grey's world behind just yet? Get to know his kids. Dakota's love story is found in Operation Fit-ish, and Kate's in Operation Annulment.

———

Need another biker fix? Keep reading for a sneak peek of *Through The Woods*, book one of the Fairest series.

Want to be the first to know when my books go on sale?
Follow me on BookBub!

For new release alerts, follow me on Amazon!

QUINN FAMILY TREE

Quinn Family Tree

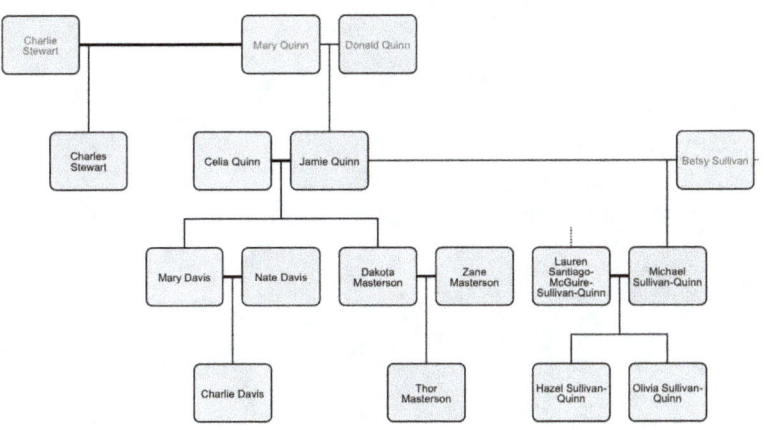

SAVIOR PLAYLIST

Seven Devils- Florence + The Machine
Gimme Shelter- The Rolling Stones
Broken Crown- Mumford & Sons
Rx (Medicate)- Theory of a Deadman
Flux- Ellie Goulding
Ride- Lana Del Rey
Basic Instinct- The Acid
The Sound of Silence- Disturbed
Heavy- Linkin Park & Kiiara
The Knowing- The Weeknd
Blood In The Cut- K. Flay
Wish You Were Here- Pink Floyd
Simple Man- Lynyrd Skynyrd
Nobody's Home- Clint Black
Heaven- Kane Brown
Poison & Wine- The Civil Wars
River- Bishop Briggs
Way Down We Go- Kaleo
Ride- Chase Rice & Macy Maloy
Eyes Closed- Halsey

H.O.L.Y.- Florida Georgia Line
Hail to the King- Avenged Sevenfold
Can't Stop- Red Hot Chili Peppers
A Hard Rain's Gonna Fall- Walk Off the Earth
Paralyzed- NF
lovely- Billie Eilish & Khalid
Knocked Up- Kings of Leon
Lay My Body Down- Rag'n'Bone Man
Mother's Daughter- Miley Cyrus
Dream- Imagine Dragons
Over The Love- Florence + The Machine
Immigrant Song- Led Zeppelin
White Flag- Bishop Briggs
Love Is Madness- Thirty Seconds To Mars & Halsey
Monsters- Shinedown
Pray For Me- The Weeknd & Kendrick Lamar
I Found- Amber Run
Never Say Never- The Fray
Beautiful War- Kings of Leon
My Kind of Crazy- Andrew Hyatt
Holy Water- Big & Rich
ocean eyes- Billie Eilish

Listen on Spotify

PREVIEW OF THROUGH THE WOODS

Once there was a princess...

Forced to run from her drug-dealing boyfriend, Neve ends up injured and alone in the middle of the Colorado wilderness. She never planned on being rescued by seven bikers and brought to their clubhouse.

While the other bikers welcome a female presence, their leader, Charm, is not impressed. As Neve recuperates, she begins to see that there's much more to this club president than she thought possible.

However, while she might've run...

She can't stay hidden forever.

Through The Woods is available now for purchase. Simply tap on the title, or read on for a sneak peek at what's to come.

THE FAIREST SERIES – BOOK 1

Through
the woods

SHANNON MYERS

THROUGH THE WOODS

Neve

"Will Clint be in a good mood when he comes home tonight?" I whispered the words as I shook the black orb in my hand.

'Don't count on it' appeared within the blue triangle and I let out a small sigh of disappointment.

So much for a peaceful evening.

Maybe relying on a Magic 8 ball to solve my problems wasn't the best use of my time, but I had nowhere else to be. I'd become what my parents had feared most—an unemployed nobody, shacked up with her loser boyfriend.

I certainly never saw it working out like that.

"You either need to buy something or leave." The store owner glared at me from the other side of the counter and I immediately felt guilty—as if I'd been doing something wrong.

"I was just browsing—" I said calmly before he interrupted.

"I know what you're doing—you're either casing the place or looking to shoplift. I don't tolerate either; so get out."

I opened my mouth to protest when he pointed to the sign hanging on the door.

'We reserve the right to refuse service to anyone.'

I tossed my purse over my shoulder and held my head high as I walked out. I guess novelty stores were cracking down on the types of customers they allowed.

The bell chimed over the door as it swung shut behind me and I turned around with a smirk, middle finger in the air. That smirk faded the minute I caught my reflection in the glass.

Is that what I looked like?

No wonder he threw me out.

My hair hung in unwashed clumps around my shoulders. My eyes were sunken in, cheeks concave. A fading yellow bruise was the only color on my ghost white skin.

I lowered my hand and turned away. I couldn't bear to stare at myself any longer. It was like staring at a stranger. The shopping center was almost empty, save for a handful of cars. Everyone was off enjoying their fourth of July weekend. I bet the Res was packed.

The Boulder Reservoir was a popular hangout spot and this weekend would be no different. In another life, I would've been out there with friends.

A lone desk chair rolled aimlessly across the parking lot as the breeze caught it and I found myself mesmerized by the sight of it.

How had something like that ended up here?

It was a great metaphor for my life. That chair and I had a lot in common. I should've graduated a couple of months ago. Instead, I was here, watching my life roll past. Looking back on it, I should've never allowed Paul to drag me upstairs. I should've thrown my beer in his face and run as far away as possible.

I'd snorted another line before I left Clint that night, with promises to meet up the next day. As I'd taken the bus back to my dorm, I'd decided that I would continue seeing him, but only use if I had a lot of studying to get done.

Unfortunately, I found that after a couple of lines, I could stay up all night. I wasn't hungry when I was using either, so my fears of gaining the 'freshman fifteen' were alleviated as well. My grades improved a lot—since I didn't require sleep, nothing could stop me.

What goes up must come down though.

I'd convinced myself that because Clint had personal feelings for me, he'd never let me get addicted. I had this crazy idea that he somehow had my best interests at heart.

I was wrong.

The man who started out being perfect, slowly became something else. In the beginning, he took me to the nicest restaurants in Denver and bought me gifts just because. By the time I realized that things weren't as they seemed, I was caught in a downward spiral. I began skipping classes in favor of getting high and having sex with him. I craved the pleasure I got from it—coke alone wasn't enough. I needed Clint just as badly.

I was beyond addicted to cocaine and him, while he'd broken his own rule and gotten hooked on cocaine and H.

Clint was no longer Clint.

In his place was a temperamental monster. The insidiousness was subtle and his skill at hiding it was better than the mob. Once I'd sobered up enough to see how bad things had gotten, it was too late. The man I loved had been taken over by addiction.

I'd known that cocaine use was highest among college-aged young adults and had always made the conscious decision to stay away from it and weed, hadn't I? I learned much later that marijuana might've been the best choice for me back then. At least it would've diminished the stress over my grades.

So, I made excuses for him—I said I'd never put up with abuse; then again, I also said I'd never do drugs. It was a bit like a lobster in a pot of water that was slowly getting hotter. By the time the lobster realized that something was wrong, it was too late—the damn thing had been boiled alive.

There weren't any shades of gray when it came to my relationship with Clint either. I'd seen enough over the years to know that I was firmly ensconced in 'accomplice territory.'

If the cops ever caught on to his illegal activities, I was going down as well.

I noticed the owner of the shop watching me suspiciously, so I moved over a few buildings before sinking down onto the sidewalk.

The breeze picked up again and the chair rolled a few feet to the left before coming to a stop. I'd never wanted to be an inanimate object more than I did in that exact moment.

A drop of crimson hit the sidewalk between my legs, quickly followed by another. I stared at it in confusion until I realized it was coming from my nose. Again. I wiped at it with the back of my hand. Instead of being concerned, it just made me crave another hit.

This had to be rock bottom. My life had become a vicious circle of white snow and blood red reminders that I needed a fix. I was headed nowhere—scratch that. I was headed toward my imminent death, yet I was too far gone to stop now.

My mind no longer raced with thoughts of 'coulda, woulda, shoulda.' It was wholly occupied only with thoughts of the next bump.

The most pathetic part was that I was friggin' content to continue living like this. At some point over the last few weeks, I'd reached acceptance. I was just like that chair, letting outside circumstances move me any which way they pleased.

It'd been so long since I'd made up my own mind on anything—so long since I wasn't under the influence of either cocaine or Clint.

I told myself I was smarter than the drug; convinced myself that I could handle it. Instead, I was completely powerless against it all.

I stood up and pinched my nostrils closed in a poor attempt to stop the bleeding. I inhaled through my mouth and immediately began coughing as the blood ran down the back of my throat.

The chair continued its path across the parking lot, not even stopping to say goodbye.

Lucky chair.

It probably didn't have a significant other, prone to murderous rages, waiting on it at home.

———

The first thing I noticed when I turned the corner onto our street was that the house was dark. I took a hesitant step closer before I noticed the second thing—Clint's truck wasn't parked in the driveway.

It didn't matter what time of day it was; the house was always lit up like a runway. A beacon on the hill in Boulder, shining its light to lost junkies in need of a fix. I looked up and down the street, waiting to hear the deep rumble of his truck, but it remained empty.

Quiet.

Too quiet.

I debated my options. I could either wait on the front porch for my boyfriend to show up, or I could put on my big girl panties and go inside to wait.

I swallowed hard, the copper taste still heavy on my tongue, and pulled the house key from my purse. The lock stuck as I turned it and I had to throw my shoulder into the door as I forced it open.

I almost fell headfirst into the living room floor, barely managing to catch myself at the last possible second. I shakily stood up and closed the door behind me; making sure it was locked in the process.

The house was silent and I laughed to myself. "Stupid, Neve. Getting scared over not—"

A hand clamped down over my mouth and spun me around, shoving my face up against the wall. A scream ripped from my throat as the hand tightened around my jaw, squeezing it until I felt like it would shatter.

"Shut the fuck up, bitch. Where is it?"

The voice was deep, but muffled, and I wondered if the person was wearing a ski mask like they did in the movies.

He slammed my head roughly against the wall. "I'm giving you one more chance. Where is it?"

Cold metal pressed into my lower spine and I fought the urge to scream again, knowing it was the quickest way to end up dead. I didn't have the slightest clue what 'it' was, but I wasn't about to let the guy holding a weapon on me know that.

"I—I don't know. Clint will be here any second and he can help you..." My voice was foreign to my ears. It spoke with a calmness I most certainly did not feel.

There'd been threats against Clint before, but no one had ever gone this far. No one was that stupid.

"Okay, bitch. You're going to pass along a message—you think you can do that?"

I nodded quickly as the metal dug into my spine.

"Good girl. Clint has twenty-four hours to get me the money. If he doesn't, what happened to you will be just the beginning. Got it?"

As my brain fought against the fear to determine what he meant, something sharp sank into my side. He quickly pulled the blade out and ran the edge of it down my throat, leaving a wet trail.

"Try to stay conscious long enough to deliver the message." The man let go of me and my knees immediately buckled.

My side burned as if it was on fire and my vision blurred from the pain. I waited until I heard him leave before crawling toward the kitchen. My tank top grew wetter with each movement and I began to feel lightheaded.

Just a few more feet and I'd be close enough to grab the phone.

I came to right outside the kitchen. The only difference was that every light in the house was now blazing around me, but I had no idea how long I'd been lying like this.

"Clint?" I whispered.

I heard his footsteps draw closer and I instinctively wanted to curl myself into a ball.

"Neve?" He gave me a puzzled look. "What the fuck are you doing on the floor?"

I pointed to my side and the carpet drenched in my blood. "There was a m-m-man—said you had twenty-four hours—stabbed me." My words were nothing more than jumbled nonsense, thanks to my tears.

He stared down at me, his eyes filled with concern and fear. "Jesus, Nevvie, you're bleeding all over the fucking place. Hold onto me."

I gave a silent prayer of thanks that Addict Clint hadn't shown up tonight. He pulled me to my feet and I swayed unsteadily against him, my grip on his shirt loosening. "Clint..."

His grip tightened on my arms as he pulled me over toward the sofa. "Sit down, baby."

I dropped back against the cushions with a loud groan of pain as Clint sat down beside me. His hands felt along my side before he gently lifted the material away from my skin. "Tell me what happened," he commanded.

I closed my eyes as exhaustion clouded my thoughts, struggling to remember even the smallest of details. "I didn't see his face. Is there

—" I paused as a wave of pain washed over me. "Is there someone you owe money to?"

Clint stared through the front window, refusing to look at me. I thought that he'd check me over again; at the very least, tell me what the hell was going on. He did none of those things. He focused on the coffee table in front of him, straightening three lines of coke with a razor blade on a large mirror lying on the surface.

"You know what we're gonna do, baby? We're gonna ask the mirror to give us the answer. You get a little snow in you and the bleeding'll stop. 'Kay?"

I nodded. Maybe he was right. I just needed a little bump to take the edge off.

Clint took the shell of a broken pen and snorted a line. Then he stared expectantly at his reflection in the mirror. He was doing that a lot more lately; staring into the damn thing as if it held the secrets of the universe.

He passed the pen over to me and held my hair back as I forced my body to bend down and slowly inhale the middle line. I pushed off the coffee table and fell back against the cushions with my eyes closed. "The trunk is most frequently stabbed in cases of penetrating trauma. However, only subcutaneous tissue is affected eighty-five percent of the time. Did you know that?" I panted through each breath, fear wrapping its tendrils around my chest.

Clint patted my head before snorting the last line and continuing his staring contest with his reflection.

Within a few minutes, my heart rate increased and I knew that he was right. The coke was healing my body—it was probably coagulating all the blood at this very moment. I didn't even hurt as badly. Maybe I wouldn't need to go to the hospital after all.

"Let's go!" Clint leapt up off the couch, startling me with the volume of his voice. He grabbed my hand and yanked me to my feet. "We're going to pick up Trev. He'll know what to do."

———

We picked up Trever and continued driving until we were out of the city and on a winding mountain road. The two men carried on a terse discussion from the front seat, while I lay in the backseat with my head against the glass.

Coke used to give me such a high, but now the euphoria only seemed to last for a few minutes. Once those few minutes were up, I was overwhelmed with sadness again.

It made me want my mom.

You know how, as a kid, moms could fix anything? That was how I felt—completely despondent and in need of my mom to step in and make everything right again.

I just needed to lay my head against her chest while she stroked my hair—well, it was definitely not going to happen in this lifetime, but I yearned for it nonetheless. Thinking of her caused my throat to tighten. I wasn't going to cry over it. Not now.

I reached down and felt my side. Blood was still trickling out, but it seemed as if it had slowed some. I was still struggling to stay awake though. Maybe Clint was taking me to a doctor.

Yeah, that was it.

He was going to find me a mountain doctor that worked with outlaws all the time. He'd know just what to do to fix a stab wound.

I closed my eyes and dozed until the truck stopped suddenly and my head hit the seat in front of me.

"Neve, wake up. We're here." Clint had the back door open before I was even fully conscious. I was completely disoriented as he pulled me from the warmth of the truck and out into the cool mountain air. It didn't matter that it was July—Colorado was always chilly at night; even more so up here in the mountains.

I wrapped my arms around myself and stumbled on the uneven ground as I fought to remain upright. We were in the middle of the woods. Maybe the doctor's place was hidden back in the trees?

Trev's face made me pause. He looked scared. I held a hand up and waved at him weakly. "I'm fine. It's just a scratch, really."

Clint wrapped his arms around my body and I leaned into him, as crickets chirped around us. "Baby, the man who came to the house—did he give you a name?"

I shook my head and snuggled closer into him. The light breeze made the hair on the back of my arms stand up and I wanted nothing more than to climb back into his truck and fall asleep again.

"What exactly did he say?" His tone was different, but in my weakened state, I was unable to determine if he was angry or not.

I held on tightly to him as I repeated the same thing I'd told him back at the house. "Well, he said you had twenty-four hours to get him the money or what he did to me would seem like nothing once he got ahold of you."

His fingers dug into my shoulder blades painfully. "He said all that, did he? Was this before or after you fucked him?"

The addict was back.

I stiffened as my brain sent out a warning, seconds too late. He shoved me and I fell back against the soft earth, cracking my elbow on a large stone as I landed. Pain shot down into my fingers and I clutched at my arm in agony.

"Clint! I didn't even know the man—I'd just gotten home—"

He was on top of me before I could finish my sentence. "Tell me the truth!" His eyes were wild and unfocused, indicating that he'd done a lot more than just coke tonight.

I shook my head and tried to pat his chest with my good arm. If I could just calm him down, he'd see how crazy this was. Trevor made no move to interrupt, choosing to turn the music up in the truck to drown out our voices instead.

Clint's hand cupped my face before moving down my body. Before I could breathe a sigh of relief, his fingers dug into my side, reopening the wound again. The breeze hit the wetness on my shirt, only making me feel colder.

"You lied, Neve. I saw it in the mirror. You were with him. How long have you been sleeping with him behind my back? Did you tell him where it was?"

Gone was my high and just like every time before, my heart broke as the madness overtook him. Why couldn't he see what he was doing to me? It hadn't mattered that I'd never once cheated on him, the Addict was convinced that I was on a mission to destroy him.

I'd just opened my mouth to reply when his hand shot up and

wrapped around my throat. I brought both arms up and attempted to break his contact, but he easily blocked me.

"I don't know who all you've been talking to, but I'm not going down because some cokehead bitch can't keep her mouth or her legs shut." He squeezed harder as tears rolled down his cheeks and fell onto my face. The cracks in my heart spread as his words pierced me until only caverns remained.

This wasn't him.

I struggled in his grip, but he didn't let up. Being choked was just one more thing that wasn't at all how it was portrayed in the movies. According to Hollywood, the person being choked would make all sorts of loud gurgling and coughing noises. That wasn't even close to real life though.

As Clint's hands squeezed, the only noises that escaped my lips were little puffs of air as it was forced from my body. I clawed at his arms and face, but still the only real sound was coming from the stereo in the truck.

Clint made small grunts as he put all of his strength into his hands. "I want to rip you apart until you hurt as badly as I do. Why'd you talk to him? I trusted you!" He roared as more tears fell from his eyes.

My vision began to blur and my bladder released. I was going to die listening to Clint sobbing above me and Eddie Vedder wailing from the truck about the lost love of his life shining like a bright star in someone else's sky.

My eyes rolled back into my head just as there was a loud metallic sound.

Heaven's made of metal and the moon's made of cheese.

"Neve, get up!" The voice sounded close by.

God?

Only good girls made it to heaven...

Yeah, I was definitely in Hell. God would've let me rest.

"Neve, wake up." The voice was insistent, even going as far as hitting my cheek.

My eyes fluttered open to Trever's face mere inches from mine. "Get up. You have to get up."

I coughed until I thought a lung would come up, my eyes streaming.

He pulled me to my feet, but my limbs didn't feel like my own. Nothing about my body seemed familiar. He shook my shoulders roughly.

"You have to run. Run, Neve! Don't stop!"

I looked down and saw Clint sprawled out on his stomach, a shovel lying nearby. Trever hooked a finger under my chin and brought my eyes up to meet his. "He brought you here to kill you. He thinks you're a nark. If he comes to and sees you here, he'll finish it. Nod if you understand."

I nodded and took a deep breath. Clint groaned from nearby and Trever shoved me toward the tree line. "Go!"

I'd thought that failing every class my first semester and losing my scholarship was the scariest thing I'd ever been through. I now realized how incredibly naïve that had been. I forced my body to move as fast as it could. Luckily, there was still enough coke and adrenaline in my system to push me along. I knew that if he caught up to me, I wouldn't get another chance.

He was probably killing Trever at this very moment.

I didn't want to die.

That thought propelled me forward and I jogged faster, low-lying tree branches and limbs scraping along my face and arms. Blood poured steadily from the wound in my side, but I refused to stop, even as my lungs felt ready to explode.

I had to keep going.

An object in motion tends to stay in motion...

Fine time for my brain to make a reappearance.

"Aghhh!"

An object in motion tends to stay in motion with the same speed and in the same direction, unless acted upon by an unbalanced force.

My ankle caught on a tree root and I cried out in a harsh whisper before slamming to the ground. My brain urged me to get up and keep running, but my body was done. I'd twisted my ankle; with my luck, it was probably broken. I was also losing a lot of blood from where Clint reopened my stab wound. On top of all of that, the bastard had just tried to choke me to death and it felt like I'd swallowed a million razor blades. My limbs were so heavy—there was no way I could move them.

What was I even running toward anyway?

I had to be a hundred miles away from Boulder and at least twenty from the nearest town.

I was done.

Just then, I heard a loud crashing sound coming from the direction I'd just run from, so I forced myself up onto my forearms and army crawled over near a fallen log. He was going to find me, but I wasn't going to lie still and wait for death. Dirt and forest debris clung to my side. If only it were fall; I could've used a pile of leaves to hide in right about now.

The crashing got louder and then stopped. I held my breath and closed my eyes, as if doing so would make me invisible. Clint had to be within five feet of me.

Right then and there, I sobered up long enough to pray that he suffered from night blindness.

Anything that would keep him from seeing me lying on the forest floor.

I continued holding my breath, even as my body pleaded for air. There was a loud retreat back into the trees and then the sounds of the forest were the only thing surrounding me again.

The air turned colder and I shivered involuntarily as I inhaled a grateful breath, my tank top and Bermuda shorts doing nothing to keep me warm. I pressed my body up against the log, seeking warmth from any source I could find.

The trees above me looked like a giant blanket, just begging to be pulled down over my body. I couldn't have chosen a more perfect place to die.

Apathy? Wasn't that a sign of hypothermia?

I fought to stay conscious, but with that thought, my vision swam and everything went dark.

———

"Fuck if I know how she got here, but we can't leave her."

"Charm's gonna flip his shit over this. We can't just bring random women back to the club—"

"Well, what do you suggest we do with her? Leave her here to die?"

The male voices continued arguing nearby as I struggled to open my eyes. My body, on the other hand, disagreed with even the mere thought of consciousness so my eyes remained closed.

I listened to the men, but their voices were unfamiliar to me. It didn't sound like Clint or Trev. In fact, I was certain I'd never heard them before in my life. He hadn't found me. That was really the only thing I had going for me at the moment.

Hands touched my throat and I stiffened in response. "She's got a pulse." From there, they moved down my side, stopping at the wound that was making me feverish and delusional. "But, she's in pretty bad shape."

Maybe I was hallucinating this entire thing. I'd fallen in the middle of nowhere. There was no way that someone had found me so soon. I'd simply conjured up a mountain doctor in my mind, a man ready to piece a cokehead like me back together. He'd probably discovered me as he'd taken his evening constitutional. I pictured him having a cane that he'd carved himself and cheeks that were permanently rosy.

I was losing it. The reality of my situation was that I'd stranded myself in the middle of the wilderness. There were no hiking trails that I'd passed as I ran for my life and it was even more impossible to assume that someone had just miraculously stumbled upon me.

"She's been stabbed. It needs to be treated." If I was going to keep with the narrative in my mind, I'd call that voice Doc. He seemed to know what he was talking about.

The faint scent of cigarette smoke and cologne hit my nostrils and for whatever reason, it reminded me of my dad, even though he'd never smoked a day in his life. This was the best hallucination I'd ever experienced—my whole body was participating. Maybe I was still high.

"Fuck, do whatever you want. It's your funeral." That was obviously Grumpy.

There was a loud sneeze followed by a curse. "Did she have to end up in a pile of flowers? Shit, my eyes are watering like a motherfucker." That one would be Sneezy.

"I think we should keep her," a chipper voice added. I'd call him Happy.

I mentally ticked off the list of my imagined rescuers. Obviously, I was still missing a few. Strong arms lifted me up off the ground and an involuntary groan of pain escaped past my lips. I felt as if I'd been forced through a meat grinder. My elbow gave a sharp protest at the movement, another reminder that last night had not been some drugged-up dream. Fingers dug into my ankle and I damn near cried out again.

An object at rest will remain at rest, unless acted on by an unbalanced force.

Hello, unbalanced force.

"Careful with her. We don't need to add to her injuries." Maybe Grumpy had a heart after all. "I, for one, don't want her staying any longer than she has to."

Maybe not.

I was jostled along uneven terrain before being placed gently in the backseat of a vehicle. I needed to sit up and take in my surroundings.

I could get a grasp of where exactly I was—maybe find a landmark. Just in case I had to run again.

The vehicle hit a bump and all plans of moving went out the window. Pain barreled through me like a locomotive and I couldn't think of anything but how badly I hurt. Beads of sweat ran down my face and I couldn't distinguish whether it was from the fever or the movement.

I flirted briefly with the idea of sitting up again before fully committing to unconsciousness.

———

Through The Woods is available for purchase now. Order it today by tapping here.

ACKNOWLEDGMENTS

A writer is only as good as the people behind her. I'm lucky enough to have an entire city.

Rebecca Pau- Bex, here it is. The HEA you've demanded for Mike and Grey. It only took two years to get here. Thank you for redesigning the covers for this series until they fit the story and for being so invested in my characters.

Beta Readers- Guys, we did it. End of the line for the Quinn family. Thank you for the feedback, even if that feedback was sometimes that you hated me.

Wander- Thank you for shooting the most perfect cover for this story. You captured everything I wanted this story to convey. Best ever!

Dani- Thank you for taking me on as a last-minute client and keeping me sane. You made it so all I had to focus on was the writing. Thank you, thank you, thank you!

Give Me Books- Thank you for your graciousness in taking on a five book series and for working around my personal life when I missed my deadline. You guys have taken the headache out of this process and made my life simple.

Ellie- Even though I'm the princess and you're the rebel, we just make it work. Thank you for not blocking me on social media and for continuing to talk to me, even when I screw up on deadlines.

Readers- Thank you for loving these characters and demanding a fitting end to the series. I bled for this book and I hope that comes through on every page.

Jen- Thank you for taking this book on for editing/proofing at the last possible second. And for correctly guessing the villain back in July and backing it up with a very convincing argument. You deserve all the awards.

Jenni- Thank you for giving me the inspiration to create a HEA for Angel, however unconventional it may be.

Laura- Bunny, we did it. I can be a normal psycho again, instead of a psycho on a deadline. I hope that this book makes you cry your eyes out. No, seriously, I hope it does. Cap can't be the only thing that gets the old tear ducts flowing.

Lily- Thank you for questioning everything, even when I compare you to Zach. You keep me constantly striving to work harder and write better. #GreedyforGrey

Wendi- Thank you for always checking in on me, and pulling me out of my writer's cave to get sun every now and then. Now, that the series is complete, let's do it more often.

Zach- We did it. End of an era, you might say. I remember it like it was only yesterday when Mike Sullivan whispered naughty things in my ear and demanded a book. You push me to dig deeper with every chapter and keep me motivated when I'm all about that nap life. I love you, and I'm excited to see where we go next. #TeamMyers

ABOUT THE AUTHOR

Shannon is a born and raised Texan. She grew up inventing clever stories, usually to get herself out of trouble. Her mother was not amused. In junior high, she began writing fractured fairy tales from the villain's point of view and that was the moment she knew that she was going to use her powers for evil instead of good.

After an unplanned surgery in 2014 and a long pity party, she decided to pen a novel about the worst thing that could happen to a person in order to cheer herself up. She's twisted like that. Thus, *From This Day Forward* was born and the rest, as they say, is history.

She resides in the Texas desert with a posse of men (nothing like she'd imagined in fantasies) and plethora of fur babies.

Find her online at: http://shannonshaemyers.com
Or in her reader group: https://www.facebook.com/
groups/630229377127363/

ALSO BY SHANNON MYERS

From This Day Forward Duet

(David & Elizabeth's Story)

From This Day Forward

Forsaking All Others

Standalone Novels

(Travis & Katya's Story)

You Save Me

Operation Series

(Dakota & Zane's Story)

Operation Fit-ish

(Kate and Nate's Story)

Operation Annulment

Silent Phoenix MC Series

(Grey & Celia's Story)

The Deserter (Book One)

The Protector (Book Two)

The Renegade (Book Three)

The Traitor (Book Four)

The Savior (Book Five)

The Mercenary (Book Six) *Coming 2022*

Fairest Series

(Charm & Neve's Story)

Through The Woods

(Killian & Ariana's Story)

Wait For It

<u>Fictioned Series</u>

(Hayden & Jake's Story)

Protagonized